MASTER OF LIES

SHANNON McKENNA

CHAPTER 1

Jed

Well, would you look at that. So Sandee was a real, live girl, after all.

I shuffled forward in my shackles, eyeing my penpal through the glass barrier with wary fascination. She hadn't noticed me yet from her place in the line by the door, but I knew her from the photos she'd sent. At least the ones that got through the prison censors. They were grubby and dog-eared by the time they made it to my cell. Letters, too. Long, gushy letters, packed with too much information, including but not limited to her hard-luck past, her loneliness, her intense longings, her sexual fantasies.

The girl was a hot mess, and desperately in need of therapy, but I'd read all of the letters multiple times. I'd pored over them, in fact.

So I had no business judging anybody else's twisted coping mechanisms.

I had plenty of empty hours in prison to study Sandee's letters and pictures. Up until right now, I'd been convinced they were a fantasy front. Just too damn pretty. Not realistic. Somebody photoshopped the living fuck out those photos. I was sure of it.

My guess had been that Sandee was some lonesome, tragically plain girl, or maybe someone housebound or disabled, looking for a virtual boyfriend. Or else maybe a guy who wanted to be a girl but was afraid to make the leap, so had chosen this way to live out his/her/their fantasy. Something along those lines.

But no. What the hell was a woman like that doing here? I couldn't see what the payoff could possibly be, the way she looked. That body, those tits, those eyes.

The pleated red plaid skirt fell a few inches above the knee, showing off bare, shapely legs. High-heeled red ankle boots. A tattoo on her ankle that I couldn't make out from here. She had hot pink streaks in her jagged blonde bob. She was rocking a rumpled, sexy anime schoolgirl look. The sweater was red, skin-tight. She'd followed the visitation modesty rules, but still managed to look like a walking wet dream. How she'd gotten through the visitor intake process like that was anybody's guess.

Worked for me, though. Oh, man. Worked great.

The glaring white light illuminated her white-blonde mop. Her full, sexy red lips gleamed hotly, all glossed up and sticky looking. If I were inclined to criticize, which I wasn't, I'd say she wore too much makeup. But she could be painted gold, for all I cared. I would lick her clean. Slowly.

Her look was so exaggerated, it had to be some kind of mask. Then again, I was probably overthinking this. I'd been undercover for too long, and prison shook a guy's grip on reality. Her letters and pictures seemed so real. So intensely vulnerable, they made me uncomfortable. And aroused. And seriously fucking confused.

According to the letters, Sandee lived in a rented trailer in a nowhere town with a shuttered factory, rampant unemployment, fentanyl, meth. She bartended at a skeevy roadhouse. Slimebag boss. No family support. And a thing for bad boys.

She'd heard about me from a friend whose husband was inside for mail fraud, and hunted down my mugshot, which was posted online on a booking photos website.

That had been unwelcome news. Like I needed any more attention.

She'd fixated on me, deciding to save some worthless fuck-up from himself by the power of her love alone. She might as well dive into a shark tank. But everybody had a right to his or her own brand of self-destruction, myself included.

Still. Something about her surprised me. I couldn't put my finger on it. That posture. Despite the sexpot outfit, she seemed elegant. Ladylike, almost. That dignified quality stuck out like a sore thumb in a maximum-security hellhole like this one. That gorgeous face, what I could see of it behind the shaggy, choppy blonde bangs. Sharp eyes, looking everywhere but at me. Like she didn't even know I was there.

The CO prodded me to enter the room. My shackles dragged and clanked as I shuffled toward the seat.

The fuck she didn't know I was there. She had positioned herself carefully, and then struck a hot, sexy pose for me. To give me a good, long gawk. That was calculated.

Sandee could be a honeypot, sent by Boer. If Boer had fingered me in here, then I was in imminent danger. Mickey, too. My team outside. They could all be in danger. I needed to contact the Unredeemables right now and put them on their guard.

I hesitated, gripped by panic, and the CO who held my arm stumbled into me with a curse. Goddamn. This was a mistake. I should have kept refusing to see her.

I'd changed my mind because I wanted to do the girl a favor by ending this fantasy of hers—definitively. To scare her to death, make her run before she drew any more unhealthy attention to herself. I wanted her miles away, back in Nowheresville, mired in whatever boring routine she was trying to escape from. *Run, Sandee, run.*

The strategy had seemed smart at the time. But now I felt danger prickle on my skin. Whether from her, or for her, I did not know. One thing was certain. I should never have touched this live wire. Not even once.

She could fuck me up. And idiot me, I'd agreed to this partly because I was bored, and curious. I had to know if she really looked that good. If anyone could.

She did. Score: one for my dick, zero for my brain.

I was so close to my goal. I'd been in Kalaharee for months, getting close to Mickey Savalletri, ingratiating myself to him by protecting him from predators. At long last, he'd agreed to give me the info I needed to run down my ex-colleague, Wex Boer.

Once I got my hands on Boer, I could torture intel about Shane's location out of that murdering shithead. I looked forward to that with every fiber of my being.

But Mickey would only provide the intel after I busted him out of the joint. That was his price, and it was time to pay up. A man had to stay focused while planning a prison break. There was no time or space for a frivolous crush on my sexpot penpal.

"… dee McGillis? For the last time! Sandee McGillis!"

Here she came, right at me. Too late to change my mind.

CHAPTER 2

Freya

I leaped forward, ankles wobbling in those ridiculous high heels.

"I'm here, I'm here!" I sang out, tottering forward. I'd been so anxious and lost in my head, I hadn't even recognized my own fake name.

Wake up, Sandee. Look sharp. And pray to God he doesn't recognize you.

The last time Jed had seen me had been years ago, when he'd come home with Shane, both of them on leave from the Ranger Regiment. I'd been almost fourteen, and he'd mostly ignored me while he was there. Or else treated me like a baby bird.

He wouldn't recognize me. Not in a million years. I looked completely different from that lovestruck, crushed out fourteen-year-old girl. Hell, I'd looked different even before I devised my Sandee disguise.

The drab visitation area reeked of sweat and frustration and despair. A final spasm of panic seized me as the tall, orange-jumper clad form shuffled forward, blurred behind the scratched panel. I was usually so cool and detached. Managing the employees in my engineering workroom required a rigorously honed alpha-female vibe. At the tender age of twenty-six, the only way to get taken seriously was to be a hardass bitch. But today, when the hardass bitchery really counted, my hands were ice cold, and my knees were like Jell-O. At least I didn't have to shake his hand. Visitation at Cell Block B at Kalaharee precluded physical contact. I'd be talking to Jed Clearwater, aka James Craig, on a phone through layers of bullet-proof glass. Safe and shielded.

Today I was not Freya Masters, chief designer and CEO of TechMasters Toys. I was Sandee McGillis, a woman who had fallen in love with him from afar. Sandee, who lived alone, with just her rescue cats for company, in her single-wide in Gholston Flats, hungering for something to give her life meaning.

I had developed a whole persona, from the ground up. Sandee's sad childhood, her trauma, her abandonment issues. I'd sent "James" reams of letters that laid it all out, every aspect of Sandee's messed up personality. I'd gone so deep into it, sometimes I felt as if I had become her. Kind of scary, considering how compromised Sandee was.

I'd been begging him to let me visit. So far, he'd always refused. Then, a few days ago, he'd finally agreed.

I froze. I couldn't even blink. God, he was huge. Bigger than I remembered. Physically massive, vibrating with power. The orange jumpsuit strained over his shoulders, his thickly muscled thighs. Shackles did not diminish him.

He was just biding his time. Waiting for his moment.

His gaze cut through the shadows that the harsh overhead lights cast on his angular face. I remembered his dark hair buzzed short. It had grown out long, thick and dark, down to his shoulders. The tribal tattoos on his neck disappeared into the jumpsuit. His blade of a nose had a bump that I didn't remember. He had a short beard. It looked good on him. But then, everything always had.

His pale gaze was so bright, like a flash of moonlight in the eyes of a nocturnal predator, observing me. Comparing, measuring, calculating. So very cold.

He sank into the chair, keeping narrowed eyes on me. One brow had been slashed at some point, leaving a diagonal scar. His full, sensual lips were grimly sealed.

I should not be reacting to him like this. This breathless, giddy feeling, that was such bullshit. No part of me should be admiring or desiring any part of him. Not one single fucking subatomic particle of him was deserving of my positive regard.

The evidence I'd found indicated that Jed Clearwater was the enemy. There was no other explanation. He was a liar and a traitor and a killer...and a resource to exploit. He could be useful —if I got him to tell me what had happened to my brother, Shane.

And for that, I had to be crafty, subtle, patient. And wildly in love with him.

His eyebrow tilted up. He jerked his chin at the phone, urging me to grab the receiver. I was deer-in-the-headlights immobilized, in spite of having practiced this scene repeatedly. I'd rehearsed the bubbling chatter. Arms outstretched, fingertips touching the glass, extended in longing. A stream of flattering blather—*Finally! Omigod you're, like, so much handsomer than your picture!* And so on.

Gone. I didn't remember a fucking word of it. Jed Clearwater blasted out a frequency that scrambled my wits. I felt vulnerable, as if I were sitting there stark naked.

The COs in the visitation were busy laying down the law, vocally and physically, to a bickering couple on the verge of a fight, so no one was monitoring us.

My nipples tightened as if his glancing look was a physical touch. The effect was extremely visible in my sweater, which was a couple of sizes too small.

Smile, Sandee. That was good. A shy, shaky smile. My body

was staying in character, helping me out by displaying a very convincing nipple hard-on. That was all.

Yeah, girl. Go on. Keep telling yourself that.

Jed picked up the phone, jerking his chin at me again. I obeyed his silent command before I could stop myself, take a breath, and deliberately choose to pick it up. Thereby proving that the action was generated by my own free will.

It wasn't. He'd given me an order, and I had followed it. *Crap.*

Bad beginning. I needed to maintain full control over a lie as deep as the one I meant to tell this man. But that lie was now taking control of me.

I knew from the start this was going to be ambiguous, messy, kind of dirty. But I hadn't expected Jed to effortlessly put himself in charge. Very slick.

I needed him to let down his guard, and let slip something that could help us find Shane. A new avenue of inquiry, a clue, no matter how slight. It was a long shot, but why not try? The guy was stuck here. Defanged. It's not like he could hurt me.

Of course, my brother, Ethan, would go ballistic if he knew. But I'd slipped my personal security detail yesterday in Portland. Ethan was probably ripping them new ones, and that was a shame, but I had never liked being shadowed by bodyguards. Or shoved around by my big brothers.

Jed gazed at me calmly, waiting for me to start. It occurred to me that he might have done this before. Gone as far as he wanted with a prison groupie. His mugshot had made the rounds, and been much noticed and remarked upon. Those piercing eyes, those amazing cheekbones, that chiseled jaw, those sensual lips. I'd seen the comments. Hell, he'd probably had refused my requests to meet before because he was already double-booked. Conjugal visits weren't allowed at Kalaharee, but they could be arranged, with the appropriate bribes, and after selling out my brother, he damn well had the money. Even if someone else managed it for him.

Yes, he'd certainly toyed with other vulnerable women before this. Because he could. *Sick opportunistic bastard.* I let the irrational anger energize me, and gathered my energy to speak.

"Um. Hi, James," I faltered.

"You made it. In spite of the weather." His voice was so deep. Resonant.

"I couldn't miss my chance to see you," I said. "You'd finally said yes."

He shrugged, a faint, amused smile at the corner of his lips. Asshole. Ironic, that I pretend to be a ditz on purpose, and then get pissed at him for buying it. So I'm contradictory. Complicated. Sure. I'm also very smart. Smarter than him.

I hope so, anyhow. Jed Clearwater was nothing if not smart. He'd decieved my brother, Shane. They'd served together in the Rangers Regiment, and went into business together afterward. Jed, Shane, and three others from the Unredeemables group from their Ranger Regiment had founded Ready Line Security after they'd left the military.

Then last year, Shane persuaded Ethan, my oldest brother, to let him use SmokeScreen, Ethan's latest and most powerful intel gathering algorithm, one that could penetrate any kind of encryption like a hot knife through butter. Ethan had agreed, on the condition that Shane alone possess the necessary security codes to operate it. According to Ethan, SmokeScreen was too powerful a tool to share. Not with national defense, not with private citizens, and certainly not with the criminal underworld. Ethan was convinced the whole world would devolve into anarchy if SmokeScreen got into the wrong hands. He hadn't wanted anyone to use it, not even his own brother.

And maybe Ethan was right, and this was a harbinger of things to come, because our lives had certainly devolved into anarchy eight months ago, when a private army had attacked the Ready Line headquarters, mowing them down and burning the place to the ground. Shane had been taken, and everyone else had been killed. Carbonized, identifiable only by dental records. Except for Jed Clearwater, who'd escaped unharmed.

Jed had insisted he had no idea what had happened to Shane. Then, scant weeks later, he'd dropped off the face of the earth. Which looked pretty damn guilty to us.

Ethan's working theory was that Jed had sold Shane to someone who wanted SmokeScreen. For the purpose of torturing the codes out of him.

And I spent my nights thinking about that, as I stared up at my bedroom ceiling.

Hacking was more restful than trying to sleep under those conditions, so I dived deeper than I'd ever gone. I hit pay dirt after I started cyber-stalking the remaining Unredeemables, when I intercepted messages between Darius, Amos and Remy Drake about placing someone in a prison. No names were mentioned, but I used facial recog to direct my search of mugshot databases, and bingo, I'd found him in the Kalaharee Correctional Facility For Men, under a fake name. Accused of first degree murder, held without bail, and still awaiting trial, according to the Kalaharee database.

I had no clue why he was there, and I didn't really care. All I wanted was to find who had taken Shane, so I could grind those fuckers into fine pink paste.

Including Jed himself. And the Drakes, too, for siding with Jed. I'd never forgive them for that. Selling my brother out, for money?

I hadn't shared my findings with Ethan, since he never shared his with me. Bitter experience had taught me that going my own way was simpler than arguing with a hyper-protective, know-it-all big brother, and I was wasting no more time.

I had patience. I could remote-work from space, or the bottom of the ocean. I had bottomless reserves of motivation. I could travel to the prison on visiting days for as long as I needed to. Build a relationship with him. Have long, winding conversations with him. Have phone sex with him. Declare my undying love. Make him dependent on me emotionally. Or on Sandee. It was important to keep Freya and Sandee very separate. Distinct.

And who knew? Something might come of it, eventually.

Of course, it was tissue-paper-thin, as plans went. The only thing that could be said for it was that it was something, not nothing. I had to do something, or I'd snap.

So far, Jed had only sent me a single brief reply to her letters, before finally agreeing to see me. A sheet of yellow legal paper, and a bold, brief penciled scrawl.

Sandee,

Thanks for the photos. You're very pretty and you seem like a nice girl, but you're wasting your time with me. Find someone who will treat you right. Don't settle.

Good luck,

James Craig

The *hell?* It was the kind of thing a good guy might have written. To an idiot. Using small words. Where the hell did he get off, acting decent and principled? It was a lie, and it pissed me off. Condescending, too. Who the hell did he think he was?

He'd had practice pretending to be a good guy. Years of it. He'd fooled Ethan and Shane. My brothers were not stupid.

So far, I hadn't seen recognition on his face, but this guy was impossible to read. I fluttered my eyelash extensions. Good thing Jed had never paid much attention to me back in the day. He sure was paying attention now, though.

Toughen up. Play the part. I gave my bleached locks a flirtatious toss. I'd paid big bucks for this style. The platinum color, the bold cut that half-covered my face. A choppy, punky look that took a good thirty points off my IQ. Very different from my usual messy ash-blonde is-it-a-ponytail-or-is-it-a-bun. I might have overdone the vampy vibe a little, but it was in keeping with the racy selfies I'd printed out for him. And I needed to look as different as possible from the Freya Masters he might or might not remember. That shy, chubby geek teenager with the braces, the zits, and the frizz.

A sharp crack made me jump. A shrill wail followed. A tired-looking woman sitting nearby had lost her patience and smacked her little boy, who'd been snorkling tear-snot the whole time I had been sitting near him.

I looked back at Jed's hooded, watchful eyes, struggling to breathe. A smile curved his sensual lips. My face was clammy. I was letting him psych me out. Stop it. The guy was neutralized. Shackled behind layers of fucking steel and plexi-glass.

He had no power over me. He was fucking *harmless.*

His gaze raked my body, and I shrank back. My intense awareness of him made my skin tingle and flush. My face must have turned cherry red in a hot instant.

Get a grip, Masters. The truth about Shane was in that man's head, and there were only so many ways to extract it. Beating it out of him would have been my first choice, but that option was out of bounds, probably for the next twenty years or so, minimum. The prison actually protected him from me. Lucky man.

That left the option of seducing him into telling me.

It might just work. He'd be lonely. He had no family to visit him. He'd be bored, restless, starved for female attention, and I would be so undemanding and sweet and welcoming and wonderful to him. I would *understand* him so well.

If it took twenty years, I would still be there every visiting day I could manage, waiting for some crumbs of truth to slip out of him. I would never lose interest. My statute of limitations would never end. I would never give up on Shane.

I lifted my chin. Put my shoulders back, sticking out my tits to showcase the nipple hard-on to best effect, and smiled.

Big deep breath...and showtime.

CHAPTER 3

Jed

Sandee clutched the phone. White-knuckled, big-eyed.

I smiled at her, and oh, Jesus. Her pupils dilated, her eyelashes fluttered and her nipples went hard against the low-cut, stretchy shirt.

Whoa. The rush of lust knocked my mind right off its tracks, and my attention arrowed in on the soft, rounded shape of her lips, the up-tilted thrust of her tits. The pulsing throb of my own dick, trapped against my thigh.

I breathed it down. Resolute. I was not doing this chick any favors by being nice to her. I should have a Surgeon General's warning label tattooed on my forehead. *Proximity to this man could be injurious to your continued existence.*

Just ask Shane. Hank. Billy. Franco.

Skip the smiling. No nicey-nice for Sandee. It was the kindest thing I could do for her. I took a deep breath. "So," I said. "Here you are." Wow. Stellar opening.

Her eyes dropped, her ridiculously long lashes casting a shadow on the curve of her cheek. "Um...ah...yeah." Lush, glossy lips, quivering.

Her voice was beautiful. Husky and feminine. It affected me pretty much the same way a warm, tender lick of her pink tongue against my cock would affect me.

"You okay?" It popped out before I could stop it. It was a reflex, nothing more. It went against my most primal instinct to be rude to any woman, let alone a girl whose tits were offered up to my eyes like a tray of creampuffs.

"I'm fine." She licked her full, plump lower lip, making my breath catch and my ass clench.

"You drove four hours from Gholston Flats this morning?" I couldn't keep the disapproval from my voice. "In the freezing rain and the snow?"

"I came in yesterday," she assured me. "Stayed at the Dew Drop Inn by the Interstate. Thanks for meeting with me. I wasn't sure you ever would."

"You shouldn't be here." I made my voice stone hard. "I told you."

"So...why did you finally agree?"

I shrugged. "I just had to see if the girl in the photos was really you."

"Did you like the pictures?" Hopeful eyes. Sweet smile. Perfect white teeth. Un-fucking-believable. I blew out a breath, keeping the stream of air slow and even.

Did I like them. Hah. They were etched into his mind. Her in the baby doll nightgown, reclining on the bed. Her in the red lace demi bra and boy shorts. Her in the ruffly shirt, no bra, shirt unbuttoned, artfully draped to hide her nipples, but leaving her belly bare, down to that itty bitty triangle of white lace stretched over—well, I couldn't call it a bush. More like a swatch. A tantalizing shadow beneath the sheer white.

"I liked them." My voice rasped. "I'd have to be dead not to like them."

Her lips curved. "Great. So, are you convinced it's me?"

Don't fall in the hole! The warning yammered in my head. Lose the crazy girl. Send her running. Outraged and terrified. Burned beyond recall. Never to return.

Do her a fucking favor, dickwad. She has to scram. Now.

I kept my eyes steely. "Show me more."

She blinked, looking bewildered. The chin went up a notch. "More?"

"Show me what you got, babe." I projected the nastiest vibe I had in my playbook. Ugly, cold. Mean as a fucking snake.

She straightened, tossed back her hair, making it bounce. Eyes locked on mine. Shoulders back.

That hot glow in her eyes did not go away. It deepened. Her slender hands pressed her belly, then drifted up, barely cupping her breasts, brushing over them.

My heartrate kicked up to a panicked gallop.

It was the look in her eyes that undid me. That hot, buzzy glow of arousal and surrender, as if she were already spreading her legs for me. Baring herself completely.

Ready to reveal her own naked, beating heart.

I had to look away, close my eyes, use all my considerable training in self-control. Silent seconds ticked by. *Back off. Simmer down. Concentrate.*

I tried to reboot the flint-eyed predator look. "Let's see the rest of it."

Her gaze faltered. Her lashes fluttered. "Rest of what?"

"You know what I mean. Let me see the goods."

A blush of pink crept up her cheeks. "Ah...how?"

I almost groaned. She was supposed to get pissed at my horndog thuggishness and tell me to fuck off and die. But she just kept fielding my shit like it was nothing.

"Your pussy," I said. "Naked. Hot and juicy. Your fingers, going in. Diddling yourself. Let me see you do it."

She glanced around, at the guards, the other visitors in the room. Gave me a panicked look.

I responded to her bewilderment with a feral smile. "Don't tell me no."

She hesitated. "I can't. They'll throw me out. But I'll talk about it. If you want. They might be listening. They spot check. A woman outside in the waiting room told me. But I'll risk it. If you want me to."

Thud. Thud. Thud. My heart was slamming.

"I wore a silk thong just for you," she began, in a voice so low it was barely audible. "If we were alone, I'd let you watch me rub my pussy with the silk part. I'd get so excited with your eyes on me. So frustrated. Because you can look...but you can't touch. Then I'd roll over onto a big pillow. I'd lift my ass up for you to look at."

I stared at her, mesmerized. Open-mouthed. Holy fucking *fuck.*

"I'll ride that pillow, just rubbing my clit against it until I'm so wet and desperate," she whispered. "Breathing hard. But I can't come yet...because you told me not to. So I make myself stop... right before I explode. Just shaking, I'm so ready. It's killing me. Then I arch back and reach around so I can stroke my bare ass cheeks. I'm so hot. Because I know you're watching me. Looking at my pussy. My ass."

I nodded, helplessly. Seeing it. All of it. My heart thudded wildly.

"And then," she murmured. "...then I spread myself wide open. So you can see absolutely everything. But I can't come without you. I need your fingers in me. And your cock. Only yours. Pushing all the way into me. Fucking me and fucking me, so deep and hard, until I'm yelling, begging, for all of you. Please. Oh please."

This was a trainwreck. I couldn't even reply. Here I was, trying to scare her away by being an asshole, and she countered by talking dirty like a seasoned professional. Which she wasn't. I was sure of that. No, she was just unhinged. And incredibly eager to please, and up for absolutely anything.

She was a force of nature. And I was right on the verge of coming.

"Why are you here?" I demanded. "I told you not to come."

"I told you," she said. "In my letters. I read about your story, and I—"

"I don't want you, Sandee," I cut in. "You know what I'm in prison for, right? You know the details of my case?"

"Of course," she said eagerly. "I read everything I could find."

"And you're not scared?"

"Of you, no! Why should I be? You didn't do it! I'm sure of it. You're innocent, and you shouldn't be here at all! You should be free! You're innocent!"

"I can't discuss that with you," I said harshly.

She leaned forward, eyes sparkling with tears. "Why not? Tell me the whole story. I could be, like, your advocate, from the outside, you know? I could find out things for you, do things for you! Whatever you wanted, whatever could help. I could prove your innocence, and we could be together! I would do anything you—"

"No!" My voice chopped down onto her eager rush of words.

"But—but—"

"The last thing I need is a brainless dollbaby messing around in my shit," I said. "I have enough problems."

Her spine stiffened. Pride flashed in her eyes. "Dollbaby? Brainless? Really?"

"You heard me," I said. "Find someone else to fixate on, bitch. I got nothing."

Her lips trembled. "I don't believe you," she said. "I have to follow my heart."

"Hearts get confused," I said. "Come on, Sandee. Wake up. You're a beautiful girl. Any man with a pulse would want you. It shouldn't be so goddamn hard."

Sandee shook her head. "You'd be surprised. Most men are pigs. Or else they're mean, or taken, or crazy. Or as dumb as a box of rocks."

"And you think a maximum security correctional facility is the place to fish for your next candidate? Seriously? You think you'll find a better class of man *here?*"

Sandee's cheeks flamed. Her gaze slid away.

It made me feel like shit, but this tack seemed to be working. "You can do better than me," I said. "I'll never even be able to touch you." I paused, and then added. "Wait. Is that what this is all about? You want a man, but you can't stand to be touched? Is that what's going on?"

She swallowed nervously. "No," she whispered. "I would love to be touched. By you, anyway."

I shook my head. "I can't. Not ever."

"Anything can happen!" she insisted. "I won't give up hope!"

"Give it up," I said. "I don't want you. Not now, not ever. Get that through your thick head."

She chewed her lip. "There are ways and ways to touch," she said, her voice barely more than a whisper.

I squinted at her. "Huh? What are you talking about?"

"Minds can touch." That hopeful, way-out-in-orbit look made me intensely uneasy. "Hearts can touch. Souls can touch. Even if bodies can't."

My head was pounding again. "Oh, for fuck's sake. Don't start."

"Don't shut me out," she pleaded. "It's true. This isn't all about sex. It could be bigger than that. You know it. You're just afraid of it."

Damn right, I was afraid.

"Listen up." I made my voice ugly. "I met with you so I could tell you to disappear. I passed those photos out to the meanest motherfuckers in this place, to jerk themselves off to. Now they all owe me favors. So thanks."

She stared at me, and for a split second, I saw it. She was angry at me. Furious. I'd finally gotten to her. Good. Now, to keep the upper hand. By brute force.

"Fuck off, Sandee," I said. "I mean it."

"James, please! Please, let me be sweet to you. It's all I want." Eyes wide. Begging, sweetly. In a heartbeat, she'd decided not to get her feelings hurt about him giving away her porno pix.

I shook my head.

Sandee tilted her head to one side. She sure could turn it on and off. The look in her eyes was almost like dreamy fascination. "You're trying to act super mean," she murmured. "But you know what? I can tell it's all just an act."

Fuck. I gritted my teeth until my jaw hurt. "You're wrong. Don't fool yourself."

"I can see right through you." She lifted her hand, and put her spread-out fingers delicately against the glass. Her nails were painted a glittery, opalescent blue.

I had the crazy urge to touch my fingertips to hers, just to see if her body heat transferred through the glass, but I killed it in time. "You only see what you want to see. You're living in a fantasy world and you're gonna get slammed."

"No." That luminous smile again. "I see more than you think. I could see more if you shared with me. Let's start over. Go slower. We can write to each other. Talk on the phone before I visit again. We could be, you know. Intimate. On the phone."

"No, we couldn't." My voice was getting thick. "I'm not interested."

"I could know you, James." Her throaty voice was low, caressing. "Like no one ever has. And you could know me." Her hands caressed the glass, silently pleading for contact. "You want to be known, underneath your super tough-guy act. And I think...I think you'd like it. If you tried it. To have someone...love you. For real."

A shudder jolted through me. Oh, please. Stop. As if this

crazy shitshow was for real. As if this silly, painted doll of a woman could see inside my head. See the gears grinding in my private darkness, and then turn around and talk to me about love.

I was getting all flustered. Breathing hard. *Get real, Clearwater.* Two possibilities. One: Sandee was a honey-pot, sent to destroy me. Two: Sandee was a lonely, dippy girl with a wild imagination and incredibly poor judgment. Either possibility was a disaster, because being cruel to her exhausted me. This chick needed to get out of my face. Right. Fucking. *Now.*

"Fuck off, Sandee," I said. "Go home. We're done here."

Her mouth tightened. "Please," she pleaded. "Don't do this. I love you."

"You're nuts. Get lost." I stood, and a CO took notice, moving toward the cubicle.

"No! I won't give up on you! I won't—"

I put the phone down. Sandee leaned forward as if she could reach through the barrier and hold on to me somehow. She knocked frantically on the glass.

A female guard appeared at her side and took her by the arms. Hustling her out, heading off trouble. An old pro.

And I felt like I'd just kicked a kitten to death.

The shackles hobbling me on the walk back to the cellblock bugged me. I'd been playing it cool, keeping my inner garbage ruthlessly organized. Keeping things slotted into their appointed boxes. Bill's and Hank's and Franco's murders, the fiery cluster-fuck at the Ready Line complex. Being betrayed by a former comrade in arms. Being framed for murder. My best friend, Shane, kidnapped and dragged off to God knew where, suffering God alone knew what. And his brother, Ethan, also my friend, convinced I had sold Shane out.

Like I'd ever given a fuck about money in my life. Like I'd betray a brother for it.

The timeline just got moved up. I couldn't articulate why, but I had stayed alive in deadly hot zones around the world by following my gut instincts, and right now, my guts were screaming at me to move, move, *move*. Get the fuck out of here. Tonight.

Sandee's arrival was a terrible omen. Even if she genuinely was exactly who she purported to be, the fact that I'd caught her attention made me feel like a fucking neon sign. If a bubblehead like Sandee had glommed on to me, who else might have? Who else had noticed James Craig's mugshot, splashed all over a public website frequented by lonely hearts? The whole thing was dangerous as all fuck, and not just for me.

I made straight for the hiding place for the cell phone I had bought from a smuggler as soon as I got here. The plan had been to contact the Drake brothers, Amos, Remy, and Darius, ten days from now, when they were scheduled to be waiting right nearby. I didn't have ten days. Maybe it was instinct, maybe just my poor delicate nerves, but I was sure of it. That hammer was coming down. Any second now.

I counted ceiling tiles from the end of the east wing, to the blind spot in the security camera, and made sure no guard was looking. I reached up, popped the tile on one side, letting the phone slide off into my other hand. When I turned it on, it still had some charge. I punched in Amos's number. He picked up swiftly. "Dude. All good?"

"It goes down tonight," I told him.

Amos whistled. "Shit, dude. We can't get there in time. You'll be on your own."

"Where are you guys?"

"Nairobi. On a mission for Hobart. Back in three days. Can it wait?"

"No," I told him, wondering how the fuck I was so sure. "Has to be tonight."

"Fuck me," Amos muttered. "We should've cleared our calendars until you were out of there."

"Not feasible," I told him. "Would have looked suspicious.

Don't sweat it. We planned this so I could pull the trigger myself if I needed to."

"I don't like it," Amos said darkly. "Too many variables."

"The Jeep is ready?"

"Yeah. Remy checked the battery ten days ago. Full tank of gas. Still completely covered in brush. Probably snow, too, at this point. The safe houses are ready."

"Good. I need you to get that money delivered to Ramon's team. The list I got you last time. Ten grand apiece. They're handling my diversion tonight."

"I'll call my guy right now and get it done," Amos said.

"Thanks. Gotta go," I said. "Hey. Dude. Thanks for believing in me. All of you. Tell the others. You know. Just in case."

"Don't get sentimental on me, man. Get the fuck out of there. Call me when you're clear. And watch yourself."

"Will do. Later."

I hung up, listening for a moment to make sure I was still alone, and stowed the phone in the pouch I'd fashioned, in the seam of the coverall's pant leg.

Breaking out of the prison without any outside backup was not optimal, but that was just too goddamn bad. I strode through the recreation area, looking around until I spotted Ramon.

I found him playing cards at one of the tables. He was a tall, lanky guy, serving a sentence for armed robbery, and one of the first allies I had cultivated here, as soon as I figured out the power dynamics among the inmates.

I met Ramon's eyes briefly, jerking my chin in the direction of the library.

He met me there a few minutes later, stopping right inside the door. I pitched my voice low. "Tonight," I said. "Cafeteria. Seven fifteen."

Ramon frowned. "Fuck. Short notice."

I shrugged. I had paid for the privilege of short notice. For months, I had been funneling large sums of money on a regular basis to Ramon's wife, Filomena, in San Jose. Enough money to cover her rent, keep all three of Ramon's kids enrolled in private Catholic school, and pay for a nursing home for his Alzheimer's-stricken father. In return, Ramon and his crew had agreed to start a prison riot for me.

"You're breaking out tonight?" Ramon asked.

I just looked at him, saying nothing. He knew better than to ask me that.

Ramon glanced around to make sure no one was listening. "I have fourteen months to go," he said quietly. "If I do this, they'll slap on more time."

"They might," I said. "That risk was factored into the deal."

"You'll send Mena money for the additional time I serve? Double for any time served beyond my original sentence. Ten grand apiece to my crew."

"As agreed," I said.

"Tonight," Ramon said, his voice flat.

I walked out of the library and headed toward my cell.

Mickey Savelletri, my cellmate, sat on the bunk, reading a paperback book from the library. His nervous leg was jittering as if it were having its own private seizure.

He looked up at me, blinking rapidly, and brandished his book. "Hey. Did you know that forests talk via fungal networks?" he asked. "Wild stuff. My brain's on fire."

"Great," I said. "Let it burn."

Mickey was a scrawny guy in his thirties, with stringy black hair, dark olive skin and huge, shadowed dark eyes. He was on the autism spectrum, and he'd had been badly in need of the protection I could offer. Prison was hard on guys like him.

After the Ready Line massacre, I'd learned that Vito Adriani, a Las Vegas crime boss, had partnered with Boer, my ex-colleague. Boer had his own security company, which occasionally had partnered with Ready Line. I'd served in the Rangers with Boer for years, but the guy had never been folded into the core Unredeemables group, for some reason I couldn't quite pinpoint. I'd pinpointed it now. Too fucking late.

Boer had faked his own death somehow. He'd ostensibly burned to death with all the others. He'd stuffed me into my car, still unconscious, and shoved it off a bridge. Framing me so it looked as if I was the one who killed everyone, and then died by accident, trying to get away from the scene of the crime. Like a blundering asshole.

Some digging had revealed that Adriani's accountant, Mickey Savelletri, had just been sentenced to four years at Kalaharee. He knew Adriani's business, and his associates' business. And my prison info-mining scheme, such as it was, took form.

I genuinely liked Mickey. He was brilliant, but had no ruthlessness to offset it. He was a numbers savant with a photographic memory. Unfortunately for him, his abilities had come to the attention of a crime boss. Mickey had been offered a job doing Adriani's accounts, and Adriani was not a guy you refused. Not if you wanted to keep your body parts attached.

Mickey wasn't a criminal, but he'd taken the most recent fall for his boss. Four years in Kalaharee for fraud, but he didn't dare rat Adriani out. He'd be dead in a day.

Mickey wanted out from under Adriani's yoke, so freedom was the coin I had offered him. In return, he had dirt he'd collected on Boer. A thumb drive chock full of evidence that Boer had faked his own death, proof that he'd framed me for murder, etc., etc. Account numbers of where he'd stashed his money. Things I could use to find him, nail him down, and eventually, clear my name. And prove to Ethan Masters that I hadn't sold out Shane Masters.

Mickey had agreed to spill the goods when I got him out, but he wouldn't give me anything before, and I didn't blame him. It took months to gain even that much trust.

Current plan: get Mickey out and keep him safe. Retrieve

Mickey's intel, which led me to Boer. Make Boer talk. Then, make Boer pay...screaming.

"It's on," I told him. "Tonight."

Mickey's eyes widened, darting nervously toward the door. "Wh-what? When?"

"After dinner," I said. "Supply closet. North wing. Seven fifteen. Don't be late."

I left the cell before he could reply and paced the corridors, rehearsing tonight's plan. My mind raced, and my dick was still buzzing from the sex kitten headcase.

Thinking about her made me want to kick the walls. I didn't want to feel bad about hurting her feelings. I didn't want to worry about her driving home in the blizzard, or think about her lips trembling. Her big eyes, full of longing. I had problems to solve. A sad girl trolling for attention did not make the cut.

I wasn't going to think about that ivory silk thong, hot and slick with her lube.

I was busy, goddamnit. I had no fucks to give.

CHAPTER 4

WHEEDON, 50 MILES FROM
KALAHAREE SPRINGS
CORRECTIONAL FACILITY FOR MEN,
LATER THAT EVENING

Red Watson fidgeted in the hard, plain chair. He had an uncomfortable sense he was about to be punished for something, but he didn't understand what, or why.

He'd done exactly as he was told to do. But the guy in the blank, freaky white mask on the other side of the desk made him so gut-twitchingly nervous, he wanted to dash for the crapper.

Red clenched his ass and mastered the urge. This should be over soon, and he could blast out of there onto the black-ice covering the roads to Kalaharee Springs. Fishtail home to his family, hopefully without ending up in a ditch and freezing to death. This was for them, he repeated to himself. For Maryellen, Kylie, and Krista.

He just had to wait for this strange guy to disappear back under whatever rock he'd crawled out from, and hope he never came back. This guy paid well, and Red prided himself on hustling for his family, but some jobs actually weren't worth the money.

His stomach growled. He'd been unable to eat at the prison, knowing he had to drive all the way out to Wheedon for this damned meeting once his shift was over. He wiped his face, sticky with a cold, clammy sweat, which not even the crackling fire in the fancy marble hearth could warm.

The man he'd been instructed to call "Mr. Jones" stared at him fixedly through the eyeholes of the mask. The effect made Red shudder, clenching harder.

"James Craig," Mr. Jones murmured. "So this woman who went by the name of Sandee McGillis came to see a man named James Craig? You're sure that was the name? It wasn't Mickey Savalletri?"

"Uh, yes, sir, I'm sure. It was James Craig, not Mickey. That's what the paperwork said," Red said. "I checked before I came. I wasn't in the visiting area today when they talked, but I have security footage of Craig in the yard with Mickey."

"Hmmph. Show me that footage."

The masked guy stared intently at the security footage Red had copied and brought with him, which made it a little easier for him to breathe, finally. Jones's blank, chilly gaze creeped Red out. So did the weird, puffy greenish color of the skin around his eyes. Like the guy was dead under there. Christ, he was psyching himself out.

Jones's female associate, who'd introduced herself as Ms. Smith, bent over the laptop keyboard. She was a beautiful woman, part Asian, high cheekbones, with a glossy, swinging black bob.

Ms. Smith tapped at the keys. Red was so wound up, he couldn't even enjoy the amazing shape of her rounded ass, sheathed in the tailored black wool pants.

"There he is," she murmured, glancing at Mr. Jones, and pointing at the screen. "The tall one, right next to Mickey. Black cap. Turning around now."

The sound that came out of Mr. Jones made Red jump in his chair. Jones leaned closer to the screen, eyes white-rimmed. "Shit!" he bellowed. "That's Jed Clearwater!"

Red looked around frantically. "Uh...uh...who..."

"Fuck!" Mr. Jones's gaze swept the room for something to blame, and inevitably, fell on Red. "Why didn't you tell me he was at Kalaharee?" He turned to Ms. Smith. "Jed Clearwater is yard buddies in the joint with Mickey Savelletri, and nobody fucking notices? Jed Clearwater chats up fucking Freya Masters on visiting day, and nobody says a word? What the *fuck* do I pay you people for?"

Red threw his hands up in a spasm of panic. "I didn't know about anyone named Jed Clearwater! James Craig is the name on his paperwork, and I had no idea—"

"How long has he been in there?" Mr. Jones bellowed.

"Ah, uh, five months, I think. Late spring, early summer maybe, more or less," Red babbled. "He was transferred from—"

"Son of a *bitch*," Mr. Jones snarled. "What the *fuck* is going on in there? How often has he seen Freya Masters?""

"Uh, who's Freya Masters? Today, he saw this Sandee McGillis woman. Look, I didn't know that he—"

"Shut up, you fucking idiot! Sandee McGillis is Freya Masters!"

Red cringed in his chair, making himself as small as a guy with a beer gut like his own possibly could. He always felt tense with these people, but now, this wasn't tension. This was bowel-loosening fear. He was way out of his depth.

"What did she talk about with him?" Mr. Jones demanded.

"Well, um, like I said, I wasn't in the visiting area today, so I—"

"So no one was listening in?" Mr. Jones's voice rose. "No one knows if she's carrying information out for him?"

"Um, let me explain, okay? It's a passive listening system, and it picks up keywords and slang that activate red flags, for drugs, gun, that kind of—"

"Can you access the archives? Pull today's recording?"

"Uh, maybe," Red faltered. "Theoretically. I'd have to ask for help."

"Then ask for fucking help, right now! Figure it out! I want to hear that recording today. Every fucking word of it. Is that clear?"

Red's mind raced. It was literally impossible. The people in admin who might have a chance in hell of knowing how to access those archives worked regular office hours, which were winding up right about now, and he was forty-five minutes away from Kalaharee Springs, way the hell out here in Wheedon. Or more like an hour, in these weather conditions. "I'll try," he offered, weakly.

"Try? That's not enough, asshole. Get it done." Mr. Jones spat the words out. He turned to Ms. Smith. "We take the Masters woman tonight. I need to question her. No more delays. Things are getting out of hand. We have to find out what he said."

Ms. Smith shrugged. "Sure," she said. "Better to nab her now when she's all alone than try when she's got her brother's corporate security hovering all over her."

Mr. Jones made an irritated sound. "Where is she now?"

Ms. Smith consulted her phone, tapping in a text. She looked up. "The team I assigned to her tell me that she's at the Red Rock Diner on Colum Creek Highway," she said. "And she's staying at the Dew Drop. We wouldn't have known she was in town at all if she hadn't turned on her phone for a few minutes last night after she checked in. That was lucky."

"I don't pay you big bucks to rely on fucking luck," Mr. Jones ground out.

Ms. Smith gave him a dazzling smile. "No, I have extreme competence and luck, combined. It's a winning combination. Don't worry. She's not going anywhere. No one's traveling on these roads tonight. You'll have her. Within hours. Don't stress yourself."

Mr. Jones turned those eerie, headlights-of-a-car eyes on Red through the freaky mask. "You have contacts in the inmate population, right? Can you organize a hit?"

Red's heart thudded. He hemmed and hawed, and gulped.

"Ah...I, um, don't want trouble. Violence, I mean. I just handle info. That's all I do. I don't want to get involved in—"

"I could care less what you want, dickhead. Shut up and listen carefully. Jed Clearwater and Mickey Savalletri have to die tonight."

Red's guts cramped horribly. "I can't be involved in something like that!"

"Red, we're talking about convicted criminals," Mr. Jones snapped. "No one gives a shit if they die. You're doing the American taxpayers a favor."

"But I...I can't..." Red's jaw flapped helpessly. "I can't possibly."

"What do you think, Ms. Smith, about Red's compensation?" Mr. Jones said. "It is a considerable risk, after all. A sixfold increase in our usual token of esteem?"

The serene face of Ms. Smith suddenly blazed into a sweet, terrifying smile. "Oh, tenfold, I think," she said. "Don't be stingy, Mr. Jones. It's unbecoming."

"Women," Mr. Jones murmured. "They do love an extravagant gesture. Well then, Ms. Smith? Do the honors."

Red watched, stunned, as Ms. Smith pulled open a canvas bag and began to take out wrapped blocks of bank notes. She set them down. Two. Four. Six. Eight.

"I can't," Red said, helplessly.

"You have to," Mr. Jones said heartily. "No choice, my friend."

"But something like that takes time to—"

"Do it for Maryellen," Ms. Smith said. "Although with what's on your plate tonight, you won't be able to pick her up at the end of her shift at the library. So sweet of her to volunteer. And in this weather, too. Brrr." She shivered, theatrically. "She'll have to take the bus. Poor thing. It's just raw out there."

Red stared at her. His jaw began to spasm.

"Yes, we know Maryellen's car is in the shop," Mr. Jones said. "Just as well, with this nasty snow, in my book. But it makes things complicated. Kylie has to be picked up from band practice. Krista from her theater rehearsal, hmm? Busy busy."

"D-d-d-don't get my family mixed up in this—"

"I'm just thinking out loud." Mr. Jones poked the canvas bag. "A little more, Ms. Smith, for his expenses. Subcontracting is expensive."

Ms. Smith gave Red a flirtatious smile, and pulled out two more blocks.

"In just a couple of years, you'll be looking at college costs for Krista." Ms. Smith's voice was a taunting lilt. "She's a good student. So she'll definitely apply to expensive schools, I'm sure. It's a disgrace, that a college education is no longer affordable for the middle class without taking on crippling debt. But it is what it is, of course. And we do what we must. Isn't that right, Red?"

"But...but..."

"Make it happen." Mr. Jones's voice was stony. "And one more thing."

Red braced himself. "What?"

"Tell your people to make those bastards sorry."

"Um...what do you mean? How, exactly?"

Mr. Jones rolled his eyes. "Be creative. Use your brain, if you have one. Now take your money and get the fuck out of here. I'm sick of looking at you."

Ms. Smith slid his money into a large manila envelope and passed it to Red with a bright, professional smile.

"Kylie would be my first choice, you know," Mr. Jones said suddenly. "I love that age. Thirteen. Chubby, budding. Super-fresh. I like redheads, too."

"Oh, Mr. Jones," the woman chided him gently. "Don't scare him. It's counterproductive." She took Red's arm, and hustled him out, through the foyer, and out onto the porch, where snow was blowing sideways in the violent gusts of wind. "He's in one of his moods," she murmured into his ear. "Don't provoke him, Red. Or disappoint him. For Kylie's sake. I'm sure you understand."

The door slammed shut. A gust of wind knocked the manila envelope from Red's hands and into the slush by the walkway, where the envelope burst apart.

The paper tape around the bundled bills split, scattering the bills everywhere.

Red stepped ankle deep into filthy slush, and crouched down to salvage what he could.

CHAPTER 5

Jed

I scanned the prison cafeteria again. Mickey was still nowhere to be seen.

Shit. Mickey wasn't even physiologically capable of forgetting a date or a detail. He was meticulous. And highly motivated. He wanted his life back.

Which meant something had gone sideways. It was that kind of day.

Timing was key. The riot would start at seven fifteen, when I'd meet Mickey in the north wing, and use my cell phone to detonate the device that would disable the locks in the north cell block, the grid that fed the electric fence and the first backup generator. The second generator would kick in quickly, but Mickey and I would have three minutes of darkness, floodlights down, to cut through the temporarily deadened electrified fence. Once through, we ran for the Jeep, hidden under a pile of brush about a mile away. It was a tight window. Also, we had no outerwear, and it was a blizzard.

I'd be fine. I'd dealt with worse. But I was worried about Mickey.

Cafeteria food was shitty, as always. Processed crap cooked in rancid fat. Barely recognizable vegetables. Mold was growing on the bread. I'd dropped thirty pounds in here, but it wasn't a problem tonight. I was too tense to eat.

I glanced at Ramon, who sat with his team, chowing down. He'd looked in my direction when I'd walked in, and given me a barely perceptible nod. We were good to go.

Amos by now would have initiated the various payments to the wives, girlfriends, etc. Ten grand apiece, which was expensive, but what else did I have to do with my money? There was nothing I gave a fuck about but this. It was everything to me.

It sucked that Mickey was late. It sucked that Sandee had hunted me down in here. Why would Boer send someone like her to sweet-talk me? It wasn't his style. A knife between the ribs would be more in character.

But she couldn't be for real. How could she have noticed me? I'd been brought into the prison with no press or fanfare. Darius Drake knew a guy with prison admin contacts who owed Darius his life from back in their time in the military. He'd quietly arranged for me to be arrested for an unsolved murder and held without bail at Kalaharee while awaiting trial. The paperwork wouldn't stand up to intense scrutiny, and no administrator at Kalaharee knew about it right now, which was how I hoped things would stay. I hadn't expected to be in so long. Courting Mickey took time.

My thoughts kept circling back to Sandee. How she must fend off propositions and tedious grab-assery every day of her life. So why fixate on incarcerated felons?

I hoped she'd gotten back to the motel safely. That she had good snow tires, and warmer clothes to change into. I also hoped all the pieces of my puzzle were still in place. Bolt cutters, sealed in heavy plastic and buried near the fence. The first backup generator had to fail exactly when I made the call, or it all went to hell. But all of these preparations had been made months ago. Too much goddamn time had passed.

I'd prepped the explosives myself, arranging to blow out just the part of the grid that controlled the door locks in the north wing, and the electric fence, all with a call from my cell phone. Three minutes was enough, if the guards were busy with a riot in the cafeteria. By the time a search was initiated, Mickey and I would long gone.

If all went well.

I sensed movement behind me, and turned. Darryl Weeks and his gang of thugs were approaching, circling around my table. Darryl led the white power contingent. They were beefy, pasty-faced guys with scraggly beards and tattooed faces, all with that flat-mouthed, dead-eyed glare. Darryl's eyes were puffy slits, and his grin showed off the rotten, discolored teeth of a methhead.

"Hey, Jimmy boy," he drawled. "So sad to see you all alone, without your little pet. But hey, man, nothing lasts forever, right? Better get yourself another fucktoy. After tonight, he'll be all used up. Might as well flush him."

"You saw Mickey?" I asked.

Darryl's smile widened. He took the brownie on my tray and crammed it into his mouth. Crumbs sprayed from his lips as he spoke. "He was heading toward the south shower room with some big, bad motherfuckers when I saw him," he said. "Shoulda kept a closer eye on your bad little boyfriend, cupcake."

I breathed down panic. Truer words were never spoken. I should have kept Mickey stuck to me like glue, but I hadn't wanted to attract attention. Mistake number one. Darryl could be lying, just to get a reaction. Or baiting a trap.

But Mickey wasn't here, and the clock was ticking. "Fuck off," I said.

The snake tattoo on Darryl's throat writhed as he swallowed.

He leered, his blackened teeth slimed with chocolate. "You're gonna be so lonely, Jimmy."

I walked away, feeling the weight of many eyes as I left the cafeteria. I had only ten or so minutes to get to the north wing. If I checked the south wing bathroom and Mickey wasn't there, I'd be cutting into our precious diversion time, having to search for him elsewhere. Was Darryl leading me into an ambush, or just rattling my cage?

It wasn't the first time I'd been forced to make a life or death decision with insufficient information. Wasn't the first time I'd fucked it up, either.

Shane could attest to that. Billy, Franco, Hank. Mom, too, for that matter.

Not helpful. I shoved that thought back into the dark before it could fuck my concentration and picked up speed, trying not to let myself sprint. Tonight was not a night to catch the attention of any of the COs. My heart galloped.

I stopped outside the bathroom. The fluorescent lights in that room buzzed like a dying bug. A shower was running. The sound was ominous.

I didn't see anyone as I walked in. The room had tiled shower stalls and toilet cubicles, chest high. The air was heavy, damp. Steam clamped around me, a smothering embrace. Every wall sweated and dripped. The place stank, but that was normal.

A dark object lay on the floor in the end of the room. As I moved closer, I realized that it was dark red, not black, with a pinkish cloud around it, and it was clogging the shower drain, causing a puddle to form. A pinkish puddle.

Get the fuck out of here. My brain stem was screaming it, shrinking from the horror, but the need to know drove me deeper into that death trap. Water from the shower was flooding out of the stall, creeping over dirty white tiles. Tinted pink.

The object in the drain was a human tongue. Oh, fuck, fuck, *fuck...*

I spun around just as Russ, Finn, Cody, and Bobby, Darryl's goons, rushed me from behind. I barely blocked the jab from the white plastic spike Russ held in time. It scored my arm, but I seized Russ's wrist, wrenching and torqueing until he howled. He bent over, spinning around, and I drove that spike into Finn's eye just as he rushed in at me with a screwdriver.

A wet sound, as the spike jabbed in deep—and Finn flopped down into the water, the spike protruding from his eye. A sharpened toothbrush. The other eye was wide in surprise. I kept twisting Russ's arm until he screamed, until I felt the wet crunch of bones, tendons, popping and splintering, and flung him away, ducking to avoid a roundhouse from Cody. I swept Cody's leg, and he hit the wet floor with a grunt.

"You know what's about to happen to your new girlfriend, right?" Darryl's taunting voice, from the door. Darryl liked to stand back and let his guys fight for him.

"I don't have a girlfriend," I said savagely.

"Aw, Jimmy boy, don't lie to Uncle Darryl. Sure you do. We know the guy at the post office. The one who opens the mail. We know about those dirty pictures she sends you."

Cody lunged at me, and I was a split second late in my countermove, barely jerking back in time, sliding and pinwheeling on the wet floor. "Don't know what the fuck you're talking about."

Darryl cackled. "Asshole. Love makes you weak. Too bad I didn't get to see that blonde bitch myself. Everyone was talking. Blonde, pink hair, pointy tits, all painted up, dressed to bend over a car and get fucked in a parking lot. Super young. Dirty boy."

"I don't know the girl who came today," I said. "She's nothing to me. And she's a fucking idiot. She came here on a dare. I made sure she won't come back."

Darryl clucked his tongue. "Well, bless her little heart. I'll pass that info on up the food chain, but ya gotta understand, Jimmy. When she came on to you, she caught the big guy's attention. Now he wants some. So if this bitch likes boning crooks, she'll be in hog heaven soon enough. They'll come for her tonight. That's what I heard."

"What big guy?" I demanded. "Who's coming for her?"

"Figure it out, shit-stain," Darryl snarled. "The one who hates your guts. The one who wants you dead. I imagine they'll treat your little bitch about like we treated your fuckboy, after they're done with her. She has that to look forward to."

"Where the fuck is Mickey?" I yelled. "What did you do to him?"

Darryl shook his head, grinning. Cody swung again. I let my rage take over. Block and grab, twist and spin. *Crunch*, I rammed the guy's head into the top of a urinal, leaving a big red splotch on the white porcelain.

I let go, and faced Bobby, the fourth guy, as Cody hit the floor. He was a tall, bald dude, sunken eyes, big yellow teeth, with face tats made him look like a skull. He lunged at me with a shard of broken glass.

A block, a stab to his eyes, a knee into his balls, and Bobby flew, hitting the floor with a wet slap. I followed up with some organ-rupturing kicks to the lower back, and he was curled into the fetal position, gasping for breath.

Darryl backed away as the water got near his feet. The men on the floor whimpered and moaned. I was ready to snap necks indiscriminately, but that motherfucker Darryl had to die first. I leaped for him, grabbed his throat, and slammed him up to the wall, squeezing his meaty throat.

Darryl clawed at my hands, but I couldn't feel it. I just squeezed harder, until his eyes were bulging, tongue protruding, face going purple—

An alarm started squealing. I heard faraway yells. Crashing.

Aw, fuck. The riot. *Mickey.*

I flung Darryl away, and splashed through the flooded room, toward the tongue.

Mickey lay in the last shower stall, inches deep in water, naked. Ah, fuck, no.

My brain refused to process all the things they had done to him. He was covered in blood. They'd cut many pieces off. I fell to my knees next to him.

He still had eyes, and he stared up at me, weeping blood from his broken capillaries. His chin and chest were slick with blood from his mouth. His jaw was shattered. His teeth were everywhere.

He reached with a trembling hand as I dropped to my knees in the water beneath him. "Mickey," I forced out. "Buddy. I'm sorry. I should have been protecting you."

Mickey grasped my wrist with a sticky, claw-like hand, coughing helplessly. He was choking on blood, spraying it on me with every desperate, mewling sound he made.

"Don't try to talk," I urged, sliding my hands beneath his shuddering body. "I'll take you to the infirmary. You need a doctor. A trauma surgeon, a transfusion."

Again, the wordless howl, the burst of blood from his mouth, and he twisted away from my grasp, touched his hand to his bloodied chin and hit the filthy tile wall, leaving a smeared hand-print. Then he began to scrawl, in a loose sprawling script, in blood. *Joe Grifo OR.* At least I thought that the last symbols were O and R. He looked at me, and then made a swirling gesture in front of his face with his stiff, shaking fingers. He made the swirling gesture again, and again, staring with wild intensity, like I should understand what he meant. Like I'd be an idiot not to.

But I didn't. Not a fucking clue. And as I watched, the desperate entreaty in his eyes faded, replaced by emptiness.

His skinny, blood-soaked chest stopped moving. Blood stopped foaming and spattering out of the corners of his mouth. The bloody letters he had scribbled had dripped down the wall in the condensation like the title font of a horror movie, no longer decipherable. I felt for his pulse. Nothing.

Mickey was gone. The mission was gone.

What the fuck did I do now? The squealing alarm penetrated my consciousness again as if from miles away.

The riot. My window. I staggered to my feet. Stumbled out, waterlogged. Numb.

Keep to the plan. Go-go-go. If I didn't leave tonight, they would regroup and kill me as they'd killed Mickey. Even if they didn't get me tonight, chances were I would take the blame for this clusterfuck. I looked guilty. Like I'd taken a bath in blood.

That would be a whole new bag of dicks to suck, and who had the fucking time.

I staggered through the fallen men in the bathroom, and headed toward the north wing, trying to make my fingers work somehow. Groping for the cell phone. I was shaking. Adrenaline, shock. My eyes were wet.

Mickey. Jesus, Mickey. That funny, wiseass little shithead. A whole life of being bullied and used and shoved around, and he'd still had dreams of being free. Of lying on a sugar sand beach someplace on a towel, reading a book in blessed peace, with no one to bug him or interrupt him. After a few months, I'd started wanting that for Mickey, too. Completely apart from the intel I needed from him. Damn, the guy had deserved to just live his life and not be fucked with, for once. It wasn't that much to ask.

But no, it was not allowed. Those filthy, greedy scum-sucking motherfuckers had gotten to him first. They had chewed him up and spat out his bones.

All because of me. I'd brought my curse along with me, just like with Shane and the others. I am shit luck to anyone who gets near me, and yet here I am, still trying to be the fucking hero of the hour, so I can prove them all wrong.

Meanwhile, people around me drop like flies.

As I turned the corner, I saw Red Watson, the CO I most despised. He was the most corrupt of the bunch. A pasty, brainless butthead. I realized, from the horrified look on his face, that he'd been doing sentry duty for Darryl. He had not expected to see me alive. His eyes went wide as I sprinted toward him. He lifted his baton, too late.

I barreled into him. We hit the floor, skidding. He howled as his head thudded the cinderblock wall. I wrenched the baton out of his hand and jammed it up under his throat. "Who hired you to take out Mickey, Red?"

He kept struggling, trying to loosen my fingers. His pale blue eyes bulged, rolling. I gave him just throat space for a single, desperate gulp of air.

"Mr. Jones!" he gasped out. "That's the name! The only name he gave me!"

"What did he look like?" I leaned my knee into his groin.

He convulsed with a shriek of pain. "I don't know!" he wailed. "He wore a mask! Ms. Smith was the other one. A hot Asian bitch. They said they'd kill my family! I had to! I had to do it!"

Oh, fuck this. There was no time to extract anything useful out of this sniveling sack of shit. I coshed him in the head with the baton, hard enough to keep him down, then staggered to my feet, and ran like hell.

Who knew if the riot was keeping them all busy. I had lost all sense of how much time had passed, but who cared. It was go time for me. I punched in the number of the cell phone wired to the explosives in the control room, and held my breath as it rang—

Boom. The blast outside was muffled, but audible. The light in the electronic lock went out. It was open. I pushed the door wide, then the outside door.

Fuck, it was cold out there. The wind sliced into me. The floodlights were dead. Just emergency lights glowed a sickly green.

I couldn't see the crooked tree through the fence in the dark and the snow. That was my reference point, so I'd know where to dig. I slipped, slid, fell into the snow, squinting through the wind, the snowflakes, for the tree, the tree, the fucking *tree...*

There it was. It looked smaller, with eighteen inches of snow covering the roots.

Damn, so fucking cold. I oriented myself, fell to the ground and dug frantically under the snow. Under dirt and leaves. The snow turned red as I scrabbled through it.

There. Heavy plastic. My hands were so stiff, I almost couldn't tear it open to get out the bolt cutters. I struggled, frantic. The backup generator was out, but the second backup generator would kick in any time now.

I got the bolt cutters in position. My hands shook and my teeth were chattering. If I got this wrong, I would fry like a pork chop, right here and now.

Snap, went the cutters through the electric fence. *Snap. Snap.* I kept at it, cutting and bending until I had made a hole big enough to crawl out. The juice would come back on any second. Maybe while I was wiggling through the hole. I was a perfect conductor of electricity right now. Soaked to the skin. Slowed down by the cold.

If it happened, I just hoped it would be quick.

I felt the prison coverall tear. My skin, too, as I dragged my ass through that jagged hole, but I was too cold to notice or care. I launched myself in a stumbling run for the tree line for cover... and *voilá*, the lights came back on. Five seconds to spare.

I plunged into the forest, and soon found that I had to slow down. The phone had a flashlight, but the beam was a weak, chilly glow that barely reached the ground. The Jeep was a mile away as the crow flew, in a gully well off the road, buried under a tarp and what looked like brush left by the floods from last year's thaw. I'd walked the route months ago, before I went inside Kalaharee, and rehearsed it in my mind every night since, but everything looked different in the dark and snow, with Mickey's mutilated body burned into my mind.

I lurched and stumbled on through the dark. I couldn't feel my feet, my hands, my face. Wind screamed. Snow stung my eyes. At least the snow would cover my tracks. Though maybe not the trail of blood.

I was almost considering the merits of just falling on my face in the soft snow and drifting off into the next life when I found the gully, by way of falling off a cliff.

Eight feet of free falling, and then *bang*, *thud*, bounce, and I was tumbling down a steep rockfall, rolling and slipping and sliding, thankfully cushioned by snow.

Once I stopped rolling, I took a moment to orient myself and figure out at what level I had intercepted the gully. From the grade of the slope, I was almost certain I was uphill from the vehicle, so I pointed myself downhill. It wasn't long until I saw the huge mounds of snow that covered the fall of dead trees where we'd hidden the Jeep.

Thank God.

I threw off the piles of brush, made heavier by heaped snow, gasping for air. My lungs were burning. I felt around for the key I had duct taped up inside the undercarriage with numb fingers. Maybe frostbitten. I could lose some of them.

Two more days, and the Drakes would have been there for backup. I could have run out the hole in the fence with Mickey, leaped into a warm car, and sped away with three tough-as-nails Unredeemables watching my back. But no. That was not to be.

Stop whining like a bitch, Clearwater. I dropped the key into snow at least twice, had to look for it in the dark with fingers that had no sensation.

Finally, I got the key and managed to open the door. I got the engine started and ratcheted up the heat. When I stowed the vehicle here, I had not counted on two feet of snow. I put it in gear, and lurched out onto the rough terrain.

I have a good visual memory, and I'd memorized every twist

and turn of the terrain, but most of my many landmarks were hidden by snow.

There. Yes. The root system of a fallen fir, reaching up high into the sky like a skeletal fan, clutching boulders in its strangling coils. That was the spot where I needed to hew hard to the left... rev up, up, up...right over the big snowdrift...and *yes.*

I was thudding over a rough but more or less level track through the trees, lurching and wallowing. Clutching the wheel with bloody claws of hands that made me think of Mickey.

Body parts, clogging the shower drain. *Don't go there. Shut it down. Just drive.*

The road ran parallel to the highway, all the way to where it intersected the powerlines. I could follow the lines down to the river road and connect with the main highway not far from the Dew Drop Inn. Where Sandee stayed, all unsuspecting.

Hoo, boy. I could feel it coming over me, like a bad rash. The urge to do something ill-considered. Self-destructive. Stupid heroics that no one had asked for.

But goddamn, that woman had done nothing to deserve what was coming for her. She'd been stupid as dirt, definitely, but not evil or greedy or cruel. She was just a weird, sweet, oversexed girl with no clue, and no discernible sense of self-preservation. Granted, she may have been cruising for a little trouble, just for the entertainment value.

But not this kind of trouble. Not the kind that landed you in the morgue.

I couldn't leave Sandee to Boer's tender mercies, and Boer knew it. They'd threatened her with harm just to make me jump. Now look at me, three feet in the air.

I just never learned. It's that sign taped to my back. "Go ahead, kick my ass."

Fuck it. What was one more rousing ass-kick. Just to make my day complete.

CHAPTER 6

Freya

I stared out the window of the diner at the gusts of snow buffeting the glass. The weather was absolute shit, and even so, I felt I'd made a mistake, deciding to stay the night. I should've hit the road the second I walked out of that prison.

I'm still too close to Jed Clearwater to even breathe. Knowing he was just a few miles away, seething in a cage, wound me up to a fever pitch.

Which, of course, made me hate myself all the more. It was so stupid.

It was just a method acting, right? Using my old crush on him to psych myself into character. Not that it had worked. He'd resisted my womanly wiles with the greatest of ease, and kicked my ass out. Brutally. So much for my powers of seduction.

It enraged me. It was dumb, and vain, but there it was. That arrogant bastard. How dare he. He could have suffered a pang of frustrated lust for me, for fuck's sake. He could have given me at least that much cheap, meaningless satisfaction.

But I couldn't rationalize away the truth right in my face. Jed Clearwater still excited me...but the feeling was not at all mutual.

Not even dolled up and tricked out as I had been. Which settled a burning question I hadn't known I was still asking.

I wanted to kill the part of myself that responded to him. Just fucking euthanize it like a rabid dog. It made me so ashamed. Talking dirty to him made me flushed, wet, weak in the knees. How could this be happening? What the fuck was wrong with me?

Jed Clearwater had set up my brother to die. For money. And look at the state I was in. God, the cognitive dissonance literally hurt my head.

I looked down at the sad tomato soup, the charred grilled cheese sandwich, the cold, weak coffee. No point. I was vibrating at too high a frequency to swallow.

I should get back to the hotel room, take a nice, long shower, wash the pink streaks out of my hair. I wouldn't need them until the next time Jed consented to let me visit, whenever that would be. Maybe never. My employees in Seattle didn't need to see the pink Sandee hair. The bleached blonde hairdo would be weird enough for them.

I took a sip of the nasty coffee, grimacing, and fished up the hem of my puffy jacket, unfastening the hidden zipper and taking out my smartphone. My Freya Masters smartphone, anyhow. I fished out the battery, too, and assembled the thing. It was time to contact Holly, my sweet little niece. Nine years old tomorrow. Shane, her dad, had disappeared off the face of the earth, so I couldn't disappear on her, too. I made a point of contacting her every day when we weren't together. But I wasn't in any state to actually talk to her. Holly was very intuitive. She'd know right away that I was all messed up. It would make her more worried, not less.

I opened up our chat, and typed in a message.

hey honey what's up

Holly responded instantly.

> finally. where r u?

I laughed softly under my breath. That girl was a Masters, through and through.

> I'm out taking care of business. Home soon.
> Just checking in on you. hugs&love
>
> But where?

Holly demanded.

> I'm in a diner, getting food. If you could call it
> that.

I snapped a quick pic of my uninspiring meal and sent it, after making sure there were no identifying symbols in it, on a napkin or a menu or a placemat, or whatever. Holly was laser sharp. She would focus right in on that.

> Not loving my meal, but whatever. Is Uncle
> Ethan with you?
>
> No he's gone 2. Sally and Angelo and Camilla
> are staying with me. come home please I
> miss you

Holly typed.

Tears prickled in my eyes. So neither of us were going to be there tomorrow for Holly's birthday. That sucked. Shitty timing, but visiting days at the prison were what they were. And when Jed finally agreed to meet, I had to jump at the chance.

> Be there soon sweetheart. Signing off. Love u.

I disassembled my phone and tucked it back into my coat

hem. Time to brave the weather. I paid for my uneaten food, and braced myself for the blast of bitter cold outside the front door, which slashed through my coat as if it wasn't there. I was grateful to get into my old Mercedes and crank up the heat. The Dew Drop was close, only a half a mile down the highway. I could have walked, if there were a shoulder on the road. If it weren't so cold. If I weren't wearing those high-heeled boots. Silly Sandee footwear.

Ironic, that I'd packed my Badass Bitch Bag of defensive doo-dads into the hidden hem pocket in my quilted coat before going to the diner. It was childish, but I felt braver and smarter when I had it on me. But I hadn't thought to change into my combat boots, which genuinely could make a difference if I had to fight or run.

By this, one could observe the Jed Clearwater effect on my brain. Like a monster dose of psychedelic drugs.

The bag was too big, puffing out the bottom of my coat, but I'd taken out all but the absolute essentials. Rose and Milla would laugh at me. I had dubbed our trio "the Badass Bitches" years ago. An aspirational name, but we did our best. Milla was the daughter of a colonel who my brothers had served under in the military, so I've known her since I was a teenager. Rose we met when we were in college. Milla was an artist, Rose was a chemist, and I had done my best to corrupt both of those fine, talented, upstanding girls into naughty badassery.

To that end, I came up with a gag gift for them three years ago. The Badass Bitch Bag. One for each of us, and I was constantly adding bits and pieces.

The BBBags, as we called them, were ostensibly travel make-up kits. Rigorously pink, decorated with hearts, stars, kittens, and rainbows, and vague and pleasant statements along the lines of "If you can dream it, you can do it."

God knows, I could definitely dream it, as paranoid and defensive as I was.

The BBBag had lots of goodies, some of which genuinely functioned as high-quality make-up. A boxcutter blade made of super-hard resin was hidden in the pressed powder of a very nice trio of rust, bronze, and gold eyeshadow. The case itself became the boxcutter's handle, and the blade snapped into its plastic housing once the powder was knocked out. There was a lipstick case—pink, of course—with a decorative ring that could be slipped onto a fingertip. It braced a sharp, serrated pop-up resin blade that a girl could hide behind her fake fingernail. There was a glittering bottle she could spray on her nails that would change their color if they were dipped into a drink that had roofies in it. There were perfumed make-up wipes treated with a powerful sedative that could bring a strong man down in seconds if she slapped it over his nose. There was a packet of eco-friendly tampons, the cotton carefully wrapped around an aerosolized bottle of Tamloxid 343, a drug I'd learned about from Rose, which worked like a truth serum, in concentrated doses. There were tracers, for tagging people who needed to be watched. All kinds of crazy stuff. Whatever would fit in the silly looking little girlie bag.

Of course, I had not brought my BBBag to the prison. Chances are, I would have made it through security with it, considering how carefully I had designed everything, but there was no point in risking it. Nothing in that bag would ever be useful to me with Jed Clearwater. There would always be a wall of glass between us.

But I liked to keep it with me whenever I could. When I had my BBBag, I felt as if I had my Badass Bitches right there with me, on my side, keeping me strong. Also, the BBBag represented Sandee's persona to a tee. Pretty and harmless, frivolous and feminine, maybe even a little silly...but underestimate her at your peril.

Of course, it was all just a mind trip to make me feel tougher. But what the hell. If it worked, I'd use it. So the BBBag lived in my coat, along with my Freya phone, my extra cards, my emergency cash.

I pulled into the Dew Drop and drove around to the small parking lot in back. The streetlight that had illuminated the lot was no longer lit. It had been when I'd left the hotel, even though it was barely dusk. I had noticed how the snowflakes blowing every which way had been lit up by its sickly orange glow.

Not anymore. The only light now was over the back door of the hotel, and with the snow blowing this thick, I could barely see it. I fished out my keycard.

The only parking spot was next to a big black van. Brrr. Classic no-no for a girl alone. I thought about driving back out in front of the Dew Drop, but the signs said No Parking, and I was too tired to be paranoid tonight. Besides, sleazy predators wouldn't be out on the prowl in weather like this. They'd be snug and warm at home, watching unsavory stuff on their computers and sipping hot tea as they plotted their evil deeds.

I was still dressed like Sandee, with those stupid shoes, so I couldn't even sprint to the back door. I was going to have to slip and slide, wobble and mince.

I couldn't wait to peel the damn things off and stuff them definitively into the garbage. *Come on, Masters. Shake your ass.*

I pushed the door open, and the wind caught it and slammed it violently wide. The snow swept in, a full frontal attack, burning against my face, blowing up my pleated skirt, stinging my bare legs. Down my neck, up my cuffs. I steadied myself against the blast and struggled out, digging my heels into the snow so I could stay on my feet in the wind. And suddenly, I heard that sound. A woman's worst nightmare.

Click. Thunk. The growling rasp of the van door sliding open, and oh, *shit...*

They boiled out before I could inhale to scream. Men in ski masks, rushing me.

I shrieked bloody murder, kicking and struggling, but the

wind and snow muffled my voice. They tossed me flat onto my back, knocking out my wind. I choked helplessly for air, and one of them grabbed my hair and jerked my head up. His breath smelled like something long dead. "Bitch," he hissed, grabbing my throat.

His voice broke off, transforming into a startled, high-pitched grunt, and after a second, he landed on top of me, right on my head. Smothering me. Unmoving.

He was massively heavy. Dead weight, crushing me into the deep, powdery snow. I wiggled desperately, gasping for air, trying to get my head out from under him just to breathe, but it was all just snow, snow, snow. Hot, sticky liquid. Blood.

Muffled grunts, thuds, gasps. Shouts. I screamed with effort as I managed to shift the heavy, bleeding thing lying on top of me just enough to lift my face to see what was happening. Fighting men were silhouetted against the dim glow of the hotel door.

I saw the largest shadowy figure leap up, delivering a chopping blow that knocked him to the ground. Another man attacked the shadow man with a hoarse bellow of rage, but the shadow seized and spun him, faster than my eyes could follow, and rammed his head into the passenger window of the van, caving in the window.

Broken glass tinkled. Someone leaped onto the shadow man's back. He flung himself and the piggy-backing guy backward against my car. He twisted and spun, grabbing the attacking man's head. *Crack...crack...crunch.* Three blows, and the guy slid down in front of the open door of my car and lay there, unmoving.

Thttp, thttp. I heard dull, thudding pops as silenced bullets peppered my car, striking the huge body that lay on top of me like hammer blows. The shadow guy hit the ground, rolling, a gun coming up, taking swift aim...

Bam. Bam. Bam, he shot back. Then, silence, for a long, breathless interval.

The shadow man rose from the ground with the seamless, effortless ease of smoke rising. I focused on the gun in his hand as he moved toward me.

I was frozen. Literally, figuratively. Trapped in the snow under a cooling corpse, my mind blank with terror. He was the angel of death. He would rip out my heart and eat it.

But he just rolled the body off me with a sharp shove of his foot. He grabbed me under the armpits and hauled me to my feet, turning me so the light fell onto his face.

He wasn't a pit of light-swallowing darkness in the shape of the man. He wore a Kalaharee prison coverall—but it was crimson, not orange. Because he was drenched with blood, head to foot. I just gazed at him, slack-jawed. Shaking violently.

"Hello, Sandee," he said quietly.

It was Jed Clearwater.

CHAPTER 7

Jed

It was official. I had a death wish. An extra special one, with a super-sized portion of stupidity piled on top. But I was too wiped out even to scold myself properly.

Sandee's eyes were huge with shock. "Wha...wha...what are you d-d-doing..."

"Don't play dumb." My voice came out sharper than I intended. "I'm trying to keep you from getting killed. God help me."

"But I...but they..."

"No time to discuss it," I said. "When those guys don't report back, he'll send reinforcements. We need to get gone."

"He? Who do you mean? Who is he?"

"Later." I picked up the pace, dragging her along, and then I noticed her shoes. Holy Jesus, those? In a fucking snowstorm?

I couldn't help her out with that, other than carrying her, which would have slowed us down too much, so I just dragged her along behind me as swiftly as I could through the snow and into the vacant field behind the Dew Drop. I'd parked the Jeep on the other side of it, hoping to keep any security cameras that the hotel might have from catching a glimpse of it. There were two inches of fresh snow already piled on top when we got there. It was coming down fast.

I had gotten to Sandee just in time. Ten more seconds, and she would've been in that van with a bag over her head. Another casualty to lay at my door. Another concrete block chained to my foot, pulling me down to the bottom of the fucking ocean. So close.

I opened the door, and she turned, flailing at me, slapping and struggling, and oh, for fuck's sake. Here I was, trying to save this girl's life, and she was pitching a fit.

"Shut up, bitch, or I'll knock you out." I put on my best super villain tone.

It worked. She went as rigid as a board. More trauma, yay. But fuck it, I'd sort out the damage later. I shoved her into the passenger seat, yanked down the seatbelt. Strapped her in. "Stay right where you are. Or you'll die tonight."

She blinked up at me, freshly terrified. Her mouth worked.

I am so sick of playing a top-shelf bad guy. Scaring people into compliance was a quick and dirty technique, time effective and convenient. The shitty downside is that I have to be prepared to follow through on my threats. I never have the stomach for it.

She was buying it for now, though, which is good enough for me. I got the Jeep into gear, braced for a sobbing, screaming meltdown, but she just huddled there, teeth chattering.

So. It would seem Sandee had not genuinely wanted her sexual fantasy to take tangible form and leap out at her like a horror move jump-scare. Wow, what a surprise. But hey, she was still breathing. That was the one point I could chalk up in my own favor today. Sandee was not dead because of my mistakes. At least, not yet.

I had to keep it that way. My conscience was burdened enough as it was.

The storm was a fucking blizzard from hell. I could barely see what constituted the road between the trees. I realized at a certain point, as if from far away, that I was letting out a constant stream of vicious profanity. It was steam, hissing out of a safety valve. A vain attempt to keep me from blowing up.

Sandee cringed against the passenger side door. Her wild mop of hair flopped with each bone-rattling *thud*.

I swallowed the profanity with some difficulty. The woman was shocked, terrified, traumatized. There was blood on her face, her coat. "Hey. You're bleeding?"

She didn't respond. I hoped she wasn't going into shock. I reached over to give her a nudge. "Hey! Sandee! Are you hurt?"

She squeaked, and recoiled.

Great. This is just so fucking typical. I had fucked myself left, right, and sideways for this girl, but I wasn't going to get any thanks for it, because she thought I was a monster. And who the fuck could blame her? This was perfect. On the lam, in a blizzard, soaked with blood, while the woman I was trying to save had a full-fledged nervous breakdown in the car next to me. Just stellar.

I gritted my teeth until my jaw ached, struggling to moderate my tone. "Don't be afraid of me," I said. "I'm not going to hurt you."

Not a peep. Like she hadn't even heard me. But at least the shitty road conditions and the shivering, sobbing, terrified girl next to me gave me something to focus on other than Mickey on the bathroom floor, bleeding out.

I made my voice ugly. "Stop whining, or I'll dump you out in the snow."

She looked over at me. I caught a hot flash of anger in her eyes. Excellent. Much better to have her furious at me than going into shock.

"Go ahead. Throw me out," she said. "Truly. Feel free. I'd prefer it."

I let out a sigh. "You'd die. We've gone too far into the mountains. You'd never find your way back in a blizzard, even if you had the right clothes and shoes. And how about those guys from the van? Do you want their B team to catch up with you?"

"I'll take my chances. I'll walk back to town and go straight to the cops."

I snorted and kept on driving. She was talking out her ass, and she probably knew it. Pointless argument. I ignored her, and she huddled into a silent, shaking ball.

The long, narrow road was nearly invisible on the satellite map, but I had driven it many times, memorizing the landmarks. But it all looked different tonight.

At the speed we had to go, it took over an hour to get to the cabin. I was so relieved when I pulled the Jeep into the car park. I'd stocked the place with everything Mickey and I might need to stage the next phase of this project. All of which, of course, had been predicated on having Mickey and his intel.

So close. So goddamn close. If I'd scheduled the riot for twenty minutes earlier, Mickey and I would've been out of there, home free. We'd been so damn close.

I killed the engine, considering different things that I could say to Sandee about what was happening to her right now, and discarding them all. I couldn't tell her about my mission. I'd already put her in mortal danger, and she hadn't demonstrated even a baseline minimum of good judgment. For fuck's sake, the girl pursued violent criminals for sexual thrills. I couldn't risk letting her know anything my business.

"Let's get inside. Get warmed up," I said.

She looked spooked. "Um. What is this place? Is this your, ah...hideout?"

I tried not to snort. "It's a place with a heater and some food. It's where we're going to spend the night. Move, Sandee. Out of the damn car."

My tone goaded her into action. I nudged her ahead of me through the snow. I could hear her teeth clacking together from the cold as I unlocked the door.

I switched on the lights once we were inside. It was freezing cold, of course, but there were a couple of space heaters and a fire laid in the woodstove. The cabin was equipped with a week's worth of provisions for two, as well as first-aid supplies and antibiotics, in case Mickey or I got injured in the prison breakout. Which was good, because I was all sliced up. There were fresh clothes for me and Mickey. Electronics and portable security equipment, so I could secure our lodgings wherever we ended up going. In the hidden safe were the guns, phones, cash, and fake IDs and credit cards, for me and Mickey. The cabin was a prison escapee's wet dream.

Sandee stood there, swaying a little on her feet. Her hands were clasped desperately tight in front of her blood-stained, puffy jacket.

I figured, the less said, the better, so I got to work making the place habitable. Got heaters fired up, ignited the fire I had laid months before. Filled the kettle on the stove, set it to boil. Pulled random packages of food from the freezer, stuck them in the microwave.

She looked shocky and faint. Her gaze followed me around, but whenever I looked in her direction, it darted away. I ignored her while I mixed up two mugs of powdered cocoa. I opened some evaporated milk, dosed it, and offered it to her.

"Drink this," I said. "It's hot. Quick sugar."

No response, just that blank stare, which worried me. I seized her upper arm, and she flinched. Good sign, I guess. She knew who I was, and she wasn't happy about it.

I pushed her toward a chair. "Sit down, Sandee." I had to keep at it to make her knees bend. She was as brittle as a china doll, but she finally collapsed into the chair.

This time she took the cup, but still didn't drink. Just stared at me with those big, startled eyes.

I sipped at my own cup, wishing there was a shot of bourbon in it.

Her face still had splatters of blood. I went into the bathroom, found a washrag, and ran water in the sink until the water heater kicked into action and warmed it. I came back and dabbed at her face. She flinched away.

"Stay still," I said, trying not to bark. "I'm just trying to see if you're cut."

"I'm okay," she quavered. "I think...the blood was from the guy on top of me."

I kept at it, wiping off the splatter. Also where it was gumming up her hair. She was right. She wasn't injured. That was a relief.

"Sandee," I said. "Listen closely, okay? I won't hurt you, and I won't touch you. All I wanted was to keep those guys from dragging you away with them. That would not have ended well for you."

She licked her trembling lips and tried several times to speak before the wobbly thread of sound came out. "H-h-how did you know that was going to happen?"

"They taunted me about it in the prison," I told her. "They told me that someone would be coming for you."

"B-b-but why?"

"To punish me," I said flatly.

"So...so those guys were, um...mad at you?"

"I'm in prison for murder, Sandee. You're surprised I have enemies?"

"But...but what do they have against me?" she faltered.

"Nothing, probably," I said. "You just got noticed by the wrong person. You came in flaunting your legs and your tits." I couldn't help my disapproving tone. "You drew attention to yourself. I tried to warn you off."

She didn't respond to that. Just looked clouded and confused.

"Just drink the fucking chocolate, Sandee," I said curtly. "You'll make my life harder if you faint, or go into shock."

There it was, that flash of anger I was angling for. "I won't faint," she said haughtily, and then took a careful sip of the chocolate drink.

I crouched in front of her, edging back when she cringed away.

"Listen up," I said. "If you're worried about what you said to me at the prison, don't be. You came on real strong during our talk, but that was just a fantasy for you, and I won't hold you to it. Understand? Tell me you understand."

Her lips were trembling. She nodded.

"We'll just hole up here until I can get us out safely," I said, trying to sound reassuring. "When I figure out someplace where you'll be safe."

"Just get me to my car," she said swiftly. "I'll go straight home. I'll never say a word, to anyone, ever. You can forget you ever met me."

"Too late for that, Sandee. Your car is full of bullet holes, and it has frozen cadavers all around it," I told her, and then the thought hit me, like a splash of ice water. Jesus, I was getting sloppy. "Shit. Have you got a phone on you?"

She just blinked at me. Anxious, confused, innocent. She had to be stalling, because of course she had a phone. "Give me your fucking phone, Sandee. *Now.*"

She moved stiffly as she unzipped her coat, holding it closed over herself as if she were afraid of giving me a glimpse of her chest She fumbled at an inside pocket, and pulled out a smartphone with a hot pink Hello Kitty phone case.

She handed it over without meeting my eyes.

I swiped the screen, and hit the passcode prompt. "What's your password?"

She shot me an embarrassed look. "FreeJamesCraig884."

Whoa. That was alarming, but I shined it on and entered the password without comment. It took me to a hot picture of Sandee dressed up in an old-time saloon girl outfit with two other girls.

Lots of cleavage and dazzling smiles on display. Sandee was the prettiest of the trio.

I looked through her chat app. There were messages from someone named Willie. He was evidently her boss at the road-house. I skimmed a series of ranting, angry texts about her not showing up for a bartending shift. There were chats with two girls named Kelly and Loretta, heavy with emojis and colorful stickers. Kelly and Loretta seemed fun-loving, man-crazy girls. No more or less than what I'd expect.

"Are Kelly and Loretta the girls in your wallpaper picture?" I asked.

She looked panicked. "You're not gonna do something bad to them, are you?"

"Nope," I said, scrolling through the chats. "I hope I never lay eyes on them."

Her fitness app told me she logged 12,000 steps a day, her heartbeat averaged around 71, and her blood pressure was well within the norm. Huh. Good for her.

I pulled the battery out of her phone and stuck it all into my bag for further study later on. "I'm going to clean up in the bath-room," I said. "Don't move, and don't touch anything. Finish your chocolate. And be good. Understand?"

She gave me a jerky nod, still not meeting my eyes.

I rifled through the boxes in the corner, a gift from my former self, five months before. Clothes, rope, tools. The guns were all stored in the safe, other than the gun I'd hidden inside the Jeep. I brought that one into the bathroom with me, along with the first-aid supplies, the fresh clothes. All I needed was to turn around and find Sandee holding my own gun to my head. Like the punchline to a bad joke.

I left the bathroom door open as I stripped off the bloody coverall. I was monitoring her in the mirror the whole time. No more surprises.

She huddled in her chair, dazed and confused. She looked

like exactly what her letters and phone suggested she was. A lost, lonely girl with no family behind her, a crap job, plenty of self-destructive tendencies, and a desperate need to overcompensate.

But she was smarter than anyone gave her credit for, and she'd gotten bored.

Boredom could be deadly.

She'd told me about her hard-luck childhood in her letters. At great length. Heart-tugging, hair-raising tales of abuse and neglect in the foster care system. One story in particular had creeped me out the most. The fanatic religious couple who had chained her up in the basement when she was seven because she was so "bad." God, who did that to a defenseless little kid? No wonder she was bouncing off the walls.

Her emotional fragility was so clear. As if she were literally advertising to be abused by a psychopathic predator. As if she actively sought the suffering that would bring her. It made me scared for her. Angry at the assholes who had hurt her.

And knowing all this? It should be a huge dick-wilting turn off for me. But no.

I could drive railroad spikes with this hard-on.

CHAPTER 8

Freya

My gaze kept skittering away from the floor show in the bathroom as he stripped off the bloody coverall and shoved it into a plastic bag. I caught a peek of his lean, muscular body as he reached up to put the gun on top of the hot water heater next to the shower, a glimpse of his taut, muscular ass...and he stepped into the shower stall.

The water started to hiss. Breath left my lungs in a shuddering rush. Good thing he'd forced me to sit. I would have hit the floor otherwise. I gulped some swiftly cooling chocolate. The sugar helped.

This disaster had stripped away my illusions. I saw very clearly now that my James&Sandee4ever prison project was a coping mechanism. A way to pretend I was doing something proactive to find Shane, and not just waiting like a good girl, hands folded in my lap, while my big brother did all the work. And it had blown up in my face.

I had been so sick of Ethan insisting I stay out of it. He'd always been overbearing. Shane too. Both my brothers were hyper-macho even before they'd joined the Special Forces, and they were overly protective of me because of the trauma that had gone down when we were kids. I get it, I do. I understand their motivations and their fears, rational and otherwise, and even so. Sitting around with my hands folded had been killing me.

The idea had come to me on tequila night with my girlfriend, Rose. After a couple of margaritas, I started thinking, what do I have that Ethan doesn't? He's smart, tough, an ex-Ranger, he's laser-focused and relentless, and he's an Unredeemable, like Shane. Those Unredeemable guys have practically superhuman capabilities.

Of course, Jed Clearwater's an Unredeemable, too. Which made this very tricky.

My brother is the most competent man I know, and he was working twenty-four-seven on finding Shane. His position was always, "Don't worry your pretty little head. You'll just get in my way."

But my pretty little head kept worrying. And so? What special thing could I contribute to this enterprise? I'm a shit-hot hacker, sure, but Ethan already has a stable of great hackers working around the clock, looking for Shane from every angle. Though arguably, none of them were as motivated as me.

What else? Well, tits and ass, of course. Big gray eyes with long, artificially lengthened lashes. I clean up well when I make an effort, and I figured, I might as well use my looks for something I cared about. I hadn't been with anyone for ages, even before my life exploded. Dating struck me as superficial and boring, and sex was underwhelming when it happened at all. Which was probably more a function of my own inhibitions, not the guy in question. I take full responsibility for how psychologically fucked up I am.

Probably the truly shitty reason that sex never worked was because none of those guys were Jed Clearwater. It was like he'd imprinted on me by being my number one crush, right when I was starting to bloom. And that was that. Permanent fixation.

Until now, the plan I'd dreamed up had seemed like better than nothing. Offer Jed attention, entertainment, flattery, ego-strokes, phone sex. Draw him in. And when his guard was down, get inside his head. It was supposed to be slow, methodical, and safe. Because the guy was incarcerated, for fuck's sake.

Now the rug had been ripped from underneath my feet. I was alone in the dark with a guy who had sold my brother out for fifteen million dollars. And what was my cover identity? Sandee, the painted-up bimbo fuckbunny who had shared her wild erotic fantasies with him only hours before.

God, I couldn't possibly be any more compromised. Not if I tried.

He was out of the shower, checking on me in the bathroom mirror, towel wrapped around his waist. He'd told me I was off the hook, sex-wise, but I'm sure he was still hoping I would deliver on the sexual promises. Why wouldn't he?

Jed Clearwater was the only sexual fantasy I'd ever been able to get off to, and he must feel that energy on some level. No one, not even me, would blame the guy for assuming I was a sure thing tonight. The bulging muscles in his back were brightly illuminated by the cold light of the bathroom. The bright highlights, the sharp shadows. Scrapes, bruises, slashes. Wow. Prison must be full of sharp edges.

I could go in there and dab disinfectant on the wounds he couldn't reach. The Florence Nightingale routine. Show him how sweet and nurturing Sandee was, cooing over his wounds. Dab-dab with the gauze and the disinfectant and the butterfly Band-aids. *Poor baby, let me kiss it and make it better.* He was beat up, stressed, exhausted. His defenses were down. That was the whole fucking point of my efforts in the first place, right? Now was the time to make a move on him. Get closer to him.

Big girl pants, Frey. Pull 'em on, cinch 'em up. God only knew what horrors Shane might be suffering. It wouldn't kill me to take this scenario all the way to its natural conclusion. See what I could glean from it. It was the obvious next step. It was just like my previous plan, except on mega-steroids. Speeded up. Intimate. Deadly.

Jed checked on me constantly as he cleaned the wounds he could reach. Those penetrating eyes, that grim, sensual mouth, those massive muscles. His sexual energy blasted out at me, rattling my every last nerve, making me breathless and confused.

But hey, breathless and confused was pretty much on-brand for Sandee.

A small part of me was yelling into the void about how this could destroy me. Well, maybe so. What of it? Wondering what Shane was suffering was destroying me anyway. Shane and Ethan had rescued me from my own hell, back in the day.

I would return the favor, or die trying.

The issue now was lack of technique. I was not versed in the arts of driving men mad with desire, having never put in the time necessary to get good at it. So I'd wing it.

My ankles wobbled in those ridiculous boots, still soaked from the snow that had melted in Jed's Jeep. I schooled the expression on my face into that spaced-out, dippy glow that said, *"Go ahead, take advantage of me. If you don't, the next guy will."*

I still had on my coat. My real cell phone was hidden in the hem of the jacket, along with the Badass Bitch Bag. Sandee had her own phone, with her own carefully constructed life on it. It would withstand a casual examination, but not an extended deep dive. Maybe I could keep Jed busy enough to not think of doing one.

I pulled the lip gloss out of my coat pocket and slicked some on. Time to turn on the juice. All that lovelorn, overheated girlish lust backed up inside me, all of that was Sandee now, begging to bust loose. *Own it. Use it.*

I slid off my coat and hung it on the back of a chair. I had to be careful Jed didn't handle it. It was heavier than it ought to be, with those secret pockets loaded with my phone and my Badass Bitch Bag stuff. If it fell, he'd hear a loud *thud*.

Jed was buckling his belt, naked to the waist. His eyes grimly focused on me as I came closer, hips swaying. Lips slightly open. *Don't overdo it, girl. He's not stupid.*

Jed turned around. "What the hell are you doing?"

"Just, you know. Looking." I pitched my voice to a throaty whisper, with a tremor that was totally justified by the circumstances. "I never thought I'd get a chance to look this close at you. And without the orange prison thing. You're...so hot."

He just stood there, speechless. His erection pressed against the denim of his jeans. And what an erection it was. I had never seen dimensions like that in any of my previous adventures. Or maybe "encounters" was a better word. "Adventure" denoted risks, thrills, high stakes. Nothing I'd ever associated with sex so far.

Just act. Offer yourself up like a virgin sacrifice. Pretend.

Hah. Like it was so easy. Sandee was a different kind of woman, the way I'd dreamed her up. Vulnerable in all the ways I wasn't, confident in all the ways I wasn't. Sandee was sexually bold, experienced, eager, wildly submissive. Sandee melted into screaming multiple orgasms at the drop of a pin. Sandee would do absolutely anything her lover wanted. She had told him so this afternoon. She'd told him in her letters, too. So the bar for this performance was set very high.

Without my coat, my arms were all over the place. Clasped in front, then behind my back, then all around, looking for pockets that didn't exist, then wrapped over my ribs, propping up my tits.

"Sandee," he said. His voice sounded thick. "You don't have to do this."

"Do what?" I leaned in the bathroom doorframe.

"Me," he said. "You don't have to do me."

Well, hell. I didn't want Jed to act decent or sensitive. That was confusing. I preferred he be an entitled, selfish, self-absorbed asshole, so my defenses would be in no danger of faltering. I did big, hurt eyes. "You...don't want me?"

He let out an explosive sound. "Of course I want you. But we shouldn't do this. You never thought you'd actually be alone in a room with me. This was just a fantasy. Fucking me for real wasn't part of your plan."

"It's a much better plan," I offered boldly. "It's my wildest dream come true."

"There's a cot over there, with blankets. Go wrap yourself up and keep your mouth shut. I won't touch you, and I'll get you someplace safe as soon as I can, but listen. If you try to fuck me up, I swear to God, I will tear you to pieces. Are we clear?"

I processed that. Those was some impressive mixed messages. On the one hand, I was perfectly safe. On the other, his enormous dick was denting out the denim of his jeans. And if I was bad, he would tear me to pieces. It was enough to make a girl dizzy.

Well. Sandee was dizzy by nature. I revved up the seduction machine, drifting closer. "I would never fuck you up, James." I undid the top button of my sweater. One button, pop. Two. Three, revealing my cleavage. Four and five showed the fastening of the blue silk balcony bra. So far, so good.

I pulled the last ones free. The sweater hung wide open.

"Sandee. Goddamnit." His voice had a grim, warning tone. "Don't."

"I can tell you want me." My voice shook, and so did my legs, but I took a tottering step forward. "I mean, the evidence is way out there. Or it would be, if you opened up those jeans and let it out of its cage. Let me see it. Let me...touch it."

"Forget it," he said curtly. "Not gonna happen."

"What, are you afraid of me?" I fluttered my lashes. "I want to feel your cock inside me. I'm so wet. I'm aching for it. You can do whatever you want."

Wow, where the hell did that come from? It scared me. As if I was becoming Sandee for real. Desperately overcompensating for my lonely, tragic, hard-luck story.

Onward. I tossed my mane of bleached hair and unfastened the front clasp of the bra, letting the cups drop. Breasts bared, nipples tight in the chilly air.

I arched my back, cupped my own breasts for him, caressing them, delicately pinching my nipples, sliding my fingers over the heavy under-curve. Lifting them for his inspection. Eyes heavy-lidded. Heart thudding double-time.

"Touch them," I said, breath coming short between my open lips. "Please."

He slowly shook his head, but he was riveted by the spectacle, so I upped the ante. Sliding my hand down to the vee of my mound, rubbing myself through the skirt. Lifting it over my bare thighs. Inch by inch. He couldn't look away.

Which was gratifying, I had to say. His eyes had glanced over me without stopping when I was a teenager with the frizzy hair, bad glasses, braces, puppy fat. But now, oh. The look on his face. As if he was afraid of me. *Yes.*

His eyes were hot. His hands clenched, flexed, shaking. I should be scared, but I'm not. Or, at least, Sandee's not. I shrugged off the sweater and bra, putting my shoulders back. *Take that, buddy. In your face.*

I reached for the hook of the pleated wool schoolgirl skirt. With one hand, I undid it, and let it fall around my ankles. I wore just a silk thong and red ankle boots.

"Sandee," he whispered. "Holy shit. Really?"

"I told you at the prison how much I wanted you. Did you not believe me?"

"I think you need urgent psychological help." His voice sounded strangled.

I kicked the skirt away. "Oh, yes, I need help, James. The kind that only you can give me."

He held his hand up. "Back off. This is not happening."

"Actually, it's already well under way." I reached out to run my finger, tipped with an opalescent blue fake nail, up the length of his stiff cock, still trapped in his jeans. Mmm, a big wet spot. Very promising.

I grabbed his belt buckle, tugged it loose. Undid the buttons. His face was a mask of tension. Blood had scabbed on the cuts on his cheekbone.

His feet were bare. Beautiful. Long, strong. But something about his naked feet, his bruises, the marks on his face...it made him seem almost vulnerable. I didn't like that at all. It was confusing. I tugged his pants down. His cock sprang out.

Oh, whoa. He was truly hung. It stood up high and proud, flushed a hot red, the veins along the shaft dark and distinct. His cockhead shone with pre-come.

He let out a thick, gasping sound as I grabbed it, milked it, squeezing out some of the silky-slick liquid and spreading it over his glans with my palm. I felt his heartbeat throb against my caressing hand.

"Sandee. You don't have to..." His voice broke off, panting. He cleared his throat. "I told you. You don't have to do this."

"Do I look like I'm not enthusiastic?" I gave him a voluptuous squeeze and a long, caressing stroke, root to tip. "Because you certainly seem, well...up for it."

"Cool it. Please. I am on a hair trigger."

Well, good. However unskilled or awkward I might be, he'll barely have time to notice before it was all over. I sank to my knees, to initiate the sex act that Sandee would definitely open with, gripping his stiff rod. His cock was so hard, the skin velvety smooth and hot, supple in my hands, practically vibrating with readiness.

He grabbed my shoulders. "Wait," he gasped out.

"Hmm? What's wrong?"

He grabbed a towel from the shelf. "Take this. For your knees."

Aw, how gallant. There he went again, pretended to be a good guy.

I wedged the towel beneath my knees. Here it was, the biggest acting challenge of my fledgling career: pretending to be a practiced fellatio artist. I could only hope once I got underway, he'd be too overstimulated to notice any clumsiness.

I started by licking his cockhead, savoring the smooth texture, the slick pre-come leaking up. Lapping it up. Warm, eager swipes. Then his shaft, getting it wet and slick for my hands to slide, up and down. So far, so good.

But I'm so turned on, I can hardly breathe.

CHAPTER 9

Jed

I'm hanging on by a fucking thread.

So good. Teasing, kittenish strokes of her tongue along my aching cock. Sweet torture. I never want it to end. It should've never even begun, goddamnit.

So stupid, to bring the blonde bombshell to my safehouse, but what the fuck else could I do with her? I couldn't leave her to be eaten alive by Boer and his goons. She was like a grenade that had been thrown into my path. And for some reason, she appeared to genuinely want this from me, in spite of the violence, in spite of the blood. I was a goddamn monster, as far as she knew. She'd seen me kill.

She sucked me in with diabolical skill, getting into the rhythm of it. Sliding her hands with that swiveling twist, sucking me deep into her throat, swirling with her tongue as my shaft slid out, hot and tight and clinging...oh God...I clasped my hands over hers, freezing her into stillness. Breathing it down.

Her eyes flicked up, questioning.

"I'm just not ready for it to be over yet," I said, by way of explanation.

She smiled with her eyes and got right back to it.

It was like a fever dream. The prettiest woman I'd ever seen, naked and glowing in the ugly little cabin. On her knees, eyes closed, sucking on my cock.

How in the fuck did we get from there to here? The whole thing was as irresistible as it was completely wrong. A girl like Sandee was so vulnerable, so needy and confused. Any righteous guy with a functioning conscience and a moral compass would back away slowly, raging hard-on and all.

But I hadn't been within shouting distance of my conscience or my moral compass in a very long time. And oh my God, those full, gleaming, rosy lips, clasping me. Those plump, pointy tits. Lush hips, round ass. Strong, smooth, graceful thighs. And her skin, so fine-grained and satiny-smooth. It had some angry red marks from the fight outside the hotel. I stroked them gently, wishing I could heal them with a touch.

My fingers wound into her hair as she sucked me deep, pulling hard. Cupping my balls, making soft, eager, welcoming sounds in her throat. Pulling on my ass, inviting me to fuck her face. So good. Best I'd ever felt or imagined. We were alone in the dark outside rules or limits, and I was taking what she offered. Hard, and repeatedly.

Being mistaken for a monster was the perfect vibe right now. Sandee might be damaged, but I had her beat by a mile. I'd forged myself into a death machine these last few months. No one had touched me, except in violence, for so long, I barely felt human anymore.

But Sandee's hot mouth working my dick...it made me feel like a god.

I just hoped when it came time to fuck her that I would have enough self-control to make her come. Already, the thundering energy inside me was picking up momentum as the world shook apart, and huge pleasure demolished me.

After some time, I remembered who and where I was again.

Insofar as anyone could. Being undercover made you realize how totally relative it all was. Just mind-fuck games. Random mask-switching. One was hardly less real than another.

More to the point, I remembered who I was pretending to be. James Craig, dirt-mean asshole, murderer, opportunist. And currently the luckiest son-of-a-bitch on earth.

Sandee still clutched my thighs, her strong fingers digging into my legs. She leaned back, letting my dick slide from her mouth, stiff as ever. She wiped her mouth, and gave him a wondering look. "Um, wow," she murmured. "You're still, ah…"

"Hard," I supplied. "Yeah. You've barely made a dent." I reached down, grabbing her hands. I hoisted her to her feet.

She backed away, looking shy. "One second," she said. "Let me just…"

She pushed past me into the bathroom and bent over the sink. I followed her in as she rinsed her mouth and splashed her face, not because I chose to, more like some huge force was dragging me, like a tow chain. I crowded her up to the sink, spun her around, pulled her against me, into a hot, ravenous kiss. As if I was drowning, and she was the last breath of air in the universe.

Her soft, tender lips, her wet face, were the sweetest thing I've ever tasted. Her shy, tender tongue retreated from mine at first, intimidated, but after a few slow, coaxing kisses, it was ready to come out and play, dancing with me. Her tits were pressed against my chest. I lifted her up, opening her legs. I've never seen such a cock-teasing outfit. Red high-heeled boots, that silk thong. A little gold locket.

I wanted to just mount up and plunge in, but no. Slow…the fuck…down.

I have to keep myself in check. She's at a huge disadvantage. She's tall and strong-looking, but I'm almost twice her size. I can't just leap on her like a bull.

So I just kept kissing her breath away, her thoughts, her fears. When I leaned back for air, I took the opportunity to admire the party-girl smeared mascara. The look of a girl who'd drunk too much and was about to make some really bad choices.

All I could do at this point was try to make those choices worth her while.

I pushed her back against the wall. The shock of the cold wall tiles made her gasp. I slid my hands down slowly, squeezing, stroking, to feel every inch of her luscious curves, every detail. The deep, sexy dip of her waist, the swell of her hips, the smooth globes of her perfect ass. I wanted to push aside the thong, reach lower. Feel those sweet, slick, secret female folds, that hot opening, yielding to my probing fingers.

Put on the brakes, dickhead. Not yet. Go slow. Go easy.

I pressed my face against her neck, her hair. I had to insert some self-control into the proceedings while still playing a believably murderous monster. It was a paradox.

I took a step back and grabbed the sink. Just to remind myself which way gravity was supposed to exert its force, because the only pull I felt was toward Sandee. "You want more?" I asked. As if I could have stopped if she said no.

Sandee licked her full, gleaming pink lips, and nodded.

"Then come for me," I said, improvising. "Show me you mean it."

"For real?" she asked, bewildered. "What do you mean? What I just did wasn't enough of a declaration to suit you? Dude, come on! What more do you want?"

I took the impulse, and ran with it. "Touch yourself. I want to watch you come."

Her eyes were startled. "Um, this is the thing. I can't do that on demand. It doesn't work that way. It's, ah...kind of mysterious. It happens, or it doesn't."

I made my voice cold and pitiless. "It's not rocket science. Put your hand on your clit and rub one out for me. That's the entry fee to this particular funhouse."

She caught her luscious lower lip between her teeth, her eyes worried.

"I want to see what you look like when you come," I told her. "The sounds you make. Your fingers all shiny from your lube. I want you to hold your pussy lips open so I can see everything. I want to suck the lube off your fingers. And then we'll see."

She blushed, eyes dilating until her irises were huge. Frozen in place. I had to get her moving. "Put your foot up onto the bathtub," I said. "Show me what you got."

Sandee straightened. Her blush had expanded down her chest. She lifted her foot, perching the high-heeled boot on the edge of the bathtub.

And whatever sexy bullshit I was about to spout just stuck right there in my throat as she slid her hand down, slowly over her breast, her belly, and lower. Down to that little decorative puff of dark blonde hair right over her clit.

She leaned back with a soft, shuddering sigh, almost a moan, spreading her pussy lips. I shifted out of the light so I could see that tantalizing glimpse of her beautiful, pink and crimson folds, like a tight furled flower. Wet and glowing. She lifted the hood of her clit, let me look. Pink, taut, gleaming, perfect. I wanted to taste it.

"Beautiful," I muttered. "Later, I'm going to suck on your clit until you scream."

That seemed to be the safest vibe. Harsh and aggressive verbally, but letting her make all the actual physical moves. I'd keep it going that way as long as I could play it.

Sandee trembled violently, gasping for breath as she touched herself. Caressing her pussy lips, then her clit with her gleaming fingers. Sliding in, out, around. In, out, around. That slow, sensual pulsing rhythm had my whole body thrumming with lust.

She gasped for breath, eyes closed. "Oh God," she quavered. "I'm going to come. I'm going to come."

"Not yet." I followed that impulse again. "Not until I say. Like your fantasy. Remember what you said at the prison? You don't come until I say you can come."

She looked distressed. "But you told me to...but...but it's killing me." Her voice vibrated. "I can't help it. I can't control it. I don't know how."

"So learn," I said. "You're doing great. You're a goddamn champion. Just be good. Just a little bit longer. You can do it. Come on...come on. So close...oh, yeah."

She was making soft, helpless whimpering sounds that almost got me off right there. I shifted closer to admire every detail of her hands down there, working her beautiful pink pussy. Close enough to feel her hot, panting breaths against my skin. See the startled look in her eyes as the pleasure started to crest.

Yes. I seized one of her hands, lube gleaming on her fingers, and slid my own hand between her legs. "Good," I murmured into her ear. "*Now.*"

As I spoke, I thrust two fingers up into her tight little hole, and sucked her wet fingers into my mouth. Her hot, sweet female taste almost made me come in my pants.

She cried out, going rigid as the orgasm blasted through her. I pinned her against the wall to keep her upright, still sucking on her fingers. Loving the hot clutching wet pulses of her pussy around my fingers. It went on and on. It was fucking incredible.

When her orgasm eased down, I scooped her up and carried her into the other room. The heater had been doing its work in the meantime, so it was no longer like a freezer, but it still wasn't warm. I set her down onto the edge of the bed. Kneeled to deal with those ridiculous red boots. Unfastening the buckles at her ankle, because she didn't appear to be up to the task herself. Not with that look on her face.

Sandee clutched the edge of the mattress with those bright blue fake fingernails, shivering. Her sharp, rapid breathing was the only sound in the room, other than the crackle of the wood in the stove, the buzz of the space heaters, the endless howling of the wind outside. We were in this little magic bubble, outside of time and space.

Fucking this girl had taken on a huge inevitability. Like a boulder rolling downhill, picking up speed, momentum, snow. Flattening everything in its path.

I pulled off her boots, massaging her chilly, gracefully shaped feet. Her nails were painted dark blue. She was a contradiction. Clearly experienced, but her response to sex was not what I'd expected. She seemed...well, blindsided by pleasure. Like she hadn't been expecting that orgasm. Like a clueless virgin, discovering it all for the first time. It made no sense at all, but I was too turned on to dwell on it.

I went over to the box of supplies that the Drakes had left for me, checking to see if Darius had left condoms. It was a running joke between us. Darius believed in being prepared for anything, but most especially for sex.

There they were. I've never been so grateful in my life for Darius's wise--ass gag. It was just a couple of three-packs, which would barely take the edge off, but they were better than nothing. I ripped one off the string and tore it open.

"Do you want this?" I asked. "You're sure?"

Sandee struggled to speak, lips still trembling, and failed. She nodded.

"Say it," I said. "Say the words. Do you want me inside you?"

"I...I want you," she said, her voice shaky but audible.

I pulled the condom from its envelope and held it out. "Then take me," I said. "Put this on and ask me for it. Loud enough so I can hear."

Her lips twitched. "I did, James," she reminded me. "Many times. I'm starting to wonder if you're feeling insecure."

"Again," I said obdurately, through clenched teeth. "Ask, every step of the way."

She cocked her head inquisitively. "Is this a power trip? Making me beg?"

I shrugged. "I don't know. Maybe, I guess. Is it working?"

She gave me a seductive glance from under her lashes. "What do you think?"

I stroked her cheek, tilted up her chin. "I assume nothing right now. It's been a long, weird day. Just fucking indulge me."

I pressed the condom into her hand. Sandee leaned forward, and I gasped as she grabbed my cock. But instead of rolling on the latex, she sucked my cockhead into her mouth again. Both hands, squeezing. That little pink tongue, flicking, sliding, swirling, suckling. God, this girl is fucking killing me.

I wound my hands into her hair, tugging it away. "No," I choked out.

Her eyes snapped open, and she retreated swiftly. "Sorry," she murmured.

I wound my hands into her hair, not letting her go. "No, no, no. I love it when you do that. It feels incredible. I just can't take any more of that without coming again."

"So come," she said. "I like it when you come. It's a huge turn-on for me."

I shook my head. "You first," I said. "I want to feel you squeezing my cock when you come the next time. Like you squeezed my fingers. I love that."

She gave me a dazzling smile that wiped my mind blank, and smoothed the latex over my cock, adjusting it with a caressing squeeze, root to tip. Stroking, twisting.

I gave her a little push, inviting her to fall backward. She leaned back onto her elbows, a shy smile on her face, gracefully opening her beautiful legs with a soft, jerky little sigh. She grabbed my hand, and pressed it against her mound.

Whoa, there I was, breathing down the excitement before it could go off like a bomb as I stroked and petted her with my fingertips. So sweet and hot and perfect, those pink pussy lips, all puffed up and swollen and slick. Sticky sweet, like honey.

Honeypot? I wondered once again if Boer could possibly have set her on me.

No way. Those bastards had attacked her to punish me. She was outside of this shitshow, and I was all done questioning my bizarre fortune. I notched my cock into her hot, slick opening, enjoying the arch and sigh and wiggle of eagerness as she lifted herself to take me deeper...and deeper, into her tight, clinging warmth.

If this was a trap, fuck it. The bastards got me.

And if it wasn't, it hardly mattered.

I was a goner either way.

CHAPTER 10

Freya

I dug my nails into his chest, but not to push him away. To trap him, to drag him closer, to keep him there, right where I wanted him. It was involuntary, like the wrenching gasps jerking out from between my lips with every deep thrust he made. Thick and hot and deep, plumbing my hot depths. Caressing, stroking, stirring me.

I hadn't known it could feel like this. He could just melt me down with pleasure and mold me into something new, someone I didn't even recognize, and couldn't control. He could turn me into Sandee for real. She was so vulnerable and compromised, so needy and desperate. Things I'd thought I wasn't. I thought I was so smart, so tough and capable. That no one could fuck with me.

I was being oh, so fucked with right now. And I was loving every second of it.

My body woke up, just for him. Glowing, aching, yearning. Each deep, sliding plunge of his cock relieved the ache, and stoked a desperate need for the next. I struggled helplessly to get closer, take him deeper. His cock stroked the melting, juicy sweet spots inside me. Making me shivering and soft. Yielding. Helpless. His.

I couldn't let myself topple like this. But I couldn't stop clutching, sobbing, lifting myself toward that thing I craved, and before I knew it, oh God...

Again, he watched me scatter into glittering pieces across the cosmos.

When I drifted back, he was on top of me, and miles inside. I could feel his swift, heavy heartbeat wedged so deep. He was still long, thick, and rock hard. Rocking, gently. Waiting until I was ready.

Not finished with me. Not by a long shot.

As our eyes locked, he started to move again. The last orgasm had sensitized me, and I gasped at the sensation, almost too much to bear, but as I stared into his eyes, he adjusted his stroke, my perception shifted, and suddenly, it was perfect. Exquisite, even. I was ravenous for more. As if he were some kind of sex god, and I was helplessly in his thrall. Coming for him, on command? Where did that come from? That was terrifying.

He was stripping me of masks I hadn't known I was wearing. I was inside out, broken parts exposed. My garbage, the godawful mess deep inside me that I had never cleaned up, because I didn't know how. I wouldn't be able to hide any of it from him.

I swallowed, to get my throat working. "Um...James? Don't you ever, you know...like, come?"

"Of course. I can go ahead and finish, if you're tired. I just love to be inside you. And I love to feel you come. Do you want to stop?"

"I'd like to see you come, too. Go ahead and finish. We can always start again."

He gave me a wicked grin as his cock pulsed deep. "Do you want to change positions? On top, from behind? Anything you like. Lady's choice."

That sounded fun, but too acrobatic in my current boneless

and quivering state. I shook my head. "This is good," I said. "Just like this."

"Yeah, it is," he said. "You're perfect. I love how it feels. That beautiful tight little hole, hugging me. Your sweet rosy tits bouncing. Your eyes, your lips. You're so fucking beautiful, Sandee."

"Ah...thank you," I faltered. "That's, ah...sweet."

His teeth flashed in the gloom, and he scooped up my knees, draping them over his elbows. Pressing me even wider open as he started in on me once again.

Slow, slick, heavy. Wickedly skillful. All the ugliness of the day had melted away. All my lies and plans and schemes, everything washed away, wiped blank as that energy started to build. He knew just how to stoke it, just how to spur me on, driving me on with those slick thrusts...waiting for me, waiting...until my pleasure throbbed through me, and he finally released his own, with a rough cry. Pouring himself into me.

That flash of bright, perfect fusion was shattering.

When I opened my eyes, my face was wet, and Jed was gazing down at me, looking worried. "Hey," he said. "You okay? Did I hurt you?'"

I shook her head. "Just tension unwinding," I murmured. "No biggie." I gave him the best smile I could muster, but he still looked unconvinced.

Jed lifted himself off, pulling out. I felt damp and small and vulnerable, alone on the bed, as he strode off to bathroom to get rid of the condom.

I was unequipped for this situation. I'd counted on my own rock-solid defenses. I thought I'd just pretend to like it, and deal with the fallout of prostituting myself later.

But actually, for real liking it? That was a goddamn disaster.

I tugged the blanket around my shivering self, but it didn't help. Water was roaring in the bathroom, and after a few minutes, Jed came back, holding out his hand.

"I ran you a bath," he said. "Come on."

I took his hand as he led me into the bathroom, which was damp and warm, lit by the glow of the kerosene lantern that sat on the windowsill. I stepped into the tub, sinking into the hot water with a sigh of pleasure.

Jed climbed in, too, which brought the water level way up high. The bathtub was a big one, but there was so much of him. He was huge, those big, powerful arms spread out wide on the edge of the tub, his bare chest gleaming.

I was speechless and shy, but Jed grabbed the soap and ran his sudsy hands slowly, sensually over every part of me that was over the level of the water, massaging, caressing. Slow, sexy, skillful. Releasing tension shuddered through my body, and when I felt shaky and soft and liquid, he pulled me up onto my knees, made his hands slippery with soap again, and reached between my legs.

He knew just exactly how to touch me there. Tender, bold, sure. I grabbed the tops of his shoulders, digging in my nails, and before I knew it, my head was flung back and I was gasping, hips jerking as he coaxed yet another explosive orgasm out of me.

What the hell? I don't know how he did it. My orgasms have always been kind of a mystery. Elusive and disappointingly shallow, ever since I started trying to have them. And my body had just randomly decided that tonight was the night to supercharge that system? While everything else in my life was going to hell at top speed?

Jed stroked his fingers inside me, a rumble of satisfied pleasure vibrating from him through me as he savored every last vibration of my climax, and then he hoisted me up, startled and dripping, to sit on the edge of the tub. My back to the wall.

Water slopped and sloshed out onto the floor, but he ignored it as he positioned himself between my legs and put his mouth to me.

Oh, he was so good. Slow and sensual, licking and sucking, flicking tenderly at my clit with the perfect tender, teasing pressure, and it wasn't just the technique, it was him, his energy, his heat, his enormous presence, making me drunk, dizzy.

I clutched at his head, his shoulders, as the waves of sensation thundered through me, over and over, in an endless, cleansing rush.

Jed pressed his lips to my belly, kissing it. I sank back into the water.

"Have you got something to prove?" I asked him.

"Nah, not really. You just have a really sweet, delicious pussy and I'm hungry for it. Just can't get enough." He got up before I could think of any snappy response, water sloshing and coursing down over his gorgeous body. Still stone hard. Droplets glittered on the thatch of hair at his groin.

He lifted me to my feet and helped me out of the tub. Dried me off with a towel. Long, gentle strokes over my arms, my legs, my back. A swift glimpse of myself in the foggy mirror made me flinch at what had become of my make-up, but it's the classic Sandee look, after all. My lips were so red, my eyes so bright. My cheeks incredibly pink. Everything so high-contrast. Extreme.

In the other room, Jed dug into a box, pulled out big black T-shirt, and tossed it to me. I put it on, and it draped off my shoulders and halfway down my thighs.

Jed opened up the bedcovers and beckoned to me. "Get some sleep," he said.

"What about you?" I asked.

"I'll keep watch on the monitors," he said. "I still have some adrenaline to metabolize. I'll crash when I crash."

"You must be tired," I said. "What monitors?"

He gestured at a table that was covered with the computer equipment. *Shit.* I'd been in such a fog of desire, I'd barely noticed all of that, and what it implied.

"Those," he said. "To keep us safe. But I doubt anyone will be chasing us in this storm."

In one swift glance, I saw two big monitors, multiple camera angles. "You've got a whole security setup out there? Jeez, what is this place?"

He didn't acknowledge the question. "Sleep easy," he said. "Nothing bigger than a fox is getting near here without me knowing about it. I'll see everything that moves."

So he must have infrared, and motion detectors, and God knows what else.

Sleep easy, my ass. This news freshly rattled me. Whatever this operation was, it was generously funded and meticulously planned, months in advance. This was not an improvisation. He had a plan, help, resources, a huge budget. Shane's disappearance was connected to it. And I couldn't say a single fucking word to him about it.

All I could do was open my legs and play dumb.

CHAPTER 11

Jed

"Dude, get real." Darius Drake's deep voice was harsh, drilling into my ear as I held up the burner phone with a half-frozen hand. "We're still in fucking Nairobi. We won't be stateside for another three days. It sucks about Mickey, and I'm sorry, but why guard this random girl? Why's she relevant? What has she got to contribute?"

I tried to keep my voice low, outside with the wind whistling by my ears. "Nothing, but that's not the issue!" I persisted. "She fell into this by chance—"

"By chance? What the fuck did she think she was doing in that prison, flirting with your dangerous, felonious ass? That was shit-for-brains stupid. We don't need stupid people draining our energy and resources. Hate to be a dickhead, my man, but I've got other things to do. Things that are more important to our cause. We all do."

"Goddamnit, that's not how—"

"I know. You feel responsible for her." Darius's voice was wry. "Of course. You feel responsible for every fucking thing that flashes through your field of vision."

"Bullshit," I snarled. "Boer had Mickey cut to pieces, and I don't want it happening to this girl! So fucking sue me!"

"Ah. Hey." Darius's voice softened, but only slightly. "Listen. I'm sorry about Mickey. For real. I know you liked the guy. Tonight must have been total shit. Hey, Amos is monitoring the cop shop, and we haven't heard about APBs or manhunts announced. So far, so good. Maybe they're trying to keep the press out of it. You off-roading to Mandan Pond tomorrow, like we planned? It's remote, and outside of any search perimeters they might establish. Go there and hang tight while we regroup."

"Fine, whatever, but you guys have to help me cover Sandee," I repeated.

"No, we don't. Boer doesn't have any reason to bother some random babe who came to visit you in prison." Darius had the overly even, controlled tone of a guy talking someone down off a ledge. "He'll forget about her. Just give her a big nice wad of cash, put her on a bus, tell her to go spend a month someplace far away from here. On a beach, maybe. She'll be fine. There's a thousand more girls where she came from. Boer won't waste time with her. He's got bigger fish to fry."

What Darius said made sense, but every instinct I had was screaming that it was dead wrong. "I heard what those guys in the prison said," I said. "He's fixated on her. By now, those assholes know everything about her. Where she lives, where she works, her friends, her social media. Every detail. She'll be dead in a day if I cut her loose."

"So what are you proposing?" Darius bitched. "A twenty-four-hour security detail until Boer is out of commission? Jesus, man. Forget it. We have no idea how long that will take, and we don't have the manpower. We have to come up with a new strategy now that Mickey's dead. Face it. Your girl is not part of our mission."

"I am real fucking sorry it's so inconvenient, but I don't want to see her die!"

Darius made a frustrated sound. "You're nuts. Wait, hold on. Is she cute?"

"What the fuck does that have to do with anything?"

Darius paused, and then chuckled under his breath. "Ahhh," he murmured. "I see. So she is cute. I'm betting you've already had a few generous helpings up there in the cabin, am I right? And you don't really feel like sharing? Is that the vibe?"

"That's not what's going on here." I growled. "I'm just trying to keep her alive."

"I understand you're sex-starved, being stuck in prison and all, but we've got more important things to do than make sure you've got a warm, wet, welcoming place to shove your—"

"Shut the fuck up, Darius. We'll talk when you're back in the country."

"After you top up, right? You want some more sugar? Ooh, baby."

I hung up on him, muttering obscenities into the wind.

Foul-mouthed, dirty-minded bastard. Darius was a relentless ballbreaker, but he wouldn't want to see an innocent girl get hurt, either. He'd come around. So would the others. But goddamn, were they ever going to make me pay for it in blood. And they couldn't help me tomorrow, in any case. They'd wouldn't be here for days.

Damn. Months of my life, locked in that hellhole, and nothing to show for it but the memory of Mickey's mutilated body to haunt me. Just what I needed. A fresh dose of crushing guilt. I was used to it by now, but fuck, it exhausted me.

So I just stood there in the snow, wondering what to do with Sandee. I couldn't just let her go as Darius had suggested. Nor could I just tell her to run, unprotected. For fuck's sake, she hadn't demonstrated even the slightest ability to look out for herself. As evidenced by her decision to throw herself onto my dick.

Not that it was fair to blame her for that. I hadn't fought very hard. My bad.

But that wasn't the point. I couldn't shake my irrational conviction that if I turned my back on Sandee, Boer and his goons would eat her for breakfast, and then I'd have her on my conscience, along all the rest. There wasn't any more room in that dark closet in my mind. It was at full capacity.

So I had to carry her. She would slow me down, have opinions, question my decisions. It would be dangerous, unwieldy, and stupid. God, I was such an asshole sometimes, I astonished myself. But I was too blasted to come up with an alternative plan of action. I'd be on the run from Boer's team and the law, no back-up, dragging a knockout blonde along with me. Way to avoid attracting attention.

I finally gave into the cold, and came back inside. I needed a couple of hours of rest, but it felt dangerous and counterintuitive to let down my guard down with Boer out there on the loose. To say nothing of a mind-blowing naked girl in my bed.

I entered quietly. Sandee was a small bump in the covers, a shock of pale hair messed over the pillow. I checked the monitors. The cameras I had placed at intervals of a half-mile all showed quiet white road, falling snow. No activity.

I stripped off my shirt and slid into the bed, trying not to wake her up, but I was too big not to cave in the mattress. Sandee slid downhill, right down into the well, fetching up next to me. Wedged up tight. Her body felt good. Soft, hot.

Her eyes fluttered, and she gazed up at me, and I was freshly struck by how ridiculously pretty she was. Those huge, hypnotic eyes. That smooth, perfect skin under the mess of smeared make-up. Those full, cushiony pink lips, puffy from being passionately kissed.

I suddenly remembered how those lips looked clasped around my dick, and instantly I was stone hard and aching again. As if I hadn't just come explosively.

She shifted against me and lifted her thigh, laying it across my erection. The soft, silky weight of her leg was a silent invitation. So was the look in her eyes, and the way her tongue flicked out to lick her full, plump red lower lip, making it gleam.

Damn. She was scary good at this. I was completely out of my league.

She touched my cheek. "Yikes. Your face is so cold. Were you outside?"

I ignored that. "Listen up." I made my voice hard. "I have to find a safe place to stash you, so tomorrow—"

"No, you don't. I don't need to be stashed."

I plodded grimly on. "Let me finish. I can't leave you alone after what happened. The guys who came after you at the hotel will finish you off. You'll have to stick with me until I can find someplace safe for you. You'll be guarded by colleagues of mine."

"Why can't I just stay with you?" She had that soft, husky, fuck-me-now voice.

"Stop," I said. "I want to keep you alive, so what I need is no back talk and no pushback. You're going to have to dress down, for starters."

Her eyes widened in alarm. "What do you mean, 'dress down?'"

"The make-up goes, the sexy clothes go. You cover up the hair. Wear a big, sloppy gray hoodie. I'll find you some bad glasses."

Sandee looked distressed. "I have to look...*ugly?* Eeeww. Can't I just, like, wear a black wig or something?"

"Not if you want us to stay alive," I said.

She stared at me for a moment, and then shifted so the cover slid down, revealing her soft, luscious tits. The tips hardened as I looked at them.

"I don't think I've ever felt this alive," she said softly. "Or this motivated to stay that way. But I want to stay with you, James. Not to get stashed someplace."

I split into two parts, reason and instinct. Reason recoiled in alarm. My dick leaped at the open invitation. Twitching with eagerness.

I shook my head slowly, and tried to keep it brutally real. "Watch yourself, Sandee," I said. "Don't get all intense about me. I've got nothing for you but a hard dick. And when I'm done, I will drop you flat."

She blinked, startled. "Wow," she said. "That's harsh."

"I won't lie to you," I warned. "Don't get your hopes up. Not for one second. I will leave you. That's a sure thing. Sooner rather than later."

She chewed her lip for a moment, and shrugged, with a crooked little smile. "At least you're honest," she said. "That's a cut above most of the guys I've ever met. And you're here now, right? It's okay. I'm used to being left. I'll survive."

I'd been half-trying to push her away, I guess. Piss her off, just to get some space. But she wasn't falling for it. By no means. Her opalescent blue-tipped fingernails were trailing down my belly, brushing my crotch through layers of blanket.

"It's worth it," she murmured, her voice husky. "I mean, who gets to have a wild adventure with a mysterious fugitive sex god? That's, like, a once in a lifetime chance. So I'm taking it. And I'll milk it for all it's worth. Like, literally."

My dick lengthened against the teasing strokes of her fingers. I couldn't push her hand away, or look away from that sexy glow in her eyes. "Don't get attached," I said.

"It's not your problem if I do," she said. "It's mine. Don't sweat it. You'll be long gone, anyhow. You won't have to watch me be all sad about it."

Bullshit. It was always my problem. That was my thing, inheriting other peoples' problems, and their punishments, too. I have a supernatural talent for it.

I remembered, abruptly, that as far as Sandee knew, I was a sociopathic monster, so I'd better man up and try to act like one.

Make her understand that she was here with me as a convenient fuck after a long dry spell.

The fact that she was turned-on by this scenario was pathological, and way too complicated for me to untangle. But like it or not, I had to stay in character.

I pulled a condom out of my pocket and jerked the cover off her naked body. I grabbed her knees, and opened her legs. Sandee let out a low, whimpering sigh and arched with athletic grace, spreading still wider.

I've been with a lot of beautiful women, but never for long. I always kept my cool, kept my distance. A shitty upbringing burns that kind of caution in real deep.

But Sandee's voluptuous surrender just got to me. Pulled at me. So raw, so unselfconscious and real. I'd never felt anything like it. It was irresistible.

I slid my hand up the velvety perfection of her inner thigh, up to the puff of dark blonde fuzz over her pussy. Everything else was waxed off, smooth as a rose petal. I ran my fingertips up and down the slick divide of her pussy lips, feeling the honey sweet moisture, like an exquisite oil, inviting me in.

I slid my fingers inside her while I tenderly caressed the bud of her clit with my thumb. I was so turned on, I could hardly breathe. She was exquisitely wet, shivers of excitement wracking her beautiful body. Turned on...for me.

No. For James. Not for me. Remember that, dick-for-brains.

I couldn't do that, not while staring into her eyes. In this raw, torn-open state, I couldn't keep up the role of the monster she wanted to save.

I got up off the bed, shoving down my pants, quickly sheathing my dick with latex. I made a brusque gesture. "Turn around," I said curtly. "Hands and knees."

Her eyelashes fluttered with doubt, but she turned, looking over her shoulder as she leaned forward on her elbows. She arched her back, parting her legs wider.

This was a mistake. I had thought it was her eyes that would melt me down, but her ass in the air, thighs open, that shadowy pink pussy luring me...if I even manage to stay conscious, it'll be a victory. I gripped her ass cheeks, caressing her slick, yielding pussy lips with my cockhead. Getting it good and wet as I nudged inside.

Pleasure wrenched a groan from me as I slid into her. So good. I could never get enough. Clinging and sweet. It made me want to lose the latex. Skin on skin. Fuck her with my naked cock, feeling everything. The heat, the wet. Then fill her with my come.

Whoa. Walk it back, bozo. None of that shit. Not going there.

I focus on sliding deep inside her, gripping her hips. Watching my dick slide out, gleaming with her balm, with the bleak realization that it didn't make any difference, fucking her from behind. The sense of intense intimacy still burned me. I reached around to cup her mound, catching her clit between my fingers. Squeezing it as I fucked her, seeking the perfect angle, the perfect stroke.

She was primed, and it didn't take long. In just a few moments, she went rigid. Wailing as her climax wrenched through her. Squeezing and milking my dick and pulling me after her. The whole universe exploding along with me as I came.

I found myself collapsed over her afterward. Crushing her into the crumpled blankets. Glued to her with sweat. Both of us panting. Trembling violently.

I was pissed. Of all things, I was angry. At her, for being so goddamn vulnerable, so stupid and unguarded. And at me for taking advantage of it. How could she let a convict, an escaped murderer, take her to a shack in the woods, strip her naked and fuck her brains out? She must have a death wish. And it bothered the living fuck out of me that she was so unprotected. Not just from me. From everyone.

Someone should be taking care of this girl. Someone should save her from herself. But it couldn't be me. I was triple booked.

Useless to her, except as a dangerous reinforcement of all her worst self-destructive instincts. And it just drove...me...*nuts.*

I went to the bathroom to get rid of the condom, came back and yanked on my jeans. Sandee was still curled up on the bed, starry eyed and rosy and tousled.

She sat up, frowning in puzzlement. "You look mad."

"Yeah," I blurted. "You shouldn't do this."

"Do what?"

I shook my head angrily, wishing I hadn't opened my mouth. This bullshit was not in character for James Craig the asshole. "Let yourself be used," I said. "Opening your legs for a no-good thug bastard like me. Begging for it. For fuck's sake."

Sandee's mouth dropped open in outrage. She slid off the bed, jumping to her feet. Magnificent and unselfconscious in her nakedness.

"I thought you liked it!" she said sharply. "It's just bullshit sex talk, you sanctimonious dickhead! What's wrong with it, if we both like it?"

I shook my head. I didn't know how to put it into words. How dangerous it was to her. How it left her wide open to be used.

"Fuck you," she said, eyes ablaze. "You're a fine one to criticize! Like someone who bitches about the calories in the cheesecake after they've already eaten the whole thing! Don't be a hypocrite, James. You ate it. You liked it. You can't say you didn't."

"You're giving your power away," I said.

"Well, there's plenty more power where that came from." She marched past me, chin up, tits out, flushed a hot red. "Get out of my way. I'm going to wash up."

She was a long time in the bathroom. Long enough for me to contemplate my sins, and feel like shit for being hypocritical. Also to ponder how different she seemed when she got really pissed at me. She got suddenly sharper, deeper. She used a different tone, different words. Of course, I'd already gleaned from her letters that she was a lot smarter than she let on. She'd probably learned how to play dumb to survive.

Sandee was right about me gobbling up the goddamn cheesecake. Why criticize her for letting me take advantage when I couldn't hold back myself? That was unfair.

I didn't have time to stress about this. I had to get rid of this girl before she took me down. Find a safe place for her that wasn't right in my face. Or riding my dick.

She finally emerged, and went straight to the T-shirt I'd given her before, pulling it on. She looked around the room as if she was searching for some other place to be.

"Get into the bed," I said.

"I'd rather take the cot." Her voice was haughty and distant.

"Too fucking bad," I said. "That ship has sailed. Tonight, your ass belongs right over here, in this bed. It wasn't a suggestion."

My tone makes her lips tighten, but she does it, thank God. The last thing I wanted to do right now was muscle around some pissed off, emotional girl.

She approached reluctantly, and I gestured for her to get in between me and the wall. Clearly, she was not thrilled to be trapped there, but tough shit. I wanted her to be right next to me while I slept. This place was full of firearms, ordnance, electronic equipment, money, documents. I didn't want her fucking with it while I was asleep.

So we were staying real cozy tonight, no matter how pissed she was at me.

"I'm turning out the light," I said. "That cool with you?"

"You're the big boss, right?" she asked, her voice sulky. "Why ask me?"

I shrugged. "You told me stuff in the letters. About those religious fanatics who locked you up in the dark when you were little. If that was me, I'd still be afraid of the dark. Just tell me, if that's the case. I don't want to have you falling apart on me with no warning."

"Oh." She wouldn't meet my eyes, just chewed on her lip, which was shaking. "Um. Well, um, I usually do sleep with a light on. If you must know. But I won't freak out if you want to turn it off. I'm not all twisted up about it. I don't have a complex or anything. It's just, you know. A preference."

"I'll leave it on, then." I dragged her close, her back to my front. Her round, luscious ass pressed against my dick had the effect one would expect, but I ignored it.

I wound my arm around her body, flung my leg over her legs. If she moved a single muscle, I would know about it.

She smelled good. Something about the way her hair tickled my nose felt good. It made something unlock inside my chest. Letting more air in.

"Your arm is too heavy," she complained. "I can't breathe."

I shifted my arm down a notch so it wasn't resting on her ribs. "Better?"

She snorted. "I guess. You're hot, though. Like a blast furnace."

"Deal with it. Now shut up and let me sleep."

She stopped talking, and I tried to calm myself down. But there was something about her that I couldn't quite put my finger on. It kept eluding me.

Something out of place. I was angry at her for being so vulnerable, so broken. Wide open to abuse. Things that weren't her fault. I, of all people, should know that.

But that didn't jive with the clear, ringing tone in her voice when she called me out for being a hypocrite. Or the cool indignation in her eyes. Or her proud posture.

And when we came together, when I felt her soul, or some crazy fucking thing, she seemed so bright. She shone like a star in that magic place in my mind. Not broken, or damaged. Ragged around the edges, maybe. Desperate, stressed, pushed to the limit.

But not broken.

CHAPTER 12

Freya

I tried for the tenth time to wiggle free of Jed's tight embrace, and failed again. He just stretched, yawned in his sleep, and tightened his grip.

I had to call Holly today. Just had to. It was her ninth birthday, and no one was there to celebrate with her but Ethan's staff. They loved her to distraction, and could be counted upon to make a birthday fuss, but even so. Poor Holly already suffered a huge blow when Shane, her dad, had disappeared. We were the only family she had left, and she needed her Uncle Ethan and me to be there for her in person in order to feel safe and whole and properly celebrated. It sucked that I wasn't there today.

Plus, I was pissed at Ethan for skiving off on his own mysterious business without sharing it with me, or thinking of Holly's birthday. He adored his little niece, but he left the organizational parenting tasks to me. Things like parent-teacher conferences, medical appointments, vaccinations, music and dance instruction, or planning for a birthday party. Those kinds of things just never occurred to him.

I needed to get my coat on, slip outside, reassemble my Freya

Masters phone, call Holly, then swiftly break the phone down and hide it all again. The ideal thing would be to get back inside and in character as Sandee before Jed even woke up.

Ambitious, risky, but a girl could try. In fact, a girl had to try.

I tried again, pulling harder. This time, Jed stirred, murmuring in protest. "What the fuck?" he mumbled. "Stop wiggling."

"Let me get up," I insisted. "I have to pee."

He made an impatient sound, but shifted his weight so I could extricate myself. My clothes were scattered around, so I scooped them up and brought them into the bathroom with me. I'd slept surprisingly well, considering everything. Maybe it was all those multiple orgasms. No matter how emotionally fraught and complicated the sex, I had never even imagined pleasure like that. I'd thought that what happened last night would make me feel bad about myself. Soiled. But it didn't.

It made me feel…hot. Again.

I'm not sure what that said about me, but screw it. I had stuff to do. I could worry about the sorry state of my psychological health later.

I took care of my business in the bathroom, then pulled on my clothes, wishing I had warmer, better ones. My BBBag with my toothbrush was in the other room, so I tried to brush my teeth with a glob of toothpaste and my finger. I had bedhead from hell, so I tried to calm it down with water and a grimy comb from the bathroom cabinet. No success. The hair just had its own unfathomable agenda.

When I crept out of the bathroom, it looked as if Jed had fallen asleep again. Yay, my golden opportunity. I tiptoed to my boots, and silently shoved my feet into them. Wishing I had underwear under my kinky schoolgirl skirt, but my skimpy thong was nowhere to be seen, and hell, it barely qualified as underwear in the best of times.

I didn't bother buckling my ankle boots. As insubstantial as they were, I might just as well be barefoot. I grabbed my coat, but didn't put it on yet, since the shiny, quilted nylon was too noisy. It puffed and chuffed with every movement I made.

I crept into the mudroom out front, and very gently opened the many locks and bolts on the door. Tiptoed out, closing it softly as I could. So far, so good.

Whoa, that ice-cold breeze on my bare nether bits under that scanty skirt was quite the sensation. And my shoes were a freaking nightmare for this deep snow. I swiftly pulled on the coat, shivering. I had to make this quick, or else lose some toes.

The storm had stopped, and everything was smooth, white, hushed. The old cabin was battered but sound-looking, perched not far from the edge of a deep, narrow canyon. The snow was still dry, and the wind had been blowing all night, so it had blown most of the snow off a rocky spine of the hillside near the cliff's edge.

It was a very beautiful place. Too bad I didn't have the time or bandwidth to enjoy it. I made my way as quickly as I could, putting my feet only where the snow wasn't, trying not to let the heels catch on the rocks and the roots, making for the nearest trees that could offer me a little cover as I fumbled at the hem, pulling my phone out and snapping in the battery. My fingers were already numb, making it difficult.

I kept the phone carefully on the side of me that couldn't be seen from the house.

If Jed looked through this phone, the jig would be up. I probably shouldn't have brought it at all, and just committed to being Sandee for the interim. That would have been the smartest thing. But who would've dreamed Jed would break out of prison on the very day I visited? And right after I'd just offered him the moon and stars, sexually speaking. Which I pretty much delivered last night.

It was silly, I knew it, but I just couldn't let Holly's birthday go by without calling her. I was such a sap. I crouched, leaning against a big rock that gave me some cover, both visually from the house and from the wind that swept through the canyon.

I pulled up Holly's number and called. She picked right up. "Auntie Frey?"

"Happy ninth birthday, baby," I said softly. "I can't believe you're so big!"

"I knew you'd call!" Holly crowed. "So where are you? Are you coming home? I hear the wind! Are you in a car with the window open? Are you on your way home?"

I couldn't help smiling. That's my girl. Only nine, but just too damn smart for her own good, and curious as hell. "I wish I was," I told her. "But I'm still pretty far away. Too far to make it back today. I just wanted to wish you a totally fabulous day. I have some birthday presents for you, but they'll have to wait until I get home."

Holly was silent for a moment. "Are you out looking for my dad?"

"Always, sweetie," I said. "Every day of my life."

Holly harrumphed. "Well, you be careful." Her voice took on a lecturing tone. "Uncle Ethan is, too. He told me before he left. But he's mad that you're not here now. And he was really, *really* mad that your phone was off all the times he tried to call."

I held back the snort of laughter with some effort. Hell, when was Ethan not mad at me? "Don't worry about it," I assured her. "It's cool. I can handle Uncle Ethan."

"He said he'd be home tonight to have some cake with me," Holly said pointedly. "So you should really call us then."

"I'm not sure if I'll be able to call tonight, sweetheart. I will try, I swear. Have a wonderful birthday, honey."

"Sandee?" Jed's furious voice, from the house. "Where the *fuck* are you?"

"Gotta go," I said, in a hushed voice. "Later, babe."

"Why are you whispering?" Holly's voice sharpened. "I hear somebody yelling. Who's that yelling? Are they yelling at you?"

"Tell you when I see you. Love you." I pried the phone open. Shoved the phone and battery into my hidden hem pocket, zipping it up with clumsy, trembling fingers.

I stumbled out from behind the rocks, waving my arms. "Hi!" I waved at him. "Over here!"

"What in the holy fuck are you doing out here?" He looked terrifyingly angry.

I put on an innocently bewildered expression. "Um...nothing much? I just wanted a little air. And, you know, to look at the view."

"The view? Yesterday a pack of fucking assassins tried to put a bag over your head! And today you waltz out into the open to make snow angels? The fuck, Sandee?"

"But nobody's here, and I didn't go far, just to—"

"Get inside!" he roared.

I stumbled through the snow as fast as I could manage in those boots, stamping it off once I got into the mudroom. "I'm sorry," I told him again as he followed me in. "I didn't go far at all. And I didn't know you'd, like, freak out about it."

Jed slammed the door, and slid the locks and bolts into place, his face grim.

I tried again. "I'm really sorry," I said. "I didn't mean to scare you. I just always stretch my legs in the morning, and I looked out the window, and it was so peaceful and pretty outside, so I thought—"

"Don't think. It's not safe. Just do what the fuck you're told, if you want to survive. Never walk out of my sight again without telling me what you're doing. Not while I'm responsible for you. Understand?"

I didn't have a leg to stand on, and I knew it. And still, I felt my spine stiffen up as I stared him down. "I did not swear to obey your every command," I said.

He looked at me thoughtfully, eyes narrowing. I realized, with a sickening shock, that anger had made me slip. That was Freya's vocal cadence, not Sandee's. Freya's clear alto voice, not the raspy, grinding vocal fry I'd learned from various female Instagram influencers, the voice I'd been practicing into my phone for months.

He had stung me into dropping my mask. *Shit.*

I shrugged off my coat and hung it on a chair, hoping to distract him with my nipple hard-on. He noticed it, but didn't lose focus.

"Don't fuck with me," he said. "Maybe you will eventually get chopped up by these assholes, despite my best efforts, but it won't be on my watch. So listen up. Do what I say, or you'll be sorry. Are we clear?"

Be Sandee. Be her right now, idiot. I fought my knee-jerk pride and anger down, and forced myself to stay in character. Sulky. Pouting. Intimidated. Maybe even a little turned on. I let my lips tremble. "I'll be good," I said, in a small, cowed voice.

He picked up a duffel bag and flung it at me. "Take this stuff and go get changed."

"Changed into what?" I opened the bag and rifled through the contents. Men's winter clothing, heavy in texture, dull in color. "Is this your stuff? I'll swim in it!"

"Not mine. It was meant for someone else. Bigger than you are, but smaller than me. You could cuff the pants, and I think there's a belt in there. Just put them on and make them work somehow."

"But why can't I just—"

"Fucking *do it!*"

CHAPTER 13

A twinge of sharp pain from her jaw shooting up to her temple reminded Nicole that she was grinding her teeth again. She'd lose some of them if she didn't stop, and that would be unacceptable. Much of her current power was based on her beauty.

Eventually, beauty faded, of course. But she had a plan. By then, she'd have extreme wealth and power. At that point, beauty and sex were no longer necessary. They were just tools, anyhow. A mirror for men's lust and ego. She looked forward to leaving that particular part of the whole sweaty, stinking mess behind her.

It had been a bad night. Wex had been furious after last night's debacle. And since the fuck-ups were frozen corpses scattered across a hotel parking lot, he'd taken it out on her, meaning she was unpleasantly sore in her nether parts. Her stomach was in knots. She kept tasting bile. It happened when she was murderously angry.

Which was to say, fairly often lately.

But she would get through this. This was her pet project, even if Wex thought he was running the show. She was the mastermind, the one who had understood what Ethan Masters was capable of during that internship she'd done with Masters Tech, Inc. a few years ago. She'd snooped into Ethan Masters's notes and been dazzled. He was a brilliant, exceptional man who needed someone like her at his side, helping him rule the entire fucking world. Since not even a man like him could possibly do it alone.

But he hadn't seen the potential in the two of them together. When she had tried to seduce him, Ethan Masters had bought her dinner, fucked her very expertly and thoroughly, and blown her off. She'd been tempted to kill him for it, but she'd held back.

He'd die for it eventually. In the meantime, she could plan all the ways she could make him suffer, and slowly devise the perfect punishment. It had been a big shame that Ethan hadn't been there when they destroyed the Ready Line facility, but he lived and worked hundreds of miles away from Shane and his company. But she hoped it stung, taking his brother away. That it made him suffer. Who knew, if a man like that even had a heart. Anyone's guess.

She was going to profit from what Ethan had created. She would take it from him. It should have been hers to begin with. *He* should have been hers.

She had finally found her entry point in Wex Boer. He'd served with the Masters brothers in the Rangers, and Ready Line Security had sometimes collaborated with Wex's security company. Shane knew the codes to open his brother's algorithms.

Wex was perfect for her purposes. He had funds, a large team of mercenaries at the ready. He was self-centered, amoral, arrogant enough to be ambitious, stupid enough to be manipulated, and he'd been absolutely on board once she'd explained the potential of the SmokeScreen algorithm to him.

Nicole had dreamed up the Ready Line massacre in every detail, but Wex and his team had executed it. She'd made the story airtight, backed up by financial data, bank deposits, forensic evidence, etc. The way it was supposed to look to the cops, Wex had burned to a crisp along with the rest of them. The fall guy was Jed Clearwater. He'd sold them all out and fled, the bastard. Or tried to. That bit was her favorite, the part the press would eat up with a spoon. How Jed had run his car off a bridge and died trying to flee the scene. Karma's immediate retribution, ka-pow! A story like that would go viral in a heartbeat. People loved when an evil asshole got his comeuppance.

Especially when he looked a fool while he was getting it.

But Jed hadn't died. Somehow, that cast-iron sonofabitch had crawled out of the totaled mess of a car under the bridge, and lived. Fucking up her perfect narrative.

Though she still had hopes of salvaging it.

Then Wex Boer, idiot extraordinaire, had boasted to his most powerful and dangerous client about his shiny new algorithm, and their captive, who held the key to it. What happened next was what any person with half a brain would predict. The bastard had swooped down and yanked Shane Masters out of their grasp. Of *course*.

God, she was so sick of cleaning up stupid men's messes.

But Shane wasn't the only one who knew the SmokeScreen codes. Ethan Masters wrote them, and persuading Ethan to give them up was going to be the most fun she'd ever had. And there were other weak points. The sister, Freya. The niece, Holly.

Yes. Fun times ahead.

The perfect conclusion would involve a river of blood and a mountain of body parts of anyone who had ever insulted her. To say nothing of hundreds of billions flowing into her personal offshore accounts. She'd be content with nothing less.

And Wex Boer...well. She was sick of his undisciplined impulses. Last night had been one tantrum too many. That new face he was so proud of, that would be his punishment. She would slowly slice all the way around it with her scalpel. Then, she would peel it off him, while he was fully conscious. Staring at her with lidless eyes. Screaming with a lipless mouth. The image gave her a stimulating rush of endorphins.

She glanced over at the computer screen, and by pure chance, she saw it flicker into being. The blip on the screen where none had been before. The little blue icon that represented Freya Masters' phone. Excitement exploded inside her.

Nicole grabbed the headset and listened to the call. The signal came from about thirty miles up into the mountains. It looked like a dead end road, and it was going to be slow going in that snow, but on the plus side, their prey would be easy to trap up there.

The conversation itself was of no particular interest. Freya calling to say happy birthday to the little girl, not ask for help or rescue. How sweet. Clearly, she cared about Holly, which was good. Beloved children were effective levers, in her experience.

And Nicole would do what was necessary to get SmokeScreen functioning. She was unbeatable with her scalpel. She'd spent a few years in medical school before they kicked her out. They were afraid of her. Too many jealous, nervous colleagues. But she had talent. She would have been a great surgeon. She had nerves of fucking steel.

Nicole paced through the house, running up to the master bedroom. Boer was lying on the bed, a damp cloth lying over his face.

"Wex," she said. "News."

"Leave me the fuck alone, you sulky cunt. I'm sick of your bullshit."

Nicole thought of some entertaining things she could do with her scalpel to certain sensitive nerve bundles in his face. His eyes, too.

"I have a fix on Freya Masters," she told him.

Wex jolted upright. The wet cloth fell. His face was red, swollen, and unpleasantly shiny from the ointment he had smeared on it, to speed the healing process. "What? Where?" he demanded.

"Up in the mountains," she told him. "It happened just now. She turned it on to make a call. To wish Holly a happy birthday. Evidently, she just turned nine today."

He laughed under his breath, grinning. The grooves in his healing cheeks looked red and painful. "What a dumb bitch," he commented. "Get everyone we have here mobilized. We should kill Clearwater and take Freya to control Ethan. Finally, you get to put these special skills you boast about to use while I watch and learn. Are you finally ready to show me what you're really made of, my killer bitch queen?"

Oh, yes. Her headache from grinding her teeth vanished as she pictured Wex's shock on that fine day when she finally showed him what she was really made of.

She gave him a blinding smile. "That sounds just perfect."

CHAPTER 14

His sharp tone cracked like a whip, making me flinch. I grabbed the duffel bag and hurried to the bathroom. Once inside, I leaned against the door, trying to calm my racing heart and get air into my lungs. This was no time for a panic attack.

The bag, the clothes. Changing into them would give me something concrete to do. Something else to react to. Activity was good. It would ground me.

I pulled out the contents, piece by piece, marveling at how butt-ugly every item was. Selected for ugliness. Heavy, awkward, vomit-tinted shades of wool, waffle weave, fleece. I guess it made sense, in a way. They made the wearer invisible.

I pulled on the items that worked the best. I had to cuff the pant legs twice, and my wrist cuffs three times. There was a pair of boots, two sizes too big, but more functional than what I had. I pulled on both pairs of socks, and laced them up tight.

The pants were three inches too big in the waist but too tight in the ass. I rolled up the cuffs and pant legs and cinched up the belt to keep it all from falling off my body. And I quietly dissolved into tears the whole time. Oh please. Not now. *Fuck.*

I kept it silent, more or less, but I couldn't stop the gasping, doubling-over, mouth-wide-open ugly-cry. Where was my inner sneaky femme fatale commando bitch when I needed her? She'd bugged out and left me sobbing in the bathroom...all because I'd gotten my tender feelings hurt by Jed-Fucking-Clearwater.

I didn't understand why I was having these feelings. As if I cared what he thought of me. Was it some freaky psychological process I couldn't control? Something inside me wanting to bond with him just because we'd had sex?

Please, please, let it not be that. I absolutely had to make that shit stop.

Because oh, dear God, that would not end well.

I finally got the sobbing to ease down, and rinsed my face in the sink. Yesterday's mascara stubbornly resisted every effort made to get rid of it. I was going to need an industrial solvent to get it off. I made another halfhearted attempt to deal with the hair, but there was a gray knit cap in the bag. I shoved my hair into it. Problem sorted.

But when I looked at myself in the mirror, oh, God help me. I looked like a ragbag on legs. My pallid, scared face with smudgy, shadowed eyes peeked out from under the oversized gray cap. I looked like a war refugee, fleeing terror and trauma.

Looking bad was dangerous on a psychological level. If I had to face the powers of evil, I preferred to look like a bad Bond girl while doing it.

But Jed was the boss right now, so no. *Suck it up, Masters.*

No, goddamnit. Suck it up, *Sandee. Keep your personae straight, girl.*

My next challenge was to work up the nerve to open that door again. After my sob-fest, I still felt raw. Not ready to face the intense energy emanating from that man.

When I finally pushed open the door, Jed turned and looked at me.

He didn't say a word. But the look in his eyes made my breath catch, and my heart speed up. As if I'd walked out and displayed myself in a slinky sequined gown.

The outfit was hideous, but he knew every detail of what was underneath those baggy clothes. He'd touched and stroked and licked and fucked it. He'd claimed it, repeatedly. And I'd loved every minute of the experience.

The way he looked at me was making me wet. I almost hoped he'd just rip all of it off me and fuck me again right this minute. Or maybe I'd rip off his.

The microwave dinged, which broke the spell. Jed grabbed a plate from the cupboard, tossed a couple of paper wrapped things onto it, and set it on the table.

"Breakfast burritos," he said. "And coffee. Come eat."

Food. What a concept. My first reaction was a nasty flop of nausea, and then my common sense kicked in. This stuff was hard, scary, extremely dangerous. It burned calories. I had to eat something if I wanted to keep going.

I sat at the table. Jed poured out a cup of coffee and set it on the table in front of me. "You do look different," he commented.

"I'll say," I muttered sourly. "Like shit, you mean?"

"That's what I was going for. I don't want you to shine. I don't want anyone to notice how fucking pretty you are."

I blushed at the compliment, which I absolutely was not braced for, and hid my confusion by unwrapping a burrito. I forced myself to take a bite, and Jed got right to work, hauling boxes out to the Jeep. That was interesting. Maybe we were on the move.

When he came in for another load, I spoke up. "Are we leaving? Where to?"

He gave me an "are-you-kidding-me-bitch" look, grabbed another armful of stuff, and went back outside.

I guess that should have put me in my place, but I was raised by two bossy, overbearing brothers, and I am stubborn to the point of idiocy. So when he came back in, I tried again.

"What is this place, anyhow?" I asked. "Did you stock it beforehand? It all seems so well organized, you know? I mean, for a jailbreak hideout. The electronics, the clothes. Breakfast burritos in the freezer, even. Like, what gives?"

"Not interested in talking about it."

"But I just wanted to know if we—"

"You don't need to know shit. Ask me no questions, and I'll tell you no lies."

He grabbed a couple of black molded plastic cases that looked like they could contain guns, or some other sort of weaponry, and toted them outside.

I just sat there, freshly seething. I knew it was totally illogical. I had invited the guy to see me as a bubbleheaded ding-a-ling, so I shouldn't get huffy about being treated like this. I was getting Sandee and Freya mixed up again. So dangerous.

A shrill beeping from one of the machines on Jed's security setup started to drill at my ear. I circled the table before I checked out the monitors. In one of the viewscreens a big black SUV was going by, wallowing in the snow. Another identical one followed it.

Yesterday's attack at the Dew Drop parking lot filled my mind, in full sensory detail, and I broke out in a cold sweat. I hurried to the front door. "Hey! James!"

Jed turned, frowning. "Get back inside, Sandee."

"Your thingie is, um, beeping? And I saw cars on the road in one of the viewscreens. Two big black SUVs."

Jed shut the Jeep and ran back to the house, straight toward the monitor. A new alarm beeped. The SUVs were passing another sensor. "Fuck me," he muttered.

"Who is that?" My voice went up into a panicked squeak, and I wasn't even faking it.

"Yesterday's assholes, taking another shot at us. How they found us, I don't know. Nobody saw us go, nobody followed us, nobody could have tagged the Jeep. Nobody knew about this place but me and my team."

My teeth were starting to chatter and my vision went dark, as if I were flat on my back in the snow again, with that huge guy crushing me, bleeding all over me.

Goddamnit, Masters. Pull yourself together. I took a deep breath, gulped. "So shouldn't we just, um…leave?"

"In the Jeep, you mean? Sure, if we want to meet them head on."

"We can't drive the other direction?"

"There is no other direction. This the end of the road. After this, it's just a logging track that peters out into nothing. The only other way out of here is a thirty-mile hike over rough country, in thigh-deep snow. And it's below zero out there."

"So…shouldn't we get started?"

Jed looked me up and down, a sharp, appraising look. "No," he said flatly. "I saw six people. They'll be heavily armed. They would run us down. I need to choose my ground, thin them out. And leave at least one of them alive to interrogate."

Something hard and implacable in his eyes chilled me to the bone.

"I think we should just run," I offered. "Like, right now. As fast as we can."

He shook his head. "We're outnumbered, outgunned, and we don't have enough lead time. I could do it alone, maybe. But not with you."

My chin went up. "I am not a weakling," I told him. "I can move fast."

He shook his head. "We've only got a few minutes, so don't waste my time. Get this on." He pulled a dark green winter coat off a hook and tossed it at me.

I caught it. The only thing I could do to help was to not be a pain in his ass, so I put it on and zipped it up. It hung to my knees. Way too big, but I had several layers on my top half, so it didn't slide around too much.

Jed rattled around in the kitchen, shoving various things into a knapsack. He slung it onto his back, grabbed a coil of rope out of a box, and took me by the arm.

"Where are we going to—"

"Shut up and hurry." Jed dragged me out the door, pulling me off my feet.

I scurried to get my feet under myself. "Hey! Dude! Slow down!"

"Listen up," he said. "We're going toward that tree, the twisted one near the edge of the canyon, but we can't leave any footprints. So stay on the rocks, where the snow's been blown off. Don't leave tracks in the snow. Understand?"

I nodded. It was more or less what I'd done when I made the phone call.

"You said you were fast," he said. "Show me. Put your feet where I put my feet."

I followed him, leaping from exposed rock to exposed rock. The wind was still whistling, blowing the snow that was as fine and dry as dust.

Jed slowed when he got to the twisted tree. He slid the coil of rope off his arm, looping it swiftly around the bottom of the tree, knotting it securely. What the hell...?

"James?" I said carefully. "Ah...what are you doing with that rope?"

"I can't have you with me when I'm hunting them." His voice was cold and distant. "You'll slow me down, make noise. You'll make me into a target."

Panic exploded inside me. Oh, shit. He was going to throw me off the cliff, to make his chances better. Oh fuck. *Fuck.*

I explode into action, but he grabs my arm with his huge hand, trapping me.

I never even got to say goodbye to Holly, to Ethan. They would never know what happened to me. I was such an arrogant idiot. Playing hero. In over my head.

I fought him, panicked, as he pulled me toward the edge. "No, no, no, James, I swear! I'll just run off into the forest. I won't make a sound! I'll hide somewhere. No one will ever see me or hear me, I swear to God!"

"They'll probably have thermal imaging. They'll find you, Sandee."

I saw, with a flash of raw panic, that he'd knotted the end of the rope into a big loop. A noose. He was going to hang me, right off that tree, off the edge of the cliff.

I fought him harder, with a burst of frantic strength—

"Goddammit, Sandee, would you stop wiggling?" he muttered, and suddenly, he jumped—with me still clamped in his arms. Oh *fuck...*

We were airborne for an instant, and I saw my life in a brilliant flash. Then Jed's feet hit a ledge on the side of the cliff, breaking our fall with a bone-rattling *thud.*

I hung there in his grasp, utterly confused. The rope was looped around his huge, powerful hand. His feet touched the ledge he'd hit, but my legs weren't long enough to reach it. I just dangled over the void below me, feet flailing over forty feet of nothing. Empty space filled with swirling snowflakes. Rocks and trees, far below.

My heart thudded so hard, I could hardly breathe. My vision dimmed....

"...dee? Sandee! Hey. Babe. Talk to me. You can't faint." Jed's voice was commanding. "Don't you dare freak out on me. I need you to be tough."

Tough. I could do tough. I blinked until I could focus. Still dangling like a spider on a thread. But alive. "What the fuck are we doing here, James?" I gasped out.

He looked relieved that I could talk in complete sentences. "Keeping you alive."

Huh. That was heartening. Contradictory, but heartening. "Um. Okay. How?"

"Look to your left, about knee level," he said. "You see that foothold there?"

I looked, searching for anything that could even remotely be categorized as a "foothold." I tapped at tiny snow-frosted notch with my toe. "You mean, this?"

"Yes, excellent. Put your toe on that," Jed encouraged. "Then reach up over my head and grab the rope. I'll push you until your weight is on it. Go on. I've got you."

He did have me. In every way that mattered. He was the difference between life and a long, horrible fall to my death. His grip was warm and reassuring. I tried not to look down at the snow-dusted treetops, swaying in the wind, far below.

It took all my nerve to release my death grip on Jed with one hand to grab the rope above his head. I felt his hand under my ass, hoisting me...and suddenly, I was draped across the slightly slanted, jagged slope of the cliff.

"It's easier from here," he said. "Look to your left. See the other two footholds, leading over to that space between that outcropping? Two steps, and you're there."

I made the steps, my legs wobbling. Jed followed along, one big warm hand still gripping me. "You see that big loop of tree root, sticking out?" he asked. "Grab it."

"Don't know if it'll hold me," I said, through chattering teeth.

"It will. It held me. Go on."

"You've been down here before?"

"Just grab it, Sandee!"

I did as I was told, and grabbed the exposed loop of root. It felt solid.

"Now look up," Jed said. "See that little overhang? It's a tiny cave. Climb up under the overhang. That's your spot. Where you're going to wait this out."

I moved my hands and legs where he told me to put them, and in a couple of minutes, he had me huddled in a shallow cave, one not deep enough to give real shelter.

"I won't be able to get back up on my own," I told him, teeth clacking.

"You can go up on the other side," he said. "There's a clear path to climb, right up over the cliff. That way's much easier than the way we came down. You don't even need a rope."

"Then why didn't we use that way down? Dude, that took years off my life!"

He grinned. "I wanted to leave virgin snow," he said. "No tracks to lead them to you. They won't find you, even with thermal imaging. Just wait them out, no matter what happens to me." He slid the backpack off his shoulder and set it on my lap. "There's a thermal blanket in there. Hot tea in the thermos. It should stay hot all day. Take these." He shoved a plastic bag into my pocket. "Butter shortbreads, some trail mix. If I don't call for you, just wait for them to get bored and leave before you come out of there. Understand? Promise me you'll do that."

"But...but what about you?" I whispered.

"I'll be fine." He pulled out a small pistol, a Walther PPK, and held it out to me. "Take this. Last resort."

I recoiled. "Oh, no, no, no. You keep it."

"I have other ones. Protect yourself, Sandee. You're worth it. Be careful."

I took the gun. "Okay," I whispered. "Thanks."

Jed hesitated, still clinging to the opening of the hiding place. It was too small for him to fit inside with me.

Suddenly, he leaned over, cupped my head...and kissed me. The kiss was long, hot, intense. And incredibly sweet. No one had ever kissed me like that before.

When he shifted away, my eyes swam with tears.

"Damn, Sandee," he said roughly. "You are something else, you know that?"

"You're quite the humdinger yourself, buddy," I told him, sniffling.

He lunged for the rope, and twisted around to look at me again. "Don't die," he said. It was not a plea, or a request. It was a flat command.

"I won't," I told him.

He launched himself out across the cliff, and started to climb. On impulse, I leaned out. "James!" I called softly.

He turned. "Yeah?"

"Fuck them up," I told him.

His teeth flashed. "That's the plan," he said.

With incredible swift grace, he scaled the cliff, and then he was gone.

The guy was giving me whiplash. I had thought he was going to murder me. But instead, he took precious time he could not afford from his defense to set me up in a hiding place. With cookies and tea and a fucking blankie. Literally.

Not quite what one would expect of a sociopath bent on destruction.

CHAPTER 15

Jed

Like an asshole, I'd spent way too much time tucking Sandee in, and my options were narrowing by the second. Boer's team had made good time, despite the snow. The monitor on my phone showed me that the first SUV had already driven past my trap before I could spring it. The next one would be there in a couple of minutes.

I sprinted down the route I'd mapped out months ago, parallel to the road, clutching the AR-15. I'd rigged some defense for the road, back when I thought Mickey and I might need to lay low here for a while before we tried to hike out. It could be activated in minutes, if I was quick.

Which I fucking hadn't been. God, stopping to kiss her goodbye and whisper sweet nothings into her ear? I may as well have read her a bedtime story while I was at it. I was a whole new level of pussy-whipped bonehead today.

I just hoped her improvised hiding place stood the test. But it was a desperate last-minute solution, and I couldn't be sure Boer wouldn't find her. He was an asshole, but he was not stupid, and he knew Sandee was with me. He'd keep on looking for her. He wouldn't give up easily.

There was also no guarantee Sandee would stay put. God knows, she had a history of being self-destructive, and ignoring direct orders.

I had to forget Sandee, and get into the zone. Nothing but the mission, which was crystal clear. Thin those bastards out, by any means necessary.

I spotted the big rock that marked the spot on the bridge where I had buried the spike strip under some pine needles, wondering if the snow would render the teeth ineffective. It was fine, dry powder, and there wasn't that much of it right here under the huge trees. Last night's wind had swept away still more. The SUVs were big and heavy, packed full of men and guns, and my spike strip was a motherfucker. Long, sharp blades to bite into those scumbags' tires, deep and hard.

I could only hope that the setup would still work, months later. Snow and all.

I heard the second SUV approaching now. The big motor growled as it rounded the bend. I shucked the rifle, hid it under a log, and dove for the huge culvert that ran beneath the bridge. It was choked with brush, but I shoved my way in, and found the wiring I'd bolted to the top of the culvert.

The grenade was in my hand already. I had to time this perfectly. I leaned out, waiting for the motor to get closer…still closer…

Now. I hit the button. The spike strip activated. *Thunk.*

The big vehicle slewed, revving its engine, and juddered to a halt. I heard men talking from inside it. Angry voices, shouting. Scolding, accusations.

Wait. Wait. I slid silently out of the culvert, staying doubled over, waiting for the sound of a door opening. Any second now. *Come on, guys.*

Clunk. The vehicle door opened, and the volume of the voices inside went up. "...the fuck happened to the tires, man? What the fuck did you do?"

"Nothing, asshole. Shut your fucking hole and let me see what's going on."

Now. I pulled the pin, leaped up, lobbed the grenade right into the open car door. Sank back down and dove right into the culvert again, wondering if I was too close to survive the blast. I heard screams of panic, all four car doors bursting open. I blocked my ears and braced myself.

Boom. The force of the blast shook the woods, jolting snow off the tree boughs.

I waited a few seconds, then scrambled out of the culvert. Heard the crackle and roar of flames. The doors, still open. Limp bodies, lying half in, half out. A balloon of smoke, bitter and greasy and black.

Four down. Good. But whoever was in the first vehicle was now closer to Sandee than I was, and that was unacceptable.

I sprinted back up the hill, feet flying.

It was the closest thing to happy Nicole had been in a very long time, lurching and bouncing through the snow on the ATV. She was going dangerously fast through the snow-frosted trees, the wind in her hair, face half frozen. The ice-cold air burned the inside of her nose. She liked the way it felt.

It was a relief to get a break from that self-involved asshole. It wasn't as if fucking Wex distressed her all that much. She had a strong stomach, and being indifferent to pain or discomfort had made it possible for her to keep him satisfied. It cost her little to give him what he craved. But it was tedious, and a poor use of her time and abilities. She got more bored and irritated with it every day that passed.

The upside was, soon she would peel off that asshole's face, and he would finally learn exactly who he was dealing with. Cheerful thought.

The cabin across the canyon came into view. Nicole pulled the ATV to a halt and got off, leaving it hidden in the trees. She crept forward, staying low.

She'd studied the satellite maps of this place on the drive over here, memorizing every detail. Boer had wanted a sniper rifle across the narrow canyon for their ace in the hole. They were temporarily short-staffed after the Dew Drop debacle, and she was excellent with a long gun, so here she was.

She hoped she'd have the opportunity to shoot someone. She loved the little jerk they made. The pink mist that came out. Such a rush. She could use a pick-me-up.

Nicole made her way stealthily through the huge, tumbled rocks at the edge of the canyon. She found the perfect place quickly, with an excellent view of the exposed house on the other side, and big, tumbled boulders for cover.

She set up her rifle and hunkered down, situating the gun barrel between two craggy granite monoliths. In her winter-camo snowsuit, no one would ever see her. As soon as Jed Clearwater wandered out into her sights, she'd—

Boom.

The huge sound shook the canyon, startling the hell out of her. Nicole's breath stopped. She grabbed the handheld and called Boer. "Wex? What the fuck was that?"

"Don't know, but the other team's not answering." Boer sounded stressed and angry. "Sounds like he blew them up. I can't wait to blast his fucking head off. Have you got a fix on him yet?"

"Not yet. I don't see a soul over there. I just got here and got myself set up."

"Well, hurry the fuck up. Use the thermal imager. Get back to me fast."

"Of course, boss," she murmured. She indulged in a pleasant

little fantasy of driving the spike heel of one of her fuck-me shoes into Boer's eye while she got out the thermal goggles, and scanned the hillside. Back and forth, with binoculars, with the thermal imager, then again...and again...and again.

She finally saw it, against the cliff face. Nothing big, just a subtle "what's-wrong-with-this-picture" feeling. That plumb line against the granite cliff face, slowly coming into focus. Too straight to be natural. Not a dangling root. It was a rope, hanging down. She followed it up with the binoculars. Someone had knotted it around that big scrub oak tree trunk that was clinging to edge of the cliff. But why? The rope didn't reach all the way down to the bottom of the gorge, so why hang it off the edge?

She put the thermal imaging goggles back on, and studied the cliff face. Back and forth...back and forth...and *yes*. A faint glow of heat in the shadowy recess beneath the overhang. It had to be Freya Masters, huddled in a hole like a frightened rodent. And Nicole was the eagle, swooping down for the kill. She felt the absurd, unprofessional desire to giggle, but squelched it, getting on the handheld again.

"Wex, good news. Freya Masters is hiding in a cave in the cliff face, right under the overhang. I've got her in my sights. I could waste her right now, if we wanted."

"We don't want," he snapped. "We need her. Kill Clearwater. Not her."

"Yeah, yeah," Nicole muttered, rolling her eyes. "There's a rope. A scrub oak tree, right near the edge of the cliff. That's how she came down. After we bag Clearwater, we could just wait her out. She'll come crawling up when she gets hungry or nervous."

"Keep your eyes on her," Boer said.

"So I kill Clearwater as soon as I see him?"

"No," he said sharply. "Wait. I want to talk to him."

"Play with him is more like it, right?" She tried not to sound disdainful. Wex was so predictable that way. He had to fuck around with his victims, just to prove his dick was bigger, before he took care of business and got on with it. So childish.

"I need information." Wex's voice was defensive. "I need to know what he knows. Who he's told. How long he's been hooked up with this bitch."

"She'd be an easier mark to interrogate than he would," she said, studying the top of the cliff. "From where I'm looking, it looks like you could get down to Masters from above and drag her out. If you wanted to entertain yourself with her. Could be fun."

"Where?" he demanded. "Give me a reference point."

"See that big round rock with the flat diagonal one leaning against it? Go around the diagonal one to your right until you're right in front of it, and she'll be right below you. If she poked her head out, you could grab her by the scruff of the neck."

She saw the flash of movement in the trees across a canyon, and focused the rifle scope on it. It was Boer, moving around the back of the house. Going toward the rocks.

The crosshairs were right on his chest. Her finger quivered on the trigger. The scope, wavering on his face, his chest. His groin.

Not yet. Wex had his uses. She still needed his resources. They ran through personnel at a very fast clip, and he had the contacts to replenish them swiftly.

She had no reason to feel put upon. She'd taken Wex Boer's measure the second she'd laid eyes on him. All he saw in her was a body to use. Her mind, her intel, her skills, all of that was secondary.

That made men like him so vulnerable. Because they never knew who they were dealing with until it was too late. And it surprised the living fuck out of them.

That part was always so entertaining.

CHAPTER 16

I huddled in my shallow cave, shivering and watching the snowflakes swirling in the air outside. I was acting like prey. Expecting to be eaten.

Well, duh. That was because I *was* prey. Get real.

It was freezing in my little aerie. There was very little real shelter, and wind rushed down the canyon, whistling in the rocks above. A bleak, miserable sound, like the howling of the damned. The wind managed to sweep in the biggest, clammiest, coldest snowflakes and smack them against my exposed neck and face.

I wished I had my own coat. This one was a lot warmer, of course, but my own had my Freya phone, and I was aching for the options it gave me. Like calling Ethan, in a worst-case scenario. Wow, what a memorable conversation that one would be. Hoo, boy.

At least I had the blanket, the hot tea, the snacks, the gun. Thanks to Jed.

The contradiction between my data sets about Jed Clearwater was confusing the living bejesus out of me. My mind hurt, trying to reason it out. What was I supposed to think? Who was I supposed to believe, or root for? I didn't want to meet anyone like the guys from last night in the Dew Drop parking lot. God knows, they were no friends of mine. So who did I trust, if I wanted to survive?

Oh, crap. Probably no one, when it came right down to it. How depressing.

Truth was, I didn't want Jed to be the one who had betrayed Shane, and I never had. I wanted him to be the man Ethan and Shane trusted without question during their Army Rangers days. The man Shane started his security company with. One of the Unredeemables. Brave and honest and incorruptible.

After what Jed had done for me, saving me in the parking lot, hiding me from whoever was driving up that hill, giving me a gun...I was tempted to think he wasn't my villain at all, and never had been. He'd compromised his own safety to keep dippy, useless, irrelevant Sandee safe. Bad guys just didn't behave like that.

Boom.

I jumped with a muffled squeak. What the hell? That was so close. So loud.

Something big had just happened. Something definitive. I wondered how long I would have to wait to find out who'd won that round.

I imagined last night's monsters prowling around above me, and no Jed to leap out of nowhere and defend me. It didn't feel good.

Part of me was convinced Jed was my hero. Selfless, noble, brave. Unfortunately, it was not a part I particularly trusted. That part was too frightened, too compromised, too hormonal. Primordial cavewoman brain. Jed had protected me from predators, and then he'd fucked me, expertly, thoroughly. Of course my inner cavewoman had glommed on to him. Of course. She wanted to stay alive...and to get some more of that excellent dick, too, while she was at it.

Please, please. Just don't be dead. I repeated it under my breath like a mantra. As if it made any difference. What had happened, had happened. It was done.

But whatever was going on out there, Jed had given me a fighting chance to survive. Even if they took him down. I was grateful for that, no matter what.

I crept forward in the cave, craning my neck out, so I could see the other side of the cave, where Jed said I could climb up to the top of the cliff without having to drag myself up a rope, which would be very hard on my own. I'm pretty strong, and I work out in the gym and use a climbing wall, but try as I might, I still suck at pull-ups.

I see and hear nothing. No one talking, no one moving. Just the wind howling.

Maybe Jed had miraculously taken them all out. A girl could hope, but hope was not a plan of action, and I needed one of those before my head exploded. How long was I supposed to wait before I sneaked up and peered over the cliff to investigate?

It made sense to wait, as Jed had directed, until he came back and gave me the all clear. But if he didn't, then clearly, the worst had happened. The unthinkable. And I had to sit tight, alone, in misery, and wait the invaders out. That was his reasoning, and it was solid. It was cold and wet in here, but with what he'd given me, I would survive.

What I might not survive were the what-ifs running through my mind. What if Jed was wounded out there, and I was just letting him bleed out in the snow while I cowered in my mouse-hole? What if there was information I could glean about the situation outside from just a swift peek over the cliff? I wouldn't even disturb the virgin snow that was my cover. They would have to be looking right at me to notice my head pop up like a prairie dog. What were the odds someone would look right then?

I had to do it. Just in case I could help. It wasn't in my nature to be passive.

I crawled out onto the ledge, and studied the snow-dusted rocks to the right of me that Jed had said were a way straight up the cliff face. I carefully clambered upward, my fingers burning as I scrabbled for purchase in the snowy, jagged rocks. Almost there—

I shrieked as someone grabbed the back of my coat, jerking me up off my feet.

I stared at the upside-down face hanging over me. It was straight out of a nightmare. A blank plastic mask, slits at nostril and mouth level for breathing. Bloodshot eyes, surrounded by puffy, purplish flesh, visible through the small eyeholes.

"Freya Masters, eh?" The ghoul spoke in a nasal, gravelly voice that scraped on my nerves like steel wool. "You should have stayed home and eaten birthday cake with Holly. Now you're deep in the shit, you dumb cunt."

Holly? Holy fuck, the guy knew everything about me. And he was so freaking strong. He dragged me up with one hand. I could have slid out of the coat, but the thought came to me too late, and I would have almost certainly tumbled to my death.

He dragged me over the sloped, rocky top of the cliff, bumping and bashing me over the boulders, and tossed me onto the stony ground, knocking out my air.

I rolled up into a ball to protect my belly as he kicked me in the thigh, hard, and oh, fuck that hurt, hurt, *hurt...*

Rough hands on my body, as he swiftly relieved me of the Walther PPK that Jed had given me. Which made me instantly hate myself for not being quick enough to pull it out and kill him with it first.

He pointed it at me. "Don't move, or I'll shoot you right in the face, bitch. Can you still talk, or did he fuck all of your brains out?"

I nodded. "Y-y-yes," I stammered, teeth chattering.

The masked guy grabbed the front of my coat and hauled me

upright, sticking the gun under my chin. I struggled to get my feet beneath me as he jerked me around.

So…hard…to breath. The pressure crushed my throat, as if he was strangling me. I stared up at the sky, because I can't do anything else. Snowflakes burned on my face, caught on my lashes. They danced in my vision, eerily detailed and clear.

"Jed Clearwater!" His sudden bellow made me gasp. "I've got your fuck-toy here, with her own gun up under her chin. Do you want her? Or do you give a shit?"

No answer. Just the wind rushing, howling in the rocks.

"I guess that's my answer. I guess I can indulge myself, then, hmm? I can start with your face. Those pretty lips. Pretty little pink ears. Like a shell. Isn't that what they say about ears? That they're like shells? We'll see if it looks like a shell when I shoot it off. More like a bloody shred of raw pork. But we'll wait to carve up the big stuff until your shithead brother is watching it on streaming. I want him to see every detail."

He grabbed my ear, yanking it hard enough to make me scream.

"Shut up, bitch," he snarled. "Hold still."

"Stop."

Jed's voice. Low and clear in the hushed stillness.

The man holding me spun around toward the direction of his voice, keeping me in front of him as a human shield.

There was Jed at the edge of clearing. He held what looked like an AR-15.

"Jed Clearwater." The masked guy's voice was an oily hiss. "Brought low by a dumb little cunt."

"Don't hurt her." Jed's gaze was locked with the guy's.

"Drop the gun," the man said. He dug the gun barrel into my cheek again. "I could just shoot off the bottom of her jaw. It wouldn't kill her."

Jed tossed the AR-15 into the snow.

The masked man studied him, suspicious. "Let's see the other guns," he said. "If you don't show me two more, I shoot her face."

Jed reached back, pulled a pistol from the back of his jeans. He tossed it into the snow. The masked guy jerked his chin. "The others."

Jed bent down, unfastening a snubbie from his boot holster and then tossing it with the others. "I'm not carrying any other guns."

"Lift your shirt," the man said. "Turn around. Show me."

Jed lifted his coat, spinning around to show he had no hidden guns holstered underneath or stuck into his pants.

"That's all." His voice was astonishingly detached.

"Back away from the guns. Hands up, dickhead."

Jed did as he was told, walking slowly backward, arms up, fingers spread. I kept my eyes on him, as if he were my salvation.

"So, what did that little whining fucker Mickey tell you, anyhow?" the masked guy said.

"Nothing," Jed said. "He was making me wait until I got him out before he gave me anything. You got there first. So I got nothing."

The masked guy was silent for a moment. "Who else did he tell?"

"Not her," Jed said, gesturing with his chin at me. "She doesn't know anything."

"That explosion," the guy said. "I assume that was my team?"

"Yes," Jed replied.

"You'll pay for that, asshole."

"Yeah, I guess. But she shouldn't." Jed jerked his chin again in my direction "She's got nothing to do with this. She's never seen your face. Let her run and hide until you're done with whatever you're going to do. She'll never say a word. Right, Sandee?"

I open my mouth to agree, and *whack*. The guy smacked the side of my head with the pistol. I yelped at the bright starburst of sickening pain.

"...dee? What Sandee? Is that the name she told you?" The man let out an evil chuckle. "This fuckbunny isn't Sandee, Jed. She's Freya-fucking-Masters. Surprise!"

Jed couldn't hide the startled flash in his eyes.

The other man saw it, too. "Oh, my fucking God," he crowed. "You actually didn't know! You were just fucking her for the fun of it! What an idiot."

Jed looked at me, asking with his eyes if it were true.

I couldn't speak. The guy's arm pressed too hard against my throat for more than a dry, soundless croak. But he saw from my face that I wasn't denying it.

"So this sneaky bitch has been trying to fuck intelligence out of you? Tough job, with someone like you, eh? The cupboard is bare." The masked guy slid the gun down my chest. "Nice titties. I could shoot those off, too."

Something inside was touched off by the guy's taunting threat.

Fuck this guy. If I had to die, it wouldn't be by having my body parts shot off.

I twisted, jerking my head around. Sank my teeth into his thick, sinewy wrist, and dropped. Dead weight.

Boom, the gun went off. Jed made some swift gesture I barely saw, but my captor jerked sharply, let out a high-pitched, grunt, and stumbled down the slope, dragging me toward the edge...

"No!" Jed ran toward us, reaching for me. Our eyes met, in that strange, suspended moment. Gravity had already won, but my body hadn't gotten the memo yet.

That moment ended, time started back up. We pitched over the edge, headlong.

But not where Jed had stashed me. Here, the slope was extremely steep, but not completely sheer. I just bounced rolled helplessly down, unable to stop.

I hit the first tree. Slim, flexible branches ripped swiftly through my hands, shredding them. Gone too fast. I hit another, hung on harder, but the masked man was grabbing my leg, and I lost that one, too. Tried for the next. Snagged it. Hung on...

But the clutching guy's weight, plus my weight was too much. This tree's wide, shallow root system was ripping loose. My shoulder joints screamed with the strain.

That grotesque white mask glared up at me, and I saw it.

That knife, sticking out of his shoulder. Jed had thrown a knife at him. That was what made the guy scream and stumble.

I howled with effort as I jerked my leg free of his grip, then lifted my boot and stomped down hard on the knife handle. He screamed, bloodshot eyes rolling madly in their sockets...and released his grip, sliding and bumping farther down the slope.

Bam. Bam. There had been shooting before, but I'd been too busy to notice.

I looked up, saw muzzle flashes. Jed's intent face. He was returning fire. The rock next to my head exploded in splinters, peppering my cheek.

Jed disappeared, ducking behind a rock. *Bam, bam, bam, bam.*

It seemed to go on forever. Then, suddenly, it stopped. I peered up, hoping desperately to see Jed. I glanced down at the masked man, and caught sight of him as he disappeared into the tree canopy far below. It was like having a venomous spider run behind the couch. Worse, when you couldn't see where it went.

The tree root came loose, and I was sliding again, helplessly... and then I hit a narrow, stony ledge with my shoulder—

And everything went black.

CHAPTER 17

Jed

Worst case scenario. I had Boer in my grasp—but I couldn't chase him, because Sandee was lying down there, motionless. She could die of exposure, or fall off the narrow shelf of rock where her still body was perched. She could have a concussion, broken bones, bullet wounds, any fucking thing my brain could dream up.

So I had to rescue her while the sniper from hell across the canyon took potshots at me. Fucking *great*.

I peered down the waving treetops, looking for Boer, but he was lost to sight. Sandee still lay on the ledge. The sniper seemed to be taking a break. I hoped to God I'd killed the sonofabitch. Or at least wounded him long enough to crawl down the cliff and haul that pain-in-the-ass woman back from certain death. Though she'd fling herself back in harm's way again at the first opportunity. I could be pretty fucking sure of that.

Sandee still wasn't moving. Sandee, Freya, whoever. I couldn't think of her as Freya right now. It rattled me. I couldn't afford to be rattled. I had to keep it simple.

I had to go down for her on the rope. Which made me a

target, if the sniper started shooting again. No way to do evasive maneuvers. No way to dive for cover. No way to return fire. Worst-case scenario.

Fuck it. That was just how I rolled these days.

I fashioned a loop at the end of the rope, hoping it was long enough. And that Sandee had enough wits left to help me when I got down there.

I launched myself off the edge and rappelled swiftly down the cliff face, hand over hand. The rope was just barely long enough to reach her. Small mercies.

I grabbed her shoulder, shaking it gently. "Sandee. Sandee? Hey."

She made a soft sound and slowly lifted her head. There was blood in her bleached blonde hair. The wound looked nasty and painful, but as far as I could see, everything important was still inside her skull. Just a bloody mess on the outside.

I hoped she hadn't dinged it too hard. That woman had enough serious personal problems to grapple with without adding a bad head injury to the list.

Sandee. Freya. The *fuck?*

Whoa, stop that shit. No rabbit holes. One thing at a time.

I find footholds, brace myself, studying the situation. Get the rope over her head and shoulders. Pull her arms through. Tuck it under her armpits. Lots of manipulation and movement, without letting her fall off the narrow ledge. Or falling myself.

And it was just a loop, not a harness. So she had to wake up, be smart and active, help me out. I couldn't hold her limp body and climb out hand over hand.

"Sandee!" I said urgently. "Babe. Wake up. I need you to help me get you out of this. We have to get back up the cliff. Sandee!"

Her eyes fluttered. "Huh?" she mumbled. "Who?"

She wasn't connecting. "Freya," I said grimly. "Wake the fuck up. *Now.*"

That snapped her eyes wide open. She blinked at me.

So it was true. Not that Boer would have had any reason to lie about something so random, so bizarre, so easily disproved. Not that it changed anything right now.

"You've got to help me," I told her. "I have to get this rope under your arms so I can pull you up, so you have to help me out. You have to hang on tight and keep the loop under your armpits, and help me with your feet whenever you can. I can't do this if you just lie there like a sack of flour. You hear me?"

"I hear you." Her voice was a thread. It quivered, which unnerved me.

"Is anything broken?" I demanded.

"I don't think so. I'm really cold. I can't feel much of anything."

"Can you move?" I asked.

She lifted her head, and peered over the edge down the cliff, then looked up and met my eyes. "I'm afraid to," she admitted.

I braced my feet in a notch I found in the rock wall. "I won't let you fall."

I hoped I could keep that rash promise as I got her ready, staying pressed against her like a bulwark against that long, empty nothing beyond the ledge.

They were extremely long, painful minutes, working the rope over her shivering body. When the loop was under her arms, I tested my knots. They were good and tight. Then I saw blood on her hands. "What the fuck? Why are your hands bleeding?"

"I grabbed onto the trees on my way down," she said faintly.

Of course she did. Whatever else she might be, this girl was one badass babe.

"So this is what'll happen," I told her. "I'll climb back up. Then I'll pull you up. Your job is to keep the rope under your arms, hang on tight to the rope, and help me with your feet, as much as you can, whenever you can. Is that clear?"

"Crystal clear," she said.

I got to the top, found some solid rock to brace myself, and started hauling her up the slope. She was tough and uncomplaining, mouth set, blood smeared over the side of her pallid face. She clung to the rope, and climbed whenever she could find footholds. There was just one harrowing part when I had to pull her over an overhang where she could find no purchase at all and had to dangle, feet waving over the emptiness. She just stared up at me, not letting herself look down. Tough babe.

And after that sweaty, nerve-wracking eternity, finally she was scrambling up over the top of the cliff. She collapsed onto the ground, panting.

"On your feet," I said. "We have to get the fuck out of here."

"Give me a second," she mumbled.

"I don't know if you noticed, but there's a sniper on the other side of the canyon. I don't know if he's dead, wounded, or reloading. On your feet." I grabbed her by the arm. She cried out sharply, and I froze. "What? Did you hurt your arm?"

"I caught myself on the trees with that arm, and the crazy mask guy was hanging off my feet," she said. "He was heavy. Messed up my shoulder, I think."

Damn, that sucked. Didn't stop her, though. She climbed to her feet without my help, but she tottered like a newborn foal.

I scooped her up, carried her to the Jeep, and deposited her into the passenger seat. Then I took off to retrieve my other guns, which still lay in the snow where Boer had forced me to throw them. The way things were going, I'd need them all, and soon.

On the way back, I was alarmed to see Freya out of the Jeep, staggering into the house.

"What the fuck are you doing?" I yelled. "We have to go, right now!"

"I need my coat," she said, breathlessly.

"Fuck your coat! I'll buy you another one! That coat's too goddamn bright anyway! You need to be invisible!"

She shot me an implacable look. "I want my goddamn coat, Jed."

First time she'd used my real name. She wasn't Sandee anymore. The tone and cadence of her voice had changed. Lower, less breathy, more steady, more musical.

Still sexy as fuck.

I followed her into the house and let her retrieve her fucking coat from the chair at the kitchen table. At which point she no longer objected to being herded back into the Jeep, thank God.

We took off as fast as conditions allowed. Boer was hiking out down the riverbed right now. If I were alone, I could stop a couple of miles down the road and hunt that fucker down, once and for all.

But I couldn't leave her behind, alone and undefended with God knows how many other murdering shitheads on the loose. I wouldn't be able to if it were Sandee beside me, and I certainly couldn't now that I knew she was Freya Masters.

There it was, the SUV Boer had driven up here. I'd spotted it first while sprinting back up the hill after blowing up his team. I jerked the Jeep to a halt, and ran toward it, pulling out my knife. I slashed all four tires. Let the fuckface find some new wheels for himself and his murdering crew. We needed a breather.

I gave Freya a worried once-over when I kicked the snow off my boots and got back into the car. Her lips were blue, her face was ashy pale. The head wound didn't seem to be bleeding, but she looked like hell.

Freya's eyes got big as we drove off the road, lurching and jolting over the frozen creek bed in order to give the bridge and its grisly load a wide berth.

We lurched back up onto the road. She stared back at the burned-out vehicle, the black smoke rising, the bodies, hanging out of the open doors, and didn't speak for several miles. She let out a sigh, as if she'd been holding her breath the whole time.

"Jed," she said. "I...I...um...thank you."

"Don't." It came out savagely loud.

Freya winced. "But I—"

"I would've had him." It was pouring out of me now, like a fire hose. "I could have gone after him and fucking nailed the bastard. But no. Because there you were, hanging off the edge of a cliff. A target for the sniper. I should've just left you there and gone after him. But like an asshole, I didn't. I just couldn't do it."

"You saved me," she whispered.

"Yeah, I did. So now, instead of him, I've got you. Useless, lying, whacked-out you. Hanging on me like a ball and chain."

"Jed, that's not fair. I didn't—"

"Hah. Shut up. Sandee. Freya. Whoever the hell you are. You fucked me up either way." I looked back at her face, trying to reconcile my memories of Shane and Ethan's little sister with the woman beside me. "I can't believe you're Freya Masters."

She snorted. "Because the last time you saw me, I was chubby, and geeky, with zits and a mouth full of metal? Classic."

"But your hair," I said. "It wasn't..."

"Yeah, you're right. It wasn't," she agreed. "I'm ash blonde, not white blond. I bleached it. I'll have dark roots soon enough. So it's just the hair that fooled you?"

"It's the vibe," I said. "I wouldn't have expected Freya Masters to be using her tits like a set of nunchucks. That's a brand new personality trait."

"You knew diddly-squat about my personality, Jed. You never saw me as a person. I only existed for you because I was attached to Shane and Ethan."

"Yes! You were a child!"

"Well, I'm not a child anymore," she said.

I shook my head. "I get that. But why fuck with my head like you did? Does Ethan know you're here?"

"There's a lot that Ethan doesn't know. And it goes both ways. He doesn't tell me shit, because he has to be the big man who handles it all alone. He won't let me contribute, or let me help with anything. So I've been investigating on my own."

"Oh, shit." I blew out a sharp breath. "So...the prison. You tracked me down."

"Yes. I hacked your friends' messaging system. Someone said something about putting someone in prison. So I searched mugshot databases, and I found you. James."

I shook my head. This clusterfuck was compounding at a terrifying rate.

"Who put you in prison, Jed?" she demanded. "Who arranged to get you out?"

"I'm not telling you jack shit," I said. "You're the one who should explain yourself to me."

"I did nothing wrong. I'm not the one who sold Shane out."

I jerked the Jeep to a halt, shocked. "You think I sold Shane out?"

She shrugged. "I've been exploring every avenue of inquiry. I followed the money, and the money says you did. So does the forensic evidence. Then you vanished, and that didn't look all that innocent, either."

"The money and the evidence were manipulated, Sandee! I mean, Freya. And I went into fucking prison, undercover, to find info on Shane!" I had to stop, breathe, fight to control myself. "You really think I'm capable of fucking over my friend?"

"I wouldn't have thought so. Ethan and Shane trusted you, and they're no dummies. But I don't know you, really. Who knows what evil lurks in the hearts of men, and all that."

I waited until I could control my voice, and started the car up again. "Why the whole seduction schtick?" I asked her. "What was all that about?"

Her face blushed faintly. "I had to establish a connection," she said primly.

"You think I would spill sensitive intel to a bubblehead like Sandee?"

"Pillow talk. People get careless. And yes, it was thin, I admit it. But it was as good a plan as anything else I could come up with. And don't badmouth Sandee. She's a sweet girl, and she means well. And after all, Jed. You fucked her."

I didn't flinch. "She said she wanted it, and I took her at her word. You can't blame me for that. Nobody told me she was a duplicitous, whoring spy."

Freya shrugged. "Well, hell. People are just full of surprises."

I bit back a sharp comment. She'd brushed up against death twice in the last twenty-four hours. I could handle a little snark. It wasn't necessary to scold her.

The world would punish her plenty without my help. It already had.

Besides, I was still reeling from the news. I had spent the night boning the innocent kid sister of my comrades-at-arms, with a carnal intensity that would make the Masters brothers pound me into sausage meat if they ever knew. Holy God.

She was blessedly silent for a few minutes, but I knew it was too good to last.

"So, who is that guy?" she asked.

"What fucking business is it of yours?" I snarled.

"Well, he almost maimed and killed me. And he knew my name, and Holly's name. That makes him my business. Does he have anything to do with Shane?"

I glanced over at her. "What do you think?"

She harrumphed. "I think you're capable of mortally pissing people off on your own merits. But I doubt he'd have reason to know my name and Holly's name if he didn't have something to do with Shane. So tell me. Who is he?"

I gave in to the inevitable. "Wex Boer is his name."

She glanced over at me, eyes widening. "Wait. I know that name. From the Ready Line massacre. Wex Boer's outfit partnered with you and Shane, right?"

"Yeah, that's right," I said. "Sometimes."

"But...but that's impossible, Jed. That can't be Boer. He's dead. Burned in the fire. Positively IDed with DNA, dental records."

"That's what he wants you to think." It was painful to say it, it sounded so much like a bullshit conspiracy theory that only an idiot would swallow. "But he faked it. I have no idea how. And I was supposed to die for real that day, in a fake car accident. They pushed my car off a bridge. I messed them up by surviving it."

She studied me intently, frowning. As if trying to read my mind. My heart.

"I was their fall guy," I said. "Someone wanted SmokeScreen. To use it, or sell it. Shane was part of the deal, because he knew the codes to open it. There was a guy doing time in Kalaharee who had dealings with Boer and was willing to bargain intel. I went into prison to cultivate him. I almost pulled it off, but then you came along. And now Boer's in the wind."

"He fell off the cliff, Jed," Freya said. "He probably broke his neck."

I shook my head. "No way. He won't die that easy. He's a tough motherfucker. He has a stab wound in the shoulder, and some bruises, but you better believe he's not dead. Just regrouping. And he's added you to his list of people to punish. Lucky you. You know, Freya, your brothers always bragged about how smart you were. The genius of the family, yada yada. But this stunt you're pulling? It does not say 'smart' to me."

"Tell me more about this Boer," she said.

The careful tone in her voice bugged me. As if she was humoring someone who was having breakdown. "Shut up and let me think," I snarled. "I'm not trusting sensitive intel to you. Not until I know how he found me. Who sold me out."

She was silent for a minute. "I think I know how he found us," she said.

That took me by surprise. "Yeah? How?"

She bit her lip, looking guilty and embarrassed. "By, um... tracking my phone. He must have hacked my phone ages ago. And followed us to the cabin with it."

"But I took your phone!" I said. "I gutted your fucking phone!"

She cleared her throat, shooting me a nervous glance. "Um, actually...you gutted Sandee's phone," she corrected. "Not Freya's."

My guts clenched. "You have another phone? You've been using it?"

"Well, of course. I'm sorry, Jed. I never dreamed anyone would track me with it. Other than Ethan, of course." She opened up a seam in her coat hem, and pulled out a smartphone. "I turned it on for maybe two minutes, max, this morning. And I guess...I guess that was enough for them to nail us down."

"So that's why you sneaked out," I said. "I assume they're still tracking us now."

"God, of course not! I've been leaving out the battery so Ethan can't track me! But I put it back when I get in touch with Holly. It must be the phone, because I didn't tell anyone where I was going. I rented a car at the airport, and no one on earth knew what I was doing."

I held out my hand. After a moment's hesitation, she reluctantly handed them over. I buzzed the window down, and flung the device out into the snow.

Freya sighed. "Oh, God, Jed. That was not necessary."

"You have the fucking nerve to say that to me, after everything that's happened? So who did you call this morning? And what did you tell them?"

She hesitated. "I didn't tell anybody anything," she said, her voice small. "It was Holly's birthday. She turned nine today. I just called to wish her a happy birthday. And tell her that I loved her."

I realized, after a moment, that my mouth hung open. Fuck.

"So you risked my whole op, and both our necks, to say happy birthday to a kid," I said.

"Yes. I'm sorry. I truly didn't know that I was on anybody's radar, at least not as Freya Masters. But listen, Jed. If what you're trying to accomplish has to do with Shane, I want to be involved. Let me be on the list of people that bastard wants to punish.

That's exactly where I belong. Bring him on." Wild anger lit up her beautiful eyes.

She wasn't scared. She wasn't cowed. Damn.

I realized right then, in a blinding flash, just how hard it was going to be to keep this woman safe.

I was in bigger trouble than I ever dreamed.

CHAPTER 18

"Nicole! Come in, you dumb bitch! Answer me! Right now! Nicole, where the fuck are you? Come in, Nicole!"

Nicole's eyes opened, blinking. Everything was red. Her eyes stung. Her head throbbed.

She touched them, and realized that they were full of blood.

The handheld lay on the ground, not far from her bloodied hand.

It all flooded back into her head. She'd been shooting at Jed Clearwater. He returned fire. He had good aim with that AR-15. She should have killed him the second he had stepped out into the clearing. Before Wex gave him that opening. That asshole couldn't have just executed him and taken the girl so they could proceed as planned.

Oh, no. The dickhead had to jerk off first. Lack of discipline would always bite you in the ass.

She slowly sat up, nausea roiling. She hated vomiting, and kept it down by grim force of will. She looked over at the other side of the gorge and saw the Jeep's taillights receding. Gone. Freya was gone. The key to controlling Ethan Masters. *Poof*, gone.

God, how she wanted to kill Wex for fucking this up for her. Wanted it so badly.

Wex was still squawking into the void. She let him babble. Her face hurt. She explored the damage. One of Clearwater's bullets had hit the lump of granite beside her head, and fragments had sprayed out. One had hit her in the temple. A few had peppered her face. Cheekbone, jaw. She was going to look like hammered shit for weeks when they scabbed up. Blood run down her neck and into her fleece shirt, sticky and hot.

One of those bleeding wounds was barely a half an inch from her eye. That made her angry. That piece of shit would pay.

As a matter of fact, he'd pay in eyes. When the time came.

"...go up there and personally shove that radio up your whore ass!"

She picked up the handheld. "Nicole here," she said. "I got knocked out."

"Are you shot?"

"No, just a ricochet. Some shards. You?"

"He threw a knife! He knocked me off a fucking cliff and shot at me!"

"Yeah, I saw you fall," she said. "I tried to take him out."

"Well, you failed, bitch!"

"You're still alive, right?" she asked. What, did he want sympathy? He should know better at this point than to ask that from her. He wasn't that stupid.

"Let's get the fuck out of here," he snarled.

"Yes. Where are you now?"

"Downstream. From the creek bed, I had a great view of Jed Clearwater taking his own sweet time climbing down to hook up Freya Masters to the rope and pull her up. It must have taken fifteen, twenty minutes. Completely unmolested by anyone shooting at them, immobilizing them, incapacitating them. Nothing. Crickets."

"I was unconscious, Wex," Nicole said, her voice expressionless.

"Good of you to come back up to consciousness just in time to watch them leave, bitch. Are you capable of operating the ATV? Or is that too much for your delicate sensibilities?"

Nicole got to her feet. Her legs were shaky, but she was upright. "I'm fine."

"Then make yourself useful. Get your ass down here and pick me up."

"I'll meet you where the rapids end," Nicole told him.

"Great," he said sourly. "I also have a dislocated shoulder."

"I'll fix it when we meet," she said.

"Get moving," he growled. "Over and out."

Nicole put the handheld back onto her belt, broke down the rifle, and got going, her good mood destroyed. The bumping of the ATV hurt now. Her head throbbed like a rotten tooth. And she hadn't even hit anyone with the gun today. So disappointing.

The only thing that kept her going was how fun it was going to be to pop Wex Boer's shoulder back into its socket.

She couldn't wait to hear him squeal.

CHAPTER 19

Freya

The route Jed was taking was impossible to follow. No rhyme or reason to it. He'd stopped the car as soon as we'd put some miles behind us, and insisted on doing some first-aid, cleaning and disinfecting the wound on my head and the scrapes on my hands. Stared into my eyes with anxious intensity to check for a concussion. Groped under my shirt to check out my shoulder, which wasn't broken or torn or dislocated, thank God. Just sore.

But after that, he had embarked on the weirdest route I could have imagined. He went offroad, through the snow, then came back up onto another road. He doubled back, he drove up riverbanks and through orchards, he favored the roughest, most abandoned roads that he could find, or so it seemed to me. At one point, we sped alongside a big highway for a few miles, and I tried to figure out which one, just to orient myself. But we plunged onto anonymous back roads again, and I missed my chance.

We didn't seem to be making any forward progress, but God forbid I question, comment, criticize, or offer suggestions. Whenever I tried it, he bit my head off.

I didn't blame him. I'd messed him up royally—if he was telling the truth.

More confusion. More uncertainty. He'd saved me from a horrible fate, at great cost to himself. He'd traded his mission for my life. He had saved me from the parking lot guys, from the masked ghoul, from the sniper, from the cliff ledge. He'd tried to ensure my safety, even if he got killed. I didn't know what to think about him now.

But if this masked guy really was Boer, as Jed insisted, what did that really prove? Only that he was Jed's antagonist. They hated each other, fine. That in itself meant nothing. Maybe they'd been partners in crime, and they'd had a falling out. Maybe they were both greedy bad actors and one of them had screwed the other one out of some money. I just didn't know, and I couldn't trust my own instincts anymore.

They were hopelessly compromised by Jed's sexual magnetism.

Not that he was vibing any of his hot, sexy energy at me now. On the contrary, he wouldn't even look at me. Any attempts I made to speak to him were met with a ferocious glare. Which made them quickly peter off into nervous silence.

Some grinding hours into that drive, he pulled a plastic bag out of the center console and tossed it at me without meeting my eyes. "Eat something, if you're hungry," he muttered. "There are some water bottles in the backseat."

The bag proved to be filled with protein bars, nut packets, and various other munchies. But the events of this morning had killed my appetite.

Jed stopped a few times at carefully chosen spots where I could have enough privacy to pee behind a tree, but not so much cover that he couldn't see to guard me. Then he hustled me back into the Jeep, growling about me being the one who had put us on the run, so don't whine. As if I were whining. I hadn't said a goddamn word.

But I was at a loss. My plan to seduce him, stick with him, get him to trust me, and reveal clues about my brother...that was all predicated on a different situation. A different Jed Clearwater. He wasn't that man. And I certainly wasn't Sandee.

So now...what were we to each other? What could we possibly be? The situation as it stood right now did not look promising.

The sun was low before I tried again. "Jed," I said. "I need to know the plan. You have to at least tell me—"

"I don't need to tell you shit, Freya."

I sighed. So it had to be like that. "That's not useful, Jed," I told him. "Could you just talk to me in a civil tone without pouting?"

"That's what you think this is? Me, pouting?"

"Yes," I said. "I know you're angry. I messed up your plans. I'm more sorry than I can tell you about the phone, and tipping that guy off to where we were. I didn't know what we were up against. But we have a couple of options here."

"Yeah? Really. I'm all ears. Illuminate me, Sandee. I mean, Freya."

I waited until my irritation at his snotty tone faded, choosing my words. "Option one, let me off at the nearest place walking distance from a town where I can buy a bus ticket, or rent a car. And you never have to see me again in your life."

"Wow, that's a real winner," he said. "I can't wait to hear option two."

I spoke through gritted teeth. "Option two is, you tell me what the fuck you're trying to do, and how you're doing it. And maybe I can help."

"Ah." He let out a harsh laugh. "She wants to help. That's sweet."

"She does," I said. "And she doesn't appreciate your sarcastic tone. If you got over your tantrum, you might realize I have resources of my own to offer."

"I assume you mean other than what's between your legs."

Ouch. Maybe I deserved that, but still. That dickhead. "Fuck you," I said crisply.

"Oh, but you did. And I'll never forget it."

"Option three, of course, consists of just dragging me along with you so that you can berate me and ignore me and insult me to no good purpose," I said. "Option three sucks. Not useful. Not fun. Big waste of our time and energy."

"Wow, Freya, thanks for laying it all out for me so clearly. There's just the small matter of you getting killed as soon as I drop you off. Which is a mathematical certainty, if you try to rent a car or buy a bus ticket."

"Whoever those guys are, they can't be watching every single bus station within a hundred miles of Kalaharee," I argued. "And no one could have followed you on the route you took. I'm in the car with you myself, and I haven't got a clue where we are, or where you're going. Do you know? Or is it random?"

He gave me his trademarked fulminating glare. "Nothing I do is random," he said. "But if Boer hacked your phone, then he hacked Ethan's and Holly's. If you call your brother, Boer will hear you. He's closer, and he'll get to you first. Count on it."

"I see." I contemplated that unnerving idea for a minute as we bumped along a snowy road that bordered a field. I saw farmhouses and barns in the distance. "This place has possibilities," I suggested. "Just let me off. I have money in the hem of my coat. I can pay someone to give me a ride out of here and never use phones at all."

He shook his head. "Too many unknowns. I can't let you off here on foot."

"I'll be fine," I assured him. "I'm very resourceful. Thanks for saving my life. If I get myself killed now, it's on me. You are one hundred percent off the hook. Okay?"

"No," he said darkly. "Too risky. Can't do it."

I felt that familiar twist of old, tired anger that dealing with my brothers so often provoked. "It's not your risk," I said wearily. "Let it go. Let me take responsibility."

"No," he said.

The man was driving me crazy. "For fuck's sake, would you just tell me what's going on!" I yelled. "Why is it risky? Who are those people? What do they have to do with Shane? Clue me in!"

Jed shook his head. "The less you know, the safer you are. You need to get someplace safe, with a security detail on you twenty-four-seven. Until you are, you stay with me. Now shut up. I'm working this through, and you're distracting me."

"Can we work through it together? I might be able to—"

"Shut up, or I'll gag you."

I subsided, fuming. The bastard was impossible to reason with. He wouldn't share, wouldn't let me help, wouldn't let me go. Plus, he was furious with me, rude as hell, and twice my size. It made me feel exhausted, and very alone.

More hours crawled by as we jolted along. It was full twilight when the Jeep turned into the shadows of a thick forest on the road so faint and overgrown, the bushes rustled and scraped loudly against the undercarriage of the vehicle.

He parked the Jeep in a car shelter next to a small, ancient house, almost hidden in the overgrown trees and shrubs that surrounded it. Shrubs that hadn't been pruned or trimmed in decades. We sat in silence for a moment.

"So, is this just someplace you found by pure chance?" I asked, because I just couldn't help myself. "Will we be trespassing on someone else's property?"

He gave me that ironic eyebrow tilt.

"Oh, I see," I muttered. "Of course it's not. It's all part of your meticulous plan. Even though you've been in prison for months, these strategically chosen, well-supplied safehouses are just waiting patiently for your convenience. Who helped you with all this? The Unredeemables? The Drake brothers?"

"How about you stop chattering and help me haul the stuff inside?"

Oh, hell with it. I'm too tired to get my back up at this point. He pulled a key from behind a weather-beaten, termite-riddled shingle, and opened the door.

It was cold in the entry hall, the air stale, but it felt weather-tight, not damp or moldy. Jed turned on a light, adjusted a thermostat. "It'll warm up soon," he said.

I set down the cases of electronic equipment and started to follow him back outside, but he stopped me in the doorway. "Stay here."

"I'd rather help," I told him. "It feels good to do something after all that sitting."

"No," he said. "Stay inside. Don't argue with me."

I knew that tone all too well, from Shane and Ethan. I also knew how to fight back and hold my ground, but maybe not tonight. I was the one in the wrong, he was furious, and I could keep my mouth shut for a little while, if I really made the effort.

But my resolve was sorely tried when Jed came back in, stomping snow off his boots, before he set down the cases. "There's food in the freezer," he said. "Go get some of it ready for us while I get the security system set up."

Oh, of course. A job perfectly suited for the little woman. I almost said something snotty about it, but then my stomach betrayed me by growling loudly.

For just the briefest second, it looked as if Jed were about to smile. Then the moment passed, and I couldn't be sure I hadn't imagined it. Wishful thinking, maybe.

Oh, to hell with it. My stomach had undermined me. I'd give him this one.

The freezer was loaded with stuff that looked really good. Real food, not packaged industrial crap. Pans of food that had been prepared by a professional caterer. The paper labels had handwritten dates that noted when they had been made and frozen.

I chose two different pans; a pot roast with vegetables and a veggie pesto lasagna. Into the microwave they went. Buttons pushed. Feminine duties performed.

Jed was hard at work messing around with his electronics, so I took myself on a tour. There were two small, chilly bedrooms with plastic wrapped bedding lying on the mattresses. I went ahead and made up one of the beds so I could fall right into it when the time came. I thought about doing Jed's too, out of courtesy, but my residual anger was too strong. The jerk could make his own damn bed when he wanted to sleep.

The bathroom was stocked with soap, shampoo, towels, toothpaste, a siren song I could not resist. Washing off the blood and the fear sweat sounded divine.

I locked the door, got the shower water running hot, stripped down, got in.

The hot water stung my scalp, but it felt good on the bruises and strains. The water ran pink for a while, but I shampooed my hair several times until it was clear, hopefully getting out the blood and the pink dye, which was no longer appropriate now that I had left Sandee and her fashion sense behind me. The hot water loosened my sore shoulder. I wanted to stay in it for hours, but nagging anxiety made me shut the water off as soon as I'd rinsed away the last of the soap. Being naked felt too vulnerable.

I toweled off my hair and pulled my clothes back on, longing sharply for some underwear. But the shower had refreshed my nerve to face up to Jed, so I strolled back to the front room, where I found Jed staring at a computer screen.

"I'm assuming this place was prepared months ago, just like the cabin last night," I said. "From before you went into the prison. Based on the dates from the food labels. They're from five months ago."

"I told you before," he said. "Ask me no questions, and I'll tell you no lies."

"He is my brother, Jed. I need to know more."

Jed leaned back in his chair. "Freya," he said. "You saw those people who came after you. You can imagine how far they're willing to go to get what they want."

"Of course," I said. "That's why I need to know—"

"Suppose I told you everything I was trying to accomplish, and how," he cut in. "Then, suppose that Boer tied you to a chair and started in on you with the bolt cutters. How long do you think you'd last?"

I stared at him, mouth agape, for an unpleasant moment, imagining it.

"Ah...probably about as long as you would," I said finally. "Let's just hope neither one of us ever has to find out. The thing is, you are underestimating me. I can help you. Whatever it is you're trying to accomplish, I would be an asset to that project."

"Like you have been so far?"

That stung, but I couldn't refute it. Then the microwave dinged.

Jed waved at me dismissively. "Go do something useful that won't get us both killed. Like setting the table."

I swallowed back my rage and got to it, since anything else I could do or say would be childish and counterproductive. I put hot pads on the table. Laid out the steaming pans of food. Found some plates in the cupboards, some forks and knives, some serving spoons. Setting the table, my ass.

"Smells good."

I looked over at Jed, taken aback by his tone. It was the first thing he had said to me in a long while that wasn't cold or antagonistic. Since the last time we'd had sex, maybe.

God knows, he'd been friendlier back in my Sandee days, which I was already kind of missing. He hadn't been so angry at

Sandee. She'd been all sweet and helpless and unthreatening, so he'd treated her far more tenderly.

But sweet, helpless, and unthreatening Freya Masters was not. By no means.

It wasn't the first time I'd disappointed a guy by letting my real personality pop out at him, like a horror movie jump scare. I'm so used to that happening, you'd think it wouldn't bug me anymore.

But it was bugging the shit out of me right now.

"Enjoy," I said coolly. "There's beer in the fridge. As I'm sure you must know, since you must've bought it, or ordered it."

"No thanks, not for me. I'm on the job," he said, pulling out a chair. "Feel free to have one yourself, though. Are you going to sit down?"

I shrugged. "I don't want to crowd you," I muttered. It seemed awkward and weird to sit down with him, as if we were friends. Or a couple. God forbid.

"Sit," he commanded. "Eat."

Resisting being pushed around and commanded ran deep in my personality, but I was really hungry, and the food was hot. So I sat down and scooped up some lasagna.

We attacked the food, eating staggeringly large helpings of each steaming dish. No dinner conversation. It was fabulous. All of it.

When we reached the smears on the bottom of the pan, I licked my fingers and decided I had the energy for one more go at him. After all, what did I have to lose? His trust? His good opinion of me? Hah.

"So," I said. "Who's Mickey?"

CHAPTER 20

Jed

I stared at Freya, motionless. My mouth still filled with potatoes. The hell?

This girl was sharp, yes. She was a Masters, after all, and her brothers were whip-smart, way smarter than me. But this was superpower scary. She could look right into my mind and effortlessly pluck stuff out with a pair of tweezers.

Like that image of Mickey in my head, curled up and bleeding on the floor, that I just could not un-see, and probably never would. It would always be with me.

I forced myself to finish chewing and swallowing the food in my mouth, with difficulty. It tasted as dry as sand, all of the sudden. "What are you talking about?"

"The guy with the mask," Freya said. "He wanted to know what Mickey told you and who else he might've told, remember? Is Mickey the inmate you were trying to make a deal with? He's the reason you went to Kalaharee, right?"

I cleared my throat, staring down at my nearly empty plate and wondered how much I dared to tell her.

"Yes," I said finally. "And it's true, what I told Boer. Mickey didn't give me any info. He wanted me to break him out first. But Boer will never believe that. He'll keep coming at me, and I don't want you to be with me for our next encounter. I need to stash you someplace before that happens. Because he will find me. Or I'll find him."

"I'm not a thing to be stashed," she said. "Tell me more about Mickey."

My body clenched up like a fist. "He's nothing to you," I said. "He's out of the picture. Forget him."

Her dark eyebrows snapped together, a little frown between them. "He seemed pretty relevant to the masked guy."

"Boer, you mean," I said. "He was relevant before. Now he's dead."

She leaned forward, eyes bright with curiosity. "When did he die? And how?"

I wondered if these revelations would come back to haunt me later. "Yesterday," I said. "Right before I left the prison. That blood on me? Most of it was his."

Her eyes got big. "Ah. I see. But...you didn't..." Her voice trailed off nervously.

I shook my head. "No, I didn't kill him myself. Boer organized the hit. I was supposed to die, too. They'll keep trying to finish the job. They'll never stop trying."

"Was Mickey a friend of yours?" she asked hesitantly.

I turned away from her worried gaze. Yeah, Mickey had been a friend. Before they chopped him into pieces and left him to bleed out alone on a filthy bathroom floor.

Some friend I was to him, though. I was the one who'd put him there. I'd baited the trap with the promise of freedom from those mobsters who held him down.

I had admired and respected Mickey. He hadn't ever bitched or whined or felt sorry for himself, in spite of his shit luck. He'd been up for anything if it gave him a chance to not be used by Adriani anymore.

He hadn't let me bully him, either. He drove a hard bargain, and I respected that.

Mickey had deserved better. His reasoning was, if he had to be on the lam for the rest of his life, at least he'd have a life.

Now he didn't. And that was on me.

Freya was still waiting. I cleared my throat. "Yeah, he was a friend."

"What happened?" she asked softly.

"We had a deal," I said. "He told me he'd left a flash drive with someone on the outside, in case something happened to him. It had all the information I needed about Boer. How he faked his death, where his money was. As soon as he was out, he'd arrange for me to get it. And it was going well. No one had noticed me. If things had gone according to plan, he would have been wearing the clothes you have on now. He would have been eating this food with me. We'd be in Phase Two, on the move."

Freya looked as if she was bracing herself, her mouth tight. "So what happened?"

"You happened," I said flatly. "You came bouncing in, flaunting your tits. Boer must have followed you via your phone to the prison. At which point, he copped to the fact that I was there, and arranged to have me and Mickey killed immediately. Consequences."

Freya's eyes widened. "Wait," she said slowly. "You're saying that it's my fault they killed Mickey? I just now found out that Mickey even existed!"

"I'm not saying you did it on purpose," I said. "But that's what happens when you fuck around with things that are above your pay grade. Mickey was barely alive when I got to him. They cut pieces off his body. He died in my arms."

Freya's face had gone deathly pale. She looked at the chunks of meat on her plate, shoved her chair back, and bolted for the bathroom.

Great. Very smooth, Clearwater. My winning personality and

charming dinner conversation had made Freya Masters toss her pot roast. That was a shame. I had no idea when or where the woman would get another decent meal.

It was so fucking stupid, to hammer on her like this, but I couldn't seem to stop myself. Something about her just yanked on my chain.

I got up and followed her. There was water running in the bathroom. I stood outside, waiting for what felt like hours. Finally, the door opened.

Her face was blotchy, her eyes red. "I'm sorry I messed things up for you."

I nodded and left it at that. It's not as if I could say, "it's no problem." That would be a lie. Or "don't worry about it." That would be really shitty advice.

"I'm glad you're starting to wake up," I said. "Took you long enough."

That brought back the spark of anger in her eyes again. Good. Better than crying or vomiting. That's one thing about me a woman can really count on. I'll be sure to piss her off on a regular basis. It's a special talent of mine.

She crossed her arms over her chest. "So, Jed. Let me ask you this. Are there any circumstances under which you would forgive me for messing up your plans?"

"Nope," I said. "None at all."

Her chin went up and her lips flattened. "Ah. Really."

"I don't have the energy for social lies." I told her. "You're getting the raw, unpolished truth. Which is more than you offered me." I turned away, heading back toward my computer set-up in the front room.

Freya followed me. "So it's the lies that bother you? Because I was pretending to be someone I'm not? You did that, too, Jed. And for the same reason."

"It is not the same," I said stonily. "I was undercover, scoring crucial intel. You were playing dress-up and fucking with my head."

"Worked, though. Is that why you can't forgive me? Because I got you?"

"I don't know what you got, besides thoroughly nailed," I said.

Freya sashayed around to the front of the table and perched on the computer table. "Do you want to know something, Jed?"

That struck me as a risky lead-in. I tried to look away from the spectacle of her round, shapely ass, smack in the middle of my field of vision. "Probably not, but I have a feeling you're going to tell me anyway."

"That unforgivable sin of sticking my tits in your business? It's the same sin that Sandee committed," she said. "But you weren't anywhere near as mad at her as you are at me. You weren't anywhere near as judgmental. Why is that?"

I shrugged. "Sandee was a fiction. How I related to her is not relevant."

"I disagree," Freya said. "Why did Sandee get a pass, but I don't? What's so different about Freya Masters fucking up? Can't I catch a break?"

I thought about it. "Sandee has an excuse," I said finally. "Sandee was a babbling simpleton. Freya Masters should have goddamn well known better."

"Why should I know better?" Her voice was impassioned. "I don't know shit! Ethan won't tell me anything. I have no option but to conduct my own investigation!"

"How did you hunt me down at the prison, anyway?" I demanded.

"I hacked the Drake brothers' phones," Freya admitted.

I clapped my hands over my eyes. "Oh God. What dickheads."

"Not at all. They were very careful, and their encryption was excellent. Just not good enough to keep me out. Not if I have weeks to crack it. That's a very high bar. The highest bar possible, really. Not to brag or anything."

"So why aren't you working for the NSA, or something like that?"

Freya snorted. "Hah. I know how that would go. I'd start off golden, and things would be great, and then I'd say something rude, make somebody powerful mad at me, and in no time, it would all go to shit. Might as well not even go down that road at all. I'm better off running my own outfit, by my own rules. I get into less trouble that way."

I remembered all the times Shane had complained about his little sister always getting into trouble. Rules and boundaries and barriers were so easy for her to break through. She never had to consider that a rule might be there for a damn good reason.

She'd certainly blown right through all my rules, barriers, and boundaries.

"I wouldn't have fucked you if I knew who you were," I told her.

"Why? Because of what my brothers would think? I'm twenty-six years old, Jed. I sleep with whoever I want. They don't have any say in that. They never did."

I shook my head. "I don't like being lied to. Or jerked around."

"You enjoyed yourself just fine, from what I could tell," she said.

"Yes, but that's over," I said. "No reason to whore yourself again."

Her eyes flashed, and she slapped her hand down onto the desk, making the keyboard rattle. "I did not whore myself." Her voice rang with conviction.

I looked up at her. "No? How do you figure that?"

"Having sex with you was never part of the plan," she said. "I didn't know about the prison break. I just wanted to establish a connection with you. I was thinking, long and winding conversations on the phone, with phone sex, at most. Then shit happened, and we were alone together. And then I realized that I...I wanted it. For real."

"Oh," I said. "So, you just lack impulse control, then. Right. Got it."

She clapped her hand over her mouth, snorting helplessly. "Don't make me laugh, or I will cry again. And you will be so sorry."

She wasn't wrong about that. I held up my hands in a warding gesture. "Don't do that to me," I begged. "It's been a shitty day so far, and I'm so done."

"I am sorry I lied to you and complicated your life," she said. "I'm especially sorry I fell off that stupid cliff and kept you from chasing Boer. He's an asshole, and I wish you'd been able to catch him, and question him, and seriously fuck him up. And I'm incredibly sorry about Mickey."

"Understood," I said.

"This flash drive that Mickey said was on the outside," she said. "You, ah...you don't have any idea where it is? Who has it?"

I shook my head silently.

She bit her lip, looking distressed. "Shit. That's... unfortunate."

"Yeah," I said, forcefully. "That puts me back to zero."

"What would it take to make you forgive me?"

Oh, come on. No hot girl could ask a normal, functioning, straight man a question like that without the obvious crass answer flashing through his mind like neon.

Which, of course, immediately transmitted to her brain. I saw it in her eyes.

"I actually wasn't suggesting sex," she said, her voice chilly. "I was thinking in terms of joining forces, helping each other. Working as a team."

"Then you weren't thinking at all," I said mercilessly. "You were dreaming. I'm unloading you the first second I can do it in a way that I judge to be safe. Which is tricky right now, but when I do pull it off, I suggest you hole up and wait this thing out. These guys play rough, and you don't have the training to take them on. You should know that after what happened today."

"I can't stand down," she said. "It's killing me."

"Oh, so you want to die quicker, then?"

She just glares at me, her color high. Whoa, genius me. I've made it worse, getting her back up. I've made her cry, made her furious, made her vomit, but here she still is, dishing it right back to me. All up in my face. So fucking pretty. We'd both be a whole lot safer if she hated my guts completely.

And to that end...it was time to let my inner asshole come out to play.

"The way I see it, the only worthwhile thing you could possibly do right now would be to pull those pants down, turn around, and bend over," I said. "Go ahead, Freya. If you're so set on making yourself useful."

Freya straightened and slid off the table, eyes blazing. She licked her lips. Her breath quickened as the air in the room caught fire. So did mine.

Now we were both turned on. Both actively thinking about it. There was too much heat between us to control. It vibrated, hummed. Made the air syrupy and heavy.

If she called my bluff now, I was toast.

CHAPTER 21

Freya

Oh, that arrogant, filthy son-of-a-bitch. It infuriated me, that he could just flip my switch like that, with nothing but a smoldering glance and a few coarse words.

But my anger didn't quench the fire one bit. It made it burn hotter. Which was embarrassing and dumb and dangerous. And I couldn't do a damn thing about it.

I wanted to smack him into next week. I also wanted to knock him down onto his back, rip off his pants, and free up that gorgeous, stiff cock. Then I wanted to mount up and ride him in a long, hard gallop, straight into wild, screaming, throbbing completion.

My hands were clenching, my thighs squeezing, toes curling.

His face was a rigid mask, with streaks of color on his cheekbones, a muscle pulsing rapidly in his jaw. I'm glad he couldn't hide his arousal. If I reached down between his legs, I was very sure he would not bat my hand away.

It came to me in a flash of sudden, visceral certainty, how he was trying to keep me out. Acting like a crude, entitled asshole to scare me away. Make me back down.

But I was past fear. I wanted inside his mind. I wanted to be sure of him, after all the data I had collected, which flatly contradicted his behavior the past couple of days. Risking his mission and himself to protect me, over and over and over, because he just couldn't help himself, no matter what it cost him…that was the knee-jerk behavior of a heroic, righteous dude, the one I'd always believed him to be.

The one I desperately wanted him to be.

I needed to know. To get closer. To make him gasp and yell and beg for mercy.

Sex was the only way through his defenses. I'd felt the real Jed last night. I'd felt him this morning, too, when he'd kissed me after depositing me into the cliff cave. I had to find that man again. Running into this cold wall over and over…it was unbearable.

I pulled off my sweatshirt, brushing wild, electrified hair out of my eyes.

"Freya," His voice was a menacing rasp. "I'm not in the mood for mind games."

"It's not your mind I want to play with." I tossed the sweater away and then undid the clasp of my bra before sending that right after it.

"Don't push me," he warned. "I won't be gentle."

"Well, thank God for that. Neither will I. Finally, something we agree on."

I unfastened my belt, let the oversized pants drop to the ground. Stepped out of them, jaybird naked, except for wool socks. The lumberjack nympho concubine vibe.

I straddled him and sat on his lap, my breasts right below his chin. Savoring the hot, angry color on his cheeks, the flash in his startled eyes.

And of course, that magnificent, hot, hard erection against my inner thigh. Excitement made my thighs clench around his. It was cold in the room, but I felt sweaty, feverish.

"Goddammit, Freya," he muttered. "You just keep pushing and pushing."

"So stop fighting, you rude, ungrateful brute." I seized his hand and put it down between my legs, letting him feel hot, slick warmth between my pussy lips. "This is the part where you make up for your bad behavior by making me come."

My words pushed him past some limit, and he made a rough sound and buried his face between my breasts. He sucked in my nipple, caressing it in his mouth with exquisite tenderness. The deep, delicate pull of his lips drew pleasure and wild magic out of me. I was full of it, an endless fountain of it.

I wrapped my arms around his neck, gasping for air. Desperate, shuddering breaths. I didn't know what was so wonderfully different from other times I'd tried this. Jed did it perfectly right, as if my body were tuned to him, as if his lips had some enchantment that made shivers race wildly over my entire body. Every kiss and swirling stroke of his tongue lifted me, filled me with light. Sweet yearning, mixed with grace.

Now he was touching me between my legs as he suckled my breasts, stroking my clit so perfectly...then sliding his fingers deeper, deeper, thrusting slowly, pressing and circling. Seeking out the spots that made me sob and wail and melt.

The tension broke. Waves of surging pleasure washed me out to a mindless, timeless state of glowing sensations, shining emotions.

When conscious thought came drifting back, I was collapsed on his shoulder, my arms still draped around his neck. He was nuzzling me, his lips sliding along my throat, then my shoulder. Licking, nipping gently. His warm, rough-textured hands stroking the length of my spine, exploring my shoulder blades as if he were mapping my body.

He pulsed his cock against my mound. I moved against him with a sigh of need.

He leaned back, giving me a narrow look. "Hey," he murmured. "A question."

My head went up, suddenly alert. "Yeah? What?"

"Nothing scary," he assured me. "A frivolous question."

I smiled at him. "I can do frivolous. Shoot."

"This," he said, sliding his fingers tenderly up and down my pussy lips, making me wiggle and gasp. "Just a little tiny little bit of fuzz up top here, and nothing else. Is that your usual style? Or was that just to get in character for Sandee?"

The question startled me into laughter, which quickly stuttered into a gasping moan as he flicked his thumb delicately around my sensitized clit. "Oh, God," I whispered. "Um, I think it started as a Sandee thing. I usually don't bother to do it, and it hurt like a bastard. But afterward? I liked the way it felt. It just feels so silky smooth, you know?"

"Oh, yeah," he rumbled. "I know."

"Do you go for that?" I asked.

It was his turn to laugh. "Sure. It drives me mad with lust. But I'm guessing a full bush would have the same effect. It's you who gets to me. The rest? Just details."

Aw. That was so sweet. "I don't think Sandee is really that much of a mask," I confessed. "She's just a side of me that I finally let loose. A more instinctive part. She's been waiting her turn, and I needed her help, so I let her come out of her cage."

"For me," he said softly. "Wow."

I felt vulnerable, having shared that with him. I moved slowly against his stiff rod, trapped in his jeans, thrumming with readiness. "Don't you want more?"

"We used up all the latex," he told me. "We didn't think ahead. Too busy."

I thought about it for just a few seconds before it burst out of me. "I have a contraceptive implant. I got it last year, but the relationship didn't pan out, so I never really had a use for it. So we could just, you know. Go for it. Full speed ahead."

His cock swelled with eagerness against me. His eyes dilated, and his hands, gripping my ass, dug in, massaging me. "Aren't you going to ask me if I'm clean?"

"Are you clean?" I echoed dutifully.

"Yes," he said. "I haven't been with anyone since before."

He didn't have to specify. The Ready Line massacre had slashed all our lives into a Before and an After. But there was something strange about his tone. I'd never offered sex without latex to any guy. Not once. I would've thought he'd be pleased.

But he looked almost angry.

"Well?" I encouraged. "What are you waiting for?"

His brows knit together. "For real? You're just going to take my word for it?"

"Shouldn't I?"

"Oh, come on, Freya." His voice was scolding. "That sounds like a classic Sandee thing to do. All instinct, no brains. You're supposed to be smart, right?"

Anger crackled through me, driving away my dreamy sexual buzz. "Well, thanks for reminding me. Just in time. You're absolutely right. Get your hands off me."

But Jed's hands tightened on my waist. "No."

I smacked his chest. "What the hell? Figure it out. You want me, you don't want me. You give me an orgasm, then you lecture me. You're giving me whiplash!"

"You shouldn't make yourself vulnerable like that," he said. "Laying yourself wide open. You should know better. It scares me that you don't."

"Oh, definitely," I agreed. "Be afraid, be very afraid. Thanks to you, I've been saved from a disaster of my own making. Yay, you. Now let me get up."

"I can't," he said starkly.

"Then why are you scolding me?"

"I don't know!" he said. "It was a dick thing to say. But I never know what I'm going to say to you. Stuff just comes out of my mouth. I'm as surprised as you are."

I stare at him thoughtfully for a moment. "Okay," I said. "Let's try this again from the top. Jed, look me in the eye. Do you have any diseases?"

"No," he said. "I'm clean."

"Well, guess what? I believe you. I'm fine, too. Haven't been with anyone in ages. Had blood work done since then. It's all good. Do you believe me?"

"Of course," he said.

"Great. That's settled. So. Do you want this?"

"Fuck yes," he said.

"Well, thank God," I said sharply. "Then shut up and take it."

He lifted me effortlessly, and with a few deft moves, got his own belt open and pants down. His cock sprang out, and he shifted me into place, holding his cock in place beneath me. Caressing me with it. His smooth, broad cockhead stroked my sensitized pussy, petting my folds, teasing them, then nudging slowly inside.

I loved that slow, tight glide as he entered me, sinking to full length. I felt so soft, so slick, honey-sweet, meltingly tender. A good thing, too, because there was a lot of him, filling me up. I rocked and squeezed around his stiff girth. He lifted me with his hands under my ass, and of course, instantly, it was perfect. The angle, the pulsing stroke, each expert thrust just running over my spot, sliding over it, stroking it, loving it.

Everything about him got to me. I loved the beard, the long, thick hair. The bruises and scratches on his face were valiant signs of heroism. His eyes were hot with arousal as he stared at me, driving me closer...closer...

Into another crashing wave of incredible, pulsing sweetness.

When I opened my eyes, he was carrying me down the corridor.

"The bed in the right-hand room is made up," I told him.

He turned to the right, leaving the door open, but didn't turn the light on, thank God. I felt too raw to be seen. The light that filtered in through the corridor from the kitchen at the end of the hall was already too much.

He sent me down on the bed, and gestured for me to turn around.

"Hands and knees," he said. "I'm going to finish."

"Okay," I whispered, but in my current blasted state, it was more like face, elbows, and knees. I braced myself against his deep thrusts. Not gentle, not rough, just perfect. Hot and lusty, and just exactly what I craved. He stirred me up, giving me all his strength, all his need, all his thick, gorgeous cock. Harder, deeper, wilder.

I realized that he was waiting, holding off on coming in order to bring me off once again before he let go...and I was right there, teetering on the edge...almost...

We exploded together.

Somehow, he managed to get us both under the covers. I had no idea how he did it. But I had the quilt pulled over us, and I was against his heat, my head under his chin.

I was too wrecked to think clearly, but a stark realization still drifted through my mind. This stunt hadn't necessarily gotten through his guard.

All it had done was completely trash what little was left of mine.

CHAPTER 22

Jed

I run through the prison, looking for something important, but I can't remember what. All the doors and gates gape open, and signs of struggle are everywhere. Blood smears and splatters on the walls, bullet holes. Something terrible happened here.

I hear water running in the bathroom as I get closer. It roars in my ears like an oncoming train. The floor is flooded. Tinted with pink. I wade through it, ankle deep, running, splashing. The bathroom seems endless. I finally find him curled up on the ground, covered in blood.

Mickey's eyes open as I approach. He lifts his head, trying to speak, but just a garbled cawing sound comes out.

I fall to my knees as he gestures toward his face, the finger spiraling. Then he makes a frustrated gesture with his hand, one that says, "don't you understand me yet? What are you, thick?" He points at his face again. And again.

Now he was holding a blank plastic mask like the one Boer had used. The roar of the falling water gets louder, like a massive waterfall. It's getting deeper, and not pink anymore. Red. A lake of blood, heaving waves, lifting Mickey's body, sweeping him away. Surging around my *knees, my thighs. Sucking and pulling at me. The mask floats on the surface, bobbing and swaying.*

I turn, and see a masked Boer blocking the bathroom door. He holds Freya in front of himself like a shield, one hand between her legs, a knife to her throat, the one I threw at him. Freya is dressed like Sandee, her tight sweater stained with blood, her skirt rucked up over Boer's hand. Her eyes are full of terror. Boer is laughing.

Boer pulls off his mask. Underneath, he has no face. Just a bloody skull, exposed muscles and tendons. Round, lidless eyes, a grinning, lipless mouth, wide open and still laughing, as the knife slashes Freya's throat. Blood spurts—

I jolted bolt upright with a sharp gasp, heart galloping. *Fuck.*

Freya sat up next to me. "What?" she asked.

I shook my head. "Bad dream," I said. "Routine for me. All those combat tours. Don't worry about it. Go back to sleep."

She didn't move, just put her hand on my arm. She could feel me vibrating from the adrenaline. "Jed," she said softly. "Please."

"I'm sorry I woke you," I said. "Just let me be. Go to sleep."

"Tell me the dream," she insisted.

"Why? So both of us can be creeped out?"

She made an impatient sound. "I'm creeped out already, so I really don't think your bad dream is going to move the dial. A burden shared is a burden halved, right?"

"No. It's a burden doubled, and I don't see the point."

She sighed in frustration. "Jed, just let me in."

"It's violent," I said. "Blood and gore. You don't need to hear it."

"Yeah? Let's have it. I'm down for some gore." She repositioned herself so she was sitting crosslegged, facing me, tugging the blankets around her. I got a swift glimpse of her nipples peeking over the quilt. Just enough light filtered in from the kitchen to show the contours of her breasts, and the flinty resolve in her eyes.

It was a piss poor idea to let my bleak, blood-soaked dreams out of the the box where I hid them. Plus, she got her throat slit at the end of it. Real buzzkill, that detail.

"You won't like it," I told her. "It doesn't end well for you."

"Duly noted," she said. "I'm not afraid of a silly old dream. Tell me."

Aw, what the fuck. Be it on her head. "It started out in prison," I said. "With Mickey, dying in the bathroom."

Freya put her hand on my hand, and I almost jumped, pulling away. The toxic violence I'd seen could transmit to her, like electricity. "He wasn't supposed to talk to me, so they cut out his tongue. To make a point. Among other parts."

I felt her flinch, just barely. "God," she whispered. "I'm so sorry." She grabbed my hand again and squeezed it, not letting me pull away. "Tell me the rest of it."

So I did. The whole disjointed mess came out. Mickey, on the floor, dying. Making that gesture with his fingers, pulling on Boer's mask, but I'm just too fucking thick to get the message. The tidal wave of blood. Boer blocking the door with a knife to her throat. The mask coming off of Boer's naked skull before he slits her throat. All of it. It was a relief to let it out. It immediately lost some of its power and dread.

Afterward, Freya just sat for a long time. I couldn't tell what she was thinking in the dim light. She looked like a statue. Calm, remote, thoughtful. She wasn't letting go of her grip on my hand, and I didn't want her to.

Then she spoke up. "The part with Mickey was just like you remembered it in real life?"

"Except for the waves of blood, and the mask," I said. "But in real life, he wrote a name on the wall. In his own blood. Joe Grifo, and then the letters O and R."

"Does that mean anything to you?"

"Not a clue. Now let's forget I said anything and go back to—"

"Shhh. I'm working it out. Don't bug me."

"It's just a dream, Freya," I said. "Dreams are irrational. It's just the brain vomiting out the stuff it can't process."

"Dreams can be garbage, yes. But they can also be high-level problem solving on a subconscious level," Freya said. "Some of mine have been. Don't discount them right away. Let's analyze this one. Think about the elements of the dream."

Shit. So she was going to fuck around with my subconscious mind, too? She was unzipping stuff, poking around inside where she had no goddanm business. "Let's not and say we did," I said grimly.

But there was no stopping this woman. "There's Mickey, making that gesture toward his face, for one—"

"He did that because they cut his tongue out. Nothing to analyze there."

"Indulge me, Jed." Her voice was gentle, but stern. "There's the mask, with Boer and Mickey both. Boer's face under the mask, with no skin. That strikes me as an important—"

"It strikes me as disgusting," I said. "I think my mind added that in just for cheap shock value. Standard nightmare bullshit theatrics."

"Don't be bad-tempered. Did you see Boer's eyes yesterday?"

I squinted at her. "Freya. He was wearing a mask. Remember?"

"I mean, through the eyeholes, Jed," she said, impatiently.

"To be honest, I was more focused on his trigger finger. He was holding a fucking gun on you, so excuse me for being distracted."

Freya snorted under her breath. "Fine. So yesterday, when he nabbed me, I happened to notice the skin around his eyes, through the eyeholes of the mask."

"Well, I didn't, so clue me in. What about it?"

"It looked swollen, kind of purple," she said. "His eyes looked bloodshot."

"Maybe he has insomnia. Or he drinks. Who the fuck knows."

Freya shook her head. "It looked like he'd been punched in both eyes."

Huh. Interesting. "Where are you going with this, Freya?"

"Nowhere yet. I'm just groping. Let me bat it around for a while. No bad ideas in brainstorming, remember?"

"Is that what we're doing?"

"It would be, if you would play along," she said, her voice sharp. "What was Mickey supposed to give you when you got out? A flash drive, you said?"

"Yeah. Mickey was an accountant for this mob boss in Vegas, Adriani. Boer partnered with him, so Mickey gathered some dirt on him. Info about his new identity, his money, things that would be useful for finding Boer, and putting him in jail. There was someone on the outside who was holding it for him."

"But Mickey didn't tell you who," she said.

I shook my head. "He didn't have a chance," I said bleakly.

"Maybe he did," she said.

I stopped breathing for a moment. "What the hell do you mean by that?"

"Well, he kept gesturing toward his face, right? And there's the mask. Boer had a mask. In the dream, Boer's face had no skin. It's all about the face."

"I wouldn't wonder about that. His tongue was cut out," I said.

She made an impatient sound. "Think about it. I had a friend who had her eyes done, and she had swollen, bruised eyes for weeks afterward. Just like Boer's eyes. What's the point of wearing a mask? You know who he is, what he looks like. Unless he's wearing his mask to hide his new face. And Mickey knew he would be."

Sudden excitement buzzed inside me. "Holy shit," I said.

"Maybe Mickey tried to tell you who has that flash drive, after all," she said. "Maybe it's Boer's surgeon. And maybe that's Joe Grifo. Where was Mickey based before prison?"

"Portland," I said. "Oregon. He had a place there. Adriani, the mob boss, was based in Las Vegas, but Mickey went home to Portland whenever he could."

"Oregon," she said. "That explains the OR. Try cross-referencing exclusive, high end cosmetic surgeons named Joseph Grifo. Start in Oregon."

I slid out of bed and went straight to the laptop in the living room, stark naked. I ran a search, and found him on the first page. Madden, Grifo, Clark, and Burns, a cosmetic surgery practice in Lake Oswego, Oregon. Grifo's first name was Joseph. There were other Grifo doctors, a James, an Angelo, a Giovanni, a Micheal, all of them with different specialties. But a Joe Grifo, in Oregon, in cosmetic surgery...that search yielded just one, single guy.

Well, fuck me.

Freya leaned over my shoulder, gorgeously smooth and warm and fragrant. "Did you find him?"

"I found someone," I said. "Doesn't mean it's him."

"Well." She shrugged. "It's a place to start. A door to knock on. Hey, look at that. Madden, Grifo, Clark and Burns are participating in the organization fundraising gala for the New Day, New Hope Foundation, a charitable foundation which seeks to improve the lives of individuals in need of reconstructive surgery, blah blah. That's happening in just a couple of days. Interesting. I wonder if our guy will be there."

In retrospect, it looked so obvious, I wish I'd figured it out for myself. But no, it had to be handed to me on a platter by a hot naked girl. Shane and Ethan always dazzled me with their big brains, too, but the sexy naked girl element gave it a special twist.

But fuck it. We couldn't all be rocket scientists. There was a place for everyone in the grand scheme of things. The world needed its grunting meatheads, too.

Like Freya had needed me today. I had made myself useful, beyond a doubt.

She gave me that incandescent Sandee smile, and tossed up

her mop of wild, tousled hair, stretching for me, arching, putting on a show. Then cupped her own breasts, sliding her fingertips down, down, down. "I think, Jed, that our work here is done for now," she said, her voice silky. "And now you should come with me into the bedroom and make up for being a jerk in that special way only you can."

She turned around and sashayed back toward the bedroom, hips swaying.

Wow. This woman was something else. Figuring out my next move by parsing my stress nightmares? She had superpowers. Like a sexy, dangerous sorceress.

And that didn't dampen down my hard-on. Oh, no. On the contrary.

She was sitting on the edge of the bed, waiting for me. I walked in and stood there, waiting for a cue. Something unmistakable, like grabbing my dick.

She did me one better, grabbing my ass with one hand, my cock with the other, sucking me tenderly into her mouth. I gasped at the intense sensation. Slow, teasing little licks and trills and swirls, taking me deeper into that hot well, caressing me with her clever tongue. She clamped her fingers around the base of my cock, squeezing tenderly while she took me in. A slow, pulsing rhythm.

I've never not liked a blowjob. What wasn't to like? But this was next level. Another universe. Life-changing, mind blowing, brain melting. I wanted to fuse with her, kiss her, fuck her. Feel her come around my dick, bathing me with her balm.

But it was so hard to stop this perfection. Only the thundering imminent orgasm made me draw back. I wanted to be inside her when I came.

I reached down, beyond speech, nudging and maneuvering her until she scooted back onto the bed, and opened her legs, holding up her arms to me.

My chest expanded, like a supernova as I entered her. So

sweet and yielding, bathing me with her hot lube at every stroke. Staring at each other. I'd never felt so completely seen, known. It felt incredible.

We clutched each other, heaving and crying out in that frantic crescendo, and then the energy blasted me open from the inside. Light was flooding into the ruins.

I was open to the brilliant, endless sky.

After my heart calmed down and I came to my senses, fear came flooding back.

This was stupid. The more attached to her I got, the more dangerous it was for both of us. I'm doubling my load and cutting my effectiveness in half. Or worse.

I couldn't wallow in all the tender fucking feelings if I wanted Freya to survive. I admired her courage and nerve, but my first priority was keeping her safe, not indulging her ego. I had to pass her over to the Drakes and have them deliver her to Ethan. Protecting and controlling her should be her brother's problem. Not mine.

I was getting swept up into the stratosphere. Which was great while I was riding the giddy updraft, but I knew it couldn't last. Gravity always had its way in the end.

And it was a long, long way back down.

CHAPTER 23

Freya

It was frustrating as hell. Confusing, too.

I couldn't understand Jed's behavior. Last night, I'd helped him. Demonstrably, measurably, materially, not just with sexual favors. Real help. A new lead, a new line of inquiry, a big step forward. At least, I hoped it would be. Please, God.

I suppose I'd thought that would automatically change my status, but it hadn't. If anything, Jed was behaving worse than he had before. More rude and grumpy, more scowling, more uncommunicative.

And I was getting my feelings hurt, which I had sworn I would not do. But damn it, the sex last night had been so intense. I thought that we'd turned a corner together. That our souls had touched, and nothing could ever be the same again.

I was embarrassed at my own foolishness. This had been a disaster begging to happen, and surprise, surprise, it had happened sooner, rather than later.

Clearly, last night hadn't meant anything to him. So I needed to grit my teeth and grow up. Right freaking *now*.

It was a good thing we were only about a seven-hour drive

away from Portland. He'd shaken me awake at four to tell me to get ready. On the long, silent drive, he'd been even more cold and unreachable than yesterday, which was saying a great deal.

We were on the outskirts of Portland slightly before noon. Jed stopped at a coffee shop, ordering sandwiches and coffee at the drive-thru without asking my preferences. He glared over at me as he pulled up to the window to pay.

"Get your head down," he said sharply. "Pull down the hat. And slump."

I oozed downward on my seat with bad grace as he paid, waiting again when we picked up the food. He passed the bags to me and pulled back out onto the freeway.

"Where are we headed?" I asked him.

"Our hotel," he said.

"I've seen a bunch of them already," I said. "They're every-where, right off the highway."

"I already picked one out last night," he said.

"Oh, really? Which one? And where? And why not tell me?"

"I didn't feel like discussing it."

I tried not to grind my teeth. There was no point even trying to be civil to that man. I pulled out one of the coffees, popped a hole in the plastic lid, and sipped.

Oh, God. Tongue-scalding, black as night, bitter as gall. Jed hadn't asked for sugar or cream, or anything contemptible and frivolous like that. I had nailed his vibe. The beverage was meant to be both bracing and punishing. A drink to kick your ass.

Dickhead. I let out a breath and braced myself. "So. What's the plan today?"

"What part of 'I don't feel like discussing it' did you not understand?"

"Oh, I don't know," I said. "Maybe the part where you fuck me until I can barely walk and then treat me like total shit the next day." There was no way to keep that one under wraps. It had to burst out, or it would eat me up from the inside.

Jed didn't look at me, but his jaw tightened under the beard. "That was a mistake," he said.

Oh, wow. That hurt more than it should have. I'd been trying to grind through all the inconvenient feelings provoked by this rude, oversexed dipshit for the last four hours, and he had just undone all that hard work in a hot instant.

"Yeah, that's clear," I said. "All ten times, or however many times we did it. I lost count. That was a whole lot of mistakes, Jed. One might actually start questioning your judgment. Maybe even your sanity."

"I'm sorry if you've decided to get your feelings hurt, but that can't be my focus right now," he said. "I'm working."

"Tell me something I don't know," I said. "Like, the plan."

"Just shut up, Freya. I'm concentrating."

Oh, man. I clenched my fists, imagining my fingers wrapped around his throat, but looking at that thick, sinewy, corded neck of his, I could probably do my absolute worst and he would barely notice the pressure. Shooting him would be more efficient.

I abandoned my attempts at conversation as we took a smaller highway which led us out into an industrial district, full of factories and warehouses, the occasional forest and field still scattered between them. He slowed down and pulled into a parking lot, with a run-down motel. "Houlihan's Motel & RV Park. Cabins. Vacancy."

"Is this one of your prepared houses?" I asked.

"I wish," he said. "I didn't know the chase would take us here, so I don't have anything ready in this area. I just picked the best I could find."

I eyed the ramshackle, decaying, 1970s era building doubtfully. "Ah, okay. What criteria did you use for choosing it?"

"I'll go get the key," he said brusquely. "Stay put. Keep down. Keep the hat on."

His voice had a warning tone. As if I were his kidnapped victim, and he was threatening me into good behavior. Asshole.

Well, hell. If he couldn't afford feelings now, neither could I. But I envied his ability to shut them off like a faucet. I wonder how he did it. What it cost him.

Maybe nothing. Maybe he was empty. Maybe it had been just sex.

But damn, that soul-fusing, overwhelming emotion I'd felt ... could it all just be me projecting my adolescent nitwit fantasies onto him? Really?

He was back soon, not meeting my eyes as he got into the car. He held an old-fashioned key hanging from a placard. No keycards or key fobs for this shabby place.

To my surprise, he directed the Jeep out past the motel building, and drove for a surprisingly long time through a thick forest of young pines and firs. There were periodic spots for RVs carved out of the woods, only a few of which were inhabited, then a loop of cabins. The place was largely deserted for the off season.

At the end of the second big loop, Jed pulled up in front of a two-room cabin in a small clearing, right off the narrow road. It had a barbecue firepit, and a trestle picnic table next to it. When I got out, I couldn't see any other cabins from where I stood.

Jed got to work with his usual routine, hauling in the boxes of computer and security equipment and setting up his security system; the motion detectors, the cameras, his grim, purposeful ritual. Then he pulled out a power drill, and swiftly installed two new and much larger, more powerful locks onto the front door of the cabin. He tested the hinges with a grunt of disgust. "Piece of shit," he muttered. "I might as well not have bothered." He proceeded to get to work on the windows.

"You can drill holes in a hotel?" I said. "Won't the management be pissed?"

"I'll give them money," he said brusquely. "They'll be fine."

Fair enough. Money did smooth over a lot of rough places. Since Ethan started making serious money in his mid-twenties, back when I was still a teenager, our lives had gotten a whole lot easier. Then Shane followed suit after he retired from the military, with Ready Line Security. Both my brothers had done very well for themselves financially, and both of them had expected to support me. Insisted on it, even.

But I had other plans. Other people's money had too many strings attached. No matter how generous my brothers were, I needed my own fonts of income. Which is why I got the engineering degrees, and developed all my many side hustles.

Jed put his tools away, and tore open the sack of food which I had left on the table in the kitchen. He pulled out the two paper-wrapped sandwiches and tossed one at me. "Eat," he said brusquely. "You need to keep your strength up."

I caught the thing, looking down at it with hostile eyes. The unchosen, un-asked-for turkey sandwich from the coffee shop. I was tempted to tell him to stick it up his ass, but that would be childish, emotional Freya talking.

Tough, calculating, grown-up Freya thought about staying strong, keeping her wits about her. That required food, so I bit back the diatribe and unwrapped it.

It pissed me off how freaking delicious it was. Right-out-of-the-oven sourdough bread, soft Havarti cheese, herbed mayonnaise, thick-sliced, fresh-baked turkey, slabs of juicy, tangy red tomato, and leaves of frilly, crunchy lettuce. I was betraying myself by enjoying it as much as I did. I ate every bite and licked my fingers. But I kept my back turned, since I'd die before giving him the satisfaction of seeing me like it.

Jed ignored me, anyway, so it hardly mattered. He ate his sandwich quickly, then ended up in the bathroom. He set the shower running. There had been no time for a shower at the crack of dawn, not with Jed hurrying me to get going.

I got an eyeful of his gorgeous naked body as he came out, running the towel over his broad, damp chest, lifting thickly muscled arms to dry thick tufts of hair under his pits. When he saw me look, he got half-hard instantly, and the usual alchemy ignited the air between us. But goddamnit, I didn't want it to.

It made me so angry. At my own body, principally. Just looking at him made me instantly wet, which of course made him go completely hard. Because he sensed it. I don't know how, but he did. He got right inside my mind. The bastard.

Then he picked up the phone, dialed. "Could you put me in touch with housekeeping? Yeah, thanks. I'm Jay Warren, staying in Cabin 34. I want to request someone come and service the cabin tomorrow morning early, at seven AM."

That was weird. I turned around to gape, and got an eyeful of his stunning, muscular ass. His broad, powerful back. Always a fresh shock to my overloaded system.

"...yes, I know...but no, we're not leaving early. I need someone there no later than seven. I need the room serviced at that hour... yeah, I know, but I'll leave a hundred-dollar tip under the lamp on the dresser for whoever gets there by that time. If no one comes by seven, no tip...yeah, exactly. So can I expect someone?...excellent. I appreciate your collaboration. So, I'll be seeing one of your staff tomorrow morning, then? Great...thank you very much. Have a great day."

"Jed?" I asked. "What the hell? Why on earth would we need maid service at that hour?"

He wouldn't look at me. "I like a clean room," he said vaguely.

"Bullshit," I said. "What are you up to? What's the point?"

He just gave me that glassy, impenetrable look, and shook his head. "Let it go."

"Fuck you, Jed Clearwater," I said.

"Anytime," he said. "I stand ready."

I couldn't look at that smirk one second longer without slapping him, so I got up and stomped past him. "Put your dick away," I snarled "It's not getting any attention from me. Ever again."

"Never? Really?" His voice was low and taunting. "You sure about that?"

"Not in this lifetime." I grabbed the bag that held all the stuff I'd pried out of my coat hem pocket, and slammed the bathroom door behind me.

The bathroom is still hot and swampy. The streaks of condensation that rolled down through the fog on the mirror showed my shocked eyes and hot-pink flush.

I looked as if I had just escaped from a burning building...and was actually considering running right back inside. The man was driving me out of my head.

I got into the shower, because why the hell not. Though when I got out, I had to get right back into the same stale, filthy clothes the luckless Mickey would never wear, which kind of canceled out the shower. Thinking of him made me feel guilty as hell, but I was not the greedy, murdering filth who had set this chain of events in motion. I was just trying to help.

I had failed, yes. Quite spectacularly. But that was my only crime.

I washed my hair, brushed my teeth, and pulled on the oversized, belted pants, the sloppy T-shirt, toweling my hair into a wild snarl of blonde tangles. When I came out, I was startled to see him already dressed. Or, more specifically, to see him dressed like that. In a costly, well-cut suit. *Yowza.*

It looked incredible on him. How could it not, with that face, that body? His hair was still wet, smoothed back and gathered into a short ponytail, and he'd trimmed and shaped the beard. He'd stopped short of a tie, and there wasn't much that could be done about the bruises and scrapes on his cheekbone, and part of his tattoo was visible over his collar on the side of his neck. And even so, he looked stunning, and memorable. Like a dangerous, drop-dead elegant billionaire mobster.

"Whoa, Jed," I said. "What are you all gussied up for?"

"I'm going to talk to Grifo," he said.

"That's the first piece of actual hard information you've given me today," I said. "You know, I was thinking. Maybe we should attend that gala."

"And how would we manage that?"

I shrugged. "Easy," I said. "We donate to their cause. It's what, ten thousand a head? For a crappy meal and a bunch of boring speeches?"

"Jesus," he muttered. "Highway robbery." He sat on the bed, opening his laptop. "I found the address of Grifo's practice. Come here for a second. I'll show you."

I hesitated out of pure stubbornness, but curiosity got the better of me. I went over to him, peering down at the laptop's screen. "If you're going to dress like that, we'll have to stop at the mall so I can pick up some decent stuff, too."

"I don't think so." He grabbed my wrist. *Snick.*

Handcuffs? The fuck? I looked at him in disbelief. Inhaled to scream.

Suddenly, his huge hand was over my mouth, and I was lifted off my feet. A sudden twirl, and *flop,* I was flat on my back in the big bed with the wrought-iron headboard. His hand lifted from my mouth to grab my other wrist. *Snick.*

Now both of my arms were handcuffed to the headboard. I craned my neck to look, flailing uselessly. The cuffs were hooked through a loop of wrought iron.

He straddled me, which squished out what breath I had left. Not enough to scream with, not with him pinning me down. My eyes had filled with tears, to my utter dismay. My breath was hitching. Goddamn him.

He slid off me quickly and lay there beside me. "I am really sorry about this," he said urgently. "I swear to God, I am. I do not like doing this to you."

I sucked in air. "Help! Help me!" I yelled.

"No one will hear you," he said. "The cabin is too far from the others, even if they were inhabited, which they're not. I checked.

That's why I requested this one. I picked this place for the iron bedframes, and the cabins with plenty of space around them. Also because it was off-season, and there's a forest. I needed a place I could hide you where you wouldn't be able to hurt yourself."

"You arrogant fucking *jerk*." I yanked at my bonds, rattling them wildly. "You cannot leave me here handcuffed! Let me go. I promise, I won't bug you, I won't follow you. I'll sit here, on my hands. Just don't do this to me. It's wrong!"

"It's the only thing," he said. "I should only be a couple of hours at the most. I have to go to this guy's private practice and see if I can talk to him. Or failing that, at least get some info from the people who worked with him."

"Hours?" My voice cracked in outrage. "You're leaving me like this for hours?"

"I've set it up very carefully. If the worst should happen, and someone killed me, two things will happen. If I don't cancel it deliberately, a timed email will go out in eight hours to the local police, alerting them of your location."

"Eight fucking hours? Are you kidding me?"

"I'll be back in two, three hours at the max. Also, the house-keeper will be here first thing in the morning to get her tip, so you're one hundred percent covered either way. I built in some redundancy, but you won't need it. I'll be back. Really soon."

"I can't do this, Jed!" My voice shook. "I can't be tied up! I can't do it!"

"I'm sorry, Freya," he repeated. "It won't be long. I was just waiting until you went into the bathroom to pee. You know, after all that coffee."

Somehow, that condescending courtesy pissed me off even more. "You asshole!" I yanked and struggled against the cuffs.

"Freya. Don't fight. You'll hurt your wrists—"

"Fuck you!" I yelled, trying to knee him, but he just rolled onto my leg.

"I hate doing this," he said. "I'm not trying to punish you.

But you don't take orders, and you don't listen to reason. I don't have anyone to watch you and keep you safe, and I can't wait until I do. I don't have time to coax and plead or wrangle you. I just have to keep you alive until I can get you back to your brother."

"Safe? You think this is safe?" My voice cracked in raw panic. "Staking me out like a fucking goat for any asshole who comes along?"

"No one will find you," he soothed. "No one knows you're here. You'll be locked in with all of my alarms connected to my phone. I'll be monitoring you. I'll know if anyone gets near you, even a rabbit or a fox. I'll send someone if there's a problem. And I'll come running back as soon as I can, I swear."

"Fuck you, Jed Clearwater!" I thrashed, trying to kick him. "Let... me...loose!"

"Goddamnit, Freya. Stop it. You'll hurt yourself!"

"You can't chain me up!" I yelled. "I can't do this! I can't stand it!"

He rolled on top of me, forcing all the air out of my chest. I tried to kick him, but ended up wound around him, with his big, solid body between my legs.

The shudder of sexual awareness made us both immobile. I tried to stop crying, avoiding eye contact, but just like that, my panic instantly transmitted into desperate heat.

And I hated myself for it. Goddamn him, for shoving it in my face like that. Humiliating me. I was so afraid of the fucked up, damaged parts of myself, messing with me. Making it so easy for him to manipulate me.

I was usually the boss bitch of the situation. I pulled all the strings, ran the whole show. I organized my whole life around that premise. That I had to be in control.

I knew I was just compensating. Trying to correct for that monstrous shitshow with Uncle Orren and Aunt Jean. As if I could ever correct for something like that.

So I was warped for life, yes, fine. I'd made as much peace with it as I could.

But I couldn't do my usual compensatory tricks with Jed. I couldn't pull strings with him. I tried to, and things moved, but never in the direction I intended. I couldn't make anything go where I wanted it to go. Jed was uncontrollable.

Kind of funny, how that was the exact same problem he had with me.

And now I was chained up again, just like when I was seven years old, in the dark basement room, and it was flooding back into me, as if it had never gone away. My aunt and uncle. The panic, the desperation. Hating on myself because they hated me. I would have done anything to please them or appease them. I just wanted to be good, so they would stop hurting me. I would be so good. I would be perfect.

That was the fucked up part. It could sink me if it mixed up with my feelings for Jed. I had no business letting myself fall in love, or even in lust. I was too messed up to ever get it right. I would just hurt myself, and the more I cared, the more it would hurt.

Now I was sobbing, and I couldn't stop. Goddammit.

"Freya." Jed's tone sounded sobered, nervous. "What the fuck?"

"That's my line, asshole," I snapped, snuffling madly. It sucked, having no way to blow my nose. "Ask yourself that question."

"I know cuffing you is horrible, and I expected you to tell me to fuck myself, but you're freaking me out. There's something else going on here."

"No, you're just an asshole," I snapped. "You simply don't understand how obscene and controlling this is, you filthy son of a bitch, because you are shit-stupid."

"I never claimed to be a genius," he said. "But I know better than to take Ethan Master's baby sister on a mission."

"I could help you," I snarled. "I am a fucking resource for you, not a bag of sand tied to your foot. I'm smart, I would see things you might not see, I know things that you might not know, and none of that will be available to you, you brain-dead son of a bitch!"

I made the huge mistake of meeting his eyes, and suddenly my nipples were hypersensitive against the fabric of my T-shirt, aching to touch his naked chest.

But I didn't want sex mixed up with the locked-in-the-dark feelings. No, no, no.

I twisted, struggling under him. He leaned down and kissed me hard, and then rolled off and got up. He straightened his clothes and stared at me, looking worried.

"I don't like upsetting you," he said. "I hate hurting you. I don't lack empathy, Freya. Sometimes I wish I did. Things would be a whole lot easier."

"Piss off, Jed. You feel bad for treating me this way? Aw, boo-hoo for you. I don't give a damn about your feelings."

"I have to do what I have to do. I just hate it that you ran into that wall."

Oh, puh-leeze. I would have spit at the guy, if I could have reached him. "Spare me the sermon, you self-righteous scumbag."

"Okay. I'm gone. We'll finish working this out later," he said.

"Oh no, we won't. We are so very done, Jed."

"Freya, please," he said wearily. He slid a pistol into the holster he wore beneath his suit jacket, then shrugged on a black wool overcoat. He pulled out his wallet, peeled out two fifties, and tucked them under the base of the lamp on the dresser. "For the housekeeper," he said. "Just in case."

I turned my face away. He went in to the front room, but as he opened the door, panic exploded inside me. "Wait!"

He turned back, looking through the open bathroom door. "What?"

"The light," I said. "Turn it on. Don't leave me in the dark. Please."

He came back to the door of the bedroom, and flipped the switch of the overhead lamp. "I should be back long before it gets dark," he said.

"Whatever," I forced out, through lips that shook. "Just...just leave it on."

I heard the door shut, and the locks engage, one after the other. Then a hollow *thud* as the Jeep door closed. The sound of the engine roaring to life.

Gravel crunched, lights flickered outside, the sound retreated...and he was gone.

He'd left me to it. Alone with my demons. The square of gray, rainy sky through the window didn't help. The dim, watery bulb of the overhead light didn't help, either, because the darkness was inside me. Memories, rushing back, of being huddled in the dark, chained up like a miserable animal in the pitch-black basement room. Rocking to soothe myself. Filthy clothes. The smelly pee and poo bucket. Nasty, spoiled food.

I had stayed down there for weeks at a time. No way to gauge how many weeks, or how many times. There was no day or night down there. It was all darkness.

It had started out normal, if anything could be called normal after Mom and Dad's car accident. The three of us, sent to stay with Uncle Orren and Aunt Jean. It wasn't home, and never would be, but we were too shocked and busy grieving to notice.

Then things got tense. Ethan and Shane quickly began to chafe at the strange, senseless rules of the place. They started mouthing off. And just like that, Uncle Orren had arranged for my big brothers to be taken off to the local reformatory.

They were gone, and it was just me, miserably afraid and alone.

I tried to run away, after a few weeks. That was when they put me in the basement for the first time. After that, the basement became the go-to punishment. Always for longer and longer times. Because they discovered that they liked it.

They said it was to make me pray for forgiveness. To make me reflect upon my sinful ways. My impure impulses. My evil feelings. I needed to pray for goodness to come into my heart and drive away the selfishness, the wickedness.

All I had to cling to was the hope that Ethan and Shane would come and save me. But they were locked up, Jean said. And they would stay locked up.

They're trash. You're all trash, like your worthless mother, and that turd she married. Zero plus zero will always equal zero. You godless little freak.

Jean would never stop ranting at me. Not until I had proved her right, and turned into a piece of garbage. Something nasty to bury at the bottom of a dark hole. Stinking, rotting, bad through and through. Because Jean was still in there, deep inside my head.

And she would never stop trying to stuff me back down into the dark.

Stay in the moment. Just breathe. Stay in the moment. You're all grown up now, and Aunt Jean and Uncle Orren are gone. This will end. You can take it. Breathe.

I used all my usual tricks and techniques to coax myself back up from that old dark pit and back to the light, and then I heard it. *Pop.*

The lightbulb had just burned out.

CHAPTER 24

My first stop was at the home address I'd found for Grifo. It was in Forest Hills, a pricey suburb of Portland. When I got to the cul-de-sac, I parked outside and walked around it. Grifo's house was handsome. Big, modern, lots of glass. Huge lawn, massive trees. Evidently the cosmetic surgery business paid well. The house looked abandoned, though. No lights, no cars visible in the garage. The grass had gotten long and shaggy. Dead leaves had blown across the front entryway, and the side patio, piling up in drifts.

I went up to the front door and gave the buzzer a try, but I wasn't surprised when no one answered. Grifo had been spooked away from his own home. Then again, Boer probably got referred to Grifo by Adriani, so chances were, Grifo had probably worked on people who were on the wrong side of the law before. He had to know the score.

He'd made a shit-ton of money, after all. This was a five-million-dollar house.

I stared up at the house, and heard Freya's voice in my mind.

The light. Turn it on. Don't leave me in the dark. Please.

The words kept repeating in my head. Or not exactly the words, but more her tone. The soul-deep desperation behind them. Something about that was all fucked up. Completely wrong. It scared me.

Well, fucking duh. Of course it was all kinds of bad to handcuff a woman to a bed and then leave her there. There was no way to spin that. It sucked. Unforgivably. Particularly after she'd helped me out like that. Stitching together information from my stress nightmares. I wouldn't have a plan at all but for her being so fucking brilliant.

But Freya was so tough and fiery, I had expected a different reaction from her. Fury, outrage, vitriol, fireworks. Sarcasm and snark. Me, getting cut down to size.

Not...whatever that was. Not her looking that vulnerable. That scared.

In any case, it made me feel like shit. I had to get this done fast, so I could let her loose and take my medicine, whatever that turned out to be. If she needed to whale on me, or scream at me, or bash me over the head with a frying pan, fair enough. I would take it. Hell, I deserved it. Every last blow. I welcomed it.

And this was just the classic problem I had with that woman. Instead of focusing on the task at hand, I was wasting time and energy wallowing in guilt, anxiety, and shame.

And doubt. Always doubt. *You think this is safe? Staking me out like a fucking goat for any asshole who comes along?*

Damn, the woman had a point. And it made me fucking tense.

The next stop was the cosmetic surgery practice right near Old Town. It was raining by the time I found the place and parked. No umbrella, but it was a short walk.

The place reeked of wealth and privilege. I walked into a great big central lobby with a vaulted ceiling, filled with big exotic potted trees and a burbling waterfall that rushed endlessly down artfully carved blocks of dark stone. Very classy. High overhead.

I walked up to the desk, which was presided over by statuesque blonde trophy receptionist. Her face had that taut, stretched look of someone who'd had some work done, but she was a fine-looking woman. Her desk had a name tag. Ramona.

She gave me a onceover, and I saw her reaction evolve over the course of two seconds. First, startled appreciation, then her smile faded as she took in the what's-wrong-with-this-picture details. Scabs on my cheekbone, the beard, the tattoo on my neck. Her red-painted lips tightened, sphincter-like. I couldn't help comparing that to Freya's soft, lush, expressive mouth, her blinding grin. Not a fair comparison.

The phone rang, and she put up her finger with a smile. "Hello, Madden, Grifo, Clark, and Burns, can I help you?" She listened for a moment. "Oh, definitely. But have the bakery switch the eclairs out for profiterole...yes. And tell Barbara in accounting there will be two catering invoices for the gala. One for the meal, from Highline Catering, and one for dessert, from the Moulin Pastisserie. Did you check on those lactose-free Neapolitan pastries?...yes, I know, but we need one for Rachelle Grifo at table one, and Dr. Maxwell at table seven, as well, and a gluten-free for Charlaine Bristol at table twelve...well, just check on it, Gary, to be sure they're on top of it! Then call me back! Okay...later, then."

She hung up, and gave me a tight, professional smile. "Hello. Can I help you?"

"I hope so," I told her, still humming from having heard the name Grifo mentioned. "I was hoping to speak to Dr. Joseph Grifo."

Ramona blinked rapidly. "Ah...he's not working here at the moment."

"He isn't?" I asked. "Since when? Where did he go?"

"I'm afraid I can't give you any information," she said. "Privacy concerns, of course. But he's not working at this practice. At the moment."

"I see. So he's not in business anymore?"

"Like I said, I can't tell you."

Damn, I should have called ahead, made an appointment with these people. I noted the subtle tension in her face, the way her eyes rolled and slid away from mine, and felt the instinct to press her. "Could I speak to someone who worked with him? Dr. Clark, for instance. The website said he was a close associate of Dr. Grifo."

"I don't think that will be possible," she said. "I doubt he's available."

I leaned down over the desk and gave her a slow, dangerous smile. "Why don't you check and see?"

Her eyes fluttered, and her lips puckered up again. Suddenly, I wondered how I had ever found her attractive at all. She looked drawn, pinched. And scared.

"I'll just, ah...go and check," she murmured. She slid her chair back and fled.

Damn. Maybe I'd overdone it. Trying to catch flies with vinegar. Not the first time I'd made that mistake.

Time to get psychologically ready to deal with the police, depending on how much I had spooked her. I hadn't done anything, except give her an arguably menacing smile. And my fake identity as Jay Warren was well developed. He was a normal, boring, blameless kind of guy. Not the type to get arrested for assault.

Ramona came back, followed by a tall bald guy with a worried frown on his face. I recognized him from his photo on the website as Dr. Milton Clark, one of Grifo's partners. He put himself protectively in front of Ramona, making her stumble back.

"Sir, I'm afraid I'll have to ask you to leave, right now," he said, in a pompous, self-important tone.

"Are you Dr. Clark? I need to speak to someone who worked with Joe Grifo."

"Sir, I'm afraid you have to leave." I sensed an edge of fear in his voice.

Damn. I wondered if they were afraid of Boer, or of Adriani. These people were definitely afraid of someone. They must think I was a mobster. I tried for a friendly smile. "I was hoping to talk to one of the partners. It would be a mistake not to hear what I have to say."

"They're all busy," Dr. Clark said. "Go, or I'll be forced to call the police."

I let out a silent sigh. "No need for that," I said. "Your loss. You folks have a great evening. Thank you for your help."

Out in the cold rain, I ran to the car, analyzing the relative idiocy of what I had just done. Yes, they were all on edge, which was good to know, but more of a vibe than hard, actionable data. Now I had put them on their guard.

One more door to bang on, and I'd head back to brave Freya's thundering wrath. I searched on my laptop for the Moulin Patisserie, and found it a few blocks away. It was a high-end bakery, relatively new, which delivered to restaurants and hotels.

I entered the warm, wood-paneled bakery, damp from the rain. The place had a retro vibe, with a soda fountain at the bar, old time stools, a long glass case that displayed a dizzying array of pastries. The smell of sugar and butter was overwhelming.

This time, I turned the collar of my coat up to hide the tattoo and put on my best "don't mind me" look. I chose a horse-faced girl with a long, tight blonde braid and heavy glasses, and approached her. Her name tag read "Jessalyn."

"Hi, Jessalyn," I said. "I'm Mike, from Madden, Grifo, Clark, and Burns. They sent me to tell you that Ramona decided to switch out the profiteroles for the eclairs, after all. Can you note that down on the order? Or is it too late to change it?"

"I don't think so," Jessalyn said. "I'll just go and check, to be sure. They wanted the early delivery, too, right?"

"Yeah. Wait, hold on. We are talking about the Tuesday event, right? The one at the Cloverdale Arms?"

Jessalyn's eyebrows arched anxiously upward. "Tuesday? I don't know anything about a Tuesday event. This order is for the gala tomorrow at the Pineview."

"Oh, yeah! Of course. Sorry." I waved my hand apologetically. "I get mixed up. Just too many details to keep track of. You know how it is."

"Oh gosh, I sure do," the girl assured me. "Tell me about it!"

I took off, waving at Jessalyn through the window, and hustled through the cold, misty drizzle toward the car. It was full dark now, and my urgency to get back to Freya had crescendoed into a wild drumroll of anxiety.

I sped out of the city toward Houlihan's, windshield wipers squeaking. I might have gathered some info, but at what cost? I still didn't know, and that drove me nuts.

Damn it. Freya had flung herself into this clusterfuck uninvited. She had no business bitching if things didn't go according to her plans.

When I got to the final loop of cabins, I turned the last corner, expecting to see light behind the bedroom curtains...and there wasn't any. The window was dark.

Fuck. I laid on the accelerator, panic stabbing deep into my gut. There was no possible way anyone could've found her here. I shoved in the key and slapped the door open, opening my mouth to—

"Aunt Jean!" A panicked, ear-splitting shriek from the bedroom. "Aunt Jean! Aunt Jean! Aunt Jean!"

CHAPTER 25

Freya

"Aunt Jean! Aunt Jean!" I bucked and fought against Uncle Orren's crushing weight, twisting away from the ugly smell of old, sour-sweet alcohol and his sweat and greasy, unwashed hair. I tried to bite him, kick him. Aunt Jean would probably scream at me, but that was better than being down here with Uncle Orren alone. Anything was better. But I just...couldn't...breathe. He was squishing me, but I would fight until I died fighting. Then, from far away, I heard a voice, repeating my name.

Not Uncle Orren. I knew that voice. My ears reached out to it eagerly.

"...fighting me! Calm down! It's me. It's Jed." His voice was low, gentle, pleading. "Please, baby. You're hurting your own wrists. You're bleeding. Stop fighting, please, so I can undo the cuffs. Please, Freya."

My trembling limbs stopped jerking and flailing. I couldn't seem to inhale. I dragged in short, sobbing breaths as the weight slowly eased. More air came in, and suddenly, I could smell him. I knew that smell. Not Uncle Orren.

The world came back into focus. My whole life reordered itself. I was an adult.

And this was Jed. Those were Jed's eyes near my face. That was Jed's voice.

He lifted himself off me, and a big gulp of air made me start coughing.

He reached up to unlock the handcuffs. My hands were cold and numb, my wrists sore. Sticky with blood. I must have had some bad moments, flashing back to that basement. But I didn't want to think about them. Please, God. Never again.

"Freya, I'm so sorry." He grabbed my wrists, looking at the red, raw ligature marks with sharp hiss of dismay. "Jesus. I didn't know…"

I pushed myself away from him into a sitting position. "Didn't know? Really?" I stammered out, mouth still trembling. "You thought leaving me handcuffed alone in the dark wouldn't bother me? Seriously, you're going to play that dumb?"

"I knew it would piss you off, of course. I'm sorry about the lightbulb burning out. I know it was bad, but I never meant to…" His voice trailed off.

"To what, Jed?" My voice was cracked and thick from screaming.

"To hurt you," he finished. "That's the last thing I want. I just wanted to keep you safe. I know how protective Ethan and Shane are about you. How much they worry. It's the same with me. Particularly since we got together."

"Together? Hah." I let out a crack of bitter laughter. "Some togetherness. My brothers always thought I should be confined, just like you do."

"That's not true," Jed said. "No one wants to confine you. They never stop bragging about you. I was always hearing about how Freya just invented a patent for this thing, or Freya just got a robotics engineering award for that thing."

"They like it that I'm smart, when it's convenient for them.

They want a toy they can show off and then put back into a box for safe storage when they're busy. But they can't protect me. Neither can you. The damage is done. It was done a long time ago."

"What damage?" he demanded. "What are you talking about?"

"Never mind," I muttered. I tried to stand up, but my legs were having none of that. I ended up just sliding off the bed and onto my knees.

Jed sank right down to the floor with me and tried to help me get up, but I smacked his hands away. "Do not touch me," I hissed.

"What damage, Freya? What are you talking about?"

"Stuff that doesn't concern you," I said. "But no man could protect me from all the bad things running around in the world, no matter how much he wants to, no matter if he thinks it's his job or not. That's just stupid, macho vanity. We all have to look out for ourselves, and I'm prepared to do that. I am fully prepared."

"Of course you can—"

"But not when I'm handcuffed to a fucking bed!" I yelled. "You made me helpless! How the fuck could you do that, Jed? How could you do that to me?"

Jed's hands fastened on my shoulders, squeezing, massaging. "Try to breathe slowly," he said. "I swear on everything that's holy, I will never do that again."

My bitter laughter turned into another coughing fit. "Oh, that's for damn sure. Fuck off, Jed Clearwater. Forever. Go to hell and stay there." I launched myself in the direction of the bathroom, and by some miracle, hit the door before my legs gave out.

Once inside, with the lock engaged, I held myself up on the sink. Not the best choice, because that meant I had to see myself in the mirror, which was a shitshow. My eyes had that gaping-windows-into-hell look, and I was still shaking violently.

I splashed my face, then closed the toilet lid and collapsed onto it, pressing my face against my knees and sobbing. Aw, poor Freya, all broken up because some man shoved her around. I should be used to it by now. I should be fighting back.

I should be fighting back.

The thought jolted me so much, it made me stop crying. I grabbed a wad of toilet paper and mopped up my eyes, blew my nose, and looked over at the small pink toiletries bag I'd left on the bathroom counter.

The BBBag, which I had taken out because I had been desperate for a toothbrush. I hadn't even considered the lethal spike hidden in the handle. It functioned perfectly well as a normal toothbrush, and I'd wanted fresh breath and white, squeaky clean teeth. Because I'd been obsessed with getting laid by that man. While I should have been thinking about getting even.

Well, halleluiah. I was cured.

I grabbed BBBag and scattered the contents out onto the counter, pawing through them, discarding this one, that one. I stopped on the pack of tampons, tucked in a pink flowered satin "modesty bag." I tore open the fluffy absorbent cotton shell of one of the tampons, prying out the tiny spray bottle I had stitched inside.

This design was my friend Rose's brainchild, my fellow badass bitch. Poor Rose was a much better human being than me, however, and she would be horrified to learn that I had actually brought this theoretical thing into being. During our tequila-fueled brainstorming sessions, Rose had told me many fascinating things about mind-bending designer drugs she was researching. Tamloxid 343 had shown promise as a treatment for chronic depression that did not respond to serotonin boosting anti-depressants, but the researchers had realized that at very high doses, involuntary truth-telling was an unexpected side effect. A possible interrogation enhancer. Big, fat can of ethical worms, torn wide open.

I'd paid a ton of money to have some Tamloxid 343 concocted for me. Super illegal. Just the thing for a badass bitch to have up her sleeve if lives were at stake.

That bastard was going to tell me the whole truth tonight. Even truths he might be hiding from himself. Chances were, I wasn't going to like it. My romantic fantasies were much more fun than the most likely truth; that he didn't give a shit about me.

And the worst possibility of all—that he'd betrayed Shane.

Seduction was the only half-assed plan my stressed out brain would suggest for getting this done. Mostly because it didn't require a great deal of thought, nor was it ever met with much resistance. But I did not feel seductive. I felt gutted.

Too fucking bad.

The tiny cylinder had a spray nozzle to push. According to my careful research, one quick pump should deliver more than enough for a full dose.

I took a swift look at myself in the mirror, and placed the slender bottle between my index and middle finger, practicing the swift, decisive flip-and-twist necessary to get the nozzle under my finger. *Zap.* Right in his face.

Then I slid it back and pushed open the bathroom door.

Jed stood there, standing at the window and staring out into the darkness. He turned to look at me, his eyes full of misery. It almost softened my resolve. Almost.

"I'm so sorry, Freya," he said. "I'll say it until my throat cracks."

"Your throat, not mine," I said.

"You won't forgive me?"

"Piss off," I said. "I've had a really horrible... how long was it? Four hours?"

"Three hours and twenty-three minutes," he said. "Never again. I swear."

I harrumphed. "What a lovely sentiment. Gee, thanks."

"Hey. Babe. Don't be that way."

"Actions have consequences, Jed."

"I was just trying to protect you," he said.

"By taking away all my agency and making me helpless? Don't do me any more favors, Jed. I don't think I'd survive another one." I sat down heavily down on the bed.

"It was the only solution I could think of to protect you from danger," he said.

"Bullshit," I said. "You were protecting yourself. Not me."

"Maybe you're right. But if you give me another chance, I'll do better."

I couldn't let myself look him in the eyes, or I wouldn't be able to go through with this. I'd have another sobbing, crying meltdown. All my nightmare memories would fly out into his face like a flock of vampire bats. And it would serve him right.

Jed sat next to me on the bed, and rested his arm on my shoulders.

There were two separate, distinct Freyas in that moment. One of them wanted to cuddle into his warmth. Wallow in his tenderness. Lean on his immense strength. A bulwark against all the bad, scary, hateful things running around out there. And there were a fuck-ton of them.

And there was the other Freya. Raging, vengeful, hurt. The pressure building up, up, up inside her, like steam, just about to reach the breaking point.

I flipped up the spray bottle, twisted—

But Jed's reflexes were lightning fast. His hands clamped down on mine, trapping the nozzle in the down position so it kept on hissing. Spraying everywhere.

Not a little tap. A long, long hiss. The drug came out in a cloud around us as we struggled. Two seconds—three—four, and I gasped in a big, honking chestful of it.

I felt the effects right away. The room wavered and distorted.

Proportions shifted and warped. The room swelled out, huge like a football field, the bed lost in the middle of it. I had become tiny, doll-like, in that vast space.

Jed's arm thudded down onto the cover next to my face. It felt like a tree falling.

"Poison?" His voice seemed distorted. Booming, but strangely far away.

I tried to speak. Tried again, and just barely got the words out. "Not poison."

"Then what? Knock-out stuff? Is someone coming for me?"

I shook my head, but was unable to lift it. "A truth serum," I whispered.

There was nothing to say but the truth. It was the only thing relevant or useful. Deceit wasn't worth my limited energy. Everything was put at the service of the truth.

Jed looked outraged. "Truth serum? I never lied to you."

"You handcuffed me." Anger gave me the energy to form words. "You tricked me. Staked me out. Left me alone in the dark. You *bastard*."

"That was a mistake. A fuck-up. Not a lie."

"Bullshit," I said. "Did you set Shane up?"

He turned his head and looked straight into my eyes. "Fuck, no," he said.

"There were fifteen million dollars deposited into an offshore account that I traced back to you," I said.

"Not mine," he said. "A set-up. Frame job."

"Fifteen million dollars? Just to gaslight us? Give me a break, Jed. That is one expensive prop. I don't buy it. Don't insult my intelligence."

"I'm not." His eyes burned with intensity. "I never had a brother. I never had a family that gave a shit about me, not before Shane and Ethan. They were brothers for me. The first family I'd ever had, and I wouldn't sell them out for fifteen million, or fifteen billion. I'd die for them. Or for you."

I stared at him, throat quivering. My eyes were wet. Not a great look for a steely-eyed interrogator.

This was my dream version of his confession. I craved these words from him. I'd gone to crazy lengths to force him to prove it, and now, even when he was stoned out of his mind on a huge dose of truth drug, I still didn't dare believe him.

He squeezed his eyes shut, cursing under his breath. "Jesus, this stuff is intense," he muttered. "How long do the effects last?"

"No idea," I admitted. "You held my finger down on the nozzle. I think we both got something like a triple dose. Maybe more."

"You must really want to punish me."

"I just needed to know if you're fucking with me," I said. "About what happened. The Ready Line massacre."

"I am not," he said. "It happened just like I said. I never lied. I tried to withhold some truths, sure, but that's useless with you. You're like a goddamn freight train." He rolled over onto his side. "This stuff is debilitating," he murmured. "I'm as weak as a kitten. Wouldn't it be fucking funny if Boer found us right now?"

I let out a snort of laughter. "About as funny as it would have been if he'd found me while I was cuffed to the headboard."

Jed's face contracted. He clapped a hand over his face.

"What, you think that's funny?" I asked, offended.

"No," he said, his voice muffled behind his hand. "*You're* funny. But that thought is really horrible. Not funny at all."

"Yup, you got that right," I agreed. "So tell me what happened, the night of the Ready Line massacre."

Jed's eyes went faraway. "It was an ambush. Shane and I were heading back to headquarters. We stopped at a downed tree, and I got out. Someone shot a tranq dart at me. I went down. When I woke up, I was upside down, and my face was stuffed into the exploded airbag of my car. I had been shoved off the bridge. The car was totaled, but I was still in one piece, maybe because the trees slowed me on the way down. I had to die in that car for their frame job to hold water, but the airbag worked too well, and I crawled away before they could get down to me and finish me off."

"Leaving you the only one still alive," I said.

"Except for Boer. He must have switched out his DNA in the database, so the charred body was identified as his. You met Boer. You know he's real."

"No, Jed," I told him. "I met a scary, murdering asshole in a mask who hates your guts. He didn't introduce himself."

"Fine. So it's my word against his." Jed's voice sounded exhausted. "The difference between us is, he tried to kill you, and I tried to save you. I can't prove anything. But I won't stop hunting him until I make him tell me where Shane is."

He sounded so real, so sincere. But just like always, I wanted this too much to let myself give in to it. He could make a fool of me so easily.

"I don't get it," I said. "I just don't understand. You cuffed me to a bed. How can you call yourself one of the good guys?"

"I don't call myself anything. I try to do the right thing, but I fuck up all the time. I've let down everyone I care about. I let that piece of shit Boer take Shane, I let him kill Franco and Bill and the others. I let him set me up like that and shove me off that bridge. It's a fluke, that I didn't die then. Things might have been simpler if I had."

"Don't you dare feel sorry for yourself, Clearwater," I warned. "You don't have that luxury."

"I got Mickey killed," he said, his voice bleak. "I got everyone killed, Freya. And then, surprise, here comes Sandee, the mystery babe, mincing around in those high-heeled boots, tits bouncing, painting a huge target on herself. I find out you're Freya Masters, and I'm like, far-fucking-out. I thought I'd hit rock bottom, but no. There's so much more damage I can do. So much further down I can go. I could get you killed, too. So I panicked, and tried to pin you down, so I would at least know where you were. It was stupid, yes. But hey, I never claimed to be a genius."

"Oh, shut up," I snapped. "I'm sick of it."

"Sick of what?"

"Your 'I'm just a dumb meathead foot soldier,' bullshit. Give it up, okay? I don't want to hear it anymore."

"Oh, I don't know about that," he said wryly. "My track record doesn't show any great trail of brilliance, Frey. So this last stunt with the handcuffs wasn't enough to convince you? You shouldn't be here with me in this shitty, insecure hotel room. You should be in Ethan's luxury bunker with Holly, guarded by his top-shelf private army of security staff. Where you'd be safe, goddamnit!"

"Yeah," I said sourly. "Living the dream. Locked in a bank vault. Yay, me."

"Don't you dare feel sorry for yourself," he said. "You don't have that luxury."

I narrowed my eyes at him. "Don't throw my words back in my face, wise-ass."

"Why not, if they fit? Come on, Frey. Don't be a baby. This is an emergency."

"It's been in an emergency all my life," I said. "At some point, I just have to pretend it's not, and get the hell on with it."

"I'd feel like shit if you got hurt. I'd do anything to keep you safe. Even if it kills me. Even if it makes you hate me. I'll pay that price if I have to."

"Don't you dare try to spin this into noble heroics," I snapped. "That's just self-righteous and annoying."

"I am in no condition to spin anything," he said wearily. "It's just the dumb, stupid, embarrassing truth. I've spent months in prison, and I have fuck-all to show for it. All I accomplished was another person that I genuinely cared about killed. So you made a fool out of me and a whore out of yourself, for nothing."

Normally, that would have enraged me, but in this weird

crucible of truth-telling, I couldn't be bothered getting uptight about it. "I wasn't whoring myself," I said.

He rolled his head around and tilted his eyebrow. "How do you rationalize that?" he asked. "I'm really stoned, Frey, so keep it simple. Use small words."

"Stop playing dumb," I said sharply. "That's a shitty habit."

"Coming from Sandee? What's sauce for the gander is sauce for the goose, babe. Don't get your back up about it. I don't judge you for trying to fuck intel out of me. I might have done the same, in your shoes, if I thought it would help. I'm just sorry for your sake that there wasn't anything in there to glean."

"I wanted you anyway," I blurted. "I've always wanted you. For years."

Jed's mouth fell open. He closed it after a moment, blinking. "Huh?"

"I'm sorry to make this weird for you, but it's the truth."

"But I haven't even seen you since you were a child," he protested. "I didn't even recognize you when I saw you as an adult."

"Adolescent, not child," I corrected. "Last time I saw you, I was fourteen. More than old enough to have naughty thoughts about the hottest guy I'd ever seen. I had a raging crush on you. I know I had frizzy hair and zits and a mouth full of metal, but my hormones were doing what they do, Jed. I know it sounds kinky, but it's the truth. Since we're doing truth tonight."

"Ah, damn," he murmured. "Weird. Makes me feel like a retroactive perv."

"Tough titties," I told him. "Suffer, bitch."

We stared at each other, and out of nowhere, we both dissolved into laughter and just lay there, snorting and choking helplessly in the blankets together.

"I don't know about this shit you dosed us with," Jed said. "Not much of a hardcore interrogation drug, with the two of us rolling around in the bed giggling like idiots. It seems more a recreational drug for a girls-gone-wild slumber party. Next up, pillow fight."

"Yeah, I think this stuff is experimental, at best," I agreed. "But me getting toasted right along with you was definitely not part of the plan. I was going to handcuff you to the bed and give you a taste of your own medicine. I was going to interrogate the shit out of you."

"Yeah?" Jed's eyes dilated, and a delighted grin spread across his face. "Wow. Cool. Did you have, you know, an outfit? Black latex? Stiletto heels? Red lipstick?"

"Don't patronize me, you oversexed son of a bitch."

"I love it when you're stern," he crooned.

That pushed us over the top again, even worse this time. The harder we tried to stifle the laughter, the worse it got. When the paroxysms finally petered out, we just lay there, facing each other, staring into each other's eyes, just drifting.

Such a strange, wide-open feeling. As if we were having a conversation without words on some level far removed from our conscious minds. I felt naked, intensely seen, as if my soul had its doors flung completely open. And he felt the same. I knew it, because I could see inside him. I could see all the way to forever. And it was beautiful.

Who knew how much time passed, in this strange floating state. I certainly couldn't track it, and I wasn't even capable of looking at a watch or a phone.

Finally, he reached out, very slowly stroking my cheek with a tip of his finger, with reverent tenderness. "Hey," he said. "Frey. Who's Aunt Jean?"

I flinched as if he'd slapped me. "What the fuck, Jed?"

He just waited. "Who is she?"

"None of your goddamn business!"

"I told you the truth," he said gently. "Now tell me yours. When I came in the door, you screamed this woman's name. Who is she? What did she do to you?"

I rolled over so my back was to him. I couldn't bear to be seen. It took me several minutes to come up with an entry point into that tangle of dark memories.

"Remember Sandee's mean foster parents?" I asked. "The ones who locked her in the basement?"

I heard his sharp intake of air. "Oh, shit! You're telling me that part of it was real?"

"Yeah, for some reason, I gave that same story to Sandee. I guess I figured it would explain her many character defects, all at once. I wasn't really thinking about what that meant for me. I was just trying to put together a believable personality."

"You succeeded," he said, his voice wry. "So, she was a relative?"

"Yeah. My aunt. Jean Winters. She and my Uncle Orren Winters. Jean was my mother's older sister, but they weren't close. Of course, you knew my parents died in a car accident when I was seven years old, right?"

He nodded. "Your brothers told me about that."

"A drunk driver," I said. "They went out to a blues festival. Never came back."

"I know how that is," Jed offered. "I was ten when my dad smashed up in his truck coming home from the bar. Except in his case, he was the drunk driver."

I winced. "I'm sorry."

He nodded acknowledgement. "So tell me about Aunt Jean and Uncle Orren."

I rolled onto my back, staring up at the ceiling. "We got sent to live with them after the accident," I said. "I was seven, Shane was almost thirteen, Ethan was fifteen."

"And they were both bad? This aunt and uncle?"

"They were terrible. Their house was a nightmare. Aunt Jean was insane. Being married to my uncle might have been what did it to her, but she couldn't have been too stable to begin with, to marry him."

"What happened with them?"

I blew out a long, calming breath. All of the giddiness from the intense closeness and the laughter had drained away, and the filthy, jagged garbage underneath was starting to make itself felt. "They were super religious, but in that toxic, scary way," I said. "They wanted to control what we thought. They hated us. The boys scared them, not that I blame them. Ethan and Shane were pretty scary. And I think Jean had been jealous of my mother, for being smarter, prettier, happier. So she hated us by reflex."

"Did they hurt you?" he persisted.

"Not at first," I said. "The situation with Ethan and Shane went south pretty fast. Uncle Orren had them accused of some stuff they never did, and got them locked up in a juvenile detention center. I tried to run away. When they brought me back, they chained me up in the basement. They left me down there in the dark. For days at a time. Weeks."

Jed looked at me in horror, but I was careful not to turn my face his way. It was hard enough, just staring up at the burnt-out lightbulb. Listening to the silence.

"Jesus, Frey," he said quietly. "That's horrific."

"Yes, it was, because then they got a taste for it. It was supposed to make me pray. Because I was such a bad girl, going straight to hell. Sometimes Orren beat me."

"Did he ever...." Jed's voice trailed off, afraid to ask the question.

"No," I said. "But I think he was working up to it. If he was down there with me alone, he would get that look on his face, and I'd start screaming for Aunt Jean. I figured, he wouldn't touch me if she was there with us. Even if she was hitting me."

"How long were you stuck in their house?"

I thought about it for a while. It had been so long since I'd let myself remember anything about that period in my life. "Maybe six months? They locked up the boys after about two months, and it took them about four months to break out of the Eagle

Crest juvenile facility. Then they busted me out. Longest four months in history."

"Your brothers never told me about that," he said.

"Yeah, they're still traumatized about it. They blame themselves. Macho idiots. They think they're supposed to be superheroes. Sort of like this other guy I know."

Jed smoothly ignored that. "So, that was a stress flashback, when I came in?"

"Yes," I admitted. "It's been a really long time since I had one. I was back in the basement, and I thought you were Uncle Orren. So I started screaming for my aunt."

"God, Frey. I am so sorry."

I turned and looked straight at him. "You should be," I said bluntly.

He looked pained, but he didn't push the reproof away. "Yeah, I know," he said. "So are they still out there?"

"Who?"

"Your aunt and uncle. Are they still alive?"

"I assume so. Why do you ask?"

"I have a few things I'd like to say to them," he said.

I shuddered. "I never want to see them again. I thought I'd put it all in the past. But they're still in there, fresh as ever. Locked in that basement room in my head and just waiting to pop out, like a Jack-in-the-box."

Jed seized my hand, pulling me toward him. "I never wanted to hurt you."

I was too wound up and tense to give in to his pull. "Nobody means to, unless they're a monster. It's just what people do. People hurt each other. Even the ones they love."

"You're the one I love," he said.

I opened my mouth, but had no words to respond to that. I started to shake. My face turned red, my eyes wet. My throat melted. Shivering too hard to speak.

I breathed carefully until I could control my voice. "Dude,

please," I said carefully. "You're under the influence of a massive dose of powerful, largely untested drug. Maybe hold off on the big declarations until you're straight again. It could get weird for you later."

"Don't push me away, Frey. Nothing will change. It's the way I felt before. I just couldn't get the door unlocked on my own. I needed you to blow it off with a shotgun. But it's open now. You're incredible. You rock my world. Tell me if you feel the same way. I know you can't lie to me now. Give it to me straight."

The words fell out. "I love you," I said. "I always have. I love you more now."

His eyes lit up, and he rolled on top of me.

Our bodies melted together, exquisitely attuned, yielding. We started shedding clothes. Unbuttoning his shirt, kicking off my shoes, unbuckling belts with breathless haste. Hungry to feel that sweet, shocking rush of hot skin against skin.

He jerked his jeans off, along with his underwear, and kicked them away. He helped me unhook my bra and fell back onto the bed, pulling me down on top of him.

I lost no time. The livewire rawness of this conversation was more than enough foreplay. I was desperate to have him inside me, already slick and soft and yielding. I petted myself with him first, sliding up and down, getting him wet with my lube. Then I nudged his cockhead between my pussy lips.

He gripped the base of his cock, holding it as I sank over the entire length of his stiff, hot shaft. Taking him in. All the way in. So full, so hot. So satisfying.

Jed clutched my hips, lifting me, dragging me close, and soon we had the perfect slow, surging, undulating ride established. Rising and falling. Deep, heavy strokes, like the slow, tender lick of a hungry tongue. Circling his thumb around my clit while stimulating that wild, live sweet spot inside me with his cock.

Driving me relentlessly to a long, pulsing climax that went on and on, until I was expanded, shimmering, liquid. Pure, shining bliss.

Jed slowly, carefully rearranged my limp body after, pulling sheets and blankets over me. He pulled me close, wrapping his arms around me. I pressed my ear to his chest, feeling the slow, heavy throb of his heartbeat under my cheek. Tasting the salt on his skin. I felt so safe and warm, wrapped in his strength.

Really? You drugged the man, you dirty girl. He'll hate you when he's clean again. He'll never trust you again, you dumb whore. Don't get too comfortable.

Jean's voice in my head. I pushed it away with all my strength. I did not have to listen to that poisonous bitch any longer. I would not let her pollute my good thing.

Whether or not she was right.

CHAPTER 26

Jed

Thud. *Thud. Thud.* Someone was knocking on the door, and the energy with which they were doing it suggested that they'd been doing it for a while. I usually slept very lightly. Whatever Freya had dosed me with must have been some serious shit.

I jerked up with a start, finding my legs wound in a tight twist with Freya's, my gun arm trapped beneath her head.

I carefully pulled myself loose, trying not to wake her, but she jolted upright, eyes wide, as I pulled my jeans on. "What? Who's that?"

Thud. Thud. Thud. Somebody was getting impatient.

"It's just someone at the door." I shoved the gun into the back of my jeans. "Stay right here." I glanced at the clock. 7:05 AM. I peeked out the kitchen curtains, and all of the air rushed out of my chest. Of course. This had all been part of my plan.

It was a square-built middle-aged woman in a uniform, hair dragged into a sparse, tight braid, with buckets, a vacuum, and case of cleaning supplies.

I had forgotten about my security set-up. I'd meant to call and cancel this request, but I had gotten blasted by a truth drug, and had gone down a rabbit hole.

One so deep, I'd probably never find my way out. Nor did I ever want to.

It was a damn good thing I'd at least cancelled that timed automatic email to the police last night while she was in the bathroom, before Freya drugged my unsuspecting ass. Wow, forgetting that little detail would have been all kinds of awkward.

I pulled the door open, wishing an instant too late that I'd taken the time to put on a shirt. The woman wore a name tag that read "Trina."

"Good morning," I said.

"Good morning," Trina said, looking me up and down with suspicious eyes. Her gaze darted anxiously past me, over my shoulder. "You called yesterday? Said you wanted the room serviced this morning, real early?"

"Yes, I did," I said. "Turns out we slept in after all. I meant to call and cancel the request last night. We got in a lot later than we anticipated."

Trina's face hardened. "You mean to say, you had me drag myself out of bed at this hour for nothing?"

"Oh, no. Not nothing," I assured her. "Wait here just a second. Hold on." I backed up so as not to show her the pistol shoved into my pants, and grabbed the two fifties I'd folded and stuck under the base of the lamp for the worst case scenario.

I handed them to her. "This is for you, and I'll be sure to tell the management how much I appreciate your willingness to collaborate. My final tip will reflect my thanks, as well. Have a great day."

Trina took the fifties, but her face was still troubled. I was a foot taller than her, but she strained up onto her toes, trying to peer around me. "Sir, is everything all right in there?" Her voice was tense. "Are you with someone?"

"He sure is, and everything is fine." Freya's voice was light. She elbowed her way past me, already dressed in her T-shirt and jeans, wrapping her arm around my waist. She smiled at Trina reassuringly. "It's just the two of us, and everything is absolutely great, but thanks for checking. That's very good of you." She gave me a sunny smile, and dropped a quick kiss onto my bare shoulder.

Trina nodded, still frowning but looking mollified. "Okay, then. So if you folks want to just call me to come and take your money again, feel free whenever."

"You bet, and thanks so much," Freya said warmly. "I'm so sorry we got you up so early."

Trina stowed her equipment in a hatchback Mazda. I turned to Freya as she pulled away. "What the hell?" I said. "Don't just pop out of nowhere without warning!"

"You were scaring her," Freya scolded. "You needed me to do my Chatty Cathy thing and make it all look normal. The poor woman probably thought something kinky was going on in the bedroom. Like, you know, somebody being handcuffed to the bed."

"Yeah, right," I said. "Or drugged against their will. Very sordid."

Freya cast a sultry look over her shoulder as she headed back into the bedroom. "If we were trying not to be noticed by the hotel staff, too bad," she said, sitting back down on the bed. "I think that ship has sailed."

"I didn't know what else to do," I said, defensive. "I needed to be sure you'd be found quickly in case Boer got a ping from one of the surgeons and had someone come after me. I needed to cover your ass. Everything comes at a cost."

"Isn't that the truth," Freya murmured. "Speaking of what things cost. I need to ask you a really embarrassing question, Jed."

I braced myself. "Okay. Hit me."

Her smile faded, and she looked down at her lap, twisting a piece of her sweatshirt. "So, would you say that you are, as of this moment, no longer in any way under the influence of Tamloxid?"

My mind took off trying to figure out where the fuck she was going with this line of questioning while I did a swift but thorough inventory of my body and mind.

"Yes," I told her. "I'm hung over, and I have a stiff neck, and a sour stomach, and probably my breath is really foul, but I'm in more or less my right mind. Or whatever passes for that on a good day."

A smile flashed over her face, but she didn't meet my eyes. "Okay, then I'll move on to the next question. When we had our talk last night, a lot of things were said. Bold, life-changing pronouncements. I just wanted to let you know that I'm, ah...not holding you to what you said. I mean, you were extremely stoned. It wouldn't be fair."

I felt my body go ice cold. My hands went clammy. I exhaled slowly, and chose my words with extreme care. "And the things you said to me?" I asked. "You were just as wasted as I was. Do you want to be released from responsibility for that too?"

She bit her lip. "Ah...not exactly."

"So what do you mean? Was it just the drug talking, for you?" My voice was hard. "I thought that shit was a truth drug. So I took you at your word last night."

"So, ah...how do you feel? About...us?" Her voice was small.

Fuck it. I just went for it. "I meant every last word I said," I told her. "I still do. More, even. A thousand percent. How about you, Frey? Did the truth drug work on you? Or are you just a better liar than I am?"

She pressed her trembling lips together. "I'm not a liar," she said. "And neither are you. I meant what I said. It was real for me. Always has been."

Thank God. I was so relieved, my knees sagged. I sank onto the bed and took a second to get my face in order. "So marry me," I said roughly.

Freya sucked in a sharp breath. "Are you serious?"

"Serious as death. If you're in, I'm in. All the way."

"But...but it's only been three days, and we're still running for our lives! It hardly seems like the time or place to make a decision like that!"

"Why not? I'm sure. You said you were, too, right?"

Freya's eyes were wet with startled tears. "Yes! It's just that from having really powerful feelings for each other to promising to get married...it's a really big jump."

She was not wrong. But I was so buzzed on that feeling inside my chest. So warm and bright and soft, this glow, as if the sun were rising right inside me.

I took her hand. So slim and strong in mine. "It is a big jump, but what the fuck," I said. "Let's take a run at it. We'll jump together. Maybe we'll get lucky and make it all the way across. We won't know unless we try. I vote for trying. Forever."

Freya's face was rosy and her eyes shone, glimmering with tears. But she wound her fingers through mine and squeezed. "Let's deal with Boer first, okay?" she urged. "With things so dangerous, it seems premature to, you know...pick out china patterns and argue about kids' names." She glanced up at me, warily. "You do want kids, right?"

"As many as you want," I said swiftly. "Bring 'em on."

She laughed at me. "Let's not get ahead of ourselves."

"What could I say that would make you less nervous?"

"I'm just afraid of jinxing it," she said. "Like I'm tempting fate by feeling this happy. It's bad luck to take anything for granted. Even this."

I nodded. That made sense to me on a visceral level. First, a guy had to slay the dragon. Then, he got the fair maiden. Then he protected her and stuck by her and hung on to her for as long as he possibly could. Preferably until death did us part.

"Yeah," I said. "First, we neutralize Boer."

"Yes. But the important thing is that we do it together." She squeezed my hand in hers, staring intently into my eyes. "We work together. Respecting each other's areas of expertise."

I narrowed my eyes at her, wary of a trap. "Ah...meaning...?"

"Meaning, we trust each other, Jed. As real partners."

"Only if you'll be reasonable about stepping back," I told her, resolute. "I'm the one with the combat training. And it's hard as hell to defend you and hunt Boer at the same time."

She nodded. "Okay. Just share your thoughts. Let me in. Like last night. I don't even know what happened after you left. Did you learn anything useful?"

"Yes, actually." I proceeded to tell her about my exploits the night before. Grifo's house, his practice, the Moulin Pastisserie. The gala, which would take place tonight. And Rachelle Grifo's lactose-free Neapolitan pastry.

"So the Grifos will be there," she said, thoughtfully. "Obviously, we have to be there, too."

"Clark and Ramona will not be thrilled to see me again," I said.

She gave me a disapproving look. "True. And I could have helped you with that last night, if you'd been thinking clearly. I could have asked all the questions and begged to see the colleagues, and I wouldn't have raised any red flags. Nobody gets intimidated by a chirping blonde. But oh, no, you had to swagger in with your brawny six-foot-three bod and your beard and your tattoo and your Viking warrior mane." She stopped short, studying me with a speculative eye. "We need to get some breakfast right away. We've got a big day ahead of us."

"Oh, do we?" I asked, alarmed. "A big day of what?"

"Shopping. You need a makeover. And then, we're going to the gala."

CHAPTER 27

"I still think you should have let me bleach it," I bitched, snipping at his hair. "It's another degree of removal from your previous look. If you think Ramona won't recognize you, even without the beard and hair, think again. Women remember hot men, even if they look scary. No, correction. *Especially* if they look scary."

"I'll try to avoid Ramona," he said.

"She'll notice you," I warned him. "Every woman in the place will notice you. The whole plan sounds haphazard with you in the mix. Let me go alone."

"I'm not letting you go anywhere alone." His tone was adamant. "Don't bother suggesting it again. I just need to drop that trace into his pocket, and then I'll get the hell out of there and follow him tonight. Find out where he's hiding."

"I'll put the trace on him," I told him. "Really. I should be the one to do that."

He made a disapproving growling sound in his throat, but he couldn't say I was wrong. It would be far simpler for me to get closer to Grifo than for Jed. Blonde cuteness combined with perky boobs, that was an unbeatable card, and I could play the shit out of that card when I wanted to.

"When did you learn to cut hair?" He was clearly trying to change the subject.

"I had two brothers," I replied. "Somebody had to groom them, or they would have looked like a couple of St. Bernards. I got pretty good at it, if I do say so myself. Okay, turn around and tell me what you think."

Jed twisted around and stared at himself in the mirror, startled. "Holy shit," he said. "That is...wow. My hair has never looked like that. Even before prison."

"It's excellent, if I do say so myself," I said, preening. "It's been years, but I've still got it. Of course, you can make an orange prison jumpsuit look good. But even so."

Truth to tell, Jed looked amazing. He had before, even with the beard, and that thick, wild mane of hair. But the crisp, elegant haircut was as good as any he'd get from a professional upmarket salon, and the smooth shave showed off every detail of his bone structure; his hawk-nose, his sharp cheekbones, his square, gorgeous jaw, his full, sexy lips, the thick, sweeping slash of his black eyebrows. Now, instead of a Viking warrior, he looked like a brooding, seductive movie vampire. Unfortunately, both of those looks were big attention-getters. But the man couldn't help being gorgeous.

Unfortunately, the cut also showcased his bruises and revealed more of his tattoo. But I had plans to remedy that. I'd gone hog-wild at the mall make-up counter.

"Go ahead and shower first," I told him. "Slather on that aftershave. Remember, tonight you are Jay Warren, a rich, ambitious, self-important businessman who thinks he is God's gift, with money to burn and tax deductions to claim. Here, try these on."

Jed took the rimless glasses I passed him, dismayed. "No way. I'll look—"

"Different," I supplied. "That's the word you're looking for. Give them a try."

Jed perched the glasses on his nose, frowning. "I feel ridiculous."

"Well, you look less like the hairy, threatening weirdo who scared Ramona and Dr. Clark out of their wits, am I right? That's the important thing. Go on, shower off the hair dust. I need time to do my make-up, and yours."

"Mine? What do you mean, mine?"

I hustled him off toward the shower, and laid out the evening gown I'd found at the mall. Shopping for tonight's event had been a challenge. I needed something that would cover my bruises, plus my scabbed up wrists, and still look sexy and elegant. A lot to ask of a dress, but I finally found something that ticked most of the boxes.

It had been a strange and wonderful day. For the first time, we were in what could almost be called harmony. We'd huddled over the computer and hacked together for hours, inventoried our stash of tricks, and come up with a plan, such as it was.

We'd gotten breakfast, shopped for phones and clothes and make-up and shoes, grabbed lunch, rented a car. We'd bought expensive tickets to the gala tonight under Jay Warren's name. We'd bickered and argued and analyzed and brainstormed every conceivable outcome, and I'd loved it. My brothers had always shut me out. Being on the inside was brain candy. Fizzy, stimulating fun.

So much so, in fact, that after our shopping trip at the mall, we returned to the cabin, tore off our clothes and tumbled into bed again, for another two hours. More pounding, melting bliss. I could never get enough.

Jed came out a few minutes later, and I lost a few minutes gaping at his clean-shaven, stunning nakedness. He'd be walking around with his own personal spotlight trained on him. He was going to attract way too much attention.

It made so much more sense for me to go to the gala alone. No one at the party had ever seen me, and I was a foot shorter. I would make far less of a stir. But predictably enough, he had laughed right in my face at the idea.

Jed took the tux down, tearing the plastic off the hanger, but I held up my hand.

"Don't put the shirt on yet," I said. "I need to cover that neck tattoo and your black eye."

"Is that really necessary?" He sounded pained.

"Absolutely," I said. "Grifo will be on the alert for a behemoth with a tattoo and bruises on his eye, and the haircut will only do so much. In any case, stay the hell away from Ramona and Clark. They'll know you in a heartbeat."

Jed sat with bad grace, flinching back a little as I got to work with my pots and powders and sponges. "Oh, stop that nonsense," I muttered. "Don't be ridiculous."

"It tickles," he complained. "And it smells funny."

But he held still long enough for me to get the job done. The neck was the easiest part, since it was just one swirl that curved up onto his neck. A little careful dabbing with my orange/red corrector and then a thick layer of high quality foundation did the job. The black eye was trickier, but I finally spun him around. "Take a look."

He frowned at himself in the mirror, leaning to study the eye, twisting to check out his neck. "Not bad," he said grudgingly. "Almost normal. If you're not too close. We'll be with a fuck-ton of plastic surgeons, though. They'll see something's off."

"You're not lingering or mingling, and you won't be hugging anyone tonight," I told him. "Just don't touch it. And try not to sweat."

I spent considerable time after my shower in front of the bathroom mirror, struggling with my hair. It was a challenge to backcomb and twist and pin the chunky blonde locks into something resembling a respectable up-do. Awkward wisps kept falling down over my face, but a crap-ton of aggressive teasing, hairpins, mousse, and choking quantities of hairspray finally got the job done.

Now for the make-up. I didn't hold back. The stress of the last few days had left their mark. I was pale, with shadows under my eyes, and that wild, manic glow, and my cheeks had a flush that made me look as if I had a fever.

My evening gown's best attribute was that it camouflaged my various injuries. I'd settled on a clinging charcoal dress of slinky knit with a subtle, glittering thread woven into it. It had a black velvet coat with long, sheer sleeves and a frill over the wrist. It showcased lots of eye-popping cleavage, and had more flash and glamour than I would've liked, since we were on a covert mission. A bland, forgettable little black dress would've been better, but every one I'd tried showed too much bruised back, arm, shoulder, or wrist. Too much skin exposed to fix with make-up.

I was surprised to note that my usual dress size was now a little loose for me. Stress, mortal danger, and grinding emotional intensity really burned it off a girl. God knows, Jed Clearwater certainly cranked up my metabolic furnace. I felt hot all the time with him. A drop of water that hit me would sizzle and hiss and turn instantly to steam.

A final slick of red lipstick, and I draped on some costume jewelry, also acquired at the mall. Glittering drop earrings. A big, sparkly pendant nestled between my boobs. That was about the best I'd be able to do right now.

I took a moment to center myself and to try to remember where my lungs were, and how they were used, since Jed often made me forget.

Then I opened the door and stepped out, and the sight of Jed in a tux fuddled me all over again. Holy freaking *crap*. Bells and whistles, dinging and whooping, alarms squealing, red alert, red alert. That man was so fine, he should come with a health warning. Everyone who laid eyes on him would remember him. Male or female.

"Looking good," I croaked out. I gathered up my skirts and emerged from the bathroom, spinning for him. "I'm ready for the ball. All I need are my glass slippers."

He was openmouthed. "Freya," he said. "You look incredible."

Aw. Sweet. I sat on the bed, reaching for the shoebox, but Jed sank to his knees in front of me and took my foot in his big, warm hand, transforming it instantly into an erogenous zone. I fought to breathe as he slid my foot into the shoe and buckled the delicate straps. "We should, um, go over the plan," I said, unsteadily.

"Absolutely," he said. "We get there late. We park in the service parking lot and slip into the back entrance where the catering staff parked their vans. We find our way to our seats without attracting attention. And when the lights are low, while they are speechifying, or dancing, or whatever the fuck else they do at these things, we cruise the place for Grifo."

"Separately," I added. "To cover more ground. And attract less attention."

He frowned. "But not far from each other. Ever. Got that? Always in eyeshot."

"Of course not. We locate Grifo, and then we look for an opportunity to get close enough to slip a trace into one of his pockets. We both have one ready. Of course, it should preferably be me, since I'll attract less attention. If a discreet opportunity presents itself, we try to talk to him."

"Bullshit you'll attract less attention," Jed scoffed. "You think Grifo would even notice I existed if he had you to look at?"

"Oh, come on—"

"If you're trying to be unobtrusive, I hate to break it to you, babe, but the Lady of the Lake outfit was not the right choice. That dress says, 'behold, mere mortal, as I lift the magic sword and draw down the lightning to open the door between worlds.'"

I laughed at him. "Don't be silly. It's dark gray, Jed. And I covered myself all the way down to my ankles and knuckles. This was the most drab, understated thing I could find in the entire store!"

"Drab, my ass. You look sexy and dangerous and memorable. Like you have garrote wire in your hair and a gun strapped to your thigh. And no underwear."

"Oh stop," I said impatiently.

"Perilously beautiful," he said, staring at my body. "I should've gone into the fitting room with you. Just to keep things real."

Aww. Sweet talk about how hot I looked was very gratifying. "Just as well you didn't," I murmured. "Picture it. Small room, locked door, wall of mirrors…"

His eyes lit up. The change of energy was so swift and intense, it made me laugh nervously. He reached for me, and I moved back "No way. It took me an hour to get my hair into this condition, and it's a house of cards at best, so don't even think about touching me. We do the job, and then we celebrate. Let's get on the road."

We weren't terribly far from the Pineview Resort. We'd spent the afternoon studying the floor plan of the place, so Jed drove without hesitation toward the service entrance parking lot. We parked in the shadows, and walked toward the building through the rustling trees. My heels clicked on the smooth granite slabs of the walkway.

I glanced at my brand new phone, and slid it back into my evening bag. "They should be about to serve dinner by now," I said. "I'll go in first."

"I'll be right behind you," Jed said.

I walked past the caterer's kitchen, letting Jed fall a few yards behind. They were in frantic busy-mode, so no one noticed me as I made my way toward the ballroom and found our out-of-the-way seats, at a peripheral table. Much better for our purposes.

We'd timed it well. The lights were low, and the orchestra played mellow, jazzy music as a halfway decent candlelit dinner was served. The food was not spectacular, but not bad, either. After the fruit plate, the room dimmed further, and a spotlight was trained on the speaker on the dais.

A tall, square-jawed guy with glasses marched up and gave a speech about the spectacular awesomeness and huge generosity of the talented surgeons who were offering their expertise to transform the lives of the less fortunate, yada yada. It was long-winded, fawning, predictable. Then they zeroed in with the spotlights on the various surgeons being honored for their contribution. One of them was Grifo.

I recognized him right away from the online images we'd pored over all day. I was closer to him, so I decided to approach him before Jed got close enough. I would be far less likely to frighten him, and I could always use my tits as a calling card, at least for the first couple of minutes. I would be Sandee for Grifo. Sandee was perfect for this situation. So unthreatening, so easy on the male ego. Besides, much as Jed tried to be inconspicuous, he had failed utterly. He looked stunning in a tux. Even the glasses set off his amazing bone structure that much more.

We caught each other's eyes across the room as I lurked near a column, not far from the band, waiting for my moment to pounce. Grifo was whispering to the brunette next to him. Black sequins, fake smile, lots of tension. Rachelle Grifo. I recognized her from online photos. She had a lot to be tense about, if she had any brains.

Grifo didn't look like the picture in his online profile. He looked thinner, grayer, older, with a strained grimace instead of a smile. He squinted in the spotlight as if it hurt him. Rachelle Grifo was younger than him by a good fifteen years. She was a good-looking, well-turned-out woman, but she still had that tight, pinched look, just like her husband. Her two young adult daughters were conspicuously absent.

They were announcing another speaker, a doctor named Coleman. The spotlight settled on a white-haired guy with a little trimmed goatee and round rosy cheeks. Coleman made his way with a bouncing gait up to the podium to give his speech.

Grifo's table was once again in the shadow. He leaned toward his wife, said something into her ear, and got up. He probably needed to take a break from being observed, maybe to cower in a bathroom stall. He was moving in my direction. Getting close to my entrance. I glanced at Jed, and moved smoothly to intercept him.

I stepped right in front of the doctor, breaking his stride so he had to stop short.

"Dr. Grifo!" I said, in a breathy whisper. "I'm so glad to see you again! Congratulations on being part of such a wonderful organization! You must be so proud."

"Thank you so much," Grifo said, his gaze dropping to my cleavage. "I'm so sorry, miss, but have we met?"

I batted my eyes at him. "Don't you remember? You did my breast lift, and my chin, and my eyes! My lids were so heavy before, but you fixed them so well!"

Grifo's eyes immediately cataloged all of the parts I had mentioned, trying to place me. "I see. I do have a very large number of patients, so I'm afraid I don't—"

"Oh, of course!" I patted his chest, and let the tiny trace fall into the breast pocket in his jacket, right behind the folded handkerchief that barely poked out of it. "There are so many grateful recipients of your talent, but only one of you, so of course you can't keep track of us all! But I'm so glad I ran into you here, because I'm desperate to ask you about a possible follow-up procedure. We never did my butt lift. At the time, we were only focused on the front view, but now that some time has gone by, I regret not getting it all done together, you know?"

"Well, now is really not the best time to—"

"But when I called your practice, I just got the runaround! I guess you're just too much in demand for a little old me."

"Actually, I've stepped back from the practice lately," Grifo's face was shiny with sweat. "But all of my colleagues are truly excellent. They can definitely—"

"No. They're not as good. No one is as good, and I won't settle for second best."

"That's very gratifying, but still, I can't help you right now."

I leaned closer. "I know about Wex Boer," I whispered. "Step out of the ballroom and go to the room at the end of the hall. We can get you out of this."

Grifo's face faded to a yellowish gray. "How do you know..."

"I'll tell you when we're there. Seriously. I'm here to help. Come with me."

I gave him a sharp tug, which made him lose his balance. He stepped out of the ballroom with me, but once in the hall outside, he chickened out, and started to pull away. "Actually, this really isn't the time or place." His voice quavered. "Let me take your number, miss. We will talk about this tomorrow, when I've have a chance to—"

"Five minutes," I insisted. "I'm not here to hurt you. We can help each other. I want Boer dead and gone. So do you. Five minutes, Dr. Grifo. It's worth it, to save your life, and your family's lives." I kept my eyes locked on his as I tugged him, trying to project conviction, sincerity and hypnotic intensity in equal measure.

The lounge across the hall was deserted. A velvet rope had blocked the door, but Jed had removed it.

I pulled Grifo into the dimly lit room. When he saw Jed, he shrank back. "Oh my God. You're that man. The thug who threatened Clark and Ramona."

Jed lifted his hands in a soothing gesture. "I never threatened anybody," he said softly. "I won't hurt you. Just listen to me. If you can help me take Boer down, you can get your life back. All of it. Everything will be just like it was before."

Grifo's eyes were rolling wildly between Jed and me. "How do I know you're not from him?" His voice was sharp with terror.

"You think you'd still be here talking to me if I was?" Jed asked.

Grifo cowered back, pulling against my clutching hand. "I need to go," he said.

"I don't know how to convince you," Jed said. "But we intend to wipe that motherfucker off the face of the earth. Thing is, we need your help to do it."

"I can't," Grifo said miserably. "He's watching me. He's probably watching right now. He'll kill my wife, my girls. Right in front of me."

"And this will be your life, from here on out," Jed said. "For you, Rachelle, Natalie, and Cecilia. Always with that sick feeling in your gut, always looking over your shoulder, waiting for the knife to sink in. Even if you run, that feeling will follow you. Every time your daughters go out on a date, you'll wonder about who they're really getting into the car with. Every time your wife goes to the spa, you'll wonder who she's going to meet in the massage room."

"Stop," Grifo pulled away. "Just...don't. Please."

"I can make it stop, if you help me," Jed said. "Together, we can take that bastard down. So he can't hurt you, ever again. And you'll be free."

"I should never have come to this goddamn thing," Grifo moaned. "I was trying to act like everything's normal, but it's not. It'll never be normal again."

"Yeah, all of you should've been on the other side of the world by now," Jed said. "But then, I wouldn't have been able to help. Look on the bright side."

Grifo's face was wretched. "I don't deserve to be punished like this. All I did was my job, damn it. I just worked on his face, that's all. Four different surgeries, the last one just four weeks ago. And I did good work. No one could have done it better."

"Yes, we know," Jed said. "You still have Mickey's flash drive, right?"

Grifo looked shocked. "What? How did you know...?"

"Mickey told me," Jed said. "You kept the flash drive because you knew you might need some leverage with that guy, right? You just didn't know how much."

Grifo's eyes were haunted. "Too much," he said, his voice hollow. "He's...he's a monster. The things he threatened us with..."

"I know," Jed said. "And if I'd been sent by Boer, I'd already be getting the location of that flash drive out of you with a long, sharp knife. But that's not me."

"Joe? Joe, who are you talking to?"

I jerked around at the sharp female voice from the door behind us. It was Grifo's wife, Rachelle. At closer range, I saw she was in her forties, but very well preserved. Having a cosmetic surgeon for a husband clearly had its perks. She'd squeezed into a sequined black sheath, and she would've been very pretty if her collagen-plumped, cherry-red mouth hadn't been puckered with anxiety.

She knew damn well her man was neck-deep in shit.

"Rachelle, I'm having a private conversation. Please leave. We'll talk later," Grifo said, but from his weary tone, it was clear she would ignore him.

"Who are these people?" she demanded. "What are you telling them, Joe? What do they want?"

I waded right in. "We want to give you a way out of this mess."

Rachelle's eyes widened. "Just exactly what mess are you referring to?"

"We know your family is in danger," Jed told her. "We've been fighting off the same man who's threatening you, and we're still alive. That's our calling card."

She turned to her husband. "I told you we should've run!" she hissed. "Weeks ago!"

"These things take time!" Grifo retorted. "Finding a safe place, getting ID, moving money around so it can't be traced—"

"Who cares about money? We'd all still be alive, right?"

Grifo let out a bark of laughter. "Oh, right. I'd love to see how little you care about money once you're in some strange foreign city and you don't have any!"

"Don't talk down to me, Joe—"

"I'm just trying to keep you all alive, and to achieve that, we have to act like everything is perfectly normal! So we attend the fucking gala! You keep on shopping, having lunch at the club, working out at the gym. The girls stay in school. If we start acting erratically, he'll notice, and we're dead! Think of the girls."

"I'm the only one who is!" Rachelle Grifo's voice was dangerously loud. "How did you get us into this mess! You got greedy? Is that what happened?"

"Me, greedy? Just chasing the lifestyle to which you have become accustomed, Shell." Grifo's voice had an ugly edge.

"Oh, so it's my fault, now? And now these strangers know our private business? This...this cheap blonde and this tattooed thug? He threatened Ramona and Clark!"

Cheap blonde? I choked back a peal of absolutely inappropriate laughter. This was so, so not the time to be a snotty bitch. Those two were teetering on a tightrope.

I barely caught Jed's swift eye-roll. "I didn't threaten anyone," he said. "They were very nervous, and they misinterpreted what I said. I swear, Mrs. Grifo. If I were working for Boer, and I had been sent to deal with you, we would not be having this conversation. The job would be done, and I would be miles down the road by now."

A terrified pause followed that statement.

"Ah...that is not reassuring," Rachelle said faintly.

"It wasn't meant to be," I told her. "We're here to help solve your problem, not to make you feel better about them." I gestured at Jed. "He is one of the good guys. And we are absolutely for real. Not some trick or some test sent from Boer. Boer has no reason to jerk you around, or play complicated mind games. The man's on a schedule."

"To do what? And who the hell are you?" Rachelle spun around to face me, her eyes wild and white-rimmed. "What the hell do you care what happens to us?"

It wouldn't be wise to give her the answer she richly deserved, so I jerked my chin at Jed. He had to field this one, or I'd get the woman's back up even more.

"We need the info your husband has on Boer," Jed said. "That's how we win."

Rachelle clapped her hands over her mouth like an opera diva. "Oh God," she moaned. "Joe, you idiot. You have evidence...? Oh, God. We are so dead."

The woman's whining was getting on my every last nerve. "Not necessarily," I said. "We're your ticket back to your real life. Your own life, here, with your house, your friends, your girls. They're, what, in college now?"

"Are you threatening my girls?" Her eyes were ringed with mascara smears.

"We're not threatening anybody, particularly not your girls," Jed said, with admirable patience. "On the contrary. If you give us the info that Mickey gave you—"

"Who's Mickey?" Rachelle shrilled. "What did he give to you, Joe? Why didn't you tell me? How can I trust you? Why have you been keeping secrets from me?"

Whoa, as if it needed to be said. The look on Joe Grifo's face made me feel almost sorry for the man, but we had no time for melodrama.

"Shut up, Shell," Grifo said miserably.

"I will not shut up! Goddamnit, I am so sick of your—"

"Stop." Jed's voice was not loud, but Rachelle cut off her rant, like a switch had been flipped. She stared at him, owl-eyed and gulping.

"There's no time for this," Jed said sternly. "Save it for when you're safe."

"We'll never be safe," Rachelle whispered.

"We can help with that." Jed turned back to Grifo. "Give me the data on Boer, and I will use it to neutralize him. In the meantime, I will provide a team of the most badass motherfuckers in the business, and they will guard your family night and day until the job is done."

Grifo's eyes look bleak, shadowed with exhaustion. He weighed his options for a few fraught seconds, and nodded. "Okay," he said. "We have a deal."

"Joe!" Rachelle exclaimed, in a screaming whisper. "No! You can't make that decision unilaterally! We have to talk. The two of us, in private!"

"I made the call, Shell," Grifo said heavily. "It's a done deal."

Rachelle overflowed again. I turned away, trying not to be a cat-bitch from hell. It was dirt mean to judge another woman for having feelings. She was suffering from chronic stress, and she was scared shitless. I knew how that felt, and I should cut her some slack. But for God's sake. Her husband was in deep shit, and she was not helping.

"I need the info asap," Jed told him. "Tonight."

Grifo nodded. "I can do that."

"You don't have it here?"

The man let out a mirthless laugh. "I don't carry it around with me, if that's what you're asking. I have to find a safe place for Shell and the girls first, and I want those badasses you talked about to meet them there and stay on them day and night until it's over. Preferably before I give you the flash drive. How long before they get here?"

"They should be in the city by six AM. They're en route now. I'll have them arrange to meet up with you as soon as they arrive at the airport."

"Joe, he'll kill us!" Rachelle sobbed. "You know nothing about these people!"

My eyes met with Jed's. In a flash, I knew we were both thinking the same thing. This gig would go down in the annals of Unredeemables history. Jed would be paying back favors to those guys for years to compensate for the epic ball-breaking they were about to experience from Rachelle Grifo.

Grifo glanced at his watch. "I'll meet you at three thirty AM. I'll text you the location later."

Jed pulled one of his burners from his pocket. "Take this phone. My number is the only one in it. Text me on that."

Grifo nodded, and slid it into his pocket. "We should get back to the party before people notice. Shell, fix your face. And stop blubbering."

Rachelle dabbed at her mascara-streaked cheekbones with her fingers. "I can't," she said, voice quivering. "I left my purse at the table."

I dug out a pack of make-up wipes from my evening bag. One of my mall purchases this morning. I would never be without make-up wipes for the rest of my life.

"I got you," I said. "Hold still." Rachelle flinched from my touch, but I persisted, wiping off the damage in a few swift strokes. At least she was trying to stop blubbering. Not success-fully, but she got points for the effort.

Grifo steered her out, and Jed and I stood there looking at each other in the sudden quiet after the door fell shut again.

"I wish his wife hadn't barged in," Jed said quietly. "I don't like the way this feels."

"Couldn't agree more," I said. "But we don't have time to second-guess ourselves now. Let's beat hell out of this place. These shoes are killing me."

Jed grabbed my hand, hauling me along as fast as I could totter. We made for the back entrance once again, and I was grateful for his arm as we hustled back to the car.

I pulled out the phone he'd gotten for me to check the time. "We should have time to get back and change into regular clothes," I said. "Of course, it all depends on where he sets the meeting, but the venue can't be too far. I want my comfy boots."

Jed took a long time to answer. "Frey," he said, in a careful tone. "About that."

My whole body contracted. I held up my hand. "Don't even start. Just don't. We've been through this. I thought we'd left it behind us. We act together now."

"We do, Frey. Always. But listen," he said earnestly. "You'd be safe in the motel. He doesn't have any way to find you there. But as soon as I go to Grifo's, I could be on Boer's radar. He has Grifo under surveillance for sure. It could be a trap."

"So? Why walk into it at all, if it's so damn dangerous?"

"We need that flash drive," he said. "It's the key to moving forward. But Grifo and his wife are weak links. They think they're doomed. They act doomed. So getting anywhere near them is bad luck. Let me do this part alone."

"If you go, I go," I said stubbornly.

"If something happens to me, you can keep looking for Shane," he coaxed. "You keep building on what we've learned, with Ethan's help. Shane has a better chance with you still out there, fighting, solving puzzles, being brilliant. This pickup is an errand any dumb grunt can do. There's no reason for you to expose yourself for this."

"Then you shouldn't expose yourself, either," I said. "You're no dumb grunt."

"This window of opportunity is about to close. Grifo is losing his nerve. He's about to bolt, or run to the cops and spill his guts, and my guess is, Boer will get him either way, and we'll lose Mickey's intel. Besides, it's time to loop your brother into this. Do it tonight while I'm gone. If Ethan saw me now, he'd shoot me in the face."

"I'll handle Ethan," I said.

"Tonight," he insisted. "While I'm with Grifo. Tell him everything. Tell him where you are. Promise me you'll do that. I don't like leaving you alone."

"So don't," I said.

He didn't answer. He didn't have to. He just drove, mouth tight, looking miserable. I just sat there, feeling the snarling dogfight deep inside me, tearing me apart.

Because he was right. I was being childish. My presence would certainly have been helpful yesterday, when he went to Grifo's practice, if he'd been smart enough to bring me. And it had made good sense for me to come to the gala. But for this meeting, I would just be tagging along because I didn't want to be alone. It would be much more practical and time-effective to hang back at the motel and get to work on Ethan.

But oh God, was it hard to swallow.

To his credit, he wasn't strong-arming me, as Ethan would have. That would've made it easier to spit in his eye and feel righteously pissed.

As it was, I just felt useless and small and scared. And abandoned.

Jed had the wisdom to leave me the hell alone as we sped through the dark. When we were on the loop road through the woods to the cabin, I finally spoke.

"Fine, then," I said, my voice small. "Go alone, if you want."

"You know I hate to leave you," he said. "You know how I feel."

"I get it. Just go, already." I hated my own bitchy tone, but couldn't control it. My choices were that, or tears, which was really no choice at all.

"You'll call Ethan?" he demanded. "You promise?"

"Yes, of course, but you have to promise something, too," I said. "Text me. Every twenty minutes. And let me put a trace in your phone."

Jed pulled to a stop in front of the cabin, and killed the

engine. "Seems a bit excessive." There was a hint of amusement in his tone, which annoyed me. "How about I just text you when I get there, and then again when I leave?"

"Twenty-minute intervals," I said, my voice icy. "Not one second more. Those are my terms, Clearwater. Read death in my eyes if you fail to comply."

"As you command, my lady."

"Oh, stop." I slammed out of the car and stalked down the gravel path to the cabin. Or tried to. It was more like a wobbling lurch. I wished I had invested more time in my tender youth learning how to function well in heels, but I had skipped those days at girly-girl school. I liked combat boots, fuzzy slippers, kicks.

Jed caught up with me by the time I pushed the door open. My face was hot, my eyes wet, and I must have had a raccoon mask to rival Rachelle. So I slapped his arm down when he made for the light switch inside the front door. "Leave it off."

He heard the tears in my voice, of course. "Oh, Frey," he whispered.

I flinched away as he tried to embrace me. "Don't. Please. I'm fine."

"You don't sound fine."

"Bummer for me," I said. "I just have to swallow the pill, and I can't pretend to enjoy it. So leave me to it and get gone."

"I'll be right back," he said. "Couple of hours, tops. Back before sunrise."

I laughed, bitterly. "Right. I've heard that song before."

He went still, blocking me against the door. "What do you mean? What song?"

I slapped at him angrily, wishing I hadn't touched that button. "Never mind," I mumbled. "Forget I said it."

"No," he said. "Tell me."

Oh, crap. There was no distracting him now. I could tell from his energy that he was going to hang on to this like a pit bull until I gave him what he wanted.

"Just me, carrying on about my trauma again," I said. "Alas, poor me."

"Skip the sarcasm. What trauma? About being left? About what happened at your aunt's house?"

I threw up my hands. "Everyone always says they'll be right back," I said. "Shane said that to Holly before the Ready Line massacre. Shane and Ethan said that to me before they were carted off to the reformatory. Mom and Dad said it before the blues festival. They all meant well, and you do, too, but it doesn't mean shit. No one can predict what'll happen. So just don't say it at all. Don't make promises you can't keep."

He jerked me closer, cupping the back of my head with his hand. "I'm in trouble, then, Frey. Because all I want in this world is to make promises to you."

I inhaled to speak, but my reply was trapped against his hot, sweet kiss.

CHAPTER 28

Jed

Every time I kissed her, that raging hunger possessed me. To know her, to understand her, to "get" her. And this time, to comfort her, even though it was the last goddamn thing I knew how to do.

I lifted my head, panting for breath, and the words just burst out of me. "I know how it feels."

"How what feels?" Her voice quavered.

"Being left," I said. "I get it. I do."

In the dimness, he could just barely make out her eyes. Her expression, the little crease of perplexity between her finely shaped dark eyebrows.

She threw up her hands. "Well, yes," she said, a little impatiently. "You were an orphan, like us, right? That was one of the things you and Shane and Ethan bonded over, back in your Army days."

"Yeah," I told her. "Did Shane ever tell you about my parents?"

"You told me about your dad," she said. "That he died in that accident when you were ten. I don't know anything about your mom, other than that she died when you were in high school."

"She left me a long time before that," I said. "To all intents and purposes."

"Ah." Her voice was low and careful. "And how is that?"

"Booze, mostly, but not only. The last few years, I supported us with the money I made working after school and weekends. It took her about seven years to kill herself, after Dad's accident. It's like, she couldn't be outdone by him. When she finally did herself in, I sold the trailer and her old beater car. I used the money to cremate her. Then I went straight to the recruitment center, and enlisted."

She looked as if she was waiting for more. "And?" she prompted.

I felt needled. "What do you mean, 'and?' That's not enough for you?"

"That's dry bones, Jed," she said gently. "Nothing about you."

Well, fuck me. "Whoa, sorry I'm not juicier," I snarled. "I don't give a shit about entertaining anyone. I choose not to think about it. That's my coping style."

"I understand," she said. "I've made extensive use of that coping style myself over the years. But what I don't understand is why you told me at all. Because this information does not help me. I don't know what to do with it."

"Maybe it's not about you, Frey," I flared. "You don't have a monopoly on abandonment, okay?"

She stiffened in my arms, pulling away. "You asshole! I never said I did!"

I hung on to her. "You act like it," I said. "So grow up."

"Fuck you, Jed Clearwater!"

She was inhaling to yell at me some more, so I just kissed her again. I was taking my life in my hands, and I knew it, but I couldn't stop myself. I was grasping for a lifeline. I was desperate, pleading, ravenous for some more of her sweet lips, her hot body, so lithe and strong and vibrant against mine. She was life, she was hope, she was my future. I had to protect that promise of a future somehow, or I was toast.

I was so grateful when she gave in and grabbed on. She held me tightly, nails, biting hard enough to draw blood, and kissed me back, fiercely, angrily. Our tongues dancing, probing, seeking each other's essence.

She turned her face away from my lips after a moment, gasping for breath.

"Damn you, Jed," she said, voice shaking. "Stop fucking with my head."

"I never invited you to jump into the middle of this cluster-fuck. That's on you, Frey. Own it."

"For a guy who wants to get lucky, you sure are being a huge pain in my ass!"

I grasped her waist and hoisted her up onto the edge of the big, heavy trestle table in the middle of the kitchen. "Then I'll use my mouth for a better purpose."

I pulled the bodice of her evening gown down with a tug, and what the neckline had been teasing all night came to pass. Her gorgeous tits popped out the top, and whatever she'd been starting to say disintegrated into a whimpering moan. I buried my face in them, worshiping them with my mouth, suckling, swirling with my tongue. Long, deep pulling suction around those tight little nipples, fingers stroking the full, plump curves, so hot and velvety and springy soft, perfumed with her scent.

She shuddered and sighed, clutching my shoulders. My body vibrated with need. I loved those low, whimpering gasps that jerked out of her mouth. I ached with lust, but I held back, because it had to be perfect for her. Every time had to be the best time. Every time had to surpass the last. That was the rule. Every time I touched her perfect body, I wanted to venture deeper into that dangerous but irresistible undiscovered territory that was Freya Masters. Infinitely dangerous, mysterious, complex, incredible. I wanted to live there. Explore it endlessly. That was what I'd been seeking, that would finally make it all come together and make sense for me. Yeah. That would be a life well spent.

I lifted her skirt, tossing up the mass of slippery fabric until I managed to slide my hand between her thighs, looking for the hot, secret sweet spots. She wore no stockings, just silken skin and tender dampness along the seam of her perfect pussy. I jerked the panties down, teasing and coaxing with my fingers until she opened for me, moving against my hand. Welcoming me into that sweet, wet warmth. Lifting and moving, hands clutching, showing me with every shivering wiggle just how to touch her, what she needed to get where she had to go.

I sank down and put my mouth to her. God, she tasted so hot, so rich and deep and inebriating. I licked around the tight little bud of her clit, sucking it carefully, sliding my tongue along the flower-petal folds, the sticky-sweet perfection of her pussy lips, caressing her with my hands. I wished the light was on, to better see every fine shading from pink to red to plum. I slid my fingers inside her, seeking out that secret magic spot that made her go wild, and whoa...yes. I found it. Oh *fuck,* yes.

She arched, writhed, crying out, and came explosively. Her hot, tight little hole seemed to suck on my fingers. It made my dick ache with jealous anticipation.

I could've done this for hours, but I was already late, and we were living on stolen time tonight. I lifted my head when the pulses of her orgasm subsided, wiping my mouth, and unfastened my belt. My dick sprang out, rock hard, desperate for action.

Freya had pushed herself up. She lifted her legs, wrapping them around my waist to clutch me closer. Grabbed my shoulders. Still panting. Still shaking.

"Now?" The voice that came out didn't even sound like mine. It was rough, scratchy. Shaking with need.

"Now." She tightened her thighs, pulling me closer.

"I love you, Frey." The words burst out of me as if they had to. As if they'd hurt me if I didn't let go of them.

She stroked my cheek. "I love you too," she said, her voice a shaky whisper.

We moaned together, foreheads touching, while I eased my cockhead with exquisite slowness into her slick, hot crevice. I loved that perfect moment when it met the clutching resistance of her body and then yielded, taking me in, like a clinging, lingering kiss. As I sank into her, I knew, for the first time in my life, without a single doubt, that I was in the right place, at the right time, doing the right thing.

Freya grabbed the lapels of my tux, pulling me closer. Letting out low, sobbing, wordless sounds as we sought out our perfect rhythm. Deep, sliding strokes, each thrust sweet, scalding perfection, following more perfection. Endless escalation. Every moment better than the last. There was no end to it. Just further, just deeper. Forever.

I kept it as slow as I could, but my self-control melted away as we merged into one wild, hot glow. The strokes grew deeper, more frenzied. We clutched each other closer, held tighter. The table squeaked and juddered, and the crashing rumble inside me grew. Something cataclysmic, that would change me for all time. No stopping it.

It overwhelmed me. Took me down. So far. So deep.

When I came back to myself, my face was pressed against the fabric of her skirt, and my face was wet. Damn.

I withdrew from her perfect body, reluctantly, grateful for the darkness. Dropped a kiss onto the soft skin between her breasts. Felt the throb of her heart, still racing.

"I have to change for the meeting," I muttered, and fled for the bedroom.

I felt as if I'd chickened out with that strategic retreat. But for fuck's sake, baby steps. I had never been good at stuff like this.

But I'd said those words again. *I love you.* They reverberated like a plucked string. I had to say it. Had to be sure she knew it before I walked away into God knows what. Just in case. No matter what happened, she would always know it.

My last words to my mother before she died were still ringing in my head. I heard them every damn day. Me, screaming at her. *Fuck you, you junkie bitch. Get out of here. Go kill yourself. You've been trying for years, so fucking finish the job.*

There had been extenuating circumstances, of course. She'd driven me over the edge for the umpteenth time. Once again, she'd found and stolen my meager hoard of cash, the one I'd saved up to pay the electricity bill, and used it for meth and a couple of gallon jugs of vodka.

Mom had taken me at my word. She'd gone to the closest high bridge she could find, and jumped off, to her death. Jesus, what was it with me and bridges?

I hadn't told her that I loved her. At least not since I was a dumb little kid who didn't know any better. But that night, she punished me forever, dying like that. Making damn sure I would never have a chance to fix it.

But I could learn from my mistakes. At least that.

CHAPTER 29

Freya

Brilliant. Miraculously, I had found a way to make this situation even worse for myself...by letting my legs fall open. The cherry on the sundae. Let the guy use his magic dick to churn me up into a total froth of wild feelings, and then, when I'm at the absolute peak of emotional vulnerability, whammo. That's when I get to watch him zip up his pants and walk away into mortal peril. Leaving me alone in the dark. Again.

Simply genius. Really, I just astonish myself sometimes.

I slid off the table and let the skirt fall. I tried to shoehorn my boobs back into the bodice for a couple of minutes before I realized how silly that was. The dress had served its purpose. It was time to take it off and put on something more practical. Jeans, a warm sweater, boots to run like hell in.

I had no idea what came next, but if Jed had his way, I wouldn't participate in it. Which was the story of my life. My two brothers were so fucked up by what had happened to me at our aunt and uncle's house, they'd been madly overcompensating ever since. Trying to keep me safe at all times, in all places. It was sweet of them, and I appreciated their anxious care as much as it annoyed me. Protecting me was a near-impossible task, considering who I am. But that didn't stop my brothers from trying.

Jed was doing the same damn thing. Maybe guys like him were all just wired up that way. Maybe that's how they all acted when they gave a shit. I had only my brothers to compare him to. None of my other boyfriends had ever behaved that way.

Of course, none of my other boyfriends had ever made the cut, either. Lightweights, to the last man. To be fair, I'd probably cherry-picked them just that way on purpose, for some reason known only to my darkest subconscious mind.

I got into my BBBag and pulled out the little pillbox that had the tiny trackers in it, so I was ready when Jed emerged from the bathroom. He was in black commando gear now, perfect for sneaking around in the dark, doing nefarious things. He had his new smartphone in his hand.

"Grifo texted me the location," he said. "An address out in Gresham. It's a forty-minute drive, and I'm meeting him in less than an hour. I should get going."

"Let me see that address," I demanded.

Jed turned the screen so I could see it. I committed it to memory, and handed him the tracker. "Load that up," I said crisply. "You promised. I've already entered the data into the app on my own phone. You just have to put in the trace."

He lifted his eyebrow at me, but got to work, prying his phone apart and inserting it without argument. "I'll take the car I rented today and leave you the Jeep," he said. "And I'll call the Drakes on the way and organize protection for the Grifos. You call Ethan and get him and his team involved. We need all hands on deck from now on."

"Yup," I said. "I will. First thing."

He put his phone away, and pulled out a six-shot snubbie. "I'll leave you this."

I recoiled. "You remember what happened the last time you gave me a gun," I said. "When we're all done with this, and we've won, I'll do some intensive training and get really good with guns. Until then, they're just another hard thing for a bad guy to bash me upside the head with. So thanks, but no thanks."

"Okay. But I'll hold you to that. About the training." He slid the gun back into whatever pocket he'd stowed it in. Then he grabbed my hand and kissed it. "Let's just claw our way to the other side of this," he said, his voice rough with suppressed emotion. "Then you and I can figure out who we are together without Boer breathing down our necks."

I kept my voice light. "Fingers crossed. Get on with it, then. Just text me every twenty minutes like you agreed. And set a timer to remind yourself. A vibrating timer, of course. I don't want to get you killed."

He tapped his phone, and held it up to show me the timer app, already programmed. "It is done, your Majesty."

I tried not to snort and roll my eyes, but failed. Jed just grabbed me, squeezing me close, and giving me another one of those sweet, breath-stealing kisses.

"Talk to you in exactly twenty minutes," he said. "And I sent you the phone numbers of the Drake brothers. Ethan has them, too. Anything happens, anything at all, you call them, first thing, got it? And call your brother, right now. Call everyone."

I was holding myself together by sheer brute force, trying to keep from shaking apart into tears. "You're starting to repeat yourself," I said tartly. "Just get gone. The sooner you go, the sooner you'll be back."

He backed away a step. "I love you, Frey," he said. "Before, I was okay with there not being anything on the other side of this whole thing. I thought, if Boer ended me, whatever. No big deal. That's not true anymore. Now, I want it all. I want you."

"Me too," I said, in a tight voice. "I love you too. But the stakes are really freaking high, and I'm all wound up, so I just can't let myself get mushy right now. Or I'll break."

He made a move as if he were going to touch me again, but I flinched back. "Go on, now. Please. You're just making it harder."

He turned away without another word and jogged off into the darkness.

The car he'd rented that day hummed into life. Headlights sliced through the trees, flickering as he accelerated away. He circled the bend, and the light was gone.

I had a brief meltdown, since he wasn't there to see me, but I got it under control quickly. I headed for the bathroom, swiftly showered off the crunchy helmet of hairspray, and swabbed off all the make-up. I put on the regular clothing we'd bought for me today, jeans and a thick, warm sweatshirt. Then I combed my wet hair back behind my ears, and that was it. No reason to wait any longer.

I dug into the stash of burner phones we'd bought today. It was an obscene hour to call my brother, but who cared. Of course, my oldest brother slept with his phone by his pillow, being twitchy by nature. He picked up instantly. "Who the fuck is this?"

Yep, that was my bro for you. "Hey, Ethan. It's me." I braced myself, and not a second too soon, because he lit right into me, with all the savagery I had fully expected from him.

"Where the *fuck* have you been?" he roared. "Why haven't you been answering your phone? I've been looking everywhere for you! I'm up in Seattle right now, grilling all of your friends, and they're all fucking useless! Did you think Holly didn't have enough to cry herself to sleep about without losing you, too?"

"She hasn't lost me," I soothed. "Listen up, Ethan. I don't have time for the lecture right now. I need to convey a lot of information very quickly, and then I need your help, and fast. Along with all the Unredeemables you can pull together. Right now."

"Frey? What the fuck are you doing?" His voice was soft with disbelief.

"I'm with Jed Clearwater," I said.

"You're...where? With who? The Jed Clearwater who sold your brother for fifteen-fucking-million dollars?"

"Ah, well. About that. He didn't, actually," I told him. "I tracked him down, after he disappeared a few months ago—"

"And never told me what you were doing."

I knew my brother well enough to feel the volcano rumbling, about to blow, but all I could do was press doggedly on. "Uh, right. Sorry about that. He was using a different name, and he was in prison, undercover, trying to make contact with a guy who could give him dirt on the person who did sell Shane. Wex Boer."

"Oh, for the love of God," Ethan snarled. "Boer's dead, Frey! His death was officially confirmed, using dental records and DNA analysis! Clearwater is playing you. He's an excellent liar. He had me fooled for years. He fooled Shane, too."

"But it's not true. Boer isn't dead. He faked his death."

"Yeah? Really? Is that what he you told you?" Ethan's voice had that dismissive, talking-down tone that always drove me mad.

"He didn't have to tell me," I said. "I met Boer myself. He tried kill me twice. I'm only alive because of Jed."

That startled him into silence, but the satisfaction was all too brief. "Where are you, Frey?"

His voice had gotten detached. He was in get-it-done warrior-mode.

"Later for that," I said. "Do you want to hear what's happening, or not?"

Ethan kept his mouth shut for the time it took to tell him the essential, abridged version of the tale, without spilling that I was wildly in love with the guy. But I might as well not have bothered to omit any details. Ethan Masters had many terrible character traits, but being unobservant was not one of them.

"Tell me something, Frey," he said, when I wrapped it up. "Jed knew that we suspected him. The evidence was stacked up against him before he disappeared into thin air. So how is it he ever agreed to see you at the prison in the first place? It seems like a piss-poor idea on his part. Pretty stupid, actually, and that guy never struck me as stupid."

I hesitated briefly. "He, ah...didn't know it was me."

"Come again?" he said, blankly. "How..."

"I'd created an alter ego," I explained. "I've been growing her for months. Her name was Sandee. She was one of those girls who fall in love with convicted felons and court them while they're behind bars. I changed up my looks, bleached out my hair, dressed differently, made myself up. And went to see him. He had no idea it was me."

"Why?" Ethan sounded shocked. "To what end? That's senseless, Frey."

"I wanted to get under his guard," I said. "I hoped to get him to spill some sort of information that could help our search for Shane."

Listening to myself, it sounded crazy in retrospect. Hell, it had sounded crazy even in forward-spect. But this was no time to fuss about my poor choices.

"And you say he didn't recognize you?"

"Nope. He hadn't seen me in years. And I was dressed, ah... differently."

"Differently how?" Ethan's voice changed.

"What does it matter?" I snapped. "He didn't know it was me. End of story."

"That's batshit, in addition to stupid," he said. "So let me get this straight. He starts a prison riot after getting this poor guy chopped up in the bathroom, cuts through an electric fence, and comes to your hotel to defend you from Boer's goons. And then he drags you off to a secluded cabin, to what purpose? And he's still thinking you're an airhead piece of easy ass who gets off on felons who are doing hard time. Right?"

I was too flustered to think of a good comeback. "Ahhh..."

"What happened in the cabin, Frey? Did he fuck you?"

I hesitated for a fraction of a second too long. "I, ah…"

"Goddamn him," he hissed. "That piece of shit. I'll kill him. No. First, I'll hurt him. Then I'll kill him."

"No," I said sharply. "You will do no such thing. It's not like that."

"Yeah? How is it, then?"

"I came on to him," I told him. "I made the moves. Not him."

"Oh, I bet he put up a big fucking fight," Ethan fumed. "What he did can't be defended. But you? Damn, I know you're stubborn and independent and wired up kind of strangely. But I really never took you for a brainless slut."

That stung, but I pushed it away. No time to get my little feelings hurt. "It's not like that," I repeated, through clenched teeth. "We're together."

"Define together," he said harshly. "You mean, still fucking?"

"Together forever," I blurted out. "For real. In love."

Ethan was silent for several horrified seconds. "Oh God," he muttered. "This is worse than I thought. He's brainwashed you. You've lost touch with reality."

"And you're not paying attention," I said impatiently. "Who I'm fucking or not fucking is irrelevant. Jed and I are trying to pin down Boer, and I'm trying to loop you in. Do you want to participate? Or do you want to keep rolling on the rug and throwing your tantrum? I can just hang up right now. The only reason I haven't is Shane."

Ethan was silent for a minute, and when he spoke again, his voice was softer.

"Hey," he said. "Frey. I know how much you miss him. How badly you want to find him. And I didn't want to tell you this, because I don't have any hard proof yet, and I don't want it to be true. But there's no reason to think Shane isn't dead. And there are a fuck-ton of reasons to think that he probably is."

That was a slam to the gut. I flopped down hard on the bed, hoping I wouldn't have to race into the bathroom to vomit.

I finally managed to get the words out. "Why didn't you tell me?"

"I didn't know how to say it." His voice was bleak. "I tried, but something always stopped me. I just didn't know what to say. Not to you, or to Holly. I was waiting for more solid proof, but I guess it was just an excuse not to face up to it."

Tears streamed out of my eyes, so I pressed my sleeve to my face. I didn't want to burble soggily when I spoke to him. "So, how did you come to that conclusion?"

"The dummy code. Our security protocol. There's an eight step process to find SmokeScreen on the dark web. And an alternate dummy code, just in case."

I gave up and went looking for tissue to soak up the tears. "How does it work?"

"We hypothesized a situation in which the user is being coerced into handing over control of the algorithm," Ethan said. "Say, someone's torturing a loved one right in front of you, etc., etc. So I wrote two different modalities. There's the straightforward one, where you freely use SmokeScreen's capabilities, and the other one, which has a different but equally complex access code. It appears to open up the algorithm, and it appears to function normally, but it also gives the prime user, in this case me, full access to the computer of whoever's running the program."

"I see," I said. "So, if Shane had been compelled to open the algorithm, you would've known instantly where he was, and been able to hack his computer."

"Yes," Ethan said. "I would've been crawling down those motherfuckers' throats instantly."

"But...he hasn't."

"No. I've been waiting, and hoping, and so far, nothing. He hasn't opened up that security hole for me to jump through and save him, and the two of us designed it together. I can't think of any reason on earth he wouldn't reach out to contact me with the dummy code. Except for the one, awful reason. The one I don't want to accept."

I swallowed multiple times to calm down the quiver in my throat. Now was not the time to get emotional. "I wish you'd told me all of this before."

"The less you knew, the safer you were," he said. "Shane got into this mess because I told him about SmokeScreen. I let him use it for Ready Line. He thought he could keep it under wraps. That it could be his and Jed's secret weapon. That was my big shit-for-brains moment. I should have buried it long ago. It's too powerful. It's the fucking kiss of death, and it would be for you, too."

"You still don't know if Shane's dead," I said. "Not yet."

I heard his sigh through the phone line. "Frey. I'm sorry." His voice was sad.

"Don't you tell me you're sorry," I said sharply. "You still don't know, not really. So until you're sure, don't say it. We have to keep hope alive. Also for Holly."

Ethan didn't answer, and the silence from the other end of the line made me incredibly anxious. And angry. "If there's a way to launch SmokeScreen with a dummy code, you should teach it to me," I said. "I'm safer if I know it, right?"

"Fuck, no," Ethan said savagely. "You'll be safer when you're here where you belong. I'll send Cade and Eli to come and get you, and you will stay here with Holly, under guard, until this shit is handled. So for the last time, Frey. Where are you?"

I let out a careful breath. Damn. I just loved the guy with all my heart, but he was a huge pain in my ass. "Your help would've been really nice to have," I said quietly. "But not at that cost. I'll call you later, big brother, when I have news. Bye."

"Frey! Don't you dare hang up on—"

I broke the connection, turned off the phone, and pried out the battery, since I didn't want my brother to hunt me down and start throwing his weight around. He was not beyond using physical force to compel me, as I knew already, to my cost. And I was not in the mood for any more posturing male bullshit.

Jed was enough to deal with. If I had to hear Ethan mansplain and beat his chest, my head would explode. Ethan could only be called as a desperate last resort.

Men had their uses, but sometimes they just seemed so damn limited to me. So hormonally hopped up. At least the ones in my family were, and Jed was neck and neck with Shane and Ethan when it came to being insanely protective and controlling.

I took out the smartphone I'd purchased today, to communicate with Jed, and checked it. *Ping*, there was his message, arriving right on time. The first message was contact info for the Drakes. The text that came after was short but sweet.

ten minutes out. love you. later.

I texted back.

love you too.

So far, so good, but damn. Pacing the floor sucked. And now I had to do it while processing this new, unwelcome information about Shane.

The dummy code, never activated. The ominous, heartbreaking silence.

Maybe I'd have been better off not knowing. Letting Ethan protect me from the truth. But that was just babying myself. Prolonging the agony. It was a bitter pill, but if my brother could swallow it, I could too.

But I would never stop looking. The Masters were stubborn as hell, even in the face of death.

CHAPTER 30

Wex Boer leaned back in the passenger seat of the SUV, scratching idly at the healing scars on his jaw. He and Nicole stared intently at the small screen that monitored Grifo's secret hideaway. Secret, hah. For a talented surgeon, the man really was staggeringly stupid sometimes. He had been in his choice of a wife, and his two simpering daughters didn't strike Wex as the sharpest knives in the drawer, either.

Not that he was complaining. It made his task easier. Boring as shit, but easier.

They heard the sound of doorbell ring on the audio. Nicole jerked her head around, startled out of her sullen reverie. "Is that him?"

It was good to hear a little energy in her voice. Nicole had been sulking ever since that shitshow at the cabin near Kalaharee, and he was sick of it. Almost tempted to just remove her from the playing board. It made sense to reduce the number of people who got a piece of the final take. Nicole had made it clear that she expected fifty percent of the haul when they got control of SmokeScreen and the billions started rolling in. She thought it was her due, for presenting the idea, working out all the details. But none of it could have happened without his muscle, his resources, his infrastructure, his inside position at Ready Line Security. He'd served in the Rangers with Clearwater and Masters, and they had trusted him enough to work with him, even if they never did invite him into their fucking elite private club.

The Unredeemables. Affectatious assholes. Not that he'd wanted to be in their stupid-ass secret society. Dumbfucks. Thought they were better than him. Always had.

He was the real player, here, with the real power. Nicole was just a concubine who doubled as a secretary. At least, she had been before. Lately, from being a seductive-sex pot up for anything, she'd become a dead-eyed robot girl with a pallid, scabbed-up face and unsightly bruises. Boring.

Then again. She was smart, ruthless, and on a good day, beautiful. When she was in top form, she was an amazing asset. It was still too soon to eliminate her.

Wex concentrated on the screen. Grifo was rushing around inside the house, freaking out, like the powderpuff asshole he was. Grifo disappeared from the screen, and reappeared moments later, followed by Clearwater.

Nicole lifted her phone, upping the volume. "...know yet where Rachelle and the girls are staying," Grifo said, his voice tight and thinner than usual. "Can you get the bodyguards in place tonight?"

"Tomorrow morning, early," Clearwater said. "The team is flying to Portland now. I'll brief them as soon as they arrive, and we'll get things in order right away."

"Hurry," Grifo bleated. "Please. Just hurry up with that."

"As soon as possible." Clearwater assured him. "Do you have the info?"

"Right here." Grifo pulled a small silver flash drive from his pants pocket. "Bank account info, photographs. Data from the lab where the DNA and blood samples are kept. Other stuff, too. Financials that only Mickey understood."

Boer sucked in a breath. "That lying prick was going to fuck me up. Maybe I will take his wife and daughters. Just on principle. Have fun with them while he watches."

"We don't have time for you to punish everyone who bugs you, Wex." Nicole sounded bored. "Shut up and let me listen."

He disliked her tone, but she had a point. They were on a tight schedule, and besides, punishing Rachelle Grifo would be tedious. He'd much rather punish Freya Masters. He'd bet good money that uppity little cunt wouldn't be tedious at all. He'd get lots of fight out of her, lots of sass. She'd be all kinds of juicy fun.

Jed Clearwater's response to Grifo was inaudible, but the flash drive went into the pocket of the man's black jacket. They shook hands.

"It's time," he said.

"I know." Nicole's voice sounded faintly annoyed. She was already opening the app on her phone, and checked the settings. She activated the gas, which began silently blasting out of all vents in the room.

The bar display on the phone app showed the concentration of soporific gas in the room rising quickly. Grifo was the first to react. He staggered, catching himself on the back of one of the couches, even though Clearwater was actually closer to the nearest vent the gas was coming from. Predictable.

Ever since their Ranger days, the bastard had been boot-leather tough in any conditions. Heat, cold, dry, wet, noise, dark, nothing took him down. Fucking Unredeemable. Thought he was such a fucking hero, up on his high horse.

He'd die knowing he was nothing more than a worthless piece of shit.

Grifo was now sprawled on the floor, only his ass currently visible in the camera. Clearwater was visibly sagging too, but still looking around for the camera that he knew had to be there. He would never see it. The Grifos certainly never had.

"You always were a sneaky little prick," Clearwater said, very clearly, as he thudded down to his knees, behind the couch, and then pitched over, out of sight.

He grabbed the two gas masks and handed one to Nicole. "Let's go. Hurry."

"What's the big hurry?" Nicole said. "We have at least twenty minutes, and that's a conservative estimate."

"This is Jed Clearwater," Boer said. "He's like a fucking cyborg. Drive up as close to the front door of the house as you can get. He's heavy. The less distance we have to drag him, the better."

Nicole drove swiftly out of the concealing foliage and up onto the driveway. She pulled up behind Grifo's SUV. They put on their gas masks, and pushed the door open.

Clearwater lay behind the couch, eyes still open, amazingly. Still conscious.

He stared up at Wex as he approached, blinking. His eyes watered. Wex aimed a hard kick to his ribs as Nicole wrenched his arms back and cuffed him.

"Hey, fuckface," Wex said. "I'm going to get that Masters girl. I'll make her scream like a little bitch. It'll be very relaxing for me, after the stress you put me through. Maybe I'll even let you watch. Think you'd like that?" He reached down into Clearwater's pocket and pulled out the flash drive, waving it in front of the other man's face. "You're going to tell me where you stashed her. Don't think you won't. Everybody breaks eventually."

Clearwater was gasping for breath, but his lips drew back, his teeth showing in a thin, dangerous smile that said everything without words. Arrogant fuck.

Nicole was busy securing Clearwater's feet, so he left her to it and strolled over to where Grifo lay sprawled, his face squashed into the parquet floor. Out cold.

Wex looked over and saw Clearwater staring at him. Trying to speak, but failing. Just conscious enough to look horrified. Small pleasures.

"You know something?" he said. "I would've let the stupid

fuckwit live, if you hadn't gotten yourself mixed up in it. So this one's on you, Clearwater." He raised his gun.

Bam. Grifo's body twitched. A pool formed behind his head on the wood floor.

Wex watched it spread as Clearwater lost consciousness. At last, that arrogant bastard would learn who was boss. Not that it would do him much good now.

It was far too late for that.

CHAPTER 31

Freya

Jed was late, goddammit. Late twice over.

I'd let the first one slide without panicking, figuring that Jed had been in the middle of some tense negotiation with Grifo. That he would of course have silenced his phone for that, to focus on what he was doing, and who could blame him.

That hypothesis was borne out by the trace on Jed's phone. It was still at the location Grifo had sent them. Jed's icon had not moved. For over an hour.

The second deadline slid by with no call. My fingernails started digging into my palms. My own messages to him were starting to pile up.

> Hey

> U r late

> We talked about this

Then, a few minutes later,

r you talking to Grifo now? Dude, catch me up.
For fucks sake.

The next appointment came and went. I texted, despairingly,

???

Jed please oh please

There was no point in writing after that. Not until he responded.

I knew what Jed would say. The smart, self-protective woman I was supposed to be would call Ethan, bleating for help and protection. She would huddle under her overbearing brother's ironclad protection, and let Ethan and his team take over, and find out what had happened at Grifo's forest hideaway.

That woman was not me. That woman would probably make a lot fewer enemies, and live a much longer, more peaceful and productive life, but fuck it.

Full speed ahead. It's not like I had any choice.

I put on my coat, wondering if I should load up with my Badass Bitches bits and pieces. They all seemed too fussy, too femmy. I wish I'd accepted the gun when Jed offered it. It wasn't stealthy, or clever, but damn, it was effective. But what I had told Jed was still true. I had no business hauling that thing around with me until I learned how to use it.

I took off in the Jeep, trying not to speed. My foot was incredibly heavy on the accelerator tonight, but the last thing I needed was to explain myself to a state trooper.

I made the trip to the location on my phone monitor in slightly under forty minutes. I cut my lights far from the house, bumping off the road into lumpy grass and coasting quietly down the slope toward the house, winding through the sparse trees.

There was a light on inside. Jed's car was nowhere to be seen, but he might have hidden it, if he was still here. There were two other cars as well.

So quiet. No sound other than the rustling of the wind in the trees. I tiptoed closer, picking my way over the uneven terrain, using the limited light available from the windows. The door was slightly open, and as I crept up the stairs to the porch, I heard a sound. A wet, pathetic little sobbing sound. Like a small child whimpering.

I pushed the door open with my elbow, and sidled inside.

A man's body was stretched out on the floor in a pool of blood. Not Jed. A woman was crumpled up on the ground next to him, sobbing.

I walked inside. She didn't hear me. Didn't move. "Rachelle," I said.

Rachelle shrieked, and scrambled to her feet with her hands up, stumbling and swaying. Her face was distorted, mouth stretched wide with helpless sobbing, blood smeared on her hands "Y-y-y-you!" she gasped out. "You got him killed! We would've been fine if you hadn't come, messing things up!"

Well, that was a classic. It was easier to blame us for everything. I ignored her as I circled the room, looking for signs of Jed. "What do you know, Rachelle? What happened here? Where is Jed?"

"I don't know and I don't care! I just found Joe. He killed my Joe!"

Then I heard it. That almost inaudible buzz of a phone, vibrating against something hard. It was time for Jed to call me, and the timer app was reminding him.

It took a few minutes of searching, and Rachelle was babbling hysterically the entire time, but I couldn't focus on what she said. Behind the couch, the sound was slightly more audible, but I still saw nothing.

I crouched, peering under the couch. There it was. I slid my hand under, nudging out Jed's smartphone. I entered his code, which he'd given to me when we bought the phones, just as I had given him mine. The phone was already open to our chat, and a message glowed on the dialog box, still unsent.

gas love u sorry run run ru

Gas. He'd been overcome by gas before he could even send it.

Terror slammed into me. Grief. I could see so clearly now, how much I loved him. How beautiful and gallant and brave and fine he was. All that wonderful, shining excellence of a man, wasted. For spite and meanness and greed.

I was so angry. A different person, now. One who could do desperate, cruel things. One who was capable of shocking, ruthless behavior. One who could kill.

I pocketed Jed's phone as I stood, and took a few steps toward Rachelle, who was still hunched over her husband's body.

"This wasn't supposed to happen," she sobbed out. "This is all wrong!"

Wrong? Hell of an understatement, from a woman weeping over her husband's bleeding body.

My mind took all the pieces, spun them around, looking for the pattern.

Gas, Jed said in his message. Which meant this house, which was supposed to be the secret hideaway, had been carefully prepped. And the Grifos were pussycats. Not hard for Boer to manage. Gas was a tool to neutralize someone deadly dangerous.

Someone like Jed.

"What a strange thing to say," I commented. "What do you know about what happened here, Rachelle? Talk to me."

Rachelle shook her head wildly back and forth. "No!" she gasped out. "No! It wasn't supposed to happen like this!"

Well, duh. Of course, it wasn't. Men weren't supposed to be gunned down in their own home. But her word choice implied that something else was supposed to happen, but had not. Some expectation had not been met.

That lying, traitorous, stupid bitch. I knew there was a reason I disliked her.

"You told Boer we were coming, didn't you?" I said.

She cringed back defensively. "You don't know anything about it!"

"I know a selfish fuckwit when I see one," I told her. "You lost your nerve, didn't you? You thought you'd be safer if you cut a deal with him yourself. You just wanted to save your own miserable skin."

"They weren't supposed to kill Joe!" she shrilled. "That wasn't the deal!"

"No, just Jed and me, right? But you sold out your own husband!"

"No!" she cried out. "I didn't! I wouldn't! They weren't supposed to hurt Joe!"

"And you thought this sonofabitch would keep his word? Wow, Rachelle. So you're stupid, as well as despicable."

Rachelle backed away unsteadily. "Don't you dare judge me! I have kids! Someone had to put the girls first! Someone had to do *something!*"

I gestured at Grifo's body. "Well, congratulations. You definitely did something."

"Don't judge me! You don't have kids, you bitch! You don't know how it is!"

I was overcome with the futility of it. I shouldn't waste my time scolding her. It was stupid and sad to have a screaming catfight with this wretched woman over her husband's cadaver. I needed to get away from her. Before I ended up punching her.

But not before getting everything I could get out of her.

"How did you communicate with Boer?" I demanded.

Rachelle backed away. "Get away from me! You're the reason Joe is dead! You and that...that awful thug!"

I had yet another moment of sharply wishing I'd taken the gun Jed had offered me while I looked frantically around for a prop to make me scary enough to bully her. Fate was kind, for once. There was a big firepit in the middle of the room, and a stand, equipped with pokers and tongs. Heavy, black rust-treated wrought-iron pokers, with a sharp little spike at the end.

I grabbed one, and hefted it up, lunging to rest the sharp spike right at the hollow of her quivering throat. "Talk to me, Rachelle. Tell me how you contacted Boer. Or your girls get orphaned."

Rachelle's jaw dangled. She looked helpless and clouded, and too fucking slow. I brandished the poker again, trying to look thuggish. "How did you do it? Did you have a phone number to call? Did he give you a burner phone?"

Her eyes flickered, so I seized onto it. "Burner phone, then. Give it to me."

"No!" she squeaked. "I can't! He'll kill us! He told me!"

I pressed the poker as hard as I dared. Breaking the skin was a line too far for me. "That's right," I said. "I can kill you now, or he can kill you later. You decide."

Rachelle squeezed her eyes shut as she shoved her shaking hand into her jacket pocket. She pulled out a flip phone. "Take it," she hissed, flinging it at me. "He said he'd leave us alone. He wasn't supposed to kill Joe! Just..." Her voice trailed off.

"Yeah, I know," I said bitterly. "Just my boyfriend. Don't expect me to feel sorry for you. What's the number?"

"There's only one number in the address function. The name is...Boss." Her voice choked a little on the word. "He said he'd leave us alone," she bleated.

"He's a liar, a cheat, a thief, and a killer, Rachelle. And you just made yourself his bitch."

"Fuck you," she said.

There I went again, haranguing her. Rachelle had to live the rest of her life with what she'd done. Or else spend all her energy stuffing it. Either way, she was fucked.

Whereas I, on the other hand, had a great deal to accomplish in a very narrow window of time. I had to come up with a brilliant plan, and be braver than I'd ever been in my life, and I was not looking forward to either thing. I was shaking in my boots.

Dawn was starting to lighten in the sky on my way back to the hotel room as I pondered the optimal moment to call Boer. He or least his minions couldn't be very far, having just killed Grifo and taken Jed. No more than a scant hour in any direction.

I also had to be extremely careful about how I timed the call to my brother. He, too, would try to take control of the situation, according to his own idea of what was most important, which wasn't necessarily mine. A careful balance had to be struck.

I pulled into the road that led to the cabin, and sat there in the car outside it, gathering my nerves. I had to do this now, swiftly. Without overthinking it.

There was one single chance I could help Jed. It was extremely slim, and it depended on many completely unpredictable variables.

I pulled out the burner and found "Boss" in the address function. I wondered if that was supposed to be funny for him. Eeew. What a nasty little jerk-off he was.

I hit "call," and waited. It buzzed five times before he picked up.

"Rachelle," Boer said. "You were explicitly instructed not to bother me. By now you've seen what happens to people who don't follow orders. Why are you calling?"

I tried to reply, but my throat was quivering too hard. I swallowed, tried again. What a cruel, self-important butthead. Bullying a bereaved woman whose husband he'd just murdered.

Boer made an impatient sound in his throat. "I have things to do Rachelle. If you have something to say, spit it out."

"I'm not Rachelle," I said.

A brief, startled pause. "Interesting," Boer said. "Freya Masters, is it? Did you kill that useless bitch Rachelle? I hoped you'd be with Clearwater when he came to Grifo's place. Cutting him into pieces won't be nearly as much fun without you watching."

"Don't," I said, involuntarily. "Don't hurt him. Please."

Boer waited, and laughed softly "Or...?" he taunted. "Or what? That's not how this works, sweetheart. You have to offer me something I want."

"SmokeScreen," I said. "I can offer you that. If you let Jed go."

"I'll be damned. I wouldn't have expected you to have any real intel. I thought you were just an empty-headed fucktoy. So? How shall we do this?"

"Let him go," I said. "And I'll open the algorithm for you."

Boer clucked his tongue. "Oh, come on. Don't insult my intelligence."

"Will you let him go? If I do?" I let my voice quaver as much as it wanted to. It was important that he took me for an airhead.

"For SmokeScreen, yes. But I still don't understand how this exchange could possibly take place. How could I secure it? I have to protect my interests."

"Let him go and you'll have me," I blurted. "I'll enter all the codes for you."

Boer thought about that. "I have a better idea," he said. "Logistically simpler. You just give me the codes right now, over the phone. And I will let him go."

His oily condescension barely touched me. "I can't," I said. "I'm sorry, but the codes are incredibly complicated and long. I have to do it in person."

"I'm sure I can manage it," he said.

"No, really," I improvised wildly. "I couldn't tell you how to do it, I swear to God. It has to be done on the fly, once you begin, everything is extremely time sensitive. You get one thing wrong and you're out."

"Try me," he said.

"But...but the program generates random patterns the user has to respond to in real time," I said. "It would take months to coach you into being able to do it. Only my two brothers and I can do it."

"Hmmm. I don't believe you, Freya. That's unfortunate for your friend Jed."

"Oh, for God sake," I said tartly. "Do you think I want to walk into your clutches? Trust me, I don't have any choice except to come and do the job myself."

Boer let me sweat while he covered the phone with his hand, conferring with someone else. He came back on the line. "Let me tell you how this will work," he said. "Clearwater doesn't know how to open the algorithm, so I have no reason not to start cutting him if I get bored and need entertainment. You, on the other hand, claim to have what I need. I know where you are right now, thanks to the location device in the burner phone I gave to Rachelle. I see where you are, and if you are not there when my people arrive, I'll take it out of Jed Clearwater. In flesh. Is that clear?"

Dread was heavy in my belly. I'd just burned my last bridge behind me.

"I'm not going anywhere," I said. "I'll wait for them."

"And if you don't come through with the code? Then it gets much worse for your fuck boy, and you get the front row seat. Close enough to catch the splatter."

"I get that," I told him

"Wait where you are," he said. "Don't talk to anyone. I'll call when it's time to come out of the cabin. When I call, you will come out with your hands raised above your head, and nothing in them but the phone. Is that clear? Keep the phone on you until I call it. Any funny stuff, Jed gets cut. Delays, Jed gets cut. Weapons, Jed gets cut."

"Got it," I repeated, robotically.

"I'll be watching you, Freya. Every fucking second."

The connection broke. I put the phone back into my pocket and got out of the car, forcing my numb legs to move.

Panic was stimulating, if you rode the crest of the wave. My first move was to tear apart the Badass Bitch Bag. I rifled through my little tricks, which seemed very lightweight and frivolous in the face of Boer and his threats. I wished I had something bigger, more lethal. But they were going to search me thoroughly.

The one thing I dared to take was the little transparent thumb ring. It braced a mechanism that had a tiny pop-out blade made out of resin that hid behind my fake fingernail. Everything else was too obvious, and would show up in a search.

But even this ring could get me and Jed killed. Another life or death decision.

Yes, to the ring. I also pulled out one of the tooth tracers. It slipped over my back molar, so anyone with the frequency could follow me. If anyone looked in my mouth, it just looked like a crown. Biting down activated the signal.

And that was it. Those were the only things in my bag of tricks that had a hope in hell of getting past Boer's security search.

On to the next hard conversation. I pulled up Ethan's number, braced myself.

My brother answered instantly. "Jesus, Frey. You hung up on me!"

"Yeah," I agreed. "Bro. I'm in trouble. I'm on a really tight schedule. So listen up."

"Frey, stop being a baby, and listen—"

"Boer's coming for me here," I said. "In just a few minutes."

"What? So go! Run! Now!"

"I have to wait. I'm letting him take me. If I don't, he starts to hurt Jed."

"No, you are not!" Ethan yelled. "Big fucking shame about Jed, but too bad!"

"I just sent you data for the transmitter I put on my tooth," I said. "When I bite down, it sends a signal. Also, get in touch with the Drake brothers. They were coming to Portland to help Jed, and they were supposed to get here early this morning, so they'll be the closest ones who can start following me. Have you got all that?"

"No fucking way! I can't let you—"

"Now give me the code," I said. "I have to be able to open the dummy version of SmokeScreen, and you need to be ready to dive through the hole I open up, right? And you'll help me any way you can. Right? Isn't that how it works?"

"Frey, no! That's insane! I never meant to actually use it, and certainly not with you! Just get in your car and get the fuck out of there! Now! Please!"

"I'm sorry, Ethan. I love you. I really do. With all my heart."

"Goddamnit, Frey. Don't do this to me." His voice cracked. "Don't let him take you too. Don't do this."

My eyes were streaming. I snorted back tears in my nose. "Too late, big brother," I said, as I saw the sweep of headlights flickering through the trees at the big loop of the driveway. "I can see their headlights. Tell me quick, or it'll be too late."

"You can't!"

"This is happening, right now." I schooled my voice to steely calm. "Either I go in there with the dummy code, or I go in there naked, nothing to bargain with, and no way to establish a connection with you. I think you know exactly how that would go."

"Goddamnit, Frey." His voice broke.

I swallowed down my tears. "They're getting closer. Tell me quick."

"Fuck!" he bellowed. "It's mom's favorite poem. You know it. Robert Frost, Nature's first green is gold. Except it's backward, and between each letter you can insert as many random numbers and symbols as you want, for as long as you want, if you need to play for time. Just don't put in more letters. Do you know the poem?"

"Shane used to recite it to me at bedtime," I said. "When I was little."

"You know the address on the darkweb. Just go to it and start entering the last line of the poem, backward, into the dialog box. Each line of the poem will get you one layer deeper. There are eight lines. You have to fill eight dialogue boxes. Start with the last line of the poem. No spaces between the words. Careful of the punctuation. And it's case sensitive."

The headlights were getting closer. "Do you mean the words are recited in backward order? Or the actual letters of the words?"

"The letters of the words," he said. "Plus the punctuation. Start with the period following the last letter of the last word of the poem."

"God, what a fucking nerd you are. I love you, big brother. Take care."

"Freya, run! Please!"

"I'm sorry, Ethan. Call the Drakes. Have them follow me. Hurry."

"Don't do this to Holly." His voice shook. "Don't do this to me. Fuck, Frey!"

That hurt, like a knife in my guts. "Sorry. Too late now. I love you. I love Holly. Tell her. Keep telling her."

"Frey—"

"Goodbye." I cut him off, turned the phone off, looked around frantically, and shoved it through a ragged hole in the baseboard, just as Rachelle's burner phone began to ring. I answered it. "Yes?"

"Take off your coat," Boer said. "There are snipers covering the cabin from two directions. Walk out with your arms in the air, holding the phone. Turn so your back is to the car. Leave four yards between you and the vehicle. Understood?"

"Understood," I said.

"Go now. I'm watching through a live stream, so do not fuck with me."

I shrugged off my coat, as he had instructed, and stepped out the door into the blinding headlights. It was very cold with just the sweatshirt. I shivered violently.

I walked out to a few yards from the lights, arms up, and turned around, the phone in my hand. The car door opening made me jump. Gravel crunched under heavy boots.

"Don't move, bitch." A gravely, unfriendly voice. Not Boer's.

I waited. The crunching got closer. I gasped as my hands were jerked behind me, plastic cuffs jerked tight. A bag went over my head, smothering me.

Pain exploded in my head. Then nothing.

CHAPTER 32

Jed

I was floating up to the surface. I could feel it happening, and I wished I could just dive deliberately back down. If only I could stay unconscious. Or better yet, die right now. Just cut loose, at will. Die on command before the horror began.

Before Boer filmed it to hurt Freya. If I could just spare her that.

But something dragged me upward like a hook, pulling me out of the miserable darkness. Noise, activity, on the other side of my bruised, swollen eyelids. It prodded and yapped at me. Boer's voice. It sounded almost jolly.

Bad sign. The guy was practically chortling. The hell bitch replied, but she just sounded bored and irritated. Something was up. Something new.

I dragged in air, which made my broken ribs flare, bright as a red-hot coal. Stabbing pains, everywhere. Blood in my throat made me cough. Another drubbing of agony. I wondered if I had perforated organs. Internal bleeding from Boer's kicking tantrum. I wondered how long it might take for that to kill me.

Too long. That would be too easy.

It didn't really matter. It would all be over, sooner rather than later. I just wished I could just cut the lights of my own accord. Take away all Boer's power by leaving him with a useless corpse. I should've gotten myself an emergency poison pill. Not my style, but hey.

Not that it would have helped me now, strung up like a side of beef. I had the long, hard road ahead, discovering the outer limits of pain. Not territory I had ever wanted to explore. It scared me shitless. But eventually I'd die. It would be over.

I heard the woman's voice again. Nicole, Boer had called her. She liked to kick too. And the toes of her boots were pointy.

She was talking to a couple of big, fleshy bearded guys. New personnel. I had personally taken eight of Boer's men off the board over the past week. Quick turnover. These guys should get hazard pay. It was a small satisfaction to cling to, before leaving this world. Hurray, I'd created frustrating logistical staffing issues for my archenemy.

Fuck, whatever. I'd take any win, however slight.

Boer's laughter had a shrill, manic sound. He'd always been kind of an annoying asshole, though very tough and competent. But the fault-lines had never showed up so clearly before.

I forced my eyes to open. A needle of artificial light slid in, stabbing into my brain, like a spike through my eyeball. I would have vomited, but I already had. Many times. Nothing left in there to heave.

I dared another spike through the brain as I opened my eyes, focused...

Oh, fuck. Oh, no. Fuck, no.

Freya. Boer was clutching her arms behind her and shoving Freya in front of himself. She was in boots and jeans and a black sweatshirt. Her hair was wild and messy, glowing pale like a candle flame in the cold fluorescent light. Smeared with blood on one side.

Her face was ashy pale, but her hazel eyes burned into mine, taking in all the damage. I tried to say it with my eyes. *Oh, baby. I love you. I love you. I'm so sorry. I would've done anything to keep this from happening to you.*

Boer was holding forth, in a loud, triumphant voice, but I was so deep in Freya's eyes, I couldn't be bothered to understand the guy. Not until Boer spun Freya around and gave her a vicious slap to the face.

"Pay attention, you dumb cunt!" Boer turned to me. "You, too, fuckface."

Freya blinked, but she kept her cool. There was an angry mark on her cheek from his slap. I wanted to hurt him for that. But I was so fucking helpless.

That was the real torture. I wondered why the guy hated us so much.

"...understand me, you stupid fuck?"

I nodded, then endured the subsequent sick throb of pain that provoked.

"I understand," I coughed out.

My voice was gravelly from yelling. Even though Boer knew I had never known the SmokeScreen codes, he liked to play with his prey just for the fun of it.

Boer had taken off his mask. The late Joe Grifo had been excellent at his job. I would not have recognized the guy in a crowd. Everything has been changed. Jaw implants, nose job, chin lift, cheek implants, eyelids, even his lips were different. His eyebrows had been reshaped. Even his hairline has been changed.

But those beady, malevolent dark eyes, those were the same, even with contact lenses. All creased up with that gloating, self-satisfied smile.

I didn't have the juice for a snappy response, so I stuck with my dull stare. Maybe I could bore him to death.

He slid his hand around, gripping Freya's breast, and his grin widened as he saw me react. No, this guy was in no danger of suffering from boredom today.

"Maybe we should wait a while to open up the algorithm," Boer said, rubbing his dick against Freya's ass. "We could have a little fun. Let you watch. What do you say, Nicole? Do you want to play? Nicole likes girls, too," he informed us.

Nicole looked over at us, her bruised face sullen and hostile. "I'm not in the mood," she said, her voice colorless. "And she's not my type. We get the algorithm running first. Fuck her all you want after that.

Boer frowned at her. "You're no fun."

"You want fun?" Nicole's mouth twisted. "Playing with this toy, that'll be fun. How shall we begin? Cut out the power grid in Dubai and see what happens? Hack into the nuclear missile silos in Russia and fuck around with them? Now *that* would be fun."

Boer's eyes gleamed. "You're on, bitch. Open that algo for us, Freya. If you damage it, or fail to deliver, I will cut chunks off your boyfriend's body and cauterize each wound with a hot iron so he won't bleed out. I'll make it last for long time. And when he finally dies of shock, I'll do the same to you while your brother watches on a livestream. I can cut off a piece just to demonstrate my commitment. What should I start with? A foot, a hand? Something more...intimate?"

"No need." Freya's voice was cool and even. "I have absolute confidence in your commitment. Let's get to work."

"Amen," Nicole said. "That's the attitude I like. Work first, play later. Stop jerking off, Wex. Get her over to the fucking computer. Let's do this thing."

"You said you'd let us go if I opened the algo for you," Freya said.

Boer snickered. "And you believed me. That's on you, sweet cheeks. You disappoint me. I'd expect that out of Rachelle Grifo, but Shane said you were smart."

"Shane?" Freya asked. "What happened to Shane? Is he dead? Do you know?"

The gloating smile vanished from Boer's surgically molded lips. "We don't have time for this."

"Please. It costs you nothing, right? We're going to die anyway. Just tell us what you know. There's no risk to you."

"Die unsatisfied, bitch," Boer said. "That's just the final fuck-you of fate. I have no clue where that asshole is. They attacked my team and took him away. Fuckers."

"Who attacked your team?" Freya's voice was sharper. "Took him where?"

"My client, who shall remain nameless, until I kill him myself. Now get to work, before I—"

"Just his name," Freya pleaded. "Just tell me who he is."

Smack. Boer knocked Freya off her feet. Then he grabbed her by the hair, dragging her over to the computer, where Nicole tapped her nails impatiently.

"The moment of truth!" Nicole said, her voice fake-sweet. "I actually have some medical training, believe it or not. I was studying to be a neurosurgeon, so I understand pain. That's my little superpower." She pulled out a knife and rested the point right under Freya's ear. "Now get to work, bitch."

"Having a knife to my throat really fucks my concentration," Freya said.

"Oh, does it? Is it hard? Oh, no! I'm so sorry!" Her hand jerked, and Freya flinched away with cry, blood flowing from a cut on her cheek.

"Get to work," Nicole said, her voice like ice. "The next cut is your eye."

CHAPTER 33

Freya

This feeling was strangely familiar. I'd done this before. Floated loose of my body, staying somewhere far outside myself, for self-preservation. It was a coping mechanism from the bad old days in the basement with Uncle Orren and Aunt Jean.

But I'd never had to perform complex intellectual activities in that state.

I barely felt the hot, ticklish streams of my own blood, running down my face and onto my sweater. Some splattered onto my hands and make the keyboard sticky.

Concentrate, Masters. Think. I had one pass at this. One. No second chances.

I entered the address of SmokeScreen on the darkweb, and the first dialog box popped up on a black screen, no explanations, no directions.

I tried to clear space in my mind for the first of the eight passwords. I had a good capacity to visualize, but I'd never tested it under conditions like these. The last line of the poem, backward. I created a visual image for reference. Huge letters, as big as buildings, on a mountaintop. The last line was "Nothing gold can stay."

So it would be .yatsnacdloggnihtoN. Got it. I fixed that image firmly in my mind. Imagined the hilltop at night. Imagined the letters illuminated, blazing with colored lights. As I entered the first letter, I just mentally switched the lights off in that letter, and let it go dark.

I began, slowly and carefully, to enter a string of numbers and symbols after it. Random filler. A clever way to buy time and look busy and compliant.

I hoped it would give the Drakes more time to find me. I'd chomped down on my tooth sensor convulsively the whole time I was in the trunk of the car. I still was biting it, probably in vain. I doubted the RF signal could escape from this place. They'd brought me down here with a hood over my head, but I had definitely gone down, down, down, three flights at least. This grotty old cinder-block room had the look and smell and mold level of an industrial sub-basement.

I couldn't look at Jed. He looked terrible. His eyes swollen shut, his lips split and bloody, his nose clearly broken for the umpteenth time. God knows what they had done to the rest of him.

Nicole hovered over my shoulders, trying to follow what I was typing. She held up her phone, filming me as I enter the numbers.

After about ten minutes, she made a suspicious sound. "Really? You committed that much code to memory? Two possibilities here, bitch. Either you're bullshitting us, or you're one of those robot freak savant types. Which is it?"

"It's sort of more the second thing, but…oh, shit. Oops, that was an q, not an a. When you threaten me, I get flustered. Sorry." I backed up, fixed it, and proceeded to insert a bunch of random numbers afterward.

"Yeah, she's definitely fucking with us." Boer was hanging

over my other shoulder now, too, squinting at the characters filling the screen. "I better get the hacksaw. I think she needs a nudge, don't you, Nicole?"

"I think that for once, Wex, you may be right," she said.

Oh fuck. I had to throw those bastards some meat. Right the fuck *now*.

I narrowed my focus to a laser point, and entered the rest of the letters I had left in that line all at once, dloggnihtoN, followed by about twenty random numbers and symbols.

I took a deep breath, my finger hovering over "enter." Please, God. Please, let me not have fucked it up and transposed something with my icy, trembling fingers.

I entered. Waited. The beach ball twirled. I held my breath... every muscle in my body rigid...and a fresh dialogue box appeared, inviting me to enter another password.

"What the fuck is this?" Boer demanded.

I shot an apologetic glance over my shoulder at him. "There are eight of them."

"This will take for-fucking-ever," Boer growled.

I turned back to the screen, and found that knife, shoved up under my eyeball again. "You do understand what happens if you disappoint us, right?" Nicole said.

I looked down the foreshortened blade that filled my field of vision. It was ice cold against my skin, the point stinging the skin under my eye. "I think I have a clue," I said. "Shall I proceed?"

She gave me a menacing stare. "Don't show me attitude, bitch," she said. "I have all the power here, and I will take it out of you, and him, in blood. And I will enjoy the fuck out of it." She pressed the knife harder under my eye. It burned. Breaking skin.

"Is that a yes to me proceeding?"

She really wanted me to cringe and grovel, and it would have been the smart thing to indulge her, but I just didn't have the energy for it. Not while also holding all this information suspended in my mind. I just simply couldn't do it.

Onward. The penultimate line of the poem was "So dawn comes down to day." I plugged it into the huge letters-on-the-hill image in my mind. .yadotnwodseognwadoS

This time, having established for them that I wasn't completely full of shit, I took the liberty of entering even more garbage numbers and symbols between each letter. Pages of them. Ethan said the first password would ping him the location of the computer, so hopefully, he knew where I was now. Who knows, he might already be able to turn on the microphone and listen to us. My task was to use this data entry job to stall, stall, stall. Which was exactly what it was designed for. My brilliant brothers.

I hoped the Drakes were able to follow the signal from my tooth sensor. But whatever. That was outside my control at this point. I had to focus on the task at hand.

"So what is this place, anyway?" I made my voice high-pitched, so it sounded like anxious babbling. "This can't be a private home, not with a concrete sub-basement. We must've gone down, what, three flights of stairs? Where are we? Is this a power station, or a bunker? Some industrial structure? Maybe a factory, or a—"

"How about you shut the fuck up and concentrate on your code, bitch?"

The knife pressed beneath my eye, and I yelped as it broke the skin again. A thread of blood trickled down my cheek and dropped off my jaw.

"Yeah, yeah, got it," I said, my voice strangled. "Don't cut me. Please. I need my eyes for this, okay?"

"No," Nicole said coolly. "You need one eye, bitch. Zip it, and get to work."

So I did. First, a bunch of numbers. Then a single letter from the poem. More numbers. Another single letter. Still more numbers and symbols. Lines and lines and lines of them. Then another letter. Doling them out like breadcrumbs in the forest.

No matter what happened to me and Jed, Ethan needed to know as much as I knew, at least. This nightmare had to serve some purpose. For Shane.

"Please," I said. "Just tell me the name of the client who stole Shane from you."

"We're not telling you shit, Masters." Boer whacked me in the side of the head, making my hands jitter on the keyboard. Which meant I had to go back, backspacing all the way to the last letter I'd entered. When the stars in my head stop spinning, the third dialog box was ready. I entered the period. It was getting harder to hold the image steady in my head for constant reference. It flickered, wavered, distorted.

No. Stay tough, girl. Five more passwords to go. Keep your shit together, for Shane. For Jed. For Holly. For Ethan.

The next line to enter backward was "So Eden sank to grief," so I inserted it into my mental image. ,feirgotknasnedEoS. I lit up the letters in my head, trying to keep the image steady, and started entering garbage numbers and symbols slowly. *Hurry, Ethan. Hurry, Drakes. I can't keep doing this. I can't go on with this. I'm going to crack.*

So many moving parts. But Ethan knew where we were. My only job was to keep Boer and Nicole too busy to cut Jed to pieces. Hah. No pressure.

I hit "enter" on the third password. Held my breath again. Another dialog box.

The fourth line from the bottom was "Then leaf subsides to leaf." That would be .faelotsedisbusfaelnehT. I inserted those onto my hilltop image. Lit them up.

Jed appeared to be unconscious. He hung there, plastic cuffs suspended from a looped chain hanging from the ceiling. His feet touched the ground but he wasn't standing on them. The cuffs had dug so deeply blood ran down his arms.

Look away. Concentrate. More numbers, more symbols. More,

more, more. I entered them grimly, until I heard Boer start to make ugly, impatient muttering noises.

I finished that one, hit "enter." It worked. Four more to go.

The next phrase was, "But only so an hour." I inserted .ruohnaosylnotuB' into my mental construct. Only three to go after this. Fuck, fuck, fuck. I had to slow down.

I started entering the fifth string of letters. I must have been at that one for twenty-five minutes of solid typing before I hit "enter." Three more to go.

And if I got to the end, and nothing happened? Then what? Oh God, then what?

"Her early leaf's a flower"...wait. Hold on. Did this line have a comma at the end, or a semicolon? On top of the rest of this horrific shitshow, I now had to make a life or death call over something as trivial as punctuation. Fuck my life.

I gritted my teeth, and decided if it were a comma, I would not have hesitated. I stopped because some part of me remembered something different. I voted for the semicolon. Betting my lover's body parts on it. ;rewolfas'fealylreareH.

I took even longer with this one. My stomach roiling with doubt. I typed in the final H and about twenty lines of random garbage after.

I exhaled, and hit "Enter." Tears slid down my face, mixing with the blood.

Yes. The dialog box appeared, for the second to last line.

Now for "Her hardest hue to hold." Which would be .dloho-teuhtsedrahreH.

Nicole and Boer were completely silent now. Nicole still pressed that bloodied knife under my eye, still holding up her phone to film what I was doing. The knife vibrated with tension against my face. I couldn't string this out too much longer. Those psychopaths were already completely unstable. The strain would make them explode.

I entered the final letter. Hit "Enter," and the very last dialog box showed up.

Last chance to stall. I had to drag this out as long as I could. Make it count.

"Nature's first green is gold," that was the first line. .dlogsi-neergtsrifs'erutaN.

I took my time like never before, but after about forty minutes of my typing, Boer spoke up. "Do you know what I think, Freya? I think you're fucking with us. What do you think, Nicole? Do you think she's fucking with us?"

"I do, Wex. I really do. I think a code this long is impossible for a human brain to memorize. So yeah. This sneaky little cunt is definitely fucking with us."

"What kind of punishment do you think she deserves?"

"Well, she still needs her eyes, at least for the moment," Nicole said thoughtfully. "But there's absolutely no reason we couldn't take one of his."

"Now you're talking." Boer chucked me under the chin. "Nicole is great with eyes. She just wiggles that knife in underneath the eyeball, and snip, she severs the optic nerve, and 'pop,' out it comes. It really is a thing to behold. But you'll see for yourself soon enough. Go ahead, Nicole. Let's show her."

I hurried up with the last few letters, and hit "Enter." "No, no, no! I'm not fucking with you, I swear. The code is really long, but this is just how our minds work. Me, my brothers. We're strange that way. Always have been."

The screen filled with scrolling numbers. Nicole leaned forward, her eyes wide.

"Are we in?" Boer asked.

"We are in." Nicole sounded excited. "Holy fucking shit, we are *in!*"

Boer reached down and squeezed my crotch so hard it made me gasp. "Good girl," he said, in that evil, oily voice. "I'll fuck you extra hard for being so obedient."

Boom. A huge, muffled explosive sound from above them.

"What the fuck..." Boer grabbed his handheld radio. "Nelson, come in. What the fuck was that? Nelson? Come in, Nelson!" He looked over at Nicole. Both of them gave me identical suspicious glances.

He turned toward the guys near the door. "Wilkes, Shelby. Go check it out."

The two men he'd called upon exited the room, leaving two men, besides Boer himself and Nicole, who leaned down over me with a menacing air. Nicole dragged the point of the knife over my cheek, then down to my mouth.

"Do you know something about this, Freya?" Boer asked. "Do you have something to share with us?"

I shook my head, trying to speak, but an unintelligible gibbering came out. I'd used up all my brain power entering that damn code. I had nothing left to be tough with.

Suddenly, the computer flashed, sparked, and the lights went out. Utter darkness.

Now. Something inside me snapped into action as if it were spring-loaded. I released the catch on the little blade hidden behind my thumbnail. Snick, it emerged, a good half-inch of lethal sharpness, pointy and serrated.

Nicole lunged for her phone, which still glowed on the desk beside us, and I jumped up and knocked it out of her hands. Then I spun around wildly, slashing the tiny blade right across Boer's face. Not a lethal blow, but I felt the contact, the friction of his skin, and the bump as it slashed over his nose. A nice, deep, nasty scratch. Good.

Boer bellowed with rage as he stumbled backward and then went for me, but I was gone, launching myself in the general direction of where Jed hung from the ceiling.

I ran right into him, making him grunt in startled pain.

"It's me," I hissed, and jumped up to grab the chain and locate the plastic cuffs. He made a sound of startled agony as my weight added to his own, which was awful, but I ignored it, sawing at the plastic with my thumb blade. It was hard, to get the right angle in the dark, and I was terrified of slicing him open, cutting a vein, a finger.

Snap. It broke, and we fell together, him on top of me. Jesus, he was so heavy. It felt as if his dead weight had crushed me into jelly. I wiggled beneath him. "Hey? Jed?"

Jed rolled off me and rose to his feet. I struggled to sit up. In the beams from cell phone flashlights, flashing and flickering, I saw him. For just a split second, I saw Jed's body, silhouetted against some fleeting light source, suspended in the air, kicking.

Fighting, again. Nothing kept that guy down.

I heard shouts, grunts, crashing furniture. Electronic equipment swept off tables, shattering on the cement floor. *Bam. Bam.* The gunfire was incredibly loud.

A cut on my forehead was bleeding, and the blood was blinding me.

Then someone landed on me like a bag of rocks, and suddenly, I was wrestling, scratching, struggling. I got a smothering mouth full of her slick, bitter-tasting hair, and choked on the smell of perfume and sweat. Nicole.

Catfight. I was giving it my all, but she was on top of me, she was fresher than me, and I was half blinded with blood. She was pounding my face. I used all of my strength to twist and wrench one hand free. I slashed my thumb blade, aiming for wherever all that panting and grunting was originating. She turned her head and jerked back, but the blade bit into flesh. I raked it hard, across her cheek.

Her thin screech sounded barely human. More flashing lights showed a stuttering strobing image of a screaming, goblin face above me, spit flying from wet lips, bloody teeth, wild eyes. I heaved myself up, shoving her off, scrambling back—

And felt it, like a massive, punch to my shoulder. It knocked me back. I hit the floor. Felt the world start to drain away into some big, bottomless hole.

Leaving only darkness and cold.

CHAPTER 34

Jed

I felt no pain, levitating through the place on a wild combat high. My body decided where to kick, when to duck, where to zig or to zag, where to punch or block. Bones were broken, but I didn't feel them.

I looked for Freya with each beam of light that flashed, but I didn't see her. I heard screams that sounded female, so I lunged in that direction. The room echoed with noise, yells, gunshots. *Bam. Bam.* Fire scored my back. The muzzle flash pinpointed the shooter, so I ducked low behind a desk, then grabbed that desk and hurled it. A *thud*, a grunt. I flung myself on the shooter while he was down, groping for his gun arm.

The guy fought like a mad dog. We writhed together on the floor, and he head-butted me on my broken nose, and everything went black—

The lights flooded back on, blinding me. I blinked, desperately.

Fuck, that was Boer. Screaming as we grappled, his face distorted with carefully landscaped fresh scar tissue, stretched into a rictus of pure rage.

We kicked and grunted and heaved, struggling for control of Boer's gun hand. He clutched a Glock 19, and the barrel kept inching up, toward my face.

Bam, the gun went off, inches from my ear. I could feel the heat radiating out of the barrel. We were eye-to-eye, sweat dripping, muscles trembling as the gun wavered, moving closer, closer...until it was right in my face.

Boer's lips stretched in a hideous grin of triumph—

Bam. Boer's head exploded.

I fell back, startled. Splattered with blood, bone fragments, wet pinkish stuff. I wiped it off my face with a bloodied, shaking hand. Fuck. Brain tissue.

The one brain that knew the name of the person who had taken Shane. Gone.

Freya. I saw shadows flickering on the periphery of my vision as my sense of time and space reactivated. "Freya!" I yelled. "Frey! Where are you?"

"Jed! Stay down, man. You're hurt bad. Let me—"

"Frey!" I ignored whoever was trying to push me down, lurching onto my feet. I wiped the blood out of my eyes. Someone grabbed my arm to steady me, but I shook them off and staggered out into the middle of the room.

Three bodies lay there in pools of blood. None were Freya.

There. I saw that black sweatshirt, the pale flash of hair. And red. Oh, shit.

I went for her, in a limping, shambling run, skidding up next to her on my knees, ready to kill whoever was leaning over her—

The guy looked up. It was Ethan Masters. He looked me up and down, cool and unfriendly. "You look like shit," he said.

"Freya?" I gasped out.

"She's shot," he said curtly. "I think it missed the lung, but she's lost a lot of blood. We need to hurry. Hey, Cade! What's the situation up top?"

Cade, one of the Unredeemables who worked on Ethan's

private team, spoke into his handheld and turned to Ethan. "All the bad guys are down," he said. "All clear."

Ethan nodded "Good. Let's get you guys to the hospital. Who was the guy I shot? The one who was trying to kill you?"

"That was Wex Boer," I said. "The one who kidnapped Shane."

Ethan looked startled. "That was Wex Boer? I didn't recognize him."

"No, you wouldn't," I said. "He'd gotten reconstructive surgery."

"He took Shane?" Ethan pushed on. "Took him where?"

I shook my head with a weary shrug. "I guess we'll never know now, will we?"

Dick move, giving the guy a hard time after he'd saved my life, and Freya's. But I forgot all that as Freya's eyes opened. I bent over her. "Hey. Frey?"

She sucked in air, wincing. "Nicole?" she croaked.

I looked up at Ethan. "Did you see Nicole? One of Boer's staff. Young, slim build, Asian, long dark hair, fights like a demon from hell. Watch out for her."

"She should have a lot of blood on her face," Freya added, with satisfaction. "Cat bitch. I got her a good one."

It looked as if Nicole had gotten in some licks as well. Freya's face was streaked with blood. Ethan relayed a directive to his team to look out for Nicole.

I tried to pick Freya up, but Ethan knocked me out of his way and grabbed her himself. I limped after him, ineffectually. Up, up, up, endless fucking flights of stairs.

Finally, Darius and Amos materialized and grabbed me under my dislocated shoulders, which made me howl and swear, but in a short time, we were packed into a van. Freya had an IV hooked up. They started in on me with the first aid, but I wasn't interested. I just wanted to stare down at Freya. Astonished that both of us were actually still alive. I couldn't fucking believe it.

"Jed," Darius said. "You're all messed up. Let me work on you."

"You guys should be hunting Nicole, not wasting time on me," I said. "We need her alive. She might know the name of the guy who took Shane."

"Ethan left a five-man team to sweep the area," Darius said. "Let them handle it. Come on, man. Let me take a look at you."

"Let him bleed if he wants to," Ethan growled.

I was too exhausted to care about Ethan hating my guts. I just stretched out my arm and grabbed Frey's bloody, sticky hand, holding it like it was a baby bird.

Her eyes opened, met mine. Her lips twitched. God, she was pale.

I just stared down at her, in awe. It blew my mind that she'd come to rescue me. All alone. She had played every card she had. All her brains and courage, put out there, on the line...for me.

I cradled her small, ice-cold hand, wondering if there could ever be any way on earth that I could possibly deserve it.

CHAPTER 35
SEVEN WEEKS LATER…

Jed

I just sat there, at the outermost gate that led up to Ethan Masters rocky fortress. It was a long and winding drive to the top, where the many-storied building was cantilevered out from sheer rock, overlooking the entire Cascade Mountain range, with views of three snow-covered volcanos. I'd been there a few times over the years. It had been pretty dazzling for a guy who had grown up in a squalid, beat-up single-wide.

It wouldn't dazzle me now. I had much more important things to be dazzled by.

I sat there, fondling my great-grandmother's ring as if it were a talisman that could confer courage or luck. I needed both. The hundred-year-old aquamarine was milky and beat up from having been worn constantly for sixty years. My great-grandmother had never taken it off, not even when she was washing dishes or doing housework, and the stone was soft and battered. But I liked the effect. The facets glowed with trapped light. The ring had a personality, history. It was an entity in itself.

At least, I hoped that was how Freya would see it. I hoped a whole lot of things.

I'd been waiting at the gate for an insultingly long time. It's not like there was any doubt about who I was. There were cameras staring down at me from every angle.

No, Ethan Masters was up there, stroking his chin, wondering if he should let me in at all. If I were him, I would do the same. As far as he was concerned, I had to be punished. Not just for banging his baby sister. More importantly, for not keeping her out of mortal danger. I was lucky to still have balls at all. Ethan Masters was a dangerous man.

I'd hoped to rack up some points out in the field, hunting for that hell-bitch Nicole, but so far, my search had born no fruit. At least I could move around in the world freely now, using my own name. With Boer's machinations revealed, my name was cleared. Nicole still wanted to kill me, but that was fine. Bring her on.

The gate was grinding open. Either Ethan was letting me in, or Ethan had decided to have me killed, one or the other. Either way, I'd finally have an end to the suspense.

I drove up the thickly forested mountainside, glimpsing cameras at every switchback. When I got to the top, there was another heavily fortified gate. I waited outside that one for several minutes as well. Probably being scanned and X-rayed.

It opened, and I drove inside, into the grounds. I parked the car on a flag-stoned square as a big, burly guy I didn't recognize came out the door. He glared at me, then turned and jerked his head for me to follow. Usually, Ethan had Unredeemables covering his private compound, but they were out in the field now, looking for Shane and Nicole. Besides, the Unredeemables didn't want to take sides in this weirdness between me and Ethan, so they kept their distance whenever possible.

I couldn't be bothered to take note of the obscene luxury of the place. Just a general sensation as I strolled through, of fine finishing, huge picture windows, stunning views, gleaming plank flooring, high-end decorating. Some of the glass-sided corridors were perched over cliffs, others opened onto patios, atriums, landscaped gardens. In one, I spotted an infinity pool and an enormous sunken hot tub. And I seemed to recall a helipad on the very top. Ethan Masters denied himself nothing.

Who cared. I just wanted to see Freya.

The big guy ushered me into a huge library. Floor-to-ceiling windows alternating with floor-to-ceiling bookshelves. If you looked hard enough, you could probably see the curve of the earth from those windows.

Ethan Masters was seated at an enormous desk. His back was to me, as he tapped at a laptop. Probably dashing off some sort of genius code he'd dreamed up while taking a dump that morning. That was a Masters for you.

I stood waiting, like a dickhead. I had no leverage here. Ethan had it all.

He finally turned, as if noticing only now that I was there, and made an impatient sound. "So? Have you got news?"

"Nothing important," I said.

His face was a cold mask. "Tell me the unimportant news."

I let out a sigh, hanging on to my patience. "We got close to Nicole a couple of times. The first time she opened the algorithm, we almost got her, but she had a bolthole and got away. We questioned her people, the ones we could pin down, but they were useless. The next time she opened the algo, it was a trap, and she almost got us. Darius is still in the hospital with shrapnel in his back. Nicole is in the wind. That's the status report."

Ethan nodded. "You could've told me that in a text," he said. "You didn't have to drive all the way up here, inconvenience my staff, and waste my time."

I shrugged. "Live and learn."

"You said Nicole might be the last person alive who might know who took Shane," Ethan said.

"She might," I said. "From the way they interacted, she seemed on equal footing with Boer."

"That's good to know, but I told you not to show your face

around here until you had something to show for the danger you put my sister through."

"I'm still working on it," I said. "But I can't wait any longer."

"Sure you can. You have to. Because it's really not up to you."

The library door opened. A little girl with long wavy blonde hair burst in. "Uncle Ethan! Could you take me to the—" Her voice broke off as she saw me. Her eyes got very big. "Oh boy! It's him, right?"

"I'm meeting with a colleague, honey. Go on out until I'm done. Off you go."

But Holly was not fooled. She gazed at me with fascination. "Are you the one that Auntie Frey broke out of jail?"

A snort of nervous laughter burst out, earning me a dirty look from Ethan. "Uh, something like that," I said.

"You're handsome," Holly said, approvingly.

"Thank you," I said.

"I'll go tell Auntie Frey!" She bolted out of the room.

"Holly!" Ethan called after her. "Don't bother Freya! She's working!"

But Holly was gone, and Ethan was cursing under his breath.

I felt something inside my chest start to relax. Thank God. At least, Freya would know I was here. I had had no way to make that happen other than trusting to luck.

"She did not need this right now," Ethan said, his voice grim. "She's still healing."

The strange thing is, I actually got why he was so angry, but I couldn't surrender. It wouldn't be Ethan's decision, whether Freya and I ended up together.

I wondered if he would ever forgive me, if I got lucky. Maybe not. He might just hate my guts until one of us croaked. That would be tedious, but whatever. If Freya would consent to be with me, I would barely notice. Ethan Masters snorting and snarling would be like a mosquito buzzing in my ear. An adverse weather condition.

An extremely brilliant and rich adverse weather condition. I was no pauper myself, but I wasn't in that exclusive billionaire club. But Freya was just as smart as her brother, and she'd freely decided to consort with the likes of me. I just had to convince her to do it again and again, for the rest of her life. And to try to make it worth her while for the rest of mine.

"Hamon," Masters called. "Bryson. You two, see Clearwater out. All the way back to his car. He needs to get gone, double-quick."

Hamon gave me an appraising look, flexing his enormous muscles and cracking his tattooed knuckles. I didn't bother to read whatever word the letters formed. The message in his eyes was clear. Another, equally huge guy with a big, bushy blond beard came into the room and joined him, also sizing me up.

"I'm not leaving," I said.

"Wrong," Ethan said. "My mistake was letting you in at all. I thought you might have a report, but no, you continue to be worse than useless. Fuck off, Clearwater."

"Not until I talk to Freya," I said.

"You're not getting anywhere near Freya," her brother said, his voice like ice. "You've done enough. You almost got her killed. She barely speaks. You already let Shane fall into a fucking hole in the earth. I won't let you inflict any more damage on my family."

I had no coherent response to that, because he was completely right. So my only option was dumb-ass stubbornness. My default setting.

"I'm not leaving until I see her," I repeated.

The energy in the room shifted as Ethan exchanged meaningful glances with his hired muscle. Hamon and Bryson moved toward me, trying to herd me toward the door.

I was in for a world of hurt, but fuck it. I was so used to pain by now, I'd barely notice. I'd rather have the shit kicked out of me ten times over then tolerate this silence any longer. She'd made no response to calls, texts, emails. Even snail mail letters.

If the answer was fuck off, it had to be verbalized, and come straight from her lips. Then I would accept it, and promptly turn around and walk right off the edge of the world. But not until then.

Hamon went for me first, his gorilla arms swinging in a lightning fast roundhouse that I barely managed to evade. It whipped right past my nose. I bobbed and wove and spun and ducked, avoiding some of the blows, catching some doozies.

Then I backed away and picked up a chair, some fancy designer thing made of bent metal and leather, and flung it at Bryson's head, dancing back just in time to avoid a crushing kick meant for my balls from Hamon's huge booted foot—

"What in the hell is going on here?"

We all froze at the sound of Freya's voice. Hamon made another lunge—

"I said *stop!*" Freya commanded, with absolute authority.

Hamon stumbled back and looked at his boss, looking confused and agonized.

"Do not touch him," she bit out. "Or you will all regret it."

Hamon stood down, giving Ethan a shame-faced, apologetic look.

At that point, I dared to lower my guard enough to turn and look at the door.

The sight of Freya Masters was a whole body experience, like jumping into water. Holy God, she was so beautiful. Different, though. So thin. Her eyes were deeply shadowed, and she'd chopped off all the bleached blonde locks, which resulted in a dark blonde raggedy pixie cut, with some paler bleached tips here and there, like some wild woodland creature. Which only accentuated all the delicate, elegant details of her face. The wounds from Nicole's knife were healed, but the scars were still an angry red against her paleness. But her eyes. So brilliant, so bright. Filled with accusation.

Well, yeah. I had let her down in every possible way. Fuck, in the end, it had been Freya who had to come and rescue me. She had to risk getting cut to pieces just to save my miserable skin. I had made every possible wrong decision, and piled incompetence upon incompetence. Boer was dead. Nicole was gone. Shane, still lost. A whole host of other people dead. No one still alive worth questioning.

My hands were empty. I was so ashamed of that. She deserved better. And even so, my eyes were starved for the sight of hers.

I couldn't look away. I felt like a prisoner in a dungeon. Desperate for the sunlight he will only see on the day that he goes to be hanged.

CHAPTER 36

Freya

What the hell? Jed, getting pounded by Ethan's security people?

I spun around to face Ethan. He had that look on his face. I knew it all too well. The look that said, "This is going to hurt, but I know what's best for you."

But I was changed by what had happened to me. I wasn't taking any of that shit from him, or anyone, ever again.

Jed looked different. Leaner, sharper, harder, but his eyes burned in his face, staring at me. The intensity was confusing, after his silence.

"Why were you attacking him?" I asked Ethan.

Ethan shrugged, his face set in stubborn lines. "He was being unruly."

"Unruly? You mean, like, he said something you didn't want to hear? Don't be a prick, Ethan!"

"Freya, he just needs to go, and then we can talk about—"

"Shut up." Something about my tone made all four men go very quiet.

I turned to Jed, keeping my back very straight. I would not

show weakness in front of this man. Even more importantly, I wouldn't show it in front of Holly. I was all she had, when it came to female role models, so I had to stop being a gibbering idiot and show her how not to be trampled. How not to let her heart get shattered in public. Like, when a guy pledges eternal love and devotion, and then after a nightmare of torture and mortal peril, *poof*. He disappears for seven weeks. Without a word.

Yeah. Like that.

I cleared my throat. "So," I said faintly. "Why are you here, Jed?"

Jed looked lost. "I had to talk to you," he said. "Since you didn't respond to my emails, or my texts. Or my letters."

I gazed at him, shocked. "Emails? Texts?" Then I turned and stared at my brother, whose arms were crossed. He had that stone-faced look. "Ethan?" I said. "Did you actually censor my communications? You dared to do that to me?"

"You didn't need any distraction," he said. "You needed peace and quiet and safety. You needed to heal. Not have some fucking idiot galumphing around and demanding your attention!"

The rage that came over me was so intense, it made me shake. I just didn't understand how this man could claim to love me and still be such a goddamn idiot.

"You thought you could decide for me," I said. "As if I was a child. That's over, Ethan. Never again. Or you will lose me, and that would be a big shame."

"I did what I thought was best," Ethan protested.

"Well, that's not your call anymore. It never really was." I turned to Jed. "So, did you have something you wanted to say to me?"

Jed glanced around the room. "Could we, ah, maybe go some-place private?"

I was about to tell him no, just to be a snotty bitch, because I was still generally pissed off at everyone, but then Ethan barged in.

"No," he said brusquely. "You can say it right here. In front of everyone."

Of course, that got my back up all over again. "Oh, shut up, Ethan," I snapped, turning to Jed. "Follow me."

"Bad idea, Frey," Ethan said.

"Did I ask for your opinion? I did not. Leave me alone."

Jed trailed me out of the room, and Holly scampered alongside until we got to the main living room on this level. Ethan followed, flat-mouthed and fuming.

I stopped at the entrance, kissed Holly on the top of her head, and shooed my brother away with a flutter of my fingers. "Excuse us," I said. "Later."

I shut the door, then leaned against it, staring at him. He looked as good as ever, in spite of the fresh marks on the side of his face, the new bump on his nose. But he had such a grim, haunted look.

"So," I said briskly. "You sent me messages. I never got them. That's classic Ethan for you. I really need to get the hell away from here, and get back to my own place in Seattle, but he's so paranoid. And I can't entirely blame him."

"Me, neither," Jed said. "You're safer here, as long as Nicole's on the loose."

I rolled my eyes at him. "Plus, there's Holly. And I was all messed up for a few weeks, so he's even more overprotective than usual." I hesitated. "And you were nowhere to be found."

"I did not hide from you," he said forcefully. "I would never. On the contrary. You'd have to drive me away with a stick, and I'd still come back for more. Ethan whisked you away to that fancy private clinic somewhere while we were both sedated. I had some surgeries, too, so I was stuck. As soon as I had my wits back, I texted you. Over and over. But I got no answer. So I started to wonder if silence was your answer."

I let that sink in for a couple of minutes. "Really, Jed?" I said. "After what I did? Calling Boer, inviting him to kidnap me? I stretched out on a fucking sacrificial altar for you. Was that not enough of a declaration of love? What do you want from me, blood? I spilled plenty of that!"

"I know," he said. "I hate it that you had to fucking rescue me, risk everything for me. I don't blame Ethan for being pissed."

"For God's sake, you saved my ass over and over! Who gives a shit who saves who?" I yelled. "And my brother is irrelevant. He does not own me. He has no authority over me. This is between you and me. He might not understand that, but he soon will."

"But...but I couldn't keep you safe. I couldn't even keep myself safe."

"I'll decide what to risk," I said. "I have the right to do dumb shit and almost get myself killed, as much as you or Shane, or anyone else does."

"I know. But Ethan told me to fuck off and go find Nicole. And that made sense to me. That seemed like an appropriate thing to do with my time and energy."

"You just trotted off to do his bidding? You didn't care enough to fight for me?"

"I thought I was fighting for you!" he protested. "I've been hunting Nicole ever since I could stand. Me and the other Unre-deemables. I just haven't bagged her yet."

"Well, good for you, for keeping busy. I would have loved to be in the loop."

Jed shook his head, his eyes full of misery. "Sorry, Frey. I thought that I should give you breathing space. A chance to know how you feel about me, about us, without all the drama and the mortal danger and the blood."

"Breathing room is way overrated," I snapped.

My voice was bitchy, but for some reason, Jed smiled. "Breathe anyway."

"Smart ass," I snapped.

"I learned from a master," he said, with another ghost of a

smile. "I was hoping to bring you back something real, babe. Solid intel about Shane, from Nicole. Nothing less would do. So you could have a way forward, or at least, some hope of closure, you know? But over and over, I came up blank, and finally, I couldn't wait any longer. I had to come here to you. Empty-handed or not."

"Empty-handed?" I stared at him, incredulous. "You thought you had to bring me a gift to approach me again? What, like, a bride price? Forty cows and forty goats?"

"I guess I was hoping to prove my worth," he admitted. "To show I can take care of you."

"Jed, for God's sake." My voice was shaking. "For this bullshit I waited all alone for seven weeks? Because you needed to prove something? We're supposed to take care of each other! I am not a fairytale princess!"

Jed put his hands up, puzzled. "Okay, got it. You're not a princess. Received."

"I'm not a prize to be won by being worthy! And I'm not anyone's possession!"

"I never thought that, not in a million years. I just think you're incredible. I'd be dead if it weren't for you."

"Newsflash," I said. "Me too. So we're even! No, actually, I'd be dead at least twice over, if not three times. So I win."

"Fine, baby. You definitely win. And you're not a princess. You're a goddess."

"Oh, stop." My eyes were leaking, which filled up my nose. *Damn.*

"Try to understand me," Jed said. "The only thing you wanted was the truth about Shane. That was your holy grail, so I tried to get it for you. Something to show for that clusterfuck we put ourselves through. I wanted to bring you that, and I failed. So here I am, with nothing to offer but myself."

I mopped at my face with a tissue, not daring to meet his eyes. I'd fall to pieces.

"It doesn't work that way," I told him. "I don't want an offering laid at my feet. Like a cat bringing me a dead bird."

He winced. "Oh, man. Not the vibe I was going for."

"I want someone who'll be there for me. Who trusts me to be there for him. Someone who's not afraid to be with me if I'm hurting, or to let me see him when he's hurting. Someone who can hold my hand through the scary parts, and the sad parts. Someone who can be with me, for real, soul to soul. I thought I had that with you. But I guess it was just a stupid romantic fantasy."

Jed took the tissues from my hand, and pulled one from the pack, dabbing gently at the corners of my eyes. "You've got everything I have," he said quietly. "The best of me, and the worst of me, too. It's all there. All my stupid stuff, my ugly stuff, my dark side. I can't just snap my fingers and make it just go away. I'm not perfect."

"I know that," I said. "Neither am I. You've seen my bad stuff."

"I know I'll let you down and piss you off, and probably disappoint you on a regular basis," he continued. "But on the plus side, I will love you until I die. And I will always put you first. I swear it, before God. This is the biggest, the most solemn, the most real thing I have ever felt. Before you, I didn't even know this kind of feeling existed. You opened my eyes to a whole other world."

I hid my face in the tissue, because it was absolutely not fit to be seen.

Then Jed reached into his jacket pocket, and pulled something out. It was delicate and small, and it flashed and glimmered as I blinked tear-blurred eyes.

"This belonged to my great-grandmother," he said. "It's an aquamarine. She wore it for her entire sixty-two-year marriage. Never took it off."

I gasped at the beauty of the gorgeous little antique ring, the delicate filigree around the stone. It had a diffuse glow, like glacial water. "It's...it's magic."

"My mom came to me one day when I was a teenager and gave it to me," he said. "She said, this is for your lady, when you pick one out. She told me to hide it someplace where she could never find it and to not tell her where I put it, no matter what she said or did. She didn't want to come back from some stupid bender and find out she'd pawned it."

"Did she...did she try to get you to tell her where it was afterward?" I immediately regretted the question when I saw the shadows in his eyes.

"Yes," he said. "But I never caved. I wrapped it up in a dish towel and then a Ziploc bag and shoved it into a hollow tree in the woods. I just went to get it a couple of days ago, and not a moment too soon. They were about to clear the woods, to build some strip mall thing. It would have been gone forever."

I stared down at it, blinking tears away again. "I'm sorry about all that," she said. "What happened with your mom. So it's been in the tree, all this time?"

He nodded. "I'm glad I found it. It seemed appropriate. A beautiful thing of great value, snatched from certain destruction at the last minute? That's our vibe."

She laughed. "It's beautiful, that your mother hid it from herself so that you would have it when you needed it. That was the best in her, wanting the best for you."

His smile was so beautiful, I was in danger of starting to cry again.

"I'll give you the best of me," Jed said. "I don't know what that is yet. I'm figuring it out, step-by-step. But I'll give you everything I've got. Will you wear it?"

He took my hand, cradling it, and waiting for my tearful, sniffling nod.

He slid the ring on, and I knew it was a silly cliché, but it fit as if it were made for me. I could feel the energy from it, rushing all the way up my arm and then straight into my heart, which felt so hot and soft, and infinitely deep. Like the whole world could fit inside it.

"It's so beautiful," I whispered. "Thank you. I'm honored."

"Not as much as me." He kissed my hand reverently. It was still covered with fading marks from our violent adventures, hardly worthy of such a perfect, glowing ring, but he leaned over my hand as if I were some sort of queen, or goddess.

And all that was romantic and lovely, but after all these weeks of lonesome pining, I needed some assurance of a more earthy kind. I stroked his face, touching the bump on his nose, the healing mark on his cheek, and tugged him close.

"Kiss me, you fool." I tried to sound commanding, but we both laughed at the waterlogged tone in my voice.

But he took me at my word, and we were off. The kiss caught fire, fueled by all the frustration, the hunger, the longing and the sweetness. The joy.

I don't know who maneuvered who, but somehow we found ourselves wound together on the nearest couch with Jed pulling me on top of him. I straddled him, winding myself around him, trying to get closer—

"What the hell? Holy crap, Frey! Does this seem the place or time?"

I lifted my head from that marvelous kiss, flushed and panting and disoriented. Looked around at the door, glaring at my interfering big brother.

Ethan was glaring at me. Holly was beside him, biting her lip and looking worried. "I'm sorry," Holly whispered loudly. "I tried to make him not come in. But you know how he is."

"Yeah, I get it. Not your fault, sweetie-pie." I slid off Jed, and off the couch. "Excuse us," I said pointedly. "Jed and I are going to go down to my apartment to talk privately for a while."

Ethan rolled his eyes. "Talk? So that's what you were doing?"

"Look!" Holly crowed. "She has a ring! So you guys are engaged now? Oh, wow, that's so romantic! It's really pretty!"

Ethan's face was a caricature of dismay. "You have got to be kidding me."

"We'll talk about this later," I said firmly.

"How about at dinner?" Holly suggested. "You guys can have champagne to celebrate! And cake! Can I ask Angela to make some cake? Or some banana pudding?"

Ethan looked at a loss for words. Holly grabbed his hand and dragged him out of the living room. He gave me a swift, speaking glance as he let himself be towed away.

When they were gone, I squeezed Jed's hand. "I apologize for Ethan," I said. "He was really freaked out. I have been contemplating escape strategies, but Holly is safest here, and I hate to leave her."

"Holly is a real piece of work," he said, his voice admiring.

"Oh, yeah," I said, stopping in front of the door to my apartment. "Holly is the best. So smart and funny and worldly wise for a nine-year-old. We love her madly. She misses Shane, but we try to make up for his absence as best we can." I paused for a moment as it occurred to me that we had never discussed this issue. "About Holly."

"What about her?"

"Well, you just need to be aware," I said. "Once I am free again to live in my own chosen space and conduct my business freely, like before, Holly will be splitting her time between me and Ethan. So, I'm sort of like a divorced mom who shares custody. And once she's back in school someplace, it'll be more than half the time. Chances are, she'll stay with me for the school year. So...you'll be a stepdad."

Jed thought about that, and smiled at me. "Okay," he said. "She seems like a great kid. It'll be fun, learning to be one of her dads. And she'll make an awesome big sister."

I gulped. "Maybe we're getting ahead of ourselves again?"

His dimples flashed. "Only if you're into it. I'm fine either way."

"There will be time for these intense conversations later. Right now, we have…" I checked my watch. "Exactly one hour and forty minutes before we go join Holly and my brother for champagne and banana pudding and heavy-duty interrogation. And in that time, you have to make up for leaving me alone for seven weeks. You've got your work cut out for you, buddy."

His smile stretched out, brilliant and happy. "Then let's get to it."

I opened the door to my apartment. We walked through it into a brand new world. One where love prevailed, and our wildest dreams came true.

Want to go to Jed and Freya's wedding? If you liked Master of Lies, join my newsletter here and get a sexy Jed and Freya novella, exclusive to my subscribers! To say nothing of other book treats destined only for my beloved super-readers! See you there!

MEET SHANNON MCKENNA

Shannon McKenna is the NYT and USA TODAY bestselling author of over thirty novels, ranging from sexy contemporary romance to action packed, turbocharged romantic thrillers. She loves tough and heroic alpha males, heroines with the brains and guts to match them, terrifying villains who challenge them to their utmost, adventure, blazing sensuality, and most of all, the redemptive power of true love.

Since she was small she has loved abandoning herself to the magic of a good book, and her fond childhood fantasy was that writing would be just like that but with the added benefit of being able to take credit for the story at the end. The alchemy of writing turned out to be messier than she'd ever dreamed, but whatever, she loves it anyway and hopes that readers enjoy the results of her experiments. She loves to hear from her readers. Contact her by email at her website, shannonmckenna.com, or find her on Facebook to keep up with all her news! Follow her on Bookbub to get new release and discount alerts!

If you'd like to know when new books will come out, and hear about discounts, giveaways and promos, join Shannon's newsletter. She has special goodies waiting for you there... exclusive bonus stories that are just for her subscribers, and a free Obsidian Files novella! She hopes to see you there!

ALSO BY SHANNON MCKENNA

The Unredeemables

Master of Lies

Master Of Secrets

Master Of Chaos

The Hellbound Brotherhood Series

Hellion

Headlong

Hellbent

Heedless

Havoc

The Obsidian Files Series

Right Through Me

My Next Breath

In My Skin

Light Me Up

The McClouds & Friends Series

Behind Closed Doors

Standing In The Shadows

Out Of Control

Edge Of Midnight

Extreme Danger

Ultimate Weapon

Fade To Midnight

Blood And Fire

One Wrong Move

Fatal Strike

In For The Kill

Standalones

Return To Me

Hot Night

www.ingramcontent.com/pod-product-compliance
Lightning Source LLC
Chambersburg PA
CBHW050018120726
47903CB00006B/1818